The Mist on The Mountain

By

Stephen Knight

Published by Stephen Knight.

First published in Great Britain in 2024 by
Stephen Knight
66 The Avenue
Pontycymer
CF32 8NA

Printed and bound by Amazon PLC.

<u>Disclaimer</u>

This is a work of fiction. Names, characters, businesses, places, events, locales, and incidents are either the products of the author's imagination or used in a fictitious manner. Any resemblance to actual persons, living or dead, or actual events is purely coincidental.

About the Book

In 1982, the Garw Valley had seen a spate of teenage murders. The Police had no leads and no suspects. DNA analysis wouldn't be invented for another three years. The villagers decide to take matters into their own hands hoping that the crimes will come to an end. After the execution of their suspect, the mutilation doesn't stop for another two years. They had the wrong man …

Forty years later the Garw is plagued by teenage murders once more. The parents of all children in the area are petrified. Once again the Police are baffled with little evidence and despite the increases in technology, the lack of DNA. The villagers want answers.

Then a national newspaper sends an investigative reporter into the locality. He feels he is getting negativity and hostility from some of the locals. Gradually he finds more than he bargained for.

He feels the wrath. Anthony Fallon also finds out that secrets can kill.

About the Author

Horror Thriller 'THE MIST ON THE MOUNTAIN' is the ninth novel from the mind of Stephen Knight who now lives in South Wales.
As well as being an Author, he is a professional musician and singer/songwriter, playing percussion from the age of ten as well as keyboards and guitar.

Check out his Author Website where there are links to buy his books and eBooks :

www.stephensamuelknight.co.uk

Chapter 1

1982. There were angry screams all around. Angry parents. Angry villagers from Pontycymer, Blaengarw, and Pant-y-gog had been under attack from an unknown entity for just over a year as six young teenagers had fallen victim to their fate. Man-made torches doused in petrol and lit brightly echoed around the sky, the fire burning heavily. The lynch mob headed towards the Avenue in Pontycymer. Chants filled the air with the same loudness as you would find at a rugby match. The surrounding mountains shadowed the village as they blocked any light trying to filter through the thousands of trees on one side and the high-rounded hills on the other. In the distance the engineering at both mines in Blaengarw and Pontycymer could be heard, the elevators running up and down the lift shafts as several coal miners with blackened faces walked away at the end of their shift totally oblivious to what was happening although they had heard that something was in the pipeline to end the slayer's reign of terror.

He was in his early twenties, but Billy Evans had already gained a reputation of trust among the people. He was always there to help out and was known to fix '*problems*'. The deaths of the children had made him make his own investigations. He wanted to know what the Police were doing about it and who their suspects were. Local bobby PC Dafydd Llewellyn, who at first worked down the mines but then chose to join the Police force instead, was happy to assist in pointing the finger.

"Kill him! Kill him!" Both fists and torches were thrust into the air as the serious, angry faces followed in lines, primed by the one man who had managed to irk up the crowds by being in a position of trust throughout the area. Before they reached their

target, Billy Evans led the mob. He stopped, turned around and held up his hands.

"STOP! STOP!" He listened to the chants which continued whilst he tried to bring the party under control. "Now listen. If anyone has doubts to what we are about to do, now is your chance to turn around! Otherwise, remember what this man has done to the community, to our children!"

Lee Jones, also in his early twenties and Billy's best friend, stepped forward to support Billy. "We must rid ourselves and our villages of this psychopath! Your children are not safe and won't be until he is gone!"

The chants continued as more residents in the Avenue looked out of their windows to see what the commotion was all about, some realising what was going on and stepping outside of their front doors to join in the lynching that was about to happen, whilst others hid behind their curtains and blinds, unsure of what to do. *"Out! Kill him! Burn the fucker! Hang him! Bastard!"*

"What about the Police, Billy?" Lee whispered into the commanders ear.

"Don't worry," Billy replied as he smiled at the answer he was about to give. "PC Llewellyn is turning a blind eye. He is back at his house to make sure that he can't be associated with what we are going to do, even though he provided the information. He is on our side." Billy looked at Lee for some reassurance that what was about to happen was right, and although the answer was silent, he noticed a slight nod of his friend's head. Looking back at the crowd of executioners he shouted, "Let's go!"

There was a sudden rush forward as every man and woman wanted to be the first to break down the door and grab the alleged psychopath Christopher Fallon. Those around him had been told that he had moved to the area to escape his divorce and live peacefully. Not long after he had bought his three-bedroom terrace house at the far end of the Avenue, children had begun to disappear, their bodies found mutilated and hanging at various places at the top of the surrounding mountains. At times, the red blood had dripped into the snow during the winter, whilst other murders had resulted in the mountain springs turning red in the water and filtering down to the lower levels of the mountain. Two of the bodies had been found face down in the streams, surrounded by a pool of blood.

They had invited Fallon to the emergency meeting just to see if he would show interest and attend, but he didn't. As the villagers were angrily discussing their plan of action, they didn't realise that another thirteen-year-old youngster had disappeared, last seen heading back after leaving his friends at the path leading up to the top of Gwendoline Street at Blaengarw. Billy had shouted at the meeting, "Friends. We know who the culprit is. He is not even here! Look around you!" He had held his hand up and pointed around the room to emphasise his point. "Fallon! What makes it worse is he was not brought up in the area! He has to go!" Those who were there were out for blood.

That was the only prompting that those present needed even though they didn't realise that the annihilation of victim number six had happened just hours before whilst they were all discussing the plan of action. The terror continued as they reached the target address on the right-hand side up near the end of the Avenue. Billy Evans noticed the curtain twitching in the living room. Christopher Fallon had heard the commotion and quickly looked unexpectedly out towards the angry crowd as the light from the torches was shining though his window.

Inside, the man was shaking. Frightened for his life. There was an angry banging on the door as several of the men tried to force it open. It sounded as though they were using something to smash the door down like a battering ram of some kind. It was. Man-made by one of the angry handy men in the area. Christopher Fallon had his home telephone receiver glued to his ear as he tried to call the Police. He never stood a chance as four heavy framed locals, Lee Jones, Ron Howells, Robert Gabriel, and Trefor Idle grabbed him whilst their wives or partners watched and screamed, each wanting a piece of the action by trying to step forward and either kick or punch the man as he was lifted up over their heads. Robert Gabriel drew a punch towards Fallon's face, in particular around the side of his head where he had held the phone to his ear. The receiver dropped to the floor, the spiral lead pulling it backwards towards the main dial, and the assailant forced his foot down on it. The phone made a crunching noise before the sign of any life disappeared and the dialling tone went silent. The four men turned around with Fallon up and above their heads.

Christopher Fallon screamed. "NO! PUT ME DOWN! ARRGGHHHH! WHAT ARE YOU DOING?"

The lynch mob didn't care about the way that they were mishandling the man, didn't care that at that moment in time he was alive as they grappled with his head, one of the men wrestling with his neck, two with each leg and one around his torso. "Fucking stop struggling you murdering bastard!"

"Wh..aaat?" Christopher screamed out in fear whilst acting as though he knew nothing about what the men were talking about.

"You are going to die for what you did!"

"PLEASE! PLEASE! NO!"

"Is that what our fucking kids screamed when you killed them?" The largest of the mob shouted as they dragged Fallon out of the front door whilst dropping him to the floor immediately outside at the top of the steps. The two men who had his legs pulled him down the steps and the back of Fallon's head banged violently on each before he reached the last. He was now screaming both with fear and pain. The crowd all rushed forward hoping to get some type of painful retribution on him whilst he wriggled in pain on the floor. Some managed to get over and either kick or stamp on his body. Christopher wrapped both arms around his head trying to protect it, but these were pulled away by the man who had previously had the hold around his neck. Fallon felt both of his hands pinned to the pavement with the feet of the men. All around him he heard the screams that had now turned into synchronised chants.

"BASTARD!"

"CHILD KILLER!"

"KILL HIM!"

Christopher Fallon was now semi-conscious and feeling as though he didn't know just where he was or what was happening to him, but yet he did. He feared for his life as suddenly his body was dragged along the ground. He felt the pain of his back being scrapped along the pavement, the kicks to his torso and head, the stamping on his legs and arms, each one becoming more and more painful, so much so that he began to accept the pain. Every parent present wanted to hurt him, to have a go at a kick, a stamp or a punch as the dragging continued to the end of the Avenue. The chants and shouts of anger continued as they reached the grass patch just before the farm. They headed down to the bottom just before the main road where five trees filled the open space, their branches hanging over most of the grassland. As the movement stopped, Christopher received another kick to the side of the head which rendered him even more semi-conscious to the terror around him. He became unable to move or understand just what was happening. Looking side to side all he could see was blurred visions of people.

Billy Evans held up his hands once more as if to demand silence from the lynchers. "Friends!" he shouted commandingly. "Our children have suffered. Tonight it ends! The Police have been powerless. We must take matters into our own hands!"

There was a grumble from the ground as Christopher Fallon made a noise which sounded like a 'no'. Lee Jones heard the plea and forced his foot into the side of the guilty man's head once more. Looking to one side he snapped his fingers at Billy's brother Julian, who was stood looking at the horror. Julian passed Lee a rope, noose tied at one end. He held it up to show the crowd and the chants started again, the torches being raised and punched into the air again as a sign of revenge. Then the second-in-command grabbed the free end of the rope and threw it over the thickest branch of one of the large, old trees. Julian grabbed it as it was thrown over. One by one the lynch mob stepped forward in quick succession for the last right to kick or punch their victim.

Billy Evans grabbed the noose and then stooped down to the body and lifted the head. "An eye for an eye, you bastard!" he exclaimed as he suddenly slipped the noose over Fallon's head.

"What are you doing?" a confused Fallon enquired. "I haven't done anything!" He was frightened beyond belief, his eyes wide and his face full of fear. He was frantic and he groaned whilst slightly unaware of what was about to happen. Billy nodded at Lee who had been joined at the rope by two of the men who had snatched Christopher from his home. They pulled at the rope.

The crowd cheered and chanted as suddenly Christopher Fallon felt the pain of the tightness of the rope around his neck, his body was leaving the ground, his feet barely touching the ground. More ropes were tied to the victims hands and legs and thrown over the smaller branches, pulled sideways and spreading his body open and sideways like a starfish. Then with one last pull the noose tightened around his neck. The victim began to choke and gurgle. Fallon knew this was the end as his face went a bright red in colour and he struggled to breathe, his eyes appeared to be bulging out of their sockets and filling with tears of pain as for one last time he looked at the lynch mob around him. The other four ropes were tightened around in the sideways direction, two to the left and two to the right. "You," he strained to talk, gurgling blood, and searching for air. "Going to die!" he gurgled once more. "I curse you all!"

"Shut the fuck up!" Lee exclaimed angrily as he punched Fallon's head one more time.

"WAIT!" Billy shouted at the crowd, once more indirectly begging them to be silent. He Watched as Lee Jones pulled out a large ballistic knife that belonged to his Father from his belt. "He will feel the full force of our children's revenge!" He looked into the semi-conscious eyes for the last time. "You did this! You never gave them a chance," he whispered loudly.

"This ... vil ...lage! Cursed!"

"Not by you, though!" Billy nodded at the psychotic Lee who stepped forward and starred into the eyes of Fallon and shook his head in disgust. He plunged the knife into Christopher's stomach.

The crowds cheered loudly once more, and the loud chants changed to *"YES! YES! DIE! DIE!"* They all looked on, again some in horror as Lee pulled the sharpened blade downwards from the top to the bottom of his torso using both hands. Blood spurted and dripped from the open wound. Then the co-leader started cutting side to side and the victims internal organs started to fall out from his stomach and hit the floor, first the intestines, then the gall bladder and finally the stomach itself. Christopher Fallon was dead. The lynch mob were still cheering, *"YES! YES!"* as they all looked over to the child killer. Some had turned their heads away as they couldn't bear to look even though they had agreed with the lynching. Finally, to ensure that

Christopher Fallon was dead, Lee struck the blade across his neck. The blood splattered everywhere. He was covered, the blood soaking into his clothes and running down his face. He then threw the blood covered knife down onto the ground. With his sleeve he began to wipe the blood splatter from his own face. In his expression, everyone could see a sense of achievement as he smiled psychotically at those around him, a smile that turned into a psychotic laugh. Then he himself shouted, "Arrrggghhhh!" He accepted the praise from the crowd who were all stood looking at their victim and continuing their chants of *'Yes! Yes! Die! Die!'* for what seemed like a few minutes. The killer turned to Billy who was now stood with a fire-engulfed torch in his hand. Robert Gabriel snatched the torch from him, waiting for the next command from the bigger man. The two of them stared at each other eye-to-eye.

Then Billy snapped, "Burn it!" Gabriel stepped forward and held the torch under the dead man's feet. The flames caught on Fallon's clothes and started to engulf the corpse. The lynch mob looked on, most of their eyes widened, most of them staring with the same psychotic eyes that Lee Jones and Billy Evans had done minutes before. They started dancing around to match their cheers as they concluded what they had set out to do on the night of evil revenge. The flames fired high. Robert looked around at the crowd. There was not one of them that looked as though they disagreed with what was happening. The fire burned the body and then ignited the trees.

Police Constable Dafydd Llewellyn heard the commotion and had stepped outside his house and walked down the street towards the crowd. He nodded his head slowly and smiled at the carnage before turning around and heading back to his home. Back to his sofa and his TV programme. There would be questions he told himself. But the village would be silent. And so would he.

The lynch mob continued their excitement for many hours into the night. Celebration of the end of the threat towards them. Or so they thought.

*****

It was 03:35 in the morning. Peter Hoskins was now in his eighties. For most of his life he had worked down in the mines in Pontycymer at the Ffaldau Colliery. He remembered the hive of activity around the many mines in the area and had seen the many changes but now hated the fact that there were rumours that the British Government were going to close every mine in the country. He knew that if the mines in the local villages closed then the area would become plagued with unemployment, that most of the men in the area didn't know any different and would struggle to find employment elsewhere. Each village would become something of a ghost town. The slogan 'close a pit, kill a community' had been used many times when the plans were overheard. Peter and many from the villages and further afield were angry that after all the hard work from thousands of men, their lives would be become more or less extinct.

Nowadays Peter just wanted an easy life to live out his days. His wife had gone, passing away of old age. Peter could not wait to join her 'in heaven' as he put it so many times every time he went to St. David's Church just up the road from where he lived. He heard all the commotion, the cheering, the laughter, the chants, and the music. He woke up and looked at the clock on his bedside table. "Bloody hell," he Mumbled to himself. "They have done it!" He knew the rumours that were circulating but he never thought that they would go through with whatever they were planning. Peter slipped his legs to the side of the bed and let his feet touch the floor. He knew that he was frail these days and had to watch his step. After a pause he pushed himself up, using his hands to balance himself on the bed. He struggled over to the window which looked out over the mountain, a scene that he had thoroughly enjoyed for several years and was one of the reasons why he had moved to Pontycymer with his lady wife. The view of the beauty and the industrial sight of the mine which he loved. He couldn't see where the noise was coming from. Wrapping his dressing gown around him Peter so carefully made his way downstairs, undid the chain on the front door and stepped outside. He knew that all he had to do was step forward and look to the right. He saw the crowds that had gathered for the execution of Christopher Fallon. He had to do something about the noise. He needed his sleep, and it was about time that they all shut up so as not to bring attention to themselves from the authorities outside of the villages.

He reached in to the table just inside the front door and grabbed his keys and then walked out closing the door behind him. He laughed as he once again realised that he wasn't as young as he used to be which was showing in his wobbly legs and stiff joints. He also realised that he was walking up the street in his pyjamas and dressing gown which made him smile. It took him just two minutes to get to the party. He looked around at the people that he knew, which accounted for most of the lynch mob. Peter looked at the fire. He gasped as he hoped that what he was seeing was just his eyes and his old mind playing tricks on him. Then he saw Billy Evans, the ringleader who appeared to be laughing and joyfully talking to those around him. Peter knew him well. In fact he knew Billy's parents who, after looking around at the crowds, he could see were up behind the trees. Billy's Father worked down the mine in Blaengarw but was due to retire due to health issues.

"Billy!" Peter exclaimed in his strained voice. "What's this then?"

"Hi Peter!" Billy replied whilst knowing that the old man could be told because he was one of those that practiced 'What happens in the village stays in the village'. "This, my friend, is for our children. We have rid our villages of the culprit. That, there," he exclaimed whilst pointing at the burning trees, "Is what is left of the killer of our kids!"

"Really?" the old man replied with wide eyes and the wrinkles on his forehead stretching upwards. "Just who did you think it was?"

"Fallon! He lived In the Avenue just up there," Billy replied whilst pointing up the hill as though the older man didn't know where the Avenue was. The fact that Peter Hoskins had lived in Pontycymer for most of his life made Billy realise what he had just done and so he quickly lowered his arm.

"Christopher? Christopher Fallon? Tell me you haven't!" Peter replied with a serious look on his face as he stared at the community leader and shook his head in defiance. "I can tell you now that it wasn't him."

"I can tell you that it was!" Billy snapped back whilst appearing slightly annoyed that the old man had ridiculed his choice of culprit to the murders. "Ever since he has been here, these atrocities have happened!"

Peter shook his head once more and laughed angrily. "Where have you been? Call yourself a pillar of the community? Chris is, or should I say was, an investigative reporter from London. He was doing a story on the closure of the mines. He was here to support us."

Confusion filled Billy's face which changed into a look of worry and then panic. Had they killed the wrong man or had Peter Hoskins got the story wrong? "Are you sure? How do you know this?"

Peter huffed and puffed. "I've seen his press card. He has even interviewed me as an old miner."

"Is he the one that has leaked each of the murders to the press then?" Billy asked worriedly.

"Well being a reporter he is hardly going to keep quiet, is he?" Peter stared once more at what was left of the body of the reporter and nodded in the direction so Billy could see. "You have just killed the one innocent man that was going to write the story to catch the real killer and also to support us miners and go against Thatcher. Just what have you done you bloody fool?" He stared seriously and the two exchanged eye contact as there was a momentary pause. "We are going to have more reporters here than I have had hot dinners now! And we know why. You had better make sure that the crowd who was here tonight keep their mouths shut. The villagers will need to know to keep this in their villages. Keep a secret and keep it away from the outside world. But stuff like this is just going to bring attention to us." He nodded at the death scene once more and there was a momentary silence. "Christopher Fallon was not your man. Believe me. Now is there any chance that you can shut this lot up so I can get some sleep?"

Billy Evans was disapprovingly silent as Lee Jones joined the pair. "Mr Hoskins. What's up?"

Peter shook his head, his face full of anger as he looked at the both of them. "I'll let brains here tell you. Goodnight!" He walked off without saying anymore, feeling disgusted at the boys and even more disgusted at the villagers who had joined in the murder.

*****

Stewart Gilmour loved his dog. Each morning the golden retriever would wake him at 06:30 hrs by jumping on the bed and usually landing on top of him. Before breakfast, 'Dave' as the dog was called much to the dismay of Stewart's wife, would demand a walk which usually turned out to be the same walk every morning along Victoria Street and down to the patch of grass on the left where Dave would roll around and do his 'zoomies'. Stewart would then take Dave down further near the Pontycymer mine.

He had put the dogs coat and lead on and then headed down the street in the direction of the mine. Stewart looked to his right which he seemed to do every morning as he reached the car park in front of the waste land. He looked across the road to the left as he prepared to cross, for Dave to play, checking for any of the speeding cars. The dog was just about to run over to his play area when Stewart focussed his eyes on what seemed to be smouldering on the ground underneath what was now a smouldering tree. It appeared that what was left of the burning trees and leaves had made a black circle around what Stewart didn't know was an execution scene. There was some smoke still echoing upwards towards the sky. He began to feel anger as he realised that his dog would not be able to run around, and that the nature had been destroyed. "Bloody hell!" he exclaimed as he stopped and looked left and right for any passing traffic. He crossed. Dave the dog started to whine and then bark. "Quiet!" Stewart exclaimed as he made a slight tug on the lead. He stepped on the grass. Then he looked closely at the remains. Most of the many ropes had been burnt away with the black marks still showing on what was left of the thick branches of the trees that hadn't burned and where Christopher Fallon had been hung before his demise. The older man looked down on the ground at the smoke and debris. The smell hit him first. There was still a smell of what seemed to be the left overs of the burning flesh and the outline of what looked like a body. But there was something more. The skeleton hadn't burned. The bones had just scattered. "Oh my God!" he exclaimed to himself as he raised his free hand to his mouth and nose both to hide the smell and his shock at the find.

15

He pulled the golden retriever back from the carcass, not wanting to disturb the scene. He knew that he had to call the Police, so pulling on the lead, he headed back home to do just that. He was frantic, the thoughts of the burning bones remaining in his head as he rushed back. He quickly put the key in the door, pulled Dave inside and then picked up the receiver. 9-9-9.

"Emergency. Which service do you require?"

"Police. Urgently! And a fire engine!"

"Putting you through to South Wales Police," she continued.

"South Wales Police."

"Call from 01656 385564," the original operator said before she cut off.

"South Wales Police. How can I help?"

Stewart cleared his throat, still shocked by the find. "I've found a skeleton and blood everywhere. Someone has been killed."

"Okay caller. Can you tell me your location?" The receptionist asked.

"Victoria Street in Pontycymer. The grass halfway up on the right-hand side. The trees and grass. It's on fire. Need a fire engine!"

"Okay Sir, we will get a unit up there as soon as we can. Can you tell me your name please?"

Stewart was still shocked but looking around to check that Dave was behaving himself. He also knew that quite soon the children would be going to school and passing the site. He wouldn't want them seeing the remains. "Sorry. It's Stewart. Stewart Gilmour."

*****

The Police came. The press joined them. The Sun newspaper tried to find their reporter who had disappeared. The investigations began. Despite the efforts of both the Police and the press, they hit a brick wall. Each villager claimed to know nothing. What happened in the village, stayed in the village. The secrets began.

PC Dafydd Llewellyn stood looking out of his living room window and down in the direction of the crime scene. Two years later in 1984, Dafydd, who had served as the local Police Constable for seven years after working down the mines for ten years, passed away. He had been diagnosed with coal workers' pneumoconiosis (CWP); a dust-induced scarring lung disease commonly called black lung.

1984. The murders stopped.

Chapter 2

It had been nearly Forty years. The villagers had all grown up. Some had passed away whilst taking the secret of the death of Christopher Fallon to the grave with them. The next generation had taken over what was now left of the area after both mines had been shut down. People had upped sticks and left. Some knew no better than Valleys life so had chosen to stay with a hope that things would get better. Some moved into the area as the economy in the Valley died, house prices dived, and entrepreneurs saw the opportunity to buy-to-let. With the next generation of villagers came the next generation of youngsters. Those who remained from the time of the murders of the teenagers and also the execution of Christopher Fallon had let the memories slip to the back of their minds.

Michael Llewelyn had moved into his parents' old house in the same year that his Father had died. 1984. He kept it like a shrine with not a thing out of place. The furniture was all the same, now old and some of it falling apart, but he felt and used to joke with himself at times that if he did away with anything, his parent's would haunt him.

He was well known now in the Blaengarw and Pontycymer area. Just like his Father, he had joined the Police Force and taken over as the community Officer, later on rising to the rank of Sergeant and based in the closed station at Pontycymer which was just used as an administrative base for him and his two PCSO's.

Deep inside, he had never forgiven the British Government for forgetting about all the miners and ex-miners who had contracted, suffered with, and died of the different illnesses contracted from working down in the mines, Coal Workers' Pneumoconiosis, silicosis, mixed dust pneumoconiosis, dust-related diffuse fibrosis, and chronic obstructive pulmonary disease. Forgetting about his Father.

At the age of fifty, he felt that he was nearing retirement. He had begun to feel tired more often. He started to hear his parent's voices in the house but put it down just to the fact that he worked too hard and lived alone. He had never married. He had been close many times but felt that many of the women that he dated would just do the dirty on him and he wouldn't want to share any of his wealth or have to sell the house to give them half of the proceeds just because he was married to them. It was his. It was his parent's house.

May 2022 had been a bad month so far. The teenagers in the area were becoming too hard to handle in the villages. Any crimes that they committed were rewarded with a slapped wrist which they proudly knew that they would receive. The Police were in effect powerless. He and his PCSO's were fed up with the verbal abuse, being spat at, and at times physically assaulted.

Tuesday evening. He came home and plonked himself down into his Dad's old Chesterfield leather armchair which seemed to be the only piece of furniture that wasn't falling apart. It was also extremely comfortable. It was silent in the house. Apart from the voices. Something was telling him to go up to the loft. He had only ever been there to place boxes of his belongings when he moved back from Cardiff having applied for the vacant post in his home village. He walked up the stairs and using the hooked stick, opened the hatch and pulled down the ladder. He climbed, carefully ensuring that his tiredness didn't make him slip or fall. As his head poked through into the darkness of the loft, he flicked the light switch before manoeuvring his legs up into the space. He could not understand why he had to come up there at such a time. Why he didn't let it wait until his day off on the following day.

Now was a good time to do some tidying, he told himself. It turned into a time to reminisce as he found himself looking in some of his parent's boxes, pulling out old photographs, papers and pictures, old electrical items that didn't work anymore but had still been kept, birthday and Christmas cards from everyone that had sent them including himself. The list was endless.

He separated and tidied the boxes. His parent's things on one side of the loft and his own on the other side of the loft. One box caught his attention. He heard a voice, like a ghostly whisper.

'Go on. Look.'

He blinked his eyes. The tiredness was getting to him, he told himself. But he heard it again.

'Go on. It's my box.'

It was his Father's voice. "Dad. Is that you?" There was no reply. He looked around as though he expected his Father to be there with him but then told himself not to be so stupid. He was tired. His hand was resting on the box. Sitting down and crossing his legs he looked in the box and smiled. This was the first time in decades that he had looked in these boxes. There was an A4 size book, plastic sleeves containing hair. A bag of black dust. He reached in and pulled out what just looked like some material. It was a suit of some kind. Slightly see-through and made from a black camouflage style material. He pulled out each item and placed them beside him. His next item was a thin black balaclava style mask. As he touched it he could feel something rough on the outside and he checked his hands after placing it on the floor. His fingertips were black with some type of dust. He began to wonder if it was the same dust that he had seen in the bag that he had already pulled out of the box. What he found next was quite worrying. Wallets. Purses. Bus passes. All belonging to children. Perhaps his Father had found them when he was a Police Officer, Michael told himself. He looked at each one. The memories took him back to 1982 and 1983. He remembered the names. These items belonged to the children that went missing and were found murdered back when he himself was only ten years old. Perhaps they were items of evidence that his Father had forgotten to return to the evidence store? He didn't know.

Michael could feel himself choking up with tears as he felt that he was actually mourning his parent's more by looking in the boxes than he had ever done as a child. He looked at the pile of things that he had taken out of the box that the voice had told him to look in. There was something else in the box. Something heavy. He reached in. Then he pulled out a small pick and looked at it, wondering whether what he saw was just a trick of the light in the dimly lit room. Dried blood. He turned the object around and around as a confused frown filled his face. He placed the object down with the rest of the items and then put his hand in the box to check if there were any more surprises. One. He pulled it out. A knife in a sheaf. He undid the clip and withdrew the blade from it's safekeeping. Slowly he took it out and then gasped. Blood. Dried blood. Just like the pick.

'The book. Look in the book.'

There was that voice again. Slowly he looked to his left. His hand reached down and picked up the book and he saw it was marked *'Journal'*. He smiled as he lightly touched the cover. His eyes still had a tear in each, although the last two items that he had taken out of the box had given him concern. He opened the journal and started to read. Each word shocked him. His Mother had died. His Father wasn't coping. The hospital appointments were bad news. His lung problems were terminal. How Dafydd had arranged for his brother Gareth to look after his child, namely him, when he finally passed away.

The journal soon turned angry. How no one was listening to the miners about the disease. There was no compensation for those that had contracted it. No additional health services for the sufferers apart from what they could get from the NHS.

Michael turned each angry page. This time he read about the teenagers that were making the villages a battle zone. Vandalism. Arson. Fighting. The violence was increasing. Bottles smashed over heads. Underage drinking. Eleven names were listed on the page in large letters that looked like they had been written by someone who in anger had dug the pen into the paper. He checked the other side of the page. The names had been written so hard that the imprint had gone right through to the next page. And the next. He flicked back to look at the names.

Owen Broderick
Bethan Cadogan
Megan Goff
Gethin Probert
Aled Bennion
Hywel Tudor
Rhys Vaughn
Bledden Cadwallader
Iwan Dacus
Taran Gittens
Lewys Meredith

Michael remembered the names. They were the names of the teenagers who were found murdered and mutilated back in 1982 and 1983. Some of the names he remembered because they went to the same school although they were in the years ahead of him. He remembered those years. Parent's, school teachers, and Police Officers were telling all the children in the area to be weary of strangers, not to go anywhere remote and make sure that they were off the streets before it got dark.

Michael read the journal some more. Each name had its own set of pages, the name underlined at the top of the first. As he read, his eyes widened, his mouth dropped, and his stomach filled with fear and shock. Each word detailed how and where each child had been killed. The words described each injury. How each was mutilated so badly. How the assailant enjoyed looking at the mutilation, Enjoyed looking at the body bleeding profusely and the organs dropping out of each. How Dafydd Llewelyn, his Father, had carried out the mutilation. How he had licked each body with his mouth and tasted the blood after each kill. The journal mentioned someone else who was with him, but no name, It indicated that someone knew about what was happening. The unknown person was apartheid to the murders. The journal mentioned how the victims were chosen for his Father. Not by him.

Michael felt sick. He dropped the book and jumped up on his feet. Immediately he placed his right hand over his mouth.

His eyes now filled with tears of fear. How could his Father carry out such atrocities?

'They had to die.'

"NO!" Michael screamed back at the voice. "THEY DIDN'T HAVE TO DIE!" he shouted loudly. "You cannot put this on me!" He reached over to some of the other boxes but this time not to tidy them but started throwing them around the loft and screaming 'ARRRGGGHHHH'. "It was you! It was you! NO!"

'Kill them, Michael! Kill them all!'

Michael Llewellyn never slept that night. There were too many voices in his head.

Chapter 3

Robert Hartland knew that he would have to get an early night if he was to get up in time to meet his friends the next morning, but he didn't want to give up playing on his PlayStation knowing that he was at a crucial level on his Black Op's shoot 'em up. He also guessed that his two friends were still up and about because he was playing with them online. He decided to send them a message.

"Hey butt. Off to bed."

"Make sure you are up for the meet," his friend Kyle replied. "I'll kick your arse otherwise."

"No problem," Robert replied with a sarcastic smirk, knowing in any case that Kyle couldn't kick his arse if he tried. Not even at Black Op's, let alone in a fight. "Later." He clicked his hand controller whilst watching the TV screen and turning off the game and then the television itself. He also knew that he had to close the curtains before he went to bed. His Dad had tried but Robert had ordered him to get out of the way because he would get shot on the game otherwise, so his Dad had told Robert to do it when he had finished.

The boy stood up and looked around, placed the controller on top of the console and then reached over to the left to pull the first side of the curtain over. It jammed on the rail, so he looked over to see what was stopping it. He froze. Outside the window it was dark, no streetlights because he and his friends had spent time using Kyle's air rifle to take pot shots at the lamps. His eyes stared and widened. There was someone stood outside the window looking in, but no face, just blackened. If it did have eyes the face was just staring at him. The figure was still, no movement. Robert froze in horror, but he was too frightened to move. He knew that he had to do something, and suddenly plucked up the courage to call for his Father's help. He took one last stare at the strange figure and then called out in his frightened voice in the direction of the stairs. "DAD! HELP!"

His Father was in bed. He had to get up earlier than his delinquent son was planning to, having to travel each morning from Pontycymer to Pontypridd to start work at 05:00 hrs. "Oh, God!" He said as he rolled over to alert his wife who was by now also stirring. "What the fuck?"

"DAD! DAD! HELP!"

Iaon slipped sideways, both of his feet stamping on the floor. "What do you want?" he shouted as he stood up.

"THERE'S SOMEONE LOOKING THROUGH THE WINDOW!" Robert shouted, as he directed his stare back to look at the figure whilst hearing his Father come down the stairs. Briefly he turned his head back towards his now angry Father.

"This had better be good!"

"There's someone outside looking through the ..." Robert stopped dead in his speech as he turned his head back to look through the glass. "There was someone there!"

"Where?" Iaon demanded to know as he moved forward to look out the window. "There's no fucker there!"

"There was someone!" Robert said with worry in his frantic voice. "It was looking at me."

"It?"

"There was no face."

"No face?" his Father replied as he stared at him with concern and then anger. He really wanted to lean over and smack his son around his head for waking him up unnecessarily. "Have you been smoking that shit again?"

"No! No! It was there! Look!" Nothing. There was nothing there. Nothing or no one. He looked outside whilst leaning on the window sill, then looked at his Father, then back outside. "It was there. I promise."

"You spend too much time on that fucking thing," his Father exclaimed angrily as he pointed at the console. "I'm going back to bed before I do something that I regret!"

Robert watched his Dad go back upstairs and then looked back outside once again. There was no one there.

*****

It was May 2022. The beautiful spring morning sunshine was just about to emerge, the sunlight pushing it's beams through the huge trees which covered most of the hillsides on the Blaengarw mountain and pushed their way upright as though they were reaching to the sky, close to each other as though they were in a crowd. In other parts the thousands of evergreen conifers which most of the children called *'Christmas trees'* looked as though they were ready to be decorated.

The three boys were all up and about which many would have found unusual on a weekend because they didn't have to get up to catch the bus which would have taken them to the out of area school. But they were on a mission.

Derryn Jones, Kyle Griffiths, and Robert Hartland were all in their prime teenage years. Fourteen, except for Robert who had just had his fifteenth birthday which he had spent most of drinking alcohol both at home in Pontycymer and with his friends at the side of the Co-op store. Like many of the teenagers in the area, they had pressganged anyone that they knew who was old enough to buy them a pack of lager or a bottle of vodka plus a packet of cigarettes. Robert had spent the money that he had gotten for his birthday.

"Come on!" Kyle shouted as he seemed to be racing ahead up the steep path ahead of the others.

"It's too fucking early for this shit!" the eldest boy replied. Robert was already puffing and panting even though he looked like the fittest boy of the three, a body frame which echoed that of a young rugby player. The fact was, he had always bowed out of any games at school, hated his teachers and was the disruptive member of his class. He had also not slept for most of the night, worrying about his experience on the previous evening. Now he was here with two friends who had the same traits. "Why couldn't we do this tonight like the last time?"

Kyle shook his head. "Because they are expecting us to do it tonight! Plus there should be no one around here yet." He watched as Derryn put his arm around Robert's shoulders to help him with the last of the incline.

"Come on, butt. This will be a good laugh."

Robert stopped once more and wiped his sweaty forehead with his sleeve. "Fuck butt. I'm fucked. If only you knew," he said as the path levelled out making it that little bit easier for him. But he knew that further on there was another incline taking them to the part of the forest where they were heading. He also knew that there was a bench coming up outside the old mine entrance where he could rest his feet before attempting the next stage. He looked to both his left and right as he struggled along. "Can't we do it here?"

"What is wrong with you?" Kyle asked angrily as he stopped to look at the slow boy.

"I haven't slept," Robert replied. "There was someone, or should I say something, stood outside my living room window last night when I finished playing Black Ops."

Derryn stopped. "Dressed in black?" he started to also shake nervously. "All dressed in black. Like he was wearing a balaclava?" He watched as Robert nodded.

"You have seen it?"

Derryn nodded. "Two nights ago. I just thought I was seeing things because I had just had a joint."

"You two wanna stop smoking that shit!" Kyle said as he looked at the pair.

"That's what my Dad keeps telling me," Robert exclaimed whilst hoping that Kyle would take it that he was comparing him to the older man.

"It scared me shitless," Derryn announced to the both of them.

Robert realised that he was getting no reaction from Kyle with his last quip, so left it alone. "I called my Dad. But whatever or whoever it was had gone by the time he came down."

"Come on." Kyle overheard the two Mumbling to each other as they continued to walk. "We will light the fire up by the wind turbine. If it spreads then the turbine will help spread the flames."

"So you haven't had anything like that, Kyle?" Derryn enquired whilst trying to put some sense to the madness that he and Robert had maybe experienced.

Kyle couldn't believe what the pair were saying. Derryn used to smoke weed like it was going out of fashion whilst he guessed that Robert was just overtired. He knew just how lazy

Robert was, knowing that his friend would catch the bus just two stops down to his house to meet him. Most of the time the driver's would shake their heads and not even charge him the bus fare because it wasn't worth it. "No. Just you two smackheads. Now just move your arses."

As they reached the seat that Robert had so wished for, he announced, "Hold on," as he sat down. "I've just got to readjust my socks in my trainers." He watched the other two boys stop and both of them look at each other and shake their heads.

"Why didn't we leave him at home?" Derryn asked, his question directed at Kyle.

"Fuck knows."

"I can hear you," Robert perked up, knowing that the three of them were best of friends. Partners-in-crime in reality. They enjoyed the thrill of setting parts of the mountain alight whilst knowing that at any time they could be seen or even caught. Hikers, dog walkers, even cyclists used the area frequently which is why they were there so early but knew that they didn't have much time before the dog walkers especially joined them on the mountain. He stood up whilst knowing that he was beginning to annoy them. "Come on then. Let's get going." Robert then moved forward quickly and actually led them for the first time since they had set out that morning.

Fifteen minutes later after the three of them had successfully attempted the two barriers which prevented the motorbikes and buggies from using the mountain paths, they eased themselves through the narrow path with the huge drop, then reached their destination. Derryn smiled as he removed his ruck sack from his back. He looked at the trees on both sides which darkened the path slightly because they were so close together. Setting the forest on fire here would easily spread what with the two wind turbines on the top to the right which today were overly active and turning at speed. "We need some dry wood. Twigs and tree branches. This stuff is too damp." He looked at the wood in and around the path that had been subject to the elements.

"I'll get them," Kyle shouted back to him as he looked left and right into the trees and tried to decide where to get them from before disappearing into the semi-darkness. He began to wish that he had brought a torch. The darkness of the trees combined with the lack of light caused by the early morning sky made his task more difficult.

"Rob," Derryn exclaimed whilst trying to get the lazy boys attention. "Get the stuff out of my rucksack." He looked on and saw his friend actually act on his command. He knew that Rob was the one who was usually the most excited when the fire was lit. His eyes always widened, and his face filled with that psychotic stare that every arsonist would give. He would also get a thrill when watching the helicopters fly over with their barrels of water whilst trying to blanch the flames.

"Fireworks? What the hell are we going to do with fireworks?" Rob was surprised at the find although didn't follow Derryn's train of thought at first.

"Announce our success once the fire has caught," Derryn replied with a laugh.

"Fucking brilliant," Rob said excitedly as he joined in his friend's laughter whilst removing two bottles of white spirit, two lighters and a box of matches. He looked inside the rucksack just to check it was empty. "We've never had fireworks before!"

"I know what is going through your mind, you psycho." Derryn looked over at him, stopping what he was doing at that moment in time to ensure that his mate didn't do anything stupid. "Wait until the fire is lit. Then you can light the fireworks."

Rob already had them in his hands, three rockets and two other huge blocks which looked like 9v batteries. "These are going to go up like a puff of smoke!"

"Where the fuck is Kyle with that wood? We only need a few dry branches and twigs. Fucking hell, there's enough of them around," Derryn snapped as he looked both sides of the path to see for himself. He began to think that it would have been quicker collecting them himself. "KYLE!" he shouted out in the direction that the boy had gone. There was no reply.

Kyle Griffiths had headed into the dense undergrowth further than he actually needed to go but he was enjoying the spookiness of the dark, imagining the woods being 'haunted' and thinking in his mind with much humour that at any moment a ghost would jump up and scare him. Many times at home his Grandparents had told him stories about the ghosts that roamed

29

around the mountain and how they petrified anyone that saw them. He smiled at the thought as he stopped. He noticed the dry small branches scattered around him and leaned down to pick them up. He heard the crackling from behind him as though someone or something was stepping on the branches that were on the ground. Footsteps around him. He stopped, scared at first as his head filled with the thought of his wish coming true. The ghost was going to get him. He laughed it off whilst under his breath calling himself a *'twat'* before continuing to pick up the dry twigs with one hand and place them into his other arm and chest. There was one last crackle from behind him.

Kyle didn't stand a chance as he turned his head around. His face filled with fear and fright, his eyes widened with terrified shock as the blackened figure thrust the blade of the pickaxe into the top of his head. In his last seconds of life he found it hard to breathe before staring at the shadow, his eyes becoming bloodshot and the blood from the heavy wound instantly dripping down his face like the water in one of the mountain springs. Momentarily the pain became suddenly apparent as for a final time he looked at the figure, as dark as the trees, blackened face, staring eyes, no expression. His breathing had become erratic what with the fear, and it quickened which made the shadow reach closer towards his face, the air inside the boys chest reducing with every inhaling breath. Kyle tried to scream as the life left his body and he fell to the ground. The dark shadow removed the pick from his head and thrust into the dead boy's stomach. The shadow hacked away at the torso before thrusting the weapon into the boys chest and pulling downwards towards the open wound on the stomach. There was a haunting gasp from the shadow's mouth as the eyes showed the excitement at the kill.

Derryn stood up and looked in the direction that Kyle had walked. "Where the hell is he? Is he walking to bloody Maesteg to get the stuff?"

Rob got up from the ground although he was still holding his fireworks as though he wasn't going to let anyone else have them. He stood shoulder to shoulder with his friend and looked down in the same direction. He couldn't see anything or anyone and so started to look around in other directions. "I can't see him."

"KYLE!"

"KYLE!" Rob joined in whilst taking a few steps forward nearer to the first of the trees. "Wakey-wakey!" He then looked at Derryn whilst taking further steps into the dark. "KYLE! FOR FUCKS SAKE!"

"Where the hell ...?" Before Derryn could finish he watched Rob drop the fireworks at the side of him and walk into the woods. The cries of *'Kyle'* slowly becoming more distant the further that Rob walked although Derryn continued to hear the crunching of the branches under Rob's feet. "Anything Rob?" he shouted.

There was a distant voice. "No. Can't see him anywhere," Rob replied as once more he stopped and turned in a complete 360-degree circle to try and hopefully see the gang member. In his heart he was much expecting Kyle to jump out on him and scare him so much that his heart would race. Rob's fate was also sealed. Making another turn, he briefly noticed the shadow that he had seen the night before, the one that had ended his friend's life moments ago. Quickly it appeared in front of him. It was a shock at first as Rob began to think that this was Kyle once more trying to scare him. "You twat!" There was nothing in reply. He was much expecting Kyle to wipe his face and burst out with laughter, but it didn't happen. Then it suddenly hit him that the figure in front of him wasn't Kyle. "Fuck! DARRYN!" He turned and tried to run but something didn't seem right. The shadow struck out at the boy as he ran, the pickaxe finding its way into Rob's head the same as it had done with Kyle. The boy screamed and started to cry out with pain. Both hands reached up to the wound which was completely open as the pickaxed had completely ripped his skull apart. He felt the extreme pain, he looked at his hand as he lowered it. Within seconds his life was extinct. There were no more screams. No more cries. No more calls for help. Just like Kyle, the pick was removed from the boys head as the body fell to the floor. The dark figure reached down and flicked the body onto its back and then raised the weapon above the head height momentarily before it was brought down with force into Rob's stomach. The boy was ripped open, his torso ripped apart. The pick was now sticking out of the area where his kidneys were. Rob's dead staring eyes look petrified as they stared up as though he was looking at the darkened assailant. For the boy it was too late. In the same way that his friend Kyle had met his fate, the darkened figure had ripped his torso from top to bottom.

Darryn stood on the path looking into the darkness. He heard his friend crying out, screaming as though he were in agony. But then silence. Nothing. Not even a bird tweeting. He didn't know what to do. What was happening? Were they being attacked by other boys from the villages around? That sometimes happened. Teenagers fight for control.

"KYLE! WHERE ARE YOU? ROB?" There was silence. "ROB? KYLE?" Nothing. Darryn began to wonder what was happening and began to think that something was happening. Something was wrong. Something to do with the black figure that he had seen outside his house. The same black figure that Rob had also seen. Suddenly a fearful look appeared on his own face, and he started slowly backing away whilst still looking in the direction that both his friends had walked. Without hesitation he turned and started to run in the direction of the wind turbines knowing that he had several choices of direction from there. Hopefully, he would come across help. The dog walkers would be out soon. But what he did know was that something wasn't right. Both his friends did not answer him and did not return from the cold dark forest. He reached the junction where he had three choices; down into the forest on the rocky path that led to the plain, straight ahead further along the path that led to the other side of the mountain and finally down to Pont-y-Rhyl, or to the right up by the wind turbines. He quickly looked around him for anything or anyone. There was no one, not even the appearance of Rob or Kyle, not even the dark figure, not even a dog walker, so he continued running as fast as he could deciding to go left and down towards the plains even though it was through the edge of the forest that Kyle and Rob had not returned from. But at the other end of the path that wasn't far away, the plains were usually occupied by the dog-walkers as they reached the top of the hillside path and continued past the Welsh flag.

Derryn ran and ran whilst stumbling several times on the uneven surface where the rocks on the ground flipped his ankles. He was halfway down now. His head was turning from side to side which didn't help his balance on the rough terrain. He began crying in fear, worried not only for himself but his friends as well. He could see the light at the end of the path. He stared forward whilst several times quickly looking behind him to check that he wasn't being followed. Derryn tripped as he felt pain around his feet and legs. The movement of his fall stopped him. He looked around and saw nothing. Not a soul in sight. His breathing was now heavy, but he told himself that he had to get out and onto the plain. "HELP! HELP ME!" he cried, hoping that he would get someone's attention, but there was no help coming. He didn't have far to go and so pushed himself upwards. There was noise of a branch cracking to his left. He turned his head slowly to see what the noise was. Out of the corner of his eye he saw the darkened figure, face covered with blackened dust, hovering towards him at a pace, pick in one hand and sharpened blade in the other. Derryn's eyes widened with fear as he froze. He screamed for several seconds, the screams echoing around the forest before silence fell once more. Life extinct.

*****

The cold mist had settled in over the forest, thick, white, which could have easily been mistaken for smoke from a distance. But that didn't stop the dog walkers who knew that no matter what the weather they had to go out come rain or shine.

Barney the German Shepherd and Rocko the American Bulldog were the best of friends and local dogwalker Kirsty Williams knew that. She could only take dogs that were *'friends'* out together through fear of having a mass brawl between the canines that she looked after. The two were running across the plains but were going too far out of sight. There were also livestock close by and she knew that Barney liked to chase the sheep although being that little bit older now would never be able to catch one. "Barney! Rocko! Wait!" The two of them were quite obedient and obeyed their recall. Kirsty often used to comment, *'They don't mess with the dog lady otherwise they don't get cwtches at the end!'* They waited until the lady was closer and then started running up the path towards the junction with the wind turbines. Halfway up the path, Barney started barking which started Rocko to do the same. At first Kirsty thought it was just dogs being dogs. They had probably seen the horses that sometimes frequented the area or were chasing the squirrels.

Kirsty stopped a few times on the rocky path to catch her breath. She looked down on the uneven terrain. Blood. It wasn't as though someone had just cut their finger or fallen over, this was quite a lot of blood. Worried that it could be one of the dogs she rushed up in the direction of the barking with increased speed. "You two! Quiet!" But in the corner of her eye on the right she saw something. Slowly turning because she didn't want it to be what she thought that she had briefly seen, she looked. There was a huge gasp from her lips. Kirsty was speechless and raised both of her hands to her cheeks and then dropped the left one across her mouth. Her eyes started to weep. "Fucking hell!" She screamed.

The three boys bodies had been strung up on the tall trees in the darkness, in the same way that you would find a skydiver, legs tied backwards, arms forward and torso hanging over the ground. She looked at the mutilation, with their internal organs hanging out, two with the intestines touching the ground. There was blood everywhere, dripping out of the corpses and spreading all over the ground, the trees around the dead, the redness standing out even in the semi-darkness and contrasting against the green and brown. The heads of the victims split open viciously. She looked whilst knowing that the boys in no way would be alive, so chose to stay where she was. Her feet were frozen to the ground in any case. Frantically she reached inside her pocket for her mobile but fumbled worriedly with it and it fell to the floor. She quickly leaned over to pick it up and as she stood up she looked at the mutilation once more. Then she dialled the emergency services. 9-9-9.

"Emergency. Which service do you require?"

"Police! Please!" She cried.

One hour later, the higher plains at the top of the rocky path that led up from the Pontycymer lake were filled with Uniformed and plain clothed Police Officers, four who had arrived by India-99, the Police helicopter that had been scattered initially from across the Valley and managed to pick up CID from the grasslands near the old Blaengarw colliery. The Police vehicles and ambulances had to negate the rough terrain on the stoney paths that twisted and turned through the various forests and plains before reaching the crime scene. Detective Chief Inspector William Gwyn, Detective Inspector Morgan Harris, Detective Sergeant Peter Ellis, and Detective Constable Aled Tello waited for the helicopter to land on the plain and then under instruction from the crew jumped out, lowering their heads as the propeller came slowly to a halt. DCI Gwyn noticed two Uniformed Officers who appeared to be waiting for them.

"Sir," PS Martin Pugh said as he noticed the DCI and his team.

"What's the story, Martin?" DCI Gwyn enquired seriously as he also looked around to search for the possible location of the crime, noticing a great deal of action to his left up in a clump of huge trees separated by a rocky path.

"Three bodies, Guv. Not a pretty sight. Boys, unrecognisable although we estimate they are in their teens."

"I guess they are up there," DI Harris mentioned whilst pointing in the direction of a group of Uniformed Officers.

"Yes," Martin replied. "We are currently drafting in more Officers to seal the area. As you can understand the forest is a huge place."

The DCI looked content that the organisation of the securing of the area was in good hands with an experienced Sergeant like Martin Pugh. "Any witnesses?"

"Only the lady that found the bodies. She is a local dog walker." He looked at his notes. "Kirsty Williams. She is over there in the squad car. Pretty shook up as you can understand. We have given her a cup of tea from one of the PC's flask."

"Might be best if we get her away. Take a statement from her back in the security of her own home."

PS Pugh nodded in agreement. "I'll get onto that now."

"What about forensics?"

"They are on their way. I spoke to Matt Robinson moments ago. As you can understand, it is not easy to access the area. Unless you have a helicopter," he smiled hoping that his humour would be accepted.

"Okay. Can you take us a bit closer?" DCI Gwyn asked as he nodded to the three other Officers in his team to follow them.

Martin Pugh led the way just as another vehicle arrived at the scene. He noticed the forensic team vehicle and as it skidded to a halt, Matthew Robinson jumped out. "Don't go anywhere near my crime scene," he shouted as he looked at the DCI. "The less contamination the better!" The large muscly ex-rugby player looked at his team who had also exited the vehicle and immediately opened the side door on the small van. The three of them started to change into their Tyvek suits. "If you want to go closer, DCI Gwyn, you will need to dress properly." He threw the senior Officer a package containing an unused outfit. "Otherwise you will need to wait."

"Can we get a bit closer just to take a look?"

"I'll let you know."

Gwyn nodded his head as he watched Matthew Robinson and his team head up the incline whilst slowly watching their footing on the rocky ground. "Okay," he said as he looked at DI Harris and then back and forward at the pair. "Let's see if Uniform know anything. They must have seen something."

"Guv," he replied. "Sergeant Pugh. Can we talk to the Officers who arrived at the scene first?"

Martin Pugh nodded and then flipped his fingers towards a young WPC who was removing a roll of cordon tape from the back of a vehicle. "WPC Baines. Can you make your way up to the top path and relieve WPC's Rowlands and Jones. Ask them to come down as CID want to talk to them. Take the long route so you don't disturb the scene of crime."

"Yes Serge," she replied.

"Oh. Take WPC Llywd with you."

The girl nodded her head and walked over towards her new colleague. "It will be a while, Guv. We have to walk around to get to the top cordon."

"No worries," Gwyn replied. "Let's get a bit closer anyway." They walked over towards the bottom of the path but were stopped by the cordon tape that forensics had put up on the way to the crime scene. "Okay," he said as he grabbed the 'Crime scene under examination – do not cross' tape. "We will stay here."

Thirty minutes later, WPC's Rowlands and Jones appeared from the forest on the left having walked around to a side path that in the other direction led down to the next Valley and further on to Pont-y-Rhyl.

"Serge. You wanted to speak to us?" WPC Jones enquired whilst being first to reach the four Officers.

"Yes. Not sure if you have met DCI Gwyn. He just needs some information from you on what you saw and found when you arrived."

Both WPC's opened their log books, Sergeant Pugh feeling happy that they had immediately taken notes which usually meant that they wouldn't forget anything. WPC Rowlands was first to perk up. "We answered the call and met the witness, a ..." she checked the name in the book. "Kirsty Williams. She led us up about halfway up the path here," she pointed behind her at the incline that the forensics team had entered and walked up before they arrived.

"That's right, Sir," WPC Jones added. "We saw three bodies hung up in the trees. They looked like boys, mid-teens but we couldn't be sure. They were completely mutilated."

"Mutilated?" DS Ellis jumped in.

Both WPC's nodded their heads as WPC Rowlands added, "Their guts and other bits hanging out of the bodies. Blood everywhere." Her eyes lowered to the ground and her voice softened as the shock of what she had seen suddenly hit her hard.

WPC Jones felt the same and knew that she had to take over the report to the CID. "We left the bodies as we found them. The only other things that we saw when we went up to cordon off the area on the top path, were a holdall, a pile of fireworks and a bottle of liquid of some kind." She looked at her fellow WPC hoping that she would snap out of her trance. "That was it really. Have you got anything to add, Ffion?" The other Officer shook her head.

"Okay," DCI Gwyn replied. "Thanks for that. I guess we will have to wait for Matt and his team to get further information. But fireworks. What is the sense of that?"

"We have had a spate of forest fires in the area recently, Sir," WPC Jones added just before she went to walk away.

"That's right," PS Pugh continued. "We have suspected it was arson but have had no leads to date."

"I think you may have found your arsonists, Sergeant," DI Harris added as he watched PS Pugh nod his head in agreement.

It was over two hours before Forensics Officer Stephen Garwood appeared at the cordon having been sent down by his manager.

"You can approach the scene now, gentlemen," he announced as he lifted the tape. The four CID Officers bowed down and stepped under, quickly followed by Sergeant Pugh. "Suits, please," he said as he handed each a bag with a white outfit in.

"About time," DCI Gwyn said with a laugh. "It will be dark soon."

After suiting up, they all walked cautiously up the path whilst being careful just in case there was any evidence on the ground that hadn't been picked up. It wasn't long before they noticed two people also in white suits kneeling down on the floor and scavenging among the foliage. As they approached, Matthew Robinson stood up and lowered his mask, pointing at the three bodies. "There we go, gentlemen," he announced, joining the five Officers in staring at the carnage.

"Oh God," DC Tello said which showed that this was the first time that he had ever seen something so bad.

"Preliminary Matt?" DI Harris said, knowing that he was probably the only one of the four CID Officers that had worked with the senior forensics Officer before.

"Males. Young teenagers I would say. Killed with an instrument like a hammer, although further examination will be needed to confirm that. Looking at the splatter patterns they were hung here after their death. Two killed in the forest in that direction," he nodded his head to his left. "There are blood trails which led us to the scene of crime. The third boy was attacked just in front of you under the cover which we have put up to keep the elements off it. Blood everywhere and splattered on the trees around the scene of crime."

"Anything else?"

"Yes," Matthew replied inquisitively as he held up a bag containing black dust. "This." He peered into the bag, his face going close to the evidence. "Under each body and around each kill scene. Black dust. I think it is coal dust." He watched as the five all filled their faces with a mixture of confusion and misunderstanding.

"Coal dust?" DS Ellis enquired confusingly.

Matthew Robinson nodded as he twisted the bag around in his fingers and stared at it. "Yes. Coal dust."

Chapter 4

Iaon Hartland stood at the bottom of the stairs. He knew that he hadn't seen his son since he had returned home from work which wasn't unusual for the normally thoughtless teenager. He imagined the sketches of *'Kevin and Perry'* and the growing pains that parents had to face, and a smile filled his face as he chuckled. He then thought to himself, *'surely the lazy bastard couldn't still be in bed?'*. He looked up to the top of the stairs.

"Robert. Are you there?" He asked whilst looking at his watch. His wife Rhiannon appeared from the living room. "Have you seen Rob today?"

She shook her head. "No. Not since he woke you last evening. What was that all about anyway?"

"He said someone was looking at him through the living room window," he laughed and shook his head.

"Has he been on the wacky baccy again?" his Mother asked her husband whilst laughing.

"Do you know that is exactly what I said," Iaon laughed once more. "No. He claimed it was a man all dressed in black and he couldn't see his face."

"Definitely hallucinating."

"ROBERT!" he shouted loudly with a bit more anger in his voice. "Shit. I'll go up. He probably has his earphones in."

"Get with the times, old man!" Rhiannon laughed. "It's EarPods these days."

"Ear ..."

"Pods," she snapped back with a smile.

"Well perhaps he has them on." He started walking up the stairs whilst still calling, "Rob! Lazy bones! Get out of bed!" Without warning he pushed open the boys bedroom door and then closed it to speak to his wife once more. "Well he isn't there. I know he was on his PlayStation until late last night, and then he saw that person outside. So he would have probably gone to bed late. He wasn't there when I left for work."

"Then I guess he is out with his friends," Rhiannon replied whilst not feeling as concerned as her husband.

"Well he hasn't come home for his tea. That's a first."

Rhiannon shook her head. "If he is not home soon I'll call his friends and see if he is around their houses. He has probably just got caught up in some game that they play."

"I'll try his mobile," Iaon snapped. "Give him a rollocking for not telling us where he is." He looked at his wife shake her head as he took his phone out of his pocket and went to his contacts. "Straight to voicemail," he exclaimed.

"He is probably out of battery. Hasn't charged it."

"Come on. He charges it every night. How many times do I have to tell him not to leave his charger plugged in?"

"Stop worrying about him. He is fifteen and can handle himself." Rhiannon went to return to the living room and have a sit down.

Iaon tapped his phone on his right hand and bit his lip. Something told him that there was something wrong. Perhaps he had upset someone. Perhaps his sighting of a man in black wasn't a hallucination after all. He sat down at the kitchen table and decided to clock watch until Rob returned home. His home telephone rang as he continued to look at the kitchen clock. It was 21:10 hrs. "Hello."

"Hello butt. This is Derryn Jones' Dad. He's a friend of your Robert. I was just wondering if he was there with him? We haven't seen him all day and he is not answering his phone."

"It's Rob's Dad here. We seem to have the same problem. Rob seems to have gone missing. The wife hasn't seen or heard from him all day either." Iaon tried to get his wife's attention by waving at her. "I haven't seen Rob since I returned home from work either."

Allan Jones was stood in his living room with his wife beside him. "I know he went out early this morning. I heard the front door bang closed."

41

"Any ideas where they would have gone?" Iaon was joined by his wife and as she stood beside him he whispered. "It's Rob's friend Derryn's Dad. He hasn't been seen either."

"No. I know they both go to school with another lad who Derryn plays a game with online. But I don't know where he lives. I think his name is Kyle."

Rob's Dad nodded his head as though the man on the other end of the phone could see him. "Yes. Kyle Griffiths. I've given him a lift to school when they have both missed the bus. Not sure where he lives though. Or his phone number."

"I'm going to call the Police," Iaon said with more than a sense of worry in his voice. "This is very worrying. I'll give you a call back."

"Great. Thanks."

*****

Up on the mountain, the area was still closed off although the search for evidence had ceased until the morning as darkness had fallen and the mist was like a shroud falling into the paths and trees especially up on the top. Police cars remained at each potential entrance in order to preserve the crime scene ready for the search to be restarted in the morning, although DCI Gwyn couldn't foresee anyone attempting to walk the mountain heights late at night. It had been a long day for the CID Officers. They had watched the Uniform Officers changeover, whilst they themselves remained there in case anything was found that may be of some importance. They were just about to get into two of the waiting squad cars to get back to the station when DI Harris' mobile burst into life.

"DI Harris," he announced.

"Hello, Sir. It's Sergeant Rollinson at CAD. We have just had a call through about two missing teenagers."

DI Harris held up his hand to try and quieten down the DCI and the two Uniform Officers who were in the squad car with him. "Do we have a description of the boys? Perhaps what they were wearing?"

"No, Sir. I've despatched a unit around to get further information."

"Okay. Keep me informed even if it means contacting me out of hours."

"Will do, Sir," Rollinson said as he ended the call.

DI Harris looked at the DCI. "That was Sierra Oscar. Sergeant Rollinson has taken a call about two missing teenagers."

"Only two?" the DCI enquired. They would need three to get names to the bodies if it were anything to do with the three bodies that they had found. He watched the DI nod his head.

"Uniform are in attendance, so hopefully we may get more by the end of today."

There was nothing. No information about the missing boys. No telephone call from the attending Officers. But the night was young. Morgan Harris and the rest of the team all decided to call it a day and go home. He didn't live far from the station which he wasn't sure whether it was a good thing or a bad thing. He could leave it until the last minute to go on duty, but if there was a problem he was always the first to be called. But he knew that the term *'Always on Duty'* was assigned to him especially. He opened his front door. The house was in complete darkness. It was 22:20 hrs and he knew that his wife would be in bed. Grabbing a can of beer from the fridge, he sat down on the sofa and picked up the remote control for the television which was on the coffee table in front of him. The news. They had picked up on the story of the three bodies. Just what he didn't want.

'We are as close as we can get to the scene of crime here in Blaengarw forest. Reports have come in that there have been three bodies found on the mountain, three young boys we have been told although that has yet to be confirmed. Sky news has contacted the Police for comment and are waiting for further information although darkness has now settled in and so we guess that investigations will be suspended until the morning.'

Morgan took a swig of his beer and shook his head. Another long day tomorrow, he thought to himself. Time for bed. After a quick shower he managed to lay down beside his lady wife and close his eyes. He didn't get much sleep as his mobile rang loudly just over two hours later.

"DI Harris? It's PC Eastman."

"I hope this is good ringing me at this time of night," Morgan Harris replied in a tired voice as he turned and looked at his bedside clock and saw that it was 01:25 hrs.

"Yes, Guv. We now have a report of three missing teenage boys. None have been seen since early yesterday morning."

Harris alerted and quickly sat up, feet now on the floor. He picked up the pen and paper that he had on his bedside table. "Do we have names?"

Flicking the pages of his notebook, PC Eastman replied, "Yes, Guv. Robert Hartland, Kyle Griffiths and Derryn Jones. Two aged fourteen and one aged fifteen. I've put all the details on CRIMEN. We are organising a search for them as soon as daylight appears."

"Did you get a description of what each boy was last wearing?"

"Yes, Guv. It's all on the system."

"Okay, PC Eastman. You may not have to worry about that search. I'll check CRIMEN but I'm sure they are the three boys found in the Blaengarw forest this morning. Thanks for letting me know." Morgan Harris' clothes were neatly folded and on the chair in the corner. He rubbed his eyes whilst wondering if he wanted to do this now or let it wait until the morning. "No time like the present," he Mumbled to himself as he reached over and started getting dressed. There were a multiple of thoughts going through his mind as he grabbed a clean shirt and tie. Should he call the DCI and the rest of the team at this time of night? They weren't needed at this moment and would all be fresh, ready, and willing to go in the morning. Plus the DCI lived over in Cwmbran which was an hour's drive in any case. No. This was something that he would handle at this moment in time.

Outside of his office window, the sun was rising, and the brightness instructed him to turn off the lights to let nature's beauty shine through the building. Harris looked at his watch. He had been there since just after 02:00 hrs and prepared everything for a team briefing first thing as soon as all the CID team arrived. As usual, DCI Gwyn was first in wearing his long expensive cashmere coat and carrying his briefcase that appeared to be bursting at the seams. DI Harris met him just as he was about to disappear into his own office.

"Morning, Guv."

"God," the DCI responded. "You look like you have been here all night." He saw the reaction on the junior Officer's face. "You have been here all night."

Harris nodded. "I got a call from Uniform. Bad news. There has been a third boy reported missing in the Garw. We now have three names. We need to get the final forensic reports. But it's not just coincidence."

The DCI looked at him seriously and lightly shook his head. "If that's the case, we will need to get something to use as a DNA sample for forensics from each family so we can match up against what they have found. Get a positive ID."

"I've called a team meeting for 08:30."

"Good idea. Disseminate the information and assign duties. We will need to be very empathetic on this one to start."

DI Harris nodded his head. "It's going to be very delicate. Just going and asking the parents for access to their boys clothes will just echo the fact that we know they are probably dead."

Gwyn nodded in agreement and turned to head into his original destination. "We had better let Matt and the team know that we may have something coming their way."

The DI nodded and then headed back to his own office.

Forty minutes later, DI Harris' office filled with an array of Officers from his team, some wide awake, others looking like they had been out on the town for most of the night. DCI Gwyn had seen them all assembling and headed in, checking to see if anyone else was coming before closing the door behind him. He nodded at Morgan giving him indication to start the meeting.

DI Harris looked around. Everyone was present. He knew that he could always trust every member of his team to turn up to work unless they were seriously ill. Several had caught Covid-19 during the pandemic and those who were able to come in picked up their caseloads. "Okay. Listen up team! You may have heard by now that there were three bodies found in the

45

Blaengarw forest yesterday." He stopped as there was a tap on the door and without invitation, SFO Matthew Robinson stepped in.

"Sorry I'm late," Matt said, although DI Harris hadn't actually expected him at the meeting and then assumed that the DCI had told him about the briefing.

"That's okay, Matt. You haven't missed much." Harris turned his attention back to the team. "Three bodies. I will let forensics give you the report on those. But firstly, overnight we had reports of three missing teenagers in the Garw area. We have names. What we don't have is identification." He looked at the SFO. "Matt. What do you have for us?"

He opened his A4 style leather folder containing his notes. "Further to the preliminary results, I can now confirm that the three corpses belonged to males, aged around twelve to fifteen. Their bodies were completely gutted and mutilated; throats had been cut. Each contained a head wound, quite deep. At first I thought it may have been a claw hammer or something like a claw hammer. However, Olivia came up with the idea that the shape of the wound resembled the shape that an old miner's pick would make. Her Grandfather was a miner up until closure of the mine up at Blaengarw. She managed to borrow his old tool that he still had in his possession." He stopped and looked around the room. "I can confirm that in all three cases, it looks like that was the murder weapon. The mutilations began after death."

"How can that be analysed?" DC Tomos Mitchell enquired whilst wondering what the significance was.

"The initial amount of blood loss and the angle at which it seemed to be thrust into the heads. On each victim, the sharp end of the pick went straight through the brain cavity."

"So the majority of the blood loss occurred after? When the mutilation was carried out?" Tomo's asked further.

"You got it. Now as I told the DCI and DI Harris, there was an amount of what we have now confirmed as coal dust, although not fine. More of a nutty slack containing small pieces of coal. Exceedingly small I may add. Coal dust itself is a fine-powdered form of coal which is created by the crushing, grinding, or pulverization of coal rock. Because of the brittle nature of coal,

coal dust can be created by mining, transporting, or mechanically handling it."

"That is strange," DC Tello added. "Where did that come from? The mines have been closed since '85."

DCI Gwyn perked up. "Which is what we need to find out, team," He responded importantly. "The Superintendent has classified this as A plus. We need results."

"Exactly," Harris exclaimed. "Now the parents of the missing boys have already had Uniform asking questions. We are going to visit them and ask for sample of hair obtainable from something like pillows, or from clothing. We must be professional and empathetic. Do not give anything away. We do not know if the three boys who have gone missing are the three boys whose bodies were found yesterday."

"It's got to be more than a coincidence though Guv," DC Harriet Lewis said whilst feeling that the link of three bodies to three corpses more or less spelled out disaster.

"We must not assume until we have valid confirmation from Matt and his department," DCI Gwyn stated whilst looking around and looking at DC Lewis in particular.

"The names and addresses are on CRIMEN. DC's Ceredig and Tello will collect forensic evidence from Derryn Jones' house. DC Earon and ADC Rees will pair up and collect the same from Kyle Griffiths parents' home. DC Mitchell and ADC Nafydd will contact the Hartlands."

"Just make sure you wear these," Matt Robinson ordered whilst throwing sealed bags containing Tyvek suits. "They will help prevent contamination. Bag all in sealed evidence bags and use pinchers to pick them up."

The six CID Officers nodded as each of them caught their packages. "The rest of us will handle a press conference, door-to-door, and confiscation of any CCTV in the area. Duties are on the attached sheets in your duty packs." Harris nodded at them. "Any questions? No? Let's get out there then." The room emptied.

DS Ellis joined the DI and DCI at the desk. "I see we are handling the press, Guv."

DCI Gwyn nodded. "It has already been speculated on by the news channels on TV. No doubt the gutter press will further speculate unless we give them an accurate headline."

"It may work in our favour, Guv," Harris exclaimed whilst looking at his boss. "Let's get them working for us."

Gwyn nodded. "It's at eleven. So meet back here 30-minutes prior. I'll see to the statement." Both junior Officers gave a 'Guv' as the DCI left the room.

*****

DC Earon and ADC Rees were the first to arrive at the Griffiths in Pontycymer. They walked up the steps, Earon leading the two of them as he reached over, noticing that the family had a *'Ring'* video doorbell.

"I've done this before," DC Earon stated as he looked at his colleague. "I'll do the talking. Whilst I am upstairs, you comfort the parents." He watched as Siwan Rees nodded his head quietly and could tell that the younger trainee was a little apprehensive about what they were about to do. The lady answered the door.

"Hello," she said, guessing who the pair were from.

"Mrs Griffiths? DC Earon," he replied whilst holding up his warrant card for her to see. "This is ADC Rees. Would you mind if we came in?"

She nodded her head and opened the door wide for the pair to enter. "Is there any news?" she asked worriedly whilst wondering why the pair were there even though the two Uniformed Officers had told her that CID would be out to see them sometime soon.

Huw Earon, a thin, small Officer who was into his running in his spare time and had the physique of a distance runner, looked the lady in the eyes. "Yes and no." He looked at the lady with an element of concern. "I didn't really want you to find out at the moment, but I wouldn't want you to find out either in the papers or on the news." He took a deep breath with the realisation of what he was about to say. "Three bodies were found up on the mountain yesterday. We need to ask you if we can take some form of sample from Kyle's bedroom in order that we can use it for DNA matching."

"You think that the three bodies found are those of the missing boys don't you?" Carli asked as she fell backwards onto the sofa behind her.

"We cannot rule it out, Mrs Griffiths. I'm not going to lie to you. Which is why we need to take something like a piece of clothing that Kyle wore recently, or a couple of hairs from his pillow. I pray that it is not your son, believe me."

There was a silence, a solemn atmosphere for a few moments as Carli Griffiths looked forward into nothingness. She knew that it was going to be bad news. So it had to be done. "I need to call my husband," she said as she grabbed her mobile from beside her. "But please. Let's get this over and done with. His room is the third door on the left up the stairs. Please be as tidy as you can. I would like to keep it in pristine order for when he returns."

Huw Earon nodded at ADC Rees as if to say that he would go and take the sample whilst he stayed and consoled the Mother. He left the living room and walked over towards the hallway. Before he ascended the stairs, he took out the Tyvek suit and quickly put it on. As he reached the top of the stairs, he looked around. Then, heading over towards the room that the lady had told him, he opened the door and walked into the bedroom that he had been given the permission to go in. He noticed just how clean and tidy it was which at times wasn't a good thing he told himself. It may restrict the samples that he could take. Had Kyle's Mother washed his clothes? He placed a pair of evidence gloves on his hands and then took out an evidence bag and a pair of tweezers that Matt Robinson had given him. Then he pulled back the duvet on the bed and looked closely at the pillow. He nodded to himself as he realised that Carli Griffiths had left the room in exactly the same way that his son had left it. There were several short hairs on the pillow. He carefully picked up four using the tweezers and placed them in the bag before sealing it tightly shut. He stopped and looked around, replacing the duvet in exactly the place that he had found it. For a few moments he began to wonder just how the parents were feeling. The thought passed as he left the room and closed the door behind him and didn't hesitate before going back down the stairs.

"All done, Serge?" ADC Rees asked the older Officer as he walked back into the living room.

DC Earon nodded. "Thank you for that, Mrs Griffiths," he said apologetically as he started to remove the white suit, struggling with the area around the feet which nearly caused him to fall over.

"So what happens now?"

"I have to get the samples of hair I have taken back to forensics," he replied as he finished removing the Tyvek suit. "As soon as we have any result your family liaison Officer will be in contact." DC Earon looked at the lady and gave her a sorrowful smile of hope.

Carli nodded. "But one of the bodies is my Kyle, isn't it?"

DC Earon didn't know how to answer. "Let's hope not," he said as he tapped her upper arm in support before heading towards the door.

"Thank you Mrs Griffiths," Siwan said as he passed her a business card. "And like I said, if you need to talk, there's my number. I mean that."

The lady nodded. "Thank you." She watched as the two Officers left.

*****

DC's Ceredig and Tello had less success contacting the parents of Derryn Jones. No one was answering the door and when DC Ceredig tried the mobile telephone numbers that Uniform had taken from them on the previous night, both numbers went straight to voicemail. He didn't leave a message mainly due to the delicate nature of their visit but decided to return later in the day thinking that both parents could have gone to work as normal and may be restricted in answering by their employers.

*****

It was quite the opposite for Robert Hartland's parents. Before the two Officers knocked on the door it opened. They had been waiting in anticipation for any news on their son's disappearance.

"Mr Hartland?" DC Mitchell enquired as he approached the front door. He took out his warrant card from his pocket and flashed it in the direction of Robert's Father. "DC Mitchell and ADC Nafydd. South Wales Police."

"I've just seen the news," Iaon stated with a look of worry on his face. "They are saying that three bodies were found up on the mountain yesterday. Is that right?"

Mitchell knew that he had an instant problem and was trying to think of what he could tell the parents at this point in the investigation. "Shall we go inside, Mr Hartland. It will be a bit more private."

Iaon Hartland opened the door wider. "Please go through."

Mitchell and Nafydd saw Mrs Hartland sat on the sofa, head in hands as she continued to watch the headlines. The murders had reached the national news on both Sky and the BBC, and Rhiannon Hartland was flicking back and forward between the two to get the most up-to-date information. "Have you seen this?" she demanded to know.

"We are aware of the situation," DC Mitchell replied sympathetically. "I can confirm that we were called to the area yesterday morning. Three bodies were removed."

Iaon Hartland shook his head and started to choke up. "It's the three boys, isn't it? It's my Robert."

"I hope not," DC Mitchell replied as he looked at the Father, although his eyes told Iaon that it was more than coincidence that three boys missing, and three bodies had been found. "It is one of the reasons we are here, Mr Hartland. To rule things out,"

"Or confirm," Iaon Hartland snapped in knowing just what the Detective was getting at, He stared at him.

"Okay. Or confirm, that it is, or isn't, Robert. we need something that we can compare in the laboratory and assess the DNA."

"Oh my God!" Mrs Hartland shouted out as she started to cry hysterically. Iaon quickly stepped around the sofa to comfort his wife.

"We need to get a sample of hair, perhaps from Robert's bed or pillow. Either that or a piece of clothing that he regularly wore that hasn't been washed since he last wore it."

Rhiannon Hartland didn't hear the request but continued to cry and Mumble, "He's dead. Rob is dead."

Robert's Father nodded at the two Detectives as he sat on the arm of the sofa and continued to cuddle his wife. "His bedroom is directly above here at the front. You will see the Wales duvet cover."

"Thank you."

"Has this got something to do with the man that Rob saw peering through the window two nights ago?" DC Mitchell stopped dead in his tracks. "A man looking through the window. Didn't the Police Officer tell you?"

"No. But we haven't managed to pick up on all the information of the case yet, Sir." Mitchell knew that was just an excuse. Why Uniform hadn't mentioned something as important as that was beyond him but once he got back to the station he would ask why.

"Rob reckoned there was a figure of a man outside looking at him. All dressed in black he said."

The thought went through DC Mitchell's mind of the presence of coal dust at the crime scene up at the mountain and a hunch was crossing his mind. Could there be anything outside on the ground? "ADC Nafydd will take a look whilst I am upstairs." He nodded his head sideways for Jon Nafydd to do just that. As the trainee Detective went to go outside, Mitchell whispered, *"coal dust"* in his ear.

"I believe Robert's friend Darryn saw the same figure, although three nights ago."

"Scrap that," Mitchell said to Nafydd. "Give forensics a call. Tell them what Mr Hartland has just told us. Get them up here." ADC Nafydd nodded his head as he stepped outside into the hallway whilst taking his mobile phone out of his pocket. "I'm going to put this on and then head upstairs if that is okay?"

Iaon Hartland nodded back to him as he wrapped his arms around his wife's head and pulled her into him. He watched as minutes later, the white suit cladded Detective run back down the stairs with four evidence bags in his hand.

"Forensics are on their way," Jon Nafydd said as he met DC Mitchell in the hallway at the base of the stairs.

"Okay, we will have to wait to meet them, Can you let the DCI know?"

ADC Nafydd nodded his head.

An hour later Stephen Garwood and Olivia Higgins appeared and took samples from outside, the ground, the external window sills, and the surrounding area. There were no fingerprints. Only elements of coal dust.

*****

Two days had passed, and the forensics team were working flat out sampling and testing all the DNA evidence from the crime scene. The DNA from the three samples taken from the boys homes were confirmed as those of the missing three boys. The information was passed to DCI Gwyn and his team. The boys had been identified as the first three victims. DCI Gwyn also knew that his team had an extremely dangerous individual out there that they had to find sooner rather than later.

It was easier said than done.

Chapter 5

Fourteen-year-old Betson Morris-Evans was the typical Valleys girl who always thought that she knew everything about growing up in Pontycymer. The boys knew her, used her as she was the most promiscuous girl around and by her age had made sure that she had sex with many boys in the area both her age and even not her age. To get through the boring nights after school she would hang around various parts of Pontycymer and Blaengarw with her so-called friends. To her anything was funny. She would kick cats until they squealed, vandalise parked cars, kick the uprights out of the pedestrian bridges that crossed the streams from the top of Blaengarw down as far as Pantygog. She didn't care and anyone who saw her would just get a mouthful of abuse. Once again the Police were helpless. She didn't listen. Betson's parents were just as bad, keeping Police Officers and PCSO's at the door when they officially visited them to talk about their delinquent daughter and then telling them to *'fuck off'* as they slammed the door shut.

The spring had definitely left the area and the normal Valleys weather for the early summer had settled in with the formation of the misty rain coming down from the mountains that surrounded the villages. Betson and her friends stood on the footbridge crossing the Pontycymer lake late one evening. The sky was dark. No one ever came around the lake that time of evening and so the group felt that they could do whatever they wanted.

Like quite a lot of the teenagers, getting alcohol was easy. Betson would take it from her Dad's supply in his fridge or take the vodka or rum from his private bar. Just like many of the younger element in the area she would also demand that some of the locals who she knew to buy her alcohol in the Coop. They wouldn't argue with her because they knew the consequences if they did say no. They would wake up the next morning with their cars scratched or wing mirrors kicked off. Buying her alcohol to them was a kind of protection money. She had them in the palm of her hand.

Delme Greening had his arm around her shoulders as the two stood looking over the lake at the ducks. He was already slightly intoxicated as he swayed and without realisation breathed over the girl. "Let's fuck," he said as he put his arm around her neck and pulled her into him.

"Fuck? Why don't you fuck off," she replied. "You are drunk. You probably couldn't even get it up."

The group of boys around him started to laugh as they listened in on the conversation. "He can't get it up when he isn't drunk," Jamie Arnett exclaimed as he laughed with the rest of them.

"Well I got it up your Mum," Delme replied whilst being quick off the ball.

Jamie laughed in reply. "I wouldn't put it past you, butt. You'd shag anything that breathes. Even Betson."

"You can fuck off as well, Jamie," the girl replied nastily whilst staring at the boy. "You are just jealous that you haven't been there yet." Delme tried to grab the bottle of vodka that was in her hand and tried to put his lips around the top to take a swig. Betson pulled it away. "You've had too much already." She reached up to his hand, grabbed his arm and pulled the neck hold away until the boy had to stand on his own two feet and use the rail on the footbridge to support himself.

"What's up? Am I not good enough for you now?"

"No," she responded sharply. "Not now I have my stalker!"

"What's that about?" Sian asked her with slight concern in her voice.

Delme intercepted whilst laughing as though he didn't believe Betson at all. "She thinks some guy has been watching her. She wishes!"

"I've seen him a few times now. Mostly in the dark evenings when I am going home."

"Are you sure it's not old Jack from across the road from you?" Dylan enquired whilst knowing of the rumours of the pervert who lived in the same street as Betson.

"She's had him already," Delme laughed and started to choke on his own humour although he was the only one who found it funny. "Come on. Let's go back to yours," he exclaimed whilst trying to make it up with her.

"Fuck off. After what you just said!" Betson replied. She looked at Dylan and Sian. "He's all dressed in black. Weirdo."

"You two would get on well then," the drunken teenager said as he realised that after that comment he wasn't going to get far with the girl so started stumbling back in the direction of the supermarket. "I'm going home," he announced as he slurred his words. "Go fuck your stalker."

"Hold on," Jamie told him. "I'll come with you. I've got to get home before my Mum goes to work. I have to look after my brother until Dad gets back from the club." Jamie headed over towards his drunken friend knowing that he would probably have to ensure that Delme got through his front door before making a move towards his own. He didn't want his mate doing something stupid on the way back like crossing a road in front of oncoming traffic and getting hit as he had done on many occasions before.

Betson watched the two boys disappear and looked at her two other friends who had remained with her. "Anyone else?" she snapped as she took another swig from her bottle.

The boy and girl in front of her realised that she too was slightly intoxicated but could obviously handle her drink that little bit more than Delme. Sian Palfrey and Dylan Chiswell both gave each other an indirect look and a light nod of their heads as if to say, 'let's go'. Neither of them were drinkers like their friend and mainly used to hang around in the gang because they went to the same school and in the evenings in the Valley there wasn't much to do. Sian decided to speak for the pair, knowing that they would get away with an excuse because they were boyfriend and girlfriend and would indicate that they wanted to get back to do what any fourteen-year-olds would want to do when going out with each other. "We are going home as well, babes. You know why. Mum and Dad are both out so we can have the house to ourselves for a bit."

Dylan nodded his head. "We are going to get chips on the way if you want to come. Up at Waunbant."

"You are all a bunch of lightweights," Betson exclaimed angrily as she walked off in the direction of Blaengarw without saying another word, watching Sian and Dylan walk in the other direction through the fenced off area at the back of the Co-op and up to Victoria Street. At first she wished that she had joined them because the chips would have sobered her up a little. But then she had an idea. She would call her other friend who was a year above her at school. She used to talk to him on the school bus. Evan lived further up than her at Blaengarw.

It took her nearly fifteen minutes to walk slowly up towards the top lake. She missed the bridge that would have let her cross the stream and let her go to Evan's house in the middle of Gwendoline Street. At first she didn't realise that she had walked right past until she saw the lake and the bench on her right that overlooked it. It had now become very dark with only the light from the nearby houses brightening up and glistening on the water. Looking at the calmness, Betson suddenly felt as though she wanted to throw up and burped as though she was about to do just that. She didn't, but continued her journey telling herself that she wouldn't miss the next bridge which was at the top end of the lake.

The trees on the right started to overshadow the path whilst the base of the mountain grasped for the height on the left. She wasn't afraid of the dark, but it did seem a little threatening at this time of night, she told herself. But she didn't care until suddenly out of the corner of her eye she saw someone. As she turned her head fully in the direction of the figure, she saw that there was nothing there, immediately thinking that her eyes were playing tricks on her due to the amount of alcohol that she had endured. "Fuck!"

In the darkness she could see the mist covering the tops of the trees up high on her left. Betson increased her speed slightly as the fresh air started to slightly sober her up. There was a *'snap!'* behind her. It sounded like a footstep standing on a twig or a branch. She stopped and turned around in the direction of the sound. "Hello? Whose there? Delme? Is that you?" There was no reply. She started to slightly panic whilst remembering that her parents and neighbours had warned all the children in the area not to walk anywhere alone until the Police had found the culprit who had murdered the three boys only weeks before. The thought also crossed her mind of the strange figure who had been stalking her. It was too late now, she thought to herself. Stopping and listening she could hear nothing but the sound of breaking wood, the whistling of the leaves on the trees and her own internal noise of sudden fear as she thought that she was being followed even though there was no one around her. "Paranoid or what?" she Mumbled to herself as she continued on towards the bridge a little way up on her right. She knew that on the left was an entrance to a zigzag path that took the dog walkers and ramblers up to the old football field that was no longer used. Well, apart from the dogs that would run around freely on the grass, as her Mother had done on several an occasion with her dog. They would continue upwards to a stream which contained clear water, clearer than the lakes which were rumoured to be polluted in some way and were always muddy and had a dirty look due to the amount of rain water crashing down from the northern direction.

Betson smiled as she continued slowly towards the junction. She stopped and leaned slightly forward putting her hands on her knees for support. Being slightly unfit had taken its toll on her but she felt a rush of energy to get to the bridge. As her breathing started to slow she pushed herself upright in order to continue her journey. She didn't stand a chance. The small pickaxe was slammed into the top of her head from behind. All she could manage was a small scream and then a gurgle as she instantly began to swallow the blood from the wound. Her body fell backwards onto the path with a loud 'THUD!'.

The Devil stood over her, one leg each side of her body which was slithering as what was left of her thoughts took in what was happening, the pain, the fear as she looked up briefly at the figure, gasped and then passed out. There was no time wasted, as the pick was brought down with force, and it pierced her chest before it ripped downwards just as it had done a month earlier to the three boys up on the mountain. The cold, darkened eyes stared down at the girl as the sharpened tool continued to rip away at the torso. Her blood splattered everywhere, the velocity of the attack forcing the red out over the path and onto the grass around her. With one final blow from the other hand, the ballistic knife with its long glistening blade was thrust into and pulled across the girls neck. The dark figure made sure that the girl was dead. Her widened eyes stared upwards.

Evan Maskell patiently waited for Betson and when she didn't arrive after thirty minutes, he gave up on her. She had let him down several times before in the same way, always getting a *'better offer'* as he so politely put it.

Betson's parents hadn't even bothered reporting her missing that evening. They knew that she would regularly not come home and would kip at one of her friend's houses or wake up with some boy in the area that she didn't know. They didn't care. She always returned. This time Betson Morris-Evans didn't return.

*****

The next morning, the light was just coming up over the mountain, the moonlight still shining on the glistening water of the lake in which the ducks were gathering and waiting for their early morning feed from residents in the area who were trying to get rid of their stale bread. Stephen Bishop didn't have any bread. His Staffordshire Bull Terrier woke him up every morning for her breakfast on the dot of 07:00 hrs, then demand a walk, although her age was now getting to her a bit as Stephen had noticed that she wasn't as nimble as she had always been.

He joined the path having come through the short cut near the visitor centre. Oreo the Staffordshire Bull Terrier had raced ahead to run down the bank and jump in the water. Stephen could hear her splashing around and he smiled as he thought of her already picking up stones from the bottom of the lake. She started barking. "Shut up, you old fool!" he shouted happily knowing that she always barked at the ducks who were in *'her lake'* as she thought. She may even be barking at the squirrels on the other side of the lake. Finally he reached the edge of the bank that led down to the water. He found that he had to focus as he noticed that the water over the other side of the lake was reddened. At first he thought that the kids had been playing with paint or red dye around there. Oreo was over there, further than she normally adventured, and she was still barking.

"Oh my God!" He suddenly exclaimed. There was a leg hanging out of the water tunnel that went under the path on the other side of the lake. The thrashing water came down from the mountain quite heavily when it had been raining. It looked like the body had jammed and rested itself against the top end of the tunnel. The water was continuing to pump red where the bodies blood mixed with it. The ducks had surrounded the body inquisitively thinking that it could be food. Oreo raced over towards them, and they flapped their wings and quickly dispersed.

Stephen knew that he had to do something. Whoever it was could still be alive. He slipped down the muddy grass bank, not worrying about getting his shoes wet but immediately wading into the coldness. The water came up to the middle of his shins and he found it slightly difficult getting over to the body with any speed. "Shit," he exclaimed as he splashed. In his mind he was telling himself that he might be able to save whoever it was with CPR. He reached across as Oreo continued to bark. Back over near the entrance to the path near the Parc Calon Lan one of the other dogwalkers whom Stephen regularly saw at the same time of morning appeared and looked down. At first he thought that his dog may be in trouble because of all the barking.

"Steve?" the man shouted. "What the hell?"

"Get an ambulance, Huw!" Stephen ordered as he momentarily watched his friend fumble with his mobile phone before looking in the end of the tunnel. He could feel the blood soaking into his own cloths as he tried to look into the dark and ascertain if there was a sign of life. Nothing. He could just make out that it was a girl. No sign of any life. He was going to grab the body and pull it out of the end of the tunnel but then realised that this was a crime scene. There was nothing that he could do. As he looked at the corpse, the injuries, the internal organs all showing, he urged and wanted to be sick, raising the back of his right hand to his mouth as he looked away and knew that it was too late. The mutilated corpse was blue with the cold, the girl's eyes still staring up to the top of the tunnel, the pool of red still washing down the small decline into the lower level of the lake and stream.

Stephen was still urging as he looked over towards Huw Jenkins. "Better get the Police as well!" he shouted in between urges. "She's dead. Looks like another one. She's been ripped apart!"

"You better get out of there, butt!"

Stephen nodded as he took a few steps away, stopped and took one last look at the carnage. "Oreo! Move! Here!"

The paramedics were the first to arrive, parking the ambulance over near the visitor centre as Huw Jenkins waved them down. They opened the back doors of the vehicle and grabbed their bags.

"Hello, Sir. You reported a body in the water. Can you show us where it is?"

"Yes," Huw replied as he quickly led the pair through the small gap whilst controlling his dog on the lead. "My friend found the body. He is down the bottom of the bank."

Senior Paramedic Paul Annett looked down and saw Stephen but then instantly saw the pool of red blood colouring most of the water in the lake over the other side. He looked at his colleague and shook his head then looked at Stephen. "Do you want to make your way up, Sir?"

Stephen was in slight shock. It hadn't hit him immediately, but it was a long time ago since he had seen something like this although just not as viciously bad. His time in Afghanistan on his tour of duty had its moments, usually open wounds on legs and arms or bumps on the fellow Regiment colleagues heads when they fell. But nothing this bad. He stared at the three men. "She's dead. She's bloody dead."

Paul Annett nodded as he reached down to grab the man's hand as he struggled with the slippery wet mud. "Come on," he said. "You are in shock. Come and sit down over here." He pointed over to the bench not far from where he climbed up. "Look after him," the Paramedic said whilst looking at his friend, who in reply nodded to him and then sat down beside Stephen.

"It's another one, Huw," Stephen exclaimed whilst staring ahead and then down at the ground.

"We are going to need Police back up," Paul said as he looked at his fellow Paramedic Laurence. "Better call it in. I can tell by the amount of blood loss that there is no sign of life." He watched as Laurence took out his mobile and stepped away from them all.

Stephen overheard what was being said. "She is dead."

"It's a she, then?" Paul asked as Stephen nodded back to him.

"Ripped apart. Like the others." Stephen started to shake and nod his head. "Blood everywhere. Look!" He turned his head and pointed to the blood on his clothes but suddenly panicked and tried to get them off.

"NO! SIR!" the senior Paramedic exclaimed loudly. "The Police will need your clothes as evidence. You will have to keep them on for the moment. Please." He held out his arm as though he was going to have to make the man keep them on. Then he looked at Huw. "Can you make sure that he doesn't take them off?"

Huw nodded as he watched Paul pick up his utility bags, firstly taking out a foil blanket and wrapping it around the shocked man before walking towards the bridge to his right. "What are you going to do?"

"I'm going to see if I can get a closer look."

"She's dead," Stephen whispered in his tremulous voice. "She's dead!"

*****

Bridgend Police Headquarters was bustling. The early morning shifts were just starting, Uniform Officers were getting their remits for the day and CID were all gathering for their morning team briefing. There was a mixture of smiling faces, *'The morning people'* as DCI Gwyn used to call them, and the others who should really only work nights because in the mornings they looked like they had been out on the town the night before. It showed what with the bags under their eyes and the lack of immediate socialisation with the others in the department. Gwyn was just about to start when suddenly with urgency DS Peter Ellis rushed into the entrance of his office.

"Guv. Looks like we have another body up in the Garw!"

The DCI dropped his briefing papers on his desk knowing that all his plans were now going out of the window. "Okay. Quickly. DI Harris, DC's Ceredig, DC Elfyn, ADC Nafydd. We will attend the scene." He looked at DS Ellis. "Did Uniform say whereabouts it was?"

"Top lake. Off Gwendoline Street near the visitor centre."

"Okay. Peter. You take charge back here working on the case of the three boys."

"Yes, Guv," the DS replied feeling somewhat disappointed that he wasn't the one attending with the team but then knowing that leading the team back at the station showed the confidence that his DCI had in him.

Forty minutes later, Gwyn found himself walking around the lake area. Blue flashing lights filled the grim sky, the rain falling making patterns on the lake. The mist covered the top of the hills covering the tops of the trees. Each of the CID Officers had their waterproof coats at the ready. They could see where the action was all taking place. Forensic Officers were already on the scene, some in waders and in the water beside the pipe where the girl was found.

"How do we get across?" DC Elfyn enquired, having never been in this part of the Bridgend County before.

One of the Uniformed Officers guarding the cordon that had been set up by Sergeant Andy Rollinson and his team lifted up the tape for the CID team to get under, most of them ducking their heads as they did so. "Up that way," he mentioned whilst pointing to his left. "There is a footbridge that crosses the river."

"Thanks," DC Elfyn replied although he had noticed that DI Harris and the DCI had already headed in that direction before the PC had told him, so he quickly caught up with them whilst hoping that he didn't appear to be the fool for asking.

They reached the other side, and DI Harris flicked his warrant card at the second cordon. The PC allowed them through, just like his colleague he lifted the tape for them to clamber under. Further down, Harris noticed his old friend Police Sergeant Rollinson directing the various PC's with tasks and Morgan overheard him already arranging the door-to-door enquiries on the other side of the lake. "Andy. How you doing?" Morgan exclaimed as he shook the Uniformed Officers hand.

PS Rollinson shook his head. "I've been better. This is a bad one mate."

"You know DCI Gwyn, don't you?" Harris said whilst introducing his boss, who in return nodded his head at the Sergeant.

"Sir," Rollinson commented in reply. "Right. Forensics are down in the water. One of them has actually clambered through the pipe on this side of the path."

"So the small tunnel goes right under the path and into the lake?" Gwyn enquired whilst guessing that was the case but just wanted his thoughts confirmed.

"Yes. Matt Robinson looked over there first due to the amount of blood on the path and surrounding area."

Morgan Harris saw the tent erected to try and keep the elements from contaminating any evidence and then saw someone dressed in white appear from the tunnel carrying a number of evidence and forensic sample bags. He reached down to grab the hand of the Officer, noting that whoever it was would have difficulty getting up on their own. "There we go," he said whilst still trying to ascertain who it was.

"Thanks," a rather wet and muddy Stephen Garwood acknowledged.

"Any preliminary for us?" DCI Gwyn enquired noticing that Garwood held more than a dozen bags in his hand.

"We think the body was placed in the rapids coming down from the mountain on this side of the tunnel. Whether or not whoever did this was hoping that the body would get stuck and never be found, we don't know." Garwood looked away as he noticed senior forensics Officer Matt Robinson scrambling up from the other side of the tunnel.

"Gentlemen," Robinson exclaimed as he brushed himself down from all the mud although the waders that he had worn to go into the water had saved him from getting too wet.

"Matt," Gwyn answered. "We were just getting the lowdown on the case from Stephen here."

"Well. I can tell you it is a girl. Age around fifteen or sixteen. Just like the three boys weeks ago, body has been viciously mutilated. We need to get the body back to the lab as soon as before the water washes away any additional evidence."

"Any idea how long she has been there?" Morgan enquired whilst looking down towards the water and guessing that the other wader-clad person in the water was Olivia.

"Hours. Body is blue. There is blood on the edges of the tunnel on this side," Matt said pointing to the side where Stephen Garwood had clambered out. "So I think the body was placed in that side. Samples from the blood splatter and pooled blood have been collected. We will need to determine that the swabs containing the small samples of dried blood are human blood, which we guess they are but need to confirm that they belong to the victim. Then we can develop a DNA profile."

"And the weapon?" Gwyn enquired as he swept back his jacket with both hands and placed his hands on his hips. "Is it the same as the one used on the boys?"

"Can't tell at this moment in time. What I can tell you is whoever did this is extremely dangerous. I think it is the same killer as the three boys but will need to confirm that."

"Why?"

Matt held up one of the evidence bags. "Black dust present at the kill scene although quite a lot of it may have probably washed away in the water."

DCI Gwyn edged forward to take a closer look whilst Morgan Harris scanned the ground around him just in case they were stepping on any further samples of the dust. Gwyn and Harris both nodded in agreement. "Okay Matt," the DCI said sympathetically. "If we can have the results ASAP."

"No worries. We have hundreds of samples to analyse. We are just going to attempt to remove the corpse now."

"Thanks," Gwyn replied as he watched both forensics Officers disappear into the tent whilst chatting away to each other. He looked at DI Harris and for a moment they maintained direct eye contact and even though nothing was said, the two could guess what each other was thinking. Harris nodded at his boss. Andy Rollinson stood beside them both.

"I have half of the team doing fingertip searching around the area. The other half on door-to-door. Have you got anyone that could help with the door-to-door?" PS Rollinson exclaimed whilst noticing that the three junior CID Officers were at the moment stood around doing nothing.

DCI Gwyn looked at the three and then turned to his DI. "Morgan. Get those three to assist PS Rollinson in whatever way they can."

"Guv," Harris replied as he turned and headed towards Ceredig, Elfyn and Nafydd. Just as he did, he looked over towards the visitor centre. A common sight. Not only the nosey neighbourhood onlookers but the press had arrived, the television crews getting their cameras out from the sides of their vans and the press already hassling the Officers at the cordon with questions and requests to get closer to the scene. "DCI Gwyn. We have another problem," he said as he nodded over towards the commotion on the other side of the lake. "They will be wanting a statement."

Gwyn shook his head. "They can wait."

Chapter 6

It was always a hive of activity in the press offices of the Sun newspaper. The Editor seemed to be juggling many things at once with various people coming into her office several times a minute at some point, from photographers trying to sell their prints to reporters clarifying their news stories and junior editors confirming that the headlines were correct and ready to go to print. The telephone didn't stop ringing and many times, the Editor-in-Chief chose to ignore it. If it were important then the people who made the call would ring back or even come down to see her in person.

Junior reporter Tony Fallon had been called into see her for reasons that he didn't know. On his way to the chief's office he felt himself wondering if he had done something wrong or reported something incorrectly. He banged on the door. "Chief. You wanted to see me?"

"Tony. Come in. Sit down." Vicky Newton called out to her receptionist. "Rachel! No calls! No visitors for the next ten minutes!" She watched the woman outside the door nod her head.

"So what's up?" Tony enquired in a light-hearted but professional manner.

"I believe that you have a vested interest in events that are happening in the Garw Valley at the moment?"

Tony nodded his head. "It's quite personal actually."

"Yes. I've heard. Read the history. We sent your Grandfather down to gather a story on the looming miner's strike in 1982 and he landed up getting a story on murders and a possible serial killer."

Tony Fallon started to choke up. "My Dad told me that one day he just suddenly disappeared. The Police found the doors of his house smashed in. They asked around but no one had seen him."

"So what is your take on it?"

"The Bridgend County Police found a body burned beyond recognition not far from the house that the paper owned. Like I said, the body was burned beyond recognition and there were no known imprints from dental records. I think it was him." Tony looked at the Editor seriously. "Perhaps he had the lowdown on the serial killer and was the next victim."

"Reading the notes, no one in the area would give any information. The whole place went silent."

Tony nodded with a sorrowful look. "Now the murders of the teens have started again. The same M.O."

"So I guess you would go and search for a common denominator?"

"There is something going on. Why forty years apart?" Tony shook his head once more. "The Police won't get anything from the villagers. Maybe I can. I can be there as a villager. Get close."

"Well you had better get your bags packed, young man. I've arranged a job for you whilst you are up there. Friend of mine owes me a favour at the McArthur Glen outlet. It's only part-time but that will give you good time to be a journalist as well."

"Thanks Vicky," Tony responded with a smile as he was happy that he was being given the task not only to get a story but to try and find out more about his Grandfather's disappearance forty years ago. Someone must know something, he thought to himself.

"I also have a contact for you who has some useful information. Ex-DCI Colin Brittain. He worked on the case forty years ago and knows it inside out. He is a personal friend of my Father. He can give you his perspective and you can decide if you want to listen to him."

"That's a great start."

"Here's his number. Give him a call. He is expecting you."

Tony took the card from his boss and looked at the number. "This is great, Vicky."

"Just make sure that you get me the story of the lifetime! You will need to keep in touch. You change my contact details on your phone to *'Mum'*. In the presence of anyone you can then say that you are ringing your Mum, or she is calling you. Ryan Parry will be your *'Dad'* seeing that he is your line manager. Regular contact!" Tony nodded once more. "The bad news is that your house in Pontycymer will be the same one that your Grandfather lived in before he disappeared." She waved out of the window towards Ryan, who was busy directing his reporters and trying to get the inner page photographs organised for the next publication. The deadline wasn't far away.

"Yes, boss," Ryan said as he poked his head in around the door.

"Two minutes," Vicky exclaimed. "Close the door."

"As quick as you can," he replied as he looked back and forth towards his boss and then back out to the action in the press office.

"You will be losing Tony here for a while. He is going under cover trying to expose what is going on in the Garw Valley."

"The serial killer?" Ryan asked seriously, the thought instantly going through his mind that such a case should be given to a senior reporter with more experience. But he also knew that he wouldn't be able to change Vicky's mind once she had made her decision and so didn't bother arguing his opinion.

"You will be his handler, Ryan. Known as Dad."

"Understood. Just make sure you do a good job, young man." He looked back at Vicky and pointed with his finger back out to the action outside.

"Go on," Vicky exclaimed. "Piss off."

*****

The Police had nothing. It worried the forensics team because the only evidence they had was the coal dust found at each scene and in front of the windows at two of the three first victims. Matt Robinson had questioned as to why it was only at two of the boys houses and not the third, and so had sent his team back to

69

see if there was something that they were missing. But their initial investigation was confirmed. There was no coal dust found at Kyle Griffith's house neither at the front or rear of the place. Matt had given the information to DCI Gwyn and questions had been raised. The two things that had been suggested were that perhaps the culprit didn't have time to stalk Kyle Griffiths in the same way. Perhaps he wasn't supposed to be a victim but was in the wrong place at the wrong time. Matt Robinson threw a spanner into the works by suggesting that whoever it was must be forensically aware.

*****

July 2022. There was a dark cloud hanging over the area in more ways than one. The villagers were fearful for the lives of their children, some more than others. It made some parents and youngsters paranoid whilst others couldn't care less. Still, the summer had come around, the Valley was filled with a mixture of sun and rain and the weather was totally unpredictable. One of the villagers regularly mentioned that you could never believe the Met Office because this was the Welsh Valleys, and they could never get the forecast right. The mist continued to form over the mountain no matter what time of year it was although in the summer months it seemed to limit itself to early mornings.

Delme Greening, Jamie Arnett, and Dylan Chiswell had all gotten over the death of Betson, in fact the only regret that Jamie regularly exclaimed was that he didn't get to fuck her, which was typical of a teenager. Dylan and Sian had parted ways which was something that happened constantly between youngsters who claimed to be going out with each other. Sian and her family had moved to the next Valley and even though Dylan had said that he would always be her boyfriend, the relationship had sizzled out and both teenagers had moved on.

The three of them were looking for something to do whilst making the most of what had been a sunny day and now the evening was drawing in and the sun was setting over the mountain. "Let's go up to Gelliron Cemetery," Delme announced as they passed the tennis courts. He had already dumped the wrapping from his chips onto the grass below the tennis courts, much to the dismay of Dylan.

"Nah, butt. I'm going home. Dad has bought me a new game for the PS5 and wants to try and beat me," Dylan replied hesitantly as he stopped and looked back towards the direction of his house. "I'll catch you two tomorrow at school." He would always see them at school. Sometimes he caught the bus with them whilst other times his Father would drop him to school as he went to work.

"Oh. Come on!" Jamie exclaimed disappointingly. "Come with us. You can play that later."

Dylan didn't want to. He was the more relaxed and law abiding one than the others and knew just what they were going to do in the cemetery because neither of them had any respect. "Nah. I'll see you later," he said as he looked at his watch and saw that it was just past 9pm. Then he walked off back down the hill.

Delme watched his friend disappear as he took a swig from his Diet Coke bottle. He knew that deep inside since Betson's death that the three of them were drifting apart as friends, Dylan especially. Before going to the cemetery the pair walked over to the end of the rear of the houses to see if the pig was out in his pen. They knew that he was usually covered in mud from head to toe but smoothed him all the same when the owner was there. When they realised that the animal was locked away for the night, they continued up to the wall that surrounded the cemetery. Both of them climbed up and over the other side. As they landed on the ground, Delme instantly kicked one of the memorial stones. "Look at this fucker!" he announced to Jamie. "So what if he was in the war. Who fucking cares. Private Michael Jones. Here's what I think of you!" He repeated his kick until the stone started to move and then it began to tilt backwards and fall over. As it hit the ground, the stone split in half.

"Fuck," Jamie said as he at first appeared disgusted at what his friend had done. "Bit disrespectful mate!"

Delme laughed as he looked back at his friend. "Come by yer now!" he ordered him. "Kick the shit out of these flowers." Delme started it off by knocking the heads off the roses and ensuring the pot that they were in was smashed.

Jamie looked at him from the corner of his eye, shook his head and then joined in the sacrilege. "I don't like this!" He looked around knowing that the two of them were nearly in complete darkness apart from the distant lights from the nearby houses. As he walked over to one of the very few graves that had remembrance flowers on them Jamie watched his step knowing that he could trip and fall in the dark. They continued to walk along and vandalise each headstone in the best way that they could. Some were impossible to break in any way due to how they were made, whilst others did not stand up to an easy kick. Suddenly Jamie saw movement about fifty metres away. At first he thought that it may be the caretaker who may have been called by one of the residents in the neighbouring houses due to the disturbance and noise. "Shit!"

"What's up?" Delme asked whilst thinking that his friend may have hurt himself whilst kicking too hard at the graves, although with little worry in his voice because he knew that his friend didn't want to damage the graves in the first place. Was it just probably something he had done? He looked at Jamie and saw him just staring ahead as he knelt down.

"Over there!" Jamie whispered whilst appearing frightened in the tone of his voice. "There's someone over there." He nodded his head in the direction of what he had thought that he had seen.

"God. Don't tell me that you are seeing things as well. Betson was seeing bloody people. Black figures."

"I'm telling you that someone is watching us!" Jamie exclaimed seriously and with worry in his voice.

"If this is your idea of a joke just to scare me, you got no chance!" Delme continued to kick the headstones. Some fell over whilst others appeared solid and held their ground.

"I'm telling you that there is someone there."

"Where?" Delme enquired cockily whilst standing up and looking in the direction that his friend had indicated that there was someone. "Look! You are imagining things, butt. There's no one there."

Jamie looked in the direction that he thought that he had first seen someone. He knelt down at the one grave that he was defacing as though to dip down and hide and then looked back to his friend, his face somewhat showing a sign of relief that his eyes may have just been playing tricks on him. But then his eyes widened in fear as he looked at Delme. "Fucking hell!" he exclaimed as he tried to scramble to his feet.

"What now?"

Delme didn't see it coming. All he saw was his mate pushing himself backwards with his two legs and staring up at him, pointing at him, his hand shaking. Then he started becoming hysterical and started to frantically scream in fear. The pick was brought down on the boy's head. The dark figure, faceless, all dressed in black, stood behind him. Delme was killed instantly, the blood spurting out of the top of his head, his brain showing through the gaping wound on top. His body slumped to the floor, his head hitting the corner stone of the grave that moments earlier he had kicked over. Jamie continued to scramble backwards whilst finding it difficult to get to his feet due to the slippery ground. His face was filled with horrific fear, his mouth letting out cries, his eyes widened with hysterical panic. Still he couldn't get up, the ground was wet, and his feet just slipped. He turned over and quickly tried to push himself up but found it hard to do so.

The darkened assailant didn't give him any chances. It dropped the pick and picked up a shovel, blackened as though it had been well used. It was above head height and brought down upon the second boys head in the same way as the pick had been used moments earlier on Delme. The noise made a loud *'CLANG!'* as it did so. Jamie slumped to the ground unconscious. The figure grabbed his left leg and dragged him over next to his dead friend.

Over two hours had passed. Jamie was beginning to come around. He started to panic, wondering who had attacked both him and Delme. Killed Delme. Why didn't whoever it was kill him? He felt the pain on the side and top of his head and tried to reach up to try and apply some relief to what he thought was just bruising. He still panicked as he began to realise that he didn't know where he was. It was totally pitch black and he couldn't see a thing. He tried to look at his watch but after a few moments realised that he couldn't move either his arms or his legs. Something was on top of him. Something was digging into his back, uncomfortable, sharp. He tried moving his head. It was dark. He couldn't see anything. He could feel something dripping down, touching his lips. He licked them but didn't recognise the taste. Perhaps it was poison. Perhaps whoever had hit him was now trying to kill him just as they had with his friend. He tried to move once more but the more he moved the more uncomfortable it became. Something was definitely digging into his back, quite sharp. Where was he? What had happened? Who had hit them? Was it the same person who had killed the other teenagers? Betson had claimed that someone in black was following her, and no one believed her. Yet the figure that he had seen attack and probably kill Delme was all dressed in black. Jamie panicked, knowing that something was still dripping quite heavily onto his face. He couldn't see anything or work out where he was. One thing that he did know was that he was confined and restricted.

"Help!" he whispered. Then he had an idea. He would just try to move his hand enough for his smartwatch to move and briefly come on, even though it would only be lit for a couple of seconds until he shook his arm again. He tried. It was hard to do. But finally the watch lit up. One. Two seconds. But it was enough. He started to panic even more as he realised that the reason he couldn't move was because there was a body on top of him and was near enough face to face with him. He shook his arm once more for the two seconds of light. The body that was dripping blood onto his own face and lips was that of Delme's. He screamed as the horror hit him. "ARRGGHHHH! HELP! HELP!" It was pitch black again. Jamie shook his hand again to give himself just enough time to see if the boy laying on top of him was actually alive or dead. He was dead. The skull had been smashed open, crushed beyond belief.

Jamie continued to shake his hand. He could see part of the boys brain. He screamed loudly. "HELP ME! HELP! HELP!" Managing to turn his head slightly he looked around in the dark, still unable to move his hands, legs, or body even though he had tried to wiggle each of them free. "I can't move!" he said to himself frantically. "I CAN'T FUCKING MOVE! HELP!" He realised that there was little room wherever he was. As he turned his head it banged against something, his hands were touching something at the side of him, his feet were touching something ensuring that he wasn't able to stretch or move. "HELP!" he shouted out. "HELP ME!"

"Where the fuck am I?" Jamie demanded to know whilst hysterically crying and becoming so frantic that he was trying to move his body which was making the space seem smaller. "HELP! HELP ME!" He continued to shout out loudly hoping that someone would hear him.

Suddenly there was light from beside him. The screen from his mobile phone burst into life and the ringtone from the Simpsons theme playing. It flickered as the boy managed to turn his head enough to see that their friend Dylan was calling. He couldn't answer in the small, confined space but the light from the phone let him see Delme's face on top of him nearly nose to nose. He saw his friend's face rippled with blood from his head wound, with most of the blood from the wound still dripping down onto his own face, quite heavily like water from a tap. The flashing light let him see just where they were. Erratically and frantically he started to scream once more as the reality of what had happened hit him. He was in a box. A coffin.

"ARRRRGGGGHHHHH!" Jamie screamed in between flashes from the screen. "HELP! PLEASE!" he shouted as he tried to wiggle himself free which made it impossible for him to even breathe.

"ARRRGGGHHHH!"

Momentarily he stopped his pleas for freedom. In between the flashing lights from the screen he turned his head to the side just enough to make out what was digging into him from behind. The skull. Bones. It confirmed his fear. The ringtone on the phone stopped. The light ceased. Jamie Arnett continued to scream in the darkness until he could scream no more. The oxygen from the coffin was becoming scarce.

*****

Dylan Chiswell had a great relationship with his Father. He also took great pleasure in beating him at every attempt on any PlayStation game that he had bought for Dylan. The boy used to accept the fact that his Dad at least tried. Even spent time with him trying to learn and sometimes understand each game.

It was approaching 00:30 hrs, and the telephone in the Chiswell's household rang loudly. Michael quickly picked up the phone whilst hoping that it had not woken up his wife, and he mouthed 'Is this for you?' before pointing at his watch to indicate the time. "Hello."

"Hello." The voice at the other end expected to speak to Dylan but realised that the tone of the voice was too deep to be him. "Is that Dylan's Dad?"

"Yes. That's right. Who is that?" he asked because he didn't recognise the voice. What he in fact wanted to ask was, *'Do you know what the time is?'* but then thought that it must be important for any adult to call this late.

"Sorry. It's Gareth Arnett here. I'm Jamie's Father. He is one of your son's friends."

"Ah right. Must be important for you to call at this time."

"Yes. Sorry. I was just wondering if Jamie was there with Dylan?"

"Hold on." Michael looked confused and then, covering the mouthpiece on the phone whispered, "Dylan. Have you seen Jamie tonight?"

"Left him and Delme about nine. Come back here to play PS5."

"I've just spoken to the boy. He said that he left Jamie and Delme about nine o'clock." Michael could imagine the man's facial expression. His son hadn't come home, and he wasn't here with whom he thought he may have been with. "I guess you have tried his phone."

"Yes. It just keeps ringing and ringing before going to voicemail. Could you ask Dylan where they were headed when he left them?"

"Hold on," Michael responded. "I'll let you speak to him." His son was already by his side listening in to the call so paused his game using the controller and then took the handset from his Father.

"Hello, Mr Arnett. I left Jamie and Delme about nine o'clock. They were heading up in the direction of the cemetery."

"Did they give any indication of where they were going?"

Dylan didn't want to get his friends into any trouble, so hesitated about telling Jamie's Dad about their real intentions for going that way. But then a thought crossed his mind. What if something had happened to them? Or was he just at Delme's house? There was a killer around who had already killed four teenagers in the area. He had to tell the truth. "I think Delme said

76

to go into the grave yard and vandalise the headstones. That is why I came home."

"He's a bad influence on you both that Delme Greening. I don't suppose you have a number for him?"

Dylan started thumbing through the contacts on his phone. "Yes, hold on. It's 07468207188."

"Okay. Thanks. And apologise to your Dad for ringing so late." He ended the call.

Dylan replaced the handset into the cradle. "I wonder where they went, then." He looked confused and his head filled with a frown.

"It doesn't matter, son," Michael exclaimed proudly. "You did the right thing by coming home if what you said was true about them vandalising the gravestones."

The boy nodded his head although appeared to be in a world of his own. "Jamie's Dad just said his phone kept ringing and ringing before going to voicemail."

"Yes."

"Well when we paused the game whilst you went upstairs, I tried to call Jamie and the same thing happened. I thought they were just pissed off with me and didn't want to speak. I'm just hoping that nothing bad has happened."

Michael Chiswell nodded his head. "Come on, Son. Time for bed. You have school in the morning, and I have to get up in," he checked his watch. "Five hours. God. I'm going to have to stop trying to beat you on that thing," he exclaimed as he nodded towards the games console.

It was 04:30 hrs. Michael Chiswell was dozing, knowing that he had to get up in about thirty minutes time and trying to decide whether to close his eyes once more for the last half hour or go downstairs for a cup of tea. He looked over at his wife who was peacefully sleeping and then decided to cancel his alarm so it wouldn't wake her, and then slowly walked downstairs for his cuppa. Suddenly there was a banging on the front door. He looked at the sleeping beauty and even though she had stirred, Sue was still in the land of nod, so quickly Michael grabbed his dressing gown and ran down the stairs. In the glass he could see the outlines of two people. He decided to leave the chain on the door just in case.

"Hello," he said as he opened the door to the best width that the chain would allow it to go. He looked and saw two Police Officer's outside, so quickly closed the door temporarily to allow him to take the chain off.

"Mr Chiswell?"

"Yes, that's right. How can I help?"

"PC Evans. This is PC Jones. We were wondering if we could have a word with Dylan."

Michael rubbed his eyes. "You two are early. It must be important."

"I'm afraid so, Mr Chiswell. Can we come inside?"

"Sure. Go into the living room. I'll go and wake Dylan." He quietly walked up the stairs still trying not to wake his wife, and then tapped on Dylan's bedroom door before instantly walking in and heading over to the sleeping teen. "Dylan," he said softly as he shook the boy's shoulder. "Dylan. Wake up. The Police are downstairs."

"Wh..what?"

"The Police are downstairs. I think it is about your two friends."

At first Dylan wasn't aware of his surroundings as though he had been woken from a deep sleep. "Where. Wh..what?" He repeated.

"You need to come downstairs. The Police want to talk to you."

Dylan heard his Dad this time and flipped both of his legs out of the side of the bed, his feet touching the floor at last. He stood, luckily already being dressed in his pyjama shorts and t-shirt. Before moving he stretched his arms. Then he headed out to the landing and down the stairs, closely followed by his Father. As he walked into the living room he noticed the two Uniformed Officers. "Hello," he said whilst wiping his tired eyes with both hands.

"Hello Dylan." PC Gareth Evans opened his notebook. "You are friends with Jamie Arnett and Delme Greening. Is that right?"

Dylan nodded. "Is this about the phone call we had earlier from Jamie's Dad?"

"We have had a report from both Jamie's and Delme's parents that neither of the boys have returned home last night," PC Evans continued. "We believe that you may have been the last to see them."

"Well I can't tell you much. Just what I told Jamie's Dad."

"I answered the phone just after midnight," Michael Chiswell added with a worried look on his face. "Has Jamie not materialised?"

"Neither boy has been seen. Their mobile phones are just ringing and ringing. Then they go to voicemail."

Dylan nodded for the Officers to see. "I told Dad that, didn't I Dad?" He watched as his Father nodded. "I tried twice and then gave up. I thought that they may have been mad with me for going home."

"Can you confirm where you last saw them and which direction that they were heading?" PC Jones asked in an official voice as though the two were playing the good cop-bad cop scenario.

"We had just gone through the field below the tennis courts. I left them both there. Delme wanted to go up and vandalise the gravestones in the graveyard." Dylan's stare went from Officer to Officer and his face looked like he wasn't being believed. "I wanted to come home and play on the PS5 with Dad."

"That's right," Michael confirmed. "I got home from work just before he arrived back home about quarter past nine."

"We don't disbelieve you, Dylan. Can you tell us what sort of mood they were both in?" PC Jones asked nicely, realising that the boy was beginning to feel threatened by both Officer's questioning.

Dylan looked at both of the Officers and then over towards his Dad. "I think they were upset that I was going home. But apart from that they were both normal."

"Like he said, Officer," Dylan's Dad added whilst intercepting the conversation to support his son. "There's not much more that he can tell you."

PC Jones closed his book and headed towards the door. "We just needed to hear it from the horse's mouth, so to speak. Thank you Dylan. If you hear from either of them, can you call me as soon as possible?" He reached inside his pocket and pulled out a business card. "You will find my name and telephone number on here. If I don't answer, someone else will and they will e-mail me any message you leave for me."

Dylan nodded as he grabbed the card and held it both hands. "Will do."

Outside, PC Jones and PC Evans went back down towards their vehicle, both looking somewhat bewildered at the disappearance of the two boys and wondering whether Dylan Chiswell could have gone missing as well if he had gone to the cemetery with his friends. But just where they were was at the moment a mystery.

"What do you think, Bry?" Gareth Evans enquired as he opened his own door on the passenger side of the car.

"I think it is too coincidental that we have had four murders and suddenly two boys go missing. It may just be that their bodies just haven't been found," he replied concerningly as he got into the car and plumped himself down in the driver's seat. "I think we need to contact CID."

The early morning was starting to pass. There was already a disturbance outside Bridgend Police Headquarters as the gutter press had all congregated wanting answers to their questions not only about the four murders but now the two missing boys.

"How the hell did they get that information so quickly?" Superintendent Saunders asked DCI Gwyn as the both of them looked out of his office window down onto the main entrance.

"We only got the call from Uniform about thirty minutes ago," Gwyn added as he shook his head in disbelief. "Someone somewhere has leaked it."

Saunders turned around and sat down in his plush leather chair. "We need to prepare a statement and organise a press conference. They will be putting two and two together to make five otherwise. You know what they are like." There was a tap on the Superintendent's door as DI Harris appeared waiting for the invitation to be able to enter the room. Superintendent Saunders flashed his fingers for Morgan to come into the room. "What's up, DI Harris?"

"I think we have problems, Guv. The community Sergeant Michael Llewellyn has just radioed in. The locals are meeting and may be arranging their own search up in Pontycymer."

DCI Gwyn looked at his junior. "Shit! That could ruin everything. We need to preserve any potential evidence."

"Bill. You and I handle the press down here. Let your DI and his team get up and handle the investigation into the two boys."

"Did you get that, Morgan?"

"Yes, Guv," DI Harris replied worriedly.

"Get some back up from Uniform, and get Sergeant Llewellyn on board," the DCI exclaimed as he watched Harris head towards the door. "Hold on, Morgan," he snapped quickly before turning his attention back to the Superintendent. "Guv, can you give authorisation for India-99? We need to beat the locals to the search and the Police helicopter hovering may deter them a bit more and who knows may even find the boys."

"Authorised. Go and see to it and then back here in thirty minutes, Bill," Alun Saunders said as he looked at DCI Gwyn.

DI Harris nodded at the DCI with an acknowledgement that more or less said, *'thanks'*.

DCI Gwyn looked over at the senior Officer as he went to leave. "We need to get these vultures off our backs as well as get them working for us."

"Yes. Can you get one of the PC's to step outside and tell them that there will be statement made in about thirty-five minutes?"

The thirty minutes went by quite fast. Superintendent Saunders had quickly put a statement together and headed out of the main entrance of the Headquarters building to face both the reporters from most of the local and national newspapers and the cameras indicating that the TV crews were there as well. Four PC's escorted the two senior Officers out of the front door. The questions were already coming thick and fast:

'Is it true that there have been another two boys go missing?'
'Is there a serial killer on the loose in the Garw?'
'Were the victims sexually abused before being murdered?'

'What are you doing about this, Superintendent?'
'Are your Officers at a loss on this case?'

Superintendent Saunders held his statement in front of him, at first waiting for the crowd to quieten down in their own time but it didn't seem to be happening and so he nodded at DCI Gwyn.

In a loud, authoritative voice, the DCI shouted, "Let's have a bit of hush," which didn't seem to work until he added, "QUIET!"

Alun Saunders jumped in quickly, making the most of the semi-controlled situation. "Ladies and Gentlemen. Thank you for coming. I have a prepared statement, after which I can take questions." He started to read.

"Last evening, two teenagers whose names we cannot provide for legal reasons, were reported missing in the Pontycymer area. Uniformed Officers have received information as to their last movements and are currently organising a search in the area. The Police helicopter India-99 has been mobilised with immediate effect to assist in the search using their infra-red on-board technology. We would ask anyone who knows of their whereabouts to contact either myself or DCI Gwyn via the 101 number. Photographs are being distributed by the PC's for your use."

The questions suddenly came thick and fast.

"Mervyn Cummings. Daily Mail. Do you think that these boys have been killed by the serial killer?"

Superintendent Saunders gave the DCI a brief look of disgust that indicated a *'Oh no, the Daily Mail'* thought. "We have no indication that the disappearance of the two boys is linked to the four murders at this time."

"David Kester. Daily Mirror. Is it not more than coincidence that another two boys have gone missing, though, Superintendent?"

"At this moment in time, we cannot speculate. We cannot assume anything until we have the facts." He pointed at one of the presenters who was in front of the TV cameras, whilst knowing that any television involvement could work for them or against them.

"Hello Superintendent. Has any progress been made so far on the murders of the four teenagers?"

"Investigations are ongoing and forensic evidence is still being analysed." The volume of a dozen questions at once being thrown at the two increased and Superintendent Saunders was beginning to find it hard to correspond what was being said and by who, so nodded at DCI Gwyn as if to say, *'end it'*.

"Ladies and gentlemen. That is it for the moment. If we have anything further, you will be first to know. Thank you." Gwyn nodded at the four PC's who instantly started to disperse the crowds, before he followed his senior Officer back into the building.

Chapter 7

Pontycymer was filled with Uniformed Police Officers, flashing lights from the Police Cars and in some cases the sirens still echoing around. The attending Police Sergeants had already been told by the area Sergeant that the locals were all gathering at the Blaengarw Rugby Club with the intention of arranging their own search. CID were on their way up to the village to take control of the investigation and assist in the search, already providing the Police helicopter India-99 which was only minutes away.

Uniformed Police Sergeant Martin Pugh led the way, instructing each unit to cordon off the area around where the boys were last seen. Members of the public were to be turned away or told to stay indoors. "We need cordons everywhere from the Tennis club upwards, Park Street, Wood Street," he ordered whilst pointing in the direction of each. "Brynhyfryd. Richard Street. Top of Alexandra Road and the top of Albany Road." He looked over and noticed the local Sergeant Michael Llewellyn approaching with two PCSO's tailing behind him.

"Martin. What do you need me, Janine, and Peter to do?" There was a sudden screech of tyres behind him, and PS Llewellyn turned around to see DI Harris and DS Ellis jump out the passenger side of one of the cars closely flanked by seven other CID Officers.

"We are out in force today," Pugh exclaimed with a thought of 'the more the merrier' crossing his mind.

"Hi Martin," Peter Ellis exclaimed to his fellow ranking Officer. "Not sure if you have heard but India-99 will be flying over us soon."

"Yes. I did hear."

"What do you need us to do?"

PS Llewellyn intervened. "I think someone needs to get down to rugby club and co-ordinate the locals. They are adamant that they are going to search. But we need to get them working for us."

"Mike, you know them. What about if you and I go down with a couple of my Officers to try and reason with them?" DI Harris questioned as he looked at the community Sergeant. Harris also had an alternative motive for suggesting it so he wouldn't be wading in the mud from any fingertip search or walking through the bushes and grasslands. He would leave that to DS Ellis and the rest of the team under the instruction of PS Pugh. "Is that okay with you, Martin?" he asked as he looked at PS Pugh.

"Sounds good to me."

DS Ellis then turned to his team who were all huddled behind him. "DC's Elfyn and Lewis. Go with the DI. The rest of you, take instructions from both me and Sergeant Pugh and assist in the search of the area." There were echoes of 'Serge' from all of the DC's. "Right. Let's go."

PS Michael Llewellyn led the three CID Officers and two other PC's into the rugby club entrance. It was already full of the residents of the local villages, who, he could tell, were showing signs of worry, fear, and anger because of the recent deaths and now the missing two boys.

Self-proclaimed community leader Billy Evans wasn't sure if the arrival of the six Police Officers into the meeting was a good thing at first but then realised that it would be a good way of getting answers to questions from worried parents and would also be a good way of getting the villagers further on his side if there were any doubts. He looked over at his fellow organiser, Lee Jones, who in return approached him, papers in his hands and then whispered, "Do they know about 1982?"

"Schhhhh!" Billy replied. "Probably not. Unless they dig deep enough. We only tell them what they want to hear!" He looked at his watch and then held up both hands to try and bring the crowd to some order. Police Officers on his right and resident John Rix and best friend Lee Jones on his left together with the local Police Sergeant Llewellyn. It was time, he thought to himself. He could hear the rowdiness of the already angry crowd. "Ladies and gentlemen. Thank you all for coming."

The noise continued and didn't appear to be getting any quieter. Ex-military man John Rix stood up and in all his military style commanded, "QUIET!" The crowd did as they were told. It was so loud that even Billy Evans jumped and stood to attention.

"Thank you all for coming. We have an urgent situation on our hands. You all know about the murders of the four teenagers. Now we have another two lads go missing. We need to get together and search for them. They might be alive, we don't know."

"Billy," PS Llewellyn exclaimed importantly as he stepped in front of the big man. "I cannot let any of you go near the place where the boys were last seen."

Gareth Arnett shouted out, "Excuse me. We have been told that our boys were last seen going up to the cemetery. That is where we are going to look, Isn't it."

"Too right," Jackie Greening added. "We are their parents. We will decide."

The crowd all cheered in agreement and feeling riled up because of the lack of action by the Police so far. DI Harris joined Sergeant Llewellyn. "Ladies and Gentlemen. My name is Detective Inspector Morgan Harris. I am one of the investigating Officers, not only in the cases of the four deaths, but now also the two missing boys. Now hopefully the latter will be found alive. But if that is not the case, we will need to preserve any evidence."

"So what are you doing that we can't?" one of the female villagers shouted from the back of the room.

"The helicopter will be flying over at any moment," Harris exclaimed worriedly. "We can get a better view from the air. It also has infrared equipment and heat seeking technology scanners. But if we have too many people tracing all over the ground we wouldn't be able to tell who is who." The three CID Officers could sense the animosity present in the room with an atmosphere that you could cut with a knife. Without looking directly at any person in particular, DI Harris cleared his throat, guessing that this was going to be quite a difficult meeting.

"Billy," PS Llewellyn added. "Can you back us up on this?" He looked briefly at the larger man before turning back to the crowd. "Please. I am asking you all, not only as a Police Officer but with most of you as your friend. Just give these guys a bit of time. If it doesn't work out, then we will search."

Billy Evans bit his lip and stared at the Sergeant who in return gave him direct eye contact that spoke a thousand words. "Okay. Let the Officers complete the search first. We will assist them and be under their control."

Micheal Llewellyn nodded and then mouthed, *'Thank you'* at Billy.

DI Harris also looked at the community leader. "Thank you, Sir," he said politely but authoritatively.

"We just want to know what you are doing! Why should we trust you to do the search when we know the area better? Not only that, the four kids who have been murdered. The Police have done bugger all so far!" Catrin Kean didn't mince her words. As direct as she always was. "Do you have a suspect? We are all worried about the kids safety!" she added angrily.

DI Harris nodded. "I can understand your worry about what has happened. There are many things happening in the background, some of which I can't discuss. Needless to say I can't tell you much at this moment in time. We have had many responses to our request for information. Several names have been repeated. We are currently looking at that." DI Harris knew he was lying just to shut the crowd up. They had no names. They had no leads. They had no DNA or evidence.

"What about the two missing boys? Their parents are here and haven't been told anything!" local busy-body Stella Edwards shouted out as the crowd all agreed with an extended *'yeehhhhh'* just like the MP's in Parliament.

Billy Evans took control. "Ladies and Gentlemen. Let's get out there and help. We can proportion blame later. Let's find Jamie and Delme before it's too late."

Outside, the Police helicopter had arrived and was hovering over the hillside where the boys were last seen. It was trying to get as close to the ground without risking the chance of disturbing the scene of any crime with the fallback from the propeller. The wind had started to pick up and the pilot had to concentrate on controlling the flight whilst his two colleagues analysed the information from the infrared and heat seeking equipment.

DI Harris was met en route to the cemetery by DS Ellis, the activity in the area showing as there was a wall of black and white Uniforms and flashing blue lights. Harris could feel the chill that was in the air, even though it was July and he felt that there should at least be some warmth from the sun above them, especially as it was a late morning in July. "Where are we, Peter?"

"India-99 are communicating with me. So far there are no sightings in the immediate area on the open ground up on the peak of the hill." He pointed up and beyond the graveyard. "They have seen a few hikers but can confirm that they are adults with hiking sticks, rucksacks and a dog."

"Let's get the helicopter closer to the last area where we know they were heading. The cemetery," Harris exclaimed as he looked over his colleagues shoulder and then around him to get the gest of what had been happening whilst he was at the meeting.

"I believe that is where they are going to try next, Guv," Ellis replied as he also joined the DI in looking around. "I'll check with them now." He clicked his radio and then raised the handset to his face. "DS Ellis to India-99."

There was a slight distortion and crackling over the airwaves but then the radio crackled into life although the reply appeared quite noisy because of the helicopter engines. "India-99. Over."

"Can we get visual over the cemetery area?"

"On route now. India-99 out."

DS Ellis looked up as he heard the buzzing of the propeller in the distance and watched it slowly fly past them from the right. Seconds later it was hovering over the cemetery area with the two crew members setting up the scan. "They are about to scan, Guv," Ellis informed the DI. Everyone in the surrounding area seemed to look upwards all at once which DS Ellis found quite illuminatingly humorous, a smile appearing on his face momentarily which he soon hid because of the nature of the circumstances. Inch by inch, India-99 moved forward, then stopped to hover, then move forward more. It appeared to Ellis to be a long-winded, but essential, process.

DI Harris nodded over to PS Pugh. "Have we had any response to requests for CCTV in the area, Martin?"

The Sergeant shook his head. "There is no Council CCTV in the area. This is the Valleys," he responded in a part humorous and a part sarcastic way whilst raising his eyebrows. "Some of the Uniform Officers are knocking on doors now."

"Where did you send my team?"

"Looking for evidence over by the farm," PS Pugh acknowledged by nodding his head towards the left. "We are also searching over by the rugby field and tennis courts in that direction."

"Guv. The dog unit are here. The Family Liaison Officers assigned to each of the parents of the missing boys have asked for clothing from them with a hope that the dogs might be able to pick up on the scent if India-99 indicates anything."

"Excellent," Harris replied as he concentrated on both situations at once, looking from side to side at both the helicopter and then the members of his team. "Best have them on standby and get them prepped up."

The inch-by-inch search was taking it's time. The summer daylight was disappearing as the grey rainclouds appeared over the tip of the mountain at the far end of Blaengarw. Seeing them, everyone knew what was coming, and were hoping to get a result before the downpour so that if there was bad news, the evidence could be preserved, and a cover placed over it. It had been two hours since India-99 had begun its search and then suddenly DS Ellis' radio crackled. "India -99."

"We might have something, Sergeant," the Officer in the helicopter working the scanner exclaimed. "There is an unusual heat source coming from the centre of the cemetery. We are hovering over it now."

"Thank you," Ellis replied before turning to DI Harris. "Guv. They may have something." DI Harris noticed the burst of bright light from the sky shine down into the grave yard. "Can the dogs go in?"

Harris nodded. "Only to confirm. We may have other problems though."

Martin Pugh stepped forward and PS Llewellyn was listening over his shoulder. "Problems?"

"Yes," DI Harris exclaimed as he turned his attention to the area that was being indicated by the helicopter. "We cannot desecrate religious grounds. Under law it is sacrilegious."

"The sensors have indicated unusual heat source though," PS Llewellyn exclaimed as he stood beside the DI who looked at him and nodded.

"I can be imprisoned for giving the order," Harris replied. "If we need to perform any dig, the exhumation can be a long process. Under law, we have to get written permission of the current owner of the Burial Licence to authorise an exhumation. The application, if granted, will normally be sent to the person applying for the exhumation."

"Fuck! That could take months!" Martin Pugh snapped.

"Fuck indeed," PS Llewellyn added worriedly. "We have dozens of locals and parents down in the rugby club, most of who are now heading down to the cordon who we will have to explain that to."

DS Ellis shook his head. "This cemetery is that old, Guv, that whoever owns the licenses might themselves be dead."

"We need to get the caretaker down here," Harris exclaimed whilst trying to think out of the box. "Meanwhile get those sniffer dogs in there."

The barking started as the canine Officers were let out of the van by their handlers. The two Springer Spaniels, Hulk and Thor, both males with beautiful brown coats, pulled at their harnesses whilst wanting their treat, the ball that each handler gave them if they provided a positive result. DS Ellis stepped forward to the handlers, knowing not to touch either dog, no matter how much he wanted to, as they were working. He passed the first Officer two evidence bags. "Clothes from the missing boys," he exclaimed.

"Thank you, Serge." PC Bettinson, an experienced specialist dog handler, took the bags and opened them, immediately allowing each dog to sniff the garments before turning to his colleague, PC Lemin, and nodding. "Let's go." With that they both headed up to the entrance and went through the gates. They both headed towards the hovering helicopter. They wouldn't let the dogs off their leads until they were close through fear of confusing them in a place where there were a thousand probable rotten corpses. PC Bettinson stopped and held the clothes up to the dogs noses once more and then about ten feet away, released Hulk whilst PC Lemin did the same to Thor. They sniffed around and it didn't take extraordinarily long before both dogs picked up the scent down where the boys had climbed over the wall. From there they followed their noses and then sat at the side of the one of the disturbed graves in the area where the helicopter light was shining down.

"Looks pretty fresh. Like it has been dug up recently," Lemin stated as he shone his own torchlight down.

"Yes. Both dogs have indicated a match. We had better get onto DS Ellis." He put the clip on his dog and watched as PC Lemin did the same. Then PC Bettinson clicked his radio. "DS Ellis."

"Go ahead, Colin,"

"Yeh. The dogs have picked up a scent at the area that the helicopter picked out."

"Thanks. We are on our way over." DS Ellis nodded to DI Harris. "It's a positive search. Dogs have indicated that the smell is where the helicopter picked out the heat."

DI Harris shook his head. "Fuck it. The boys could still be alive."

"Your decision, Guv."

Harris bit his lip and then looked down at the crowd gathering at the cordon down by the tennis court. "Buggered if I do and buggered if I don't. But I would never forgive myself if the boys were still alive. Let's see what's underneath all that earth."

Ellis turned to the waiting Officer who had suited up in overalls. "Go for it. DI Harris has authorised the graves to be exhumed." He watched the team follow in the footsteps of the dog handlers and head over to the grave in question. Then he and DI Harris followed them.

DI Harris stopped as he approached the area. "Coal dust," he stated as he looked down on the ground and then leaned down to point at the blackened powder. He then looked over to the dogs. The Officers immediately started digging with urgency. They had to take it that the boys were buried there and that they could still be alive. The spades were digging into the earth and the soil thrown in a pile to the right, with two Officers digging and the other making sure that the earth was clear of the dig. Suddenly there was a *THUD!* One of the spades had hit the lid of the wooden coffin. The Officers immediately removed the earth from the lid of the coffin and quickly dug around the side.

DS Ellis was just as frantic as DI Harris, wanting to get the top off of the coffin with a hope that they had saved a life, or even two. He watched the diggers jump down and then use the spades to break to lid of the coffin off, and then throw it up beside the mound of earth. PC Powell leaned forward, feet either side of the coffin and then dipped down. He noticed the gaping wound on the head of the boy and put his fingers on the blood splattered neck to feel the carotid artery. Nothing. As expected from the sight of the wound the boy was dead. But then he saw a face underneath the first body, and it didn't look like there were any serious injuries. He did the same. Leaned down to take a pulse. He was sure that he felt something.

"Guv, I think we have a live one!" He didn't care. He had to get the body out. PC Eastman, also in scrubs separated his feet.

"I got the legs," Eastman screamed. "After three!" He watched Powell grasp the top of the corpse the best that he could. "One-two-three! Lift!" They pulled up the corpse from the top and turned it to one side of the coffin, quickly reaching down afterwards to pull up the second boy.

"Get an ambulance!" Powell ordered with urgency and a hope that they might be able to save the second boy.

"He's alive, Guv!" DS Ellis said excitedly to the DI.

"AMBULANCE!" Harris announced to the Officers behind him. "We need Paramedics now. I said NOW!"

DC Mitchell was on the radio as fast as he could as PC's Powell and Eastman, with the aid of the two dog handlers raised the body. Eastman took his jacket off and wrapped it around the boy, knowing that he had to get him warm. His lips were blue having been in the cold coffin for some time. There was only a slight pulse, and his breathing was terribly slow and erratic, but PC Powell told himself that a slight pulse was better than no pulse.

The ambulance was close, parked up in Bettws. They heard the call and had to ditch their coffees to answer the call. Ten minutes later, the sirens and the flashing lights announced the arrival of the Paramedic team. Right behind them was a quick response vehicle and a Doctor assigned to the team. They all jumped out, grabbed their medical equipment, and headed right over towards the area where all the action was taking place. Dr Bullman saw DS Ellis who was waving him in the right direction. The two Paramedics carried the stretcher over whilst watching their footing on the uneven ground around the graves.

As they reached the action on the ground, the first paramedic Conor Morrisey looked at the body with the horrendous injuries. "No sign of life," he shouted before pointing towards the second teenager Jamie Arnett who was currently being kept warm. "Is that one alive?"

PC Eastman looked at his colleague PC Powell who was taking his turn in trying to raise his temperature. "Still a slight pulse," he shouted back. "Very faint."

The second paramedic Laurence Wilson took over from PC Powell. Doctor Bullman knelt down. "We will work on this one only," he shouted at his team. "He's breathing but let's get a mask on him!" Conor pulled it out of his kit bag and placed it over his face then started to squeeze the bag to assist with the oxygen flow. "Let's try and raise the boy's temperature. Laurence. Line in. Sodium Chloride to start."

Seconds later, the senior paramedic was placing a cannula into the boys vein on his left arm which was closest to him. Then the fluids. "All done," the senior paramedic exclaimed with relief. Doctor Bullman placed the stethoscope on the boys chest and listened to the heart beating. "Once the temperature is back at an acceptable level we can assist with atropine if his pulse is still slow. Right now, let's get him back to the ambulance!"

DI Harris looked at DS Ellis and nodded his head before turning and heading back towards the car park. "One is better than none."

Ellis nodded in respect at his DI. "You made the right decision, Guv. A couple of minutes more and we would have had two dead bodies." He saw Harris nod his head.

Sergeant Llewellyn was eagerly waiting at the entrance to the cemetery and watched as the two CID Officers walked out, about to walk right by without any acknowledgement. "The missing boys?"

DI Harris nodded silently and continued walking whilst DS Ellis stopped and looked at the Sergeant. "One dead. Mutilated just like the others. The second, although we don't know which one of the boys it is at the moment, is alive for now." He nodded over towards the ambulance.

Llewellyn shook his head. "Shame about the one we lost. Guess we will have to tell the parents as soon as we know who it was."

Ellis couldn't believe the lack of sympathy and the hardness of the Sergeant's comment but just shook his head and started to follow the DI.

The crowd that had gathered in the rugby club an hour earlier and threatened to complete the search for the boys were now all gathered at the cordon at the bottom of Gwaun-Bant. Two PC's tried to keep an element of order even though on many occasions a few of the protesters had tried to break the cordon to get up to the crime scene. They had seen the arrival of the ambulance and had to disperse either side of the street in order that the Police could let it through, so they knew that something was going on. In amongst them, the press and television cameras were out in force, parking over at the Co-op car park and bringing their reporters over to get the reactions from the crowd. Many of the journalists from the tabloids had decided to try and get closer to the scene by taking one of the many unmanned shortcuts which took them up to the rugby field, over the stile and right over the mud, through the hedgerows and closer to the top end of the cemetery. The flashing of their cameras only alerted the Officers close by who had been given the instructions to arrest on sight, even if they were reporters.

DI Harris knew at any moment that there would be interest in what was happening. The forensic team had arrived some time ago and were waiting in the wings to take over at the crime scene even though it had been disturbed in a big way by the order given by him. *'The needs of the one outweigh the needs of the many'* he told himself before making the important decision. He also knew that he would have to give a statement soon to the press because they were becoming impatient with the amount of information that they were receiving what with all the action going on. He looked at his Sergeant. "I have another hard decision, Peter." They both looked down to the cordon.

"I guess that they will be expecting a statement, Guv."

"The press and the villagers. The only problem we have is that we do not know which boy is which. Should we wait and get an ID on the boy that has been taken in the ambulance? Should we tell the parents of the two boys first? We know they are part of the crowd down there at the cordon." DI Harris had already made one difficult decision that day. He didn't have to say that it was the two missing boys. Just that they had found two boys, one of whom was alive and on his way to hospital in the ambulance as the medical services had had a response at the moment. The identification of the bodies would come later, even though the parents of the two missing boys would know that it was their boys who were found. They weren't daft and they would certainly believe in coincidence. At that time there were no other reports of missing boys in the area.

"Why don't we get both sets of parents away and take them down to ED. As for the rest, just tell them what you want them to hear, Guv. No questions. Short and sweet."

Harris nodded. "Good Idea. Get three of the DC's to assist you. Separate the parents in their own car with two CID Officers." Inside he was hoping that he would have had good news for both sets of parents. There hadn't been any identification yet, so he couldn't say for sure that which boy was alive or even if the two bodies belonged to Delme Greening or Jamie Arnett. But deep inside he knew. No one had to be a Detective to realise the inevitable.

"Will do, Guv."

"I'll handle the statement then I'll be down with you," Harris exclaimed. "No time like the present."

The closer that the DI Harris got to the cordon, the louder it seemed to get. Harris looked at the angry villagers who were being riled up by Billy Evans, Lee Jones, and John Rix mainly because in the meeting earlier they had been given the impression that the Police would be completing the search and in return they hoped that they would be kept informed of the developments. As he approached, the volume of the chants, screams and shouting increased, so much so that any questions thrown their way by the press could not be heard. DI Harris remembered DS Ellis' words. Short and sweet. As they approached the cordon, he held his hands up as if to try and get some order. He watched as his DS jumped into one of the unmarked cars. "Right go for it whilst I distract the crowd. Get both sets of parents down to the hospital and try to identify which boy is alive."

"Yes, Guv. I'll try and do that as discreetly as possible."

Harris shook his head as he realised that there was some humour in DS Ellis' reply. He hesitated. "Good luck with that," he said as he approached the crowd.

"Ladies and gentlemen. Please. I have a statement. At this moment in time I cannot answer any questions."

"Why not?" Billy Evans exclaimed as though he were shouting out to try and cause an uprising among the villagers just as he had done in 1982.

The DI chose not to rise to any comments like that. He ignored the call. "My name is Detective Inspector Harris. I am one of the senior investigating officers on the case. About thirty minutes ago, Officers found the bodies of two males. One of the males was already deceased whilst the second male has received urgent medical attention and is currently en route to the Princess of Wales hospital."

'Are the bodies the two missing boys, Detective?'
'Which boy is alive?'
'How were they killed?'
'Do you think it is the serial killer's latest victim?'
'Were they sexually assaulted?'
'Were the injuries identical to those on the four murdered teenagers?'

DI Harris had already said that no questions would be answered and again ignored the shouting from all corners of the cordon. He noticed DS Ellis talking to the parents and without the knowing of Billy Evans they were just led away to the two waiting cars. The PC's continued guarding the cordon.

Billy Evans perked up. "You owe it to both sets of parents who are here to confirm that the bodies are those of their children." His comments were echoed with loud *'yeeehhhh'* from the angry crowd. But then Billy looked around. The parent's had gone and all he could see were two cars speeding away from the cordon.

"No identification has been made on the two boys yet and therefore I cannot confirm or deny who they are and if I could, I cannot say which boy was saved. Further information will be given as and when we have it. Thank you." The angered villagers started to chant louder. They wanted answers.

Chapter 8

Jamie Arnett had been placed in a private room in the Children's ward at Princess of Wales Hospital. At the request of Superintendent Saunders, the room was guarded by a Uniformed Officer and would be twenty-four hours a day. The Police were hoping that when the boy became conscious he may be able to identify his attacker although knowing the circumstances in which he was found the incident would probably have a deep psychological effect on him for many years. Right now, he was stable although still comatose enforced by the medical staff to aid his recovery. His parents were sat at his bedside with his Mother Jan holding his hand with hers, hoping that he would know by doing so that both his parents were with him.

The Police Sergeant knew what he was doing. After getting through the security of the ward via the intercom and using his Police status, Michael Llewellyn headed down the corridor to the reception desk. "I'm here to visit Jamie Arnett and his parents," he said officially.

"Down on the left," the male nurse replied as he pointed towards the room. "You can't miss it. There is a Police Officer outside."

"Thanks," Llewellyn said as the thought went through his mind of who had authorised a Police Officer to be outside the room. Some form of protection. It must have come from orders above, but they hadn't told him. He walked down the corridor. He was here to visit the boy. That was his explanation. He was the community Policeman after all. The parents would welcome his thoughtfulness. He knew that in reality he had an alternative motive. He had cocked up. He was supposed to suffocate. The boy may be able to finger him. Had the boy seen his face? He doubted it very much because when he conducted the atrocities he was masked. But with a Uniformed guard outside, his reasons for being there were going to make his job that little bit harder.

The PC outside of the room noticed the Sergeant approaching. "Serge," he said as he acknowledged PS Llewellyn.

"It's okay. It's okay," Llewellyn exclaimed as he noticed the Officer had more of less stood to attention as he approached him. "I'm not here on official business. I'm the community Sergeant. I just wanted to check on both the parents and the boy. How long have the parents been here?"

The PC relaxed. "They came in a few hours ago after he was identified whilst in the E.D."

"And you?"

"Chief Inspector Williams and Superintendent Saunders have requested twenty-four-hour Uniform presence. They think that whoever did this may come back to finish the job."

"What? They think that he was supposed to be killed as well?"

"It looks that way, Serge. The DI thinks that whoever did this wanted him to suffocate in the coffin before he was found. Some kind of sick fantasy."

Llewellyn nodded his head. Inside he was telling himself that this was going to be a problem. The boy had to die. He was wishing in his mind that his sick and twisted plan was different to the sexual thrill he was getting out of burying the kid alive with his mutilated best friend. The boy should have suffocated. The grave should not have been desecrated in the way it was by DI Harris's order. He looked through the large observation window into the room and tapped on the glass.

Immediately Gareth Arnett, Jamie's Father, turned to see who was making the noise. He saw the Sergeant and got up from his chair and walked across the room. Then he opened the door, stepped outside, and closed the door behind him. "Sergeant."

"Hello, Mr Arnett. I just thought I would check in to see how Jamie was doing."

Gareth nodded his head in slight gratitude. "Well he's stable but still in a bad way. He was without oxygen for some time, and they don't know if it has caused any damage to the brain. They have kept him in an induced coma to aid his head injuries at the moment."

"That is sometimes for the best."

The parent nodded. "I guess they know what they are doing."

"If your car needs an MOT, you take it to a garage," Llewellyn replied. "Medical care, let the Doctor's handle it."

Mr Arnett nodded after seeing the Sergeant's analysis. "Yes. Exactly what I said to the wife."

"How is she doing?"

"Well," Gareth replied whilst joining the Sergeant in looking through the window at them, "I know this sounds bad, but she is feeling blessed that Jamie survived."

"The other boy was Delme Greening."

"Yes. We know. His parents had to join us in order to identify which boy was which."

Llewellyn shook his head. "It must have been a very traumatic time for you both." He watched the Father nod. "Well, listen. I won't keep you. I just wanted to show my face and let you know that if there is anything that I can do, call me." He handed Gareth his card. "I've written my personal mobile number on the back."

"Thank you, Sergeant."

"You had better get back to your family." He watched Gareth Arnett nod and then return to the room. He stared in through the glass once more momentarily before turning to the young PC and saying, "Thanks. I'll be off."

"Serge."

Half an hour later, Sergeant Llewellyn returned to Pontycymer and noticed that the cordons that closed most of the bottom end had now been lifted which allowed the locals to carry on with their lives.

Tracey Edwards had managed to re-open her fish and chip shop and found that there was a sudden increase in business mainly because the residents in the area were more interested in the latest goings on than they were about cooking their own meals.

Catrin Kean headed inside but found herself having to queue out of the door. She noticed Tracey and her Mum busy behind the counter as the wait time started to refine down until she was next to be served. "Hello Trace," she said as she stood in front of the owner who was sweating what with the heat of the fryers and the unexpected stress that they had been under. "Two fish and chips please."

"Don't fancy helping," Tracey said jokingly. "Any news on the boys?"

"Police are taking statements and knocking on doors."

"As long as they don't come down here and expect us to stop," Tracey said as she wrapped the food individually and then passed them over to Catrin. "16.20 please, doll."

"You know I am surprised that Sergeant Llewellyn didn't see anything. I saw him out in the area when I was walking the dog. We were up the rugby field. He even waved to me." She handed over the cash.

"When was that then?" Tracey enquired with a frown appearing on her face. "Mind you, he is as much use as a dose of the clap sometimes."

"Last night. The night that the boys went missing. I'm surprised that he didn't see them." She looked on as Tracey shook her head. "They have to do something soon."

"Listen, I'll catch up with you later. I'm getting the evil eye from Mum!"

"No worries." She left and went to get into her car when suddenly she saw the very man that she had been talking about moments earlier walking down Gwaun-Bant acting as though he didn't have a care in the world. Catrin held her door open, one foot in the driver's side of her Dacia Logan. "Any news, Sergeant? Do we know which of the boys survived?"

He nodded his head. "Jamie Arnett. I've just been to see him in the hospital," he replied as he walked over towards the car. "Tragic though. Very tragic."

"I guess he is in a bad way. I was just saying to Tracey in the chippy that I'm surprised that you didn't see the boys last night. I was up the rugby field with the three dogs and saw you walking that way."

"That's right. I remember. You waved to me. You know me. If I haven't got my Uniform on, I'm like the walking dead." He laughed, that kind of false laugh that only he knew had a different meaning. What he was really thinking was that someone had seen him in the wrong place at the wrong time. If she had seen him, who else had seen him? "How are those three beauties, anyway?" He asked whilst trying his hardest to change the subject and not draw attention to the fact.

"Looking forward to their walk," she said whilst looking at her watch. "Although it won't be extremely far tonight. All being well we can go up top in the morning if the weather is okay."

"I would say I would join you, but I don't go up there unless I have to," Michael replied whilst nodding up towards the flag. "So enjoy. I have a difficult job now. Going around to see the parents of Delme Greening. I hate that side of the job."

Catrin nodded. "It must be terrible. Those poor parents. At least the boys have been identified."

"I think from the start that we knew it was more than coincidence, don't you think? Have a good night." He started to walk on down the street towards the Co-op. His face was filling with both worry and anger. Someone had seen him. Close to the crime scene. What if she told CID? Had she been interviewed yet? He needed a plan.

*****

The next morning, the dog walkers were out in force. The Police were still maintaining a presence in the area around the Gelliron Cemetery, tennis courts and rugby field and needless to say, no one was allowed in these areas as evidence could still be present.

It was dry and the summer sun was rising over the north-west hill by the Blaengarw forest. Catrin Kean had met her friend Rhian Bevan, and they were heading up the steep zig-zag path to the top. The two were talking about the events from the previous evening as they watched their dogs inquisitively nose around the greenery and in the trees, sometimes becoming alert as they thought that there was something in the forest, normally wildlife or birds breaking the twigs off to make their nests.

"Five teenagers so far," Catrin exclaimed worriedly.

"It is very worrying Cat. I mean, just why? Why teenagers?"

Catrin looked around, somewhat frightened by the recent happenings that had gone on and knowing that they were approaching the area where the three boys were found. "Well at least they have one still alive. Sergeant Llewellyn told me it was Jamie Arnett that survived."

"Yes. So I believe. The word is getting around. But I heard on the grapevine that there were similar murders back about forty years ago. Billy Evans told me that the village lost faith in the Police back then and a lynch mob took the law into their own hands. But it didn't stop the murders. Then suddenly, nothing."

"Was it kids that were murdered?" Catrin filled her face with confusion and worry, her forehead showing her great concern.

Rhian nodded her head but was more concerned with her two mischievous giant Newfoundland's, as black as night apart from a white paw on one and weighing enough to flatten you if they jumped up. Otto and Betty were 'up to no good' looking into the forest because something had grasped their inquisitiveness. "What are those two up to? OTTO! BETTY! ON THE PATH PLEASE!" She looked back at Catrin wondering if her friend had seen the nodding gesture. "Yes. Eleven of them so I was told." The two women walked on whilst not mentioning any more about the murders as their attention was now taken up by the dogs.

On the other side of the path, the forest went in an upward direction and the three nosey brown Ridgebacks stood beautifully tall and proud and were running in and out of the foliage, looking back to their 'Mum' to check that they weren't being watched in order that they could get into mischief. "They will be jumping into the water up by the mine soon, I can tell you that." Catrin laughed at the thought of the same routine of her dogs. "I had a word with Tracey down the chippy yesterday. I told her that I was surprised that Sergeant Llewellyn didn't see the two boys who went missing. Both he and I were in the vicinity. Although I was up the rugby field. He was heading through Park Street over towards that direction."

"He might have just missed them then."

"Exactly what I thought. Minutes later he could have saved their lives, who knows." Catrin looked at her dogs once more. She noticed the youngest of the three, Sula, racing on towards the water. "Sula! Wait there!" The other two were slightly older and sometimes could not keep up with the baby of the three. "Come on you two," she said as she noticed that they weren't taking any notice of her at first. "Layla. Raffi. Come!" They turned and started chasing the other dog.

"You can tell that it is getting colder," Catrin exclaimed as she looked up in the direction of the wind turbines near the top of the Blaengarw forest. "That mist is starting to settle again."

"I love it when it is like that."

"What, when you can't see hand in front of face?" Catrin laughed at her friend. "It's lucky we know the way."

"You mean the dogs know the way." Rhian rubbed her arms which even through her warm coat had picked up that the temperature had dropped because of the mist falling on the forest. They approached the mine entrance where Sula had already jumped in the water which, no matter what time of the year, appeared to be cold. It was also always unhygienically brown in colour, but this didn't deter two of the three Ridgebacks, with the eldest Raffi not bothering, standing, and watching the other two playing, his face giving the impression that he was saying *'bugger that'*. Meanwhile Otto and Betty just didn't seem to be interested and had decided to lay down beside the stone bench which overlooked the Valley. "Look at these two. I might join them," Rhian said as she turned around to look in the direction of the mine entrance and plonked her backside down on the cold stone, realising that it was just as cold as the misty mountain. Catrin stood beside Raffi looking into the water, and suddenly the older dog joined the two giants in resting by laying down whilst continuing to look at the other two.

"Look at this pair," Catrin exclaimed happily as she watched the other two dogs splashing around and play fighting each other for any stone that they had pulled up from the bottom of the pool of water. She turned her head, a smile on her face and a laugh in her voice quickly turned into a look of horror. She pointed her hand and suddenly screamed whilst freezing in her posture. "Arrggghhhhh!"

"Wh…" Rhian didn't have the time to reply as the dark figure had appeared behind her and slammed the now sharpened pick into the back of the woman's head. It pierced the top of her skull, the length of the blade disappearing deep into the brain and beyond. She didn't stand a chance as the Devil had hit her in exactly the way that he wanted to and as he removed it, the blood spurted out from the wound and the body fell forward, lifeless. Otto and Betty jumped up and looked at their master laying on the floor, then looked up at the assailant, back down to Rhian, their timid ways not registering on what to do next or what had happened to their Mum.

Catrin panicked, her feet seemed to still be frozen in fright to the ground. Raffi could feel her fear and turned his head as he heard the noise from the slaying of his dog Mum's best friend. The dog saw the hidden faced figure, jumped up and ran towards the black covered killer, teeth showing and a growl appearing as he jumped up. His age didn't help him as the Devil swung the pick sideways with shear strength and it threw the dog sideways. Raffi yelped in pain as he landed on his side to the right. He wanted to get up again, but his age made the task that little bit slower. Betty and Otto just stood and watched the assault whilst not understanding what was happening. Catrin wanted to save her dogs. Layla and Sula stopped playing, hearing their Mum's scream and panic and the yelp from their brother. They jumped up beside her and instantly looked at the figure who was now heading towards Catrin with the pick in a threatening position as though the killer was ready to strike once more. Catrin wanted to run but didn't know which direction. She needed to hide but knew that the dogs would follow and give her away if she didn't silence them. Layla and Sula ran towards the approaching dark figure just as Raffi had done moments earlier. The older dog managed to bite the arm whilst Sula was hit with the sharpened end and was wounded although not fatally, a large gash striking along the dogs right hand side of the torso, and she was also thrown sideways and landed close to Raffi but unlike the older dog was rendered slightly semi-conscious by the strike and moaned with the pain. Layla decided to stalk the killer. Her Mum noticed that the protection was taking the dark figures attention away from her and so decided to run to the left in the direction that they had come as it was mostly all downhill. She was chased although her assailant was also chased by the remaining protective dog Layla who was growling as she ran. The dark figure realised that the chase was on so stopped and turned just as the dog jumped up to try and disable the stranger by flattening them to the ground. The pick was raised, and Layla's stomach was pierced by the edge just as Rhian's head had been. The dog fell to the ground, the paws scrapping on the ground as she felt the pain and yelped in agony.

The Devil noticed the two bigger dogs Otto and Betty already sniffing the three disabled dogs whilst trying to understand what was happening. Looking down at the latest casualty, the blackened character didn't waste any more time but turned and looked around for the target. She was in the distant, had picked up speed. But then she was being chased. The fiend had one advantage. The speed. Catrin was panicking, crying frantically, momentarily looking back to see where the assailant was. Each time she looked the closer the darkness appeared to be. She was hoping that the mist would hide her but knew that she had to get off the track, into the tall trees where both the darkness and the lowered mist would hide her. She could camouflage herself whilst hiding. Lay low. She looked right into the downhill forest and then threw herself into the step declining foliage, the brambles scratching different parts of her body and ripping her clothes. At last she was on the same level as the trees, but whilst looking back each time and running downhill she found herself going headfirst into one of the uprights which knocked her senseless and she fell sideways, and she felt a pain in her forehead and nose. Forgetting about the chase and with the frantic fear from ending up the same way as her best friend, she started to cry from the mixture of the pain and the knowing that running into the tree had stopped her escape and put her closer to being slain. She was on her knees. The dark became darker. The dark figure had caught up with her. It was stood over her and had paused as though it was playing with her. Then with one strong blow the pick was swung sideways which took half of the woman's face off, the jaw was protruding, the nose had left the face, one of the eye's had been hit and landed over at the base of a tree. Catrin screamed one last scream as the feat was repeated although from the left-hand side of her head only this time the point from the weapon hitting her head and piercing the side through the ear.

The dark figure left it inside her head for a while as the blood spurted out of each wound and onto the surrounding dark green and brown bark, leaves, pines and the twigs and branches on the ground. Finally he removed his net mask hoping that she was still alive to see who had killed her, but it was too late. Catrin was dead. With one final thrashing of the pick he thrust it into her torso and pulled it downwards which exposed the contents of her stomach, her lungs, her kidneys, her intestines. There was blood everywhere. He left her there and headed back to the scene of his first kill of the day.

The killer looked at the carnage near the mine entrance. The three Ridgebacks were laying disabled, whining in pain but he knew that they would live. The two Newfoundland's still looking around at each other and at their friend's and trying to understand what had happened. To rub salt into the wounds he rubbed the big dogs heads and ruffled their fluffy coats before heading over to Rhian. Just as he had done with Catrin moments earlier, he raised the pick above his head and brought it down with all his might into Rhian's chest, the cavity opening up as he pulled it downwards, her ribs crunching as it snapped each and exposed the contents of her stomach. He smiled psychotically and then grabbing her right leg, he dragged the body over towards the water that the dogs had played in. Once the corpse was beside the water, he kicked the side of the body and rolled it into the shallow water. Then he turned and surveyed the carnage. Blood trailed from the bench where he had killed her, all the way over to the water's edge. The water had turned red and was continuing to flow down the stream to whatever destination it would land. The black outfit was quickly removed whilst the black figure looked around to check that he hadn't been seen. He knew that there was no one. Time for him to escape.

Chapter 9

Tony Newton made his way to Wales along the M4 and turned off at the turning for Bridgend. He was told that his house was ready for him in Pontycymer, but before he went there he needed to visit the contact that Vicky had supplied to him. Ex-DCI Colin Brittain actually worked on the case back in 1982 and Colin had told her that he still had his own personal notes and his own personal views on the suspects.

Tony had trouble finding the house. It was in a secluded spot in Blackmill and off the beaten track but the one thing that Tony had that he guessed that the man he was going to visit never had even now was a sat nav. He headed up the gravel driveway. He had already called ahead, as had Vicky, to let the respected man know that he was coming. Speaking to him on the phone, he felt that the older man seemed glad to be able to speak to someone about Police work and investigations once again. He was now in his eighties but appeared switched on. Like a true gentleman he was sat outside waiting for his visitor to arrive, and as the car came to a halt, the ex-Police Officer got up, with what it seemed to Tony with no problems as though the older man kept himself in shape.

The reporter walked over holding out his hand. "Mr Brittain?" he enquired with a smile.

"You must be Tony. Vicky has told me all about you."

"All good I hope," Tony replied jokingly as he shook his hand.

"Come in, come in," the host said as he lead the way. "Now it's a bit too early for a glass of whiskey, plus you are driving. So will coffee or tea suffice?"

"Coffee sounds great. White, one sugar."

"Good. Well you go and take a seat in there," Colin said as he watched Tony respecting his house and taking his shoes off, which he much appreciated because usually with visitors he had to request them to do so, sometimes much to their dismay.

"Thanks, Sir." Tony said, heading into the room on his left. He noticed the spotless décor, cherry wood bookcases filled with old books, a leather sofa and two chairs, buttoned backs, firm and all polished. Tony thought that he was going to be afraid to sit on them. There were paintings on the other wall opposite from the bookcase. He stood there looking at them for some time, thinking how beautiful they were. Tony enjoyed the galleries in London, something he did to relax on his days off from the hustle and bustle of the newspaper environment, so he was feeling the same sort of comfort looking at these.

"Beautiful, aren't they?" The old man said as he appeared in the doorway carrying a tray of drinks.

"Here, let me take that for you," Tony said as he prepared to walk over to his host.

"I'm not dead yet," Colin replied whilst showing his independence. "Come, sit down. Those paintings are by an artist called Robert Lenkiewicz. I've tried so hard to get more, but the poor man passed away some years ago and his other paintings are every collector's wish." He put the tray down on the coffee table.

"I thought I recognised them. I went to an exhibition of all his work when he died."

"Their value has soared because of his death. I don't mind, but I don't care. They will never be for sale. I admire them too much."

"I don't blame you." He acknowledged Colin Brittain as the old man passed him his cup and saucer, instantly thinking that he would have preferred a mug but then noticing the peculator on the tray which would have meant a refill.

"Help yourself to biscuits."

"Thanks. I love biscuits. Too much in fact!"

"Snap." Colin took a sip of his drink. "So how can I help? Vicky said you are investigating things that are going on in the Garw at the moment. She also told me that it was your Grandfather Christopher Fallon that disappeared when the first spate of murders were happening in the early eighties."

109

Tony put his cup and saucer back down on the table and then turned to look at Colin. "I have thoroughly read up on the case the best that I can. I was hoping that you could shed some light."

"What do you know?"

"Six murders of teenage boys up until the time that my Grandfather went missing. Then another five afterwards. It appears the injuries to the victims were quite horrific."

"Gut-wrenching. Of course back in 1982, DNA testing was extremely limited. Still in its early stages and in some ways not accurate enough to be of any use."

"Yes. I studied that at University. It wasn't until 1984 that Mr Jeffreys actually admitted to have discovered it," Tony replied. "I wasn't even born then."

"Well. The whole of Scotland Yard got excited," Colin laughed. "If only he had invented it a couple of years earlier. It would have made our jobs that little bit easier."

"So I believe there was a body burned to smithereens?"

"Yes. One of the residents found it early one morning. I remember it well. It was under some trees. No ID or anything. The body had been that severely burned that we couldn't even get a fingerprint match or link the teeth to any dentistry."

"The report I read said that my Grandfather went missing after that incident."

"Yes. The Uniform units were called to a house in a long street called the Avenue. Very original name for a street, I know," Colin joked as he shared a smile. "Well, the front door had been forced and was all smashed. The inside of the house looked like a bomb had hit it. The looters had been in and took things that weren't smashed and were of value, which from we could make out were truly little."

Tony nodded as he once again picked up his drink. "Well originally, the records back at the paper state he was there to do a story on the way the miners were feeling about the Government's proposal to close the mines. He was there to fight their case."

"So I was told." He looked at the younger man and saw that his cup was empty. "There is a whole jug of coffee there. Help yourself, otherwise I will have to drink it and at my age that will mean I will be running to the toilet."

Tony laughed as he filled his cup and then took a biscuit from the plate. "Of course whilst he was there the murders started."

"And I guess being a reporter he wasn't going to miss such a high-profile story. I would have done exactly the same."

"So the records say. I have looked at the mesh of all the newspapers around that time."

Colin followed the younger man's lead and took a biscuit. "Well our hands were tied. We could only assume that the body in the ashes was your Grandfather. The story ended after the disappearance. We thought he either went back to the newspaper or he was the victim. And when the house was reported as ransacked it became apparent that there was something bad going on."

"Can I ask. Did you have any suspects in mind?"

"It wasn't so much that we had suspects. There was an air of silence throughout. Only the very few would speak to us. We think those who hadn't been involved. But otherwise, no one would speak to us. We had nothing to go on."

Tony shook his head. "You sometimes find that in communities. One of my colleagues had the same up in Norfolk when a rapist who had walked free from court was found murdered."

"I hate to say this as an ex-Police Officer, but sometimes you like to agree with them and turn a blind eye. But don't quote me on that."

Tony laughed. "I would too if I was sure of their guilt."

"Exactly. All I can tell you about your investigation is the animosity towards the Police given at the time by a number of individuals. I remember their names even now. As an old school copper you used to look at someone and tell yourself that certain people knew more than they were letting on. Or some had something to do with it."

"I bet some just echoed guilt?"

"Of course. One of them, Robert Gabriel, lives in the local village here in Blackmill. He was one of a number of guilty acting youngsters at the time of your Grandfather going missing and the fire. He lived in Blaengarw at the time but moved here just after."

Tony shook his head. "Running away?"

111

Colin nodded. "He is a bad 'en alright. Involved in everything that is wrong here in the village. Car thefts. Burglaries. Stolen goods. You name it, he has done it. You would think that at the age of sixty-something he would have given up the crime. But that is not the case."

The reporter poured himself yet another cup of coffee, again thinking that it would have been easier for the old man to give him a big mug like the one that he had at work. "What about the others?"

Colin reached over to the small table beside him that seemed to contain magazines and a coaster that was there to hold his glass of whiskey on an evening. He flicked through the various documents and came across a folder. "I'm going to loan you this. I used to keep my own notes, mainly because things in 1982 were all paper. No computers back then. Because it was all paperwork, things had a habit of going astray."

Tony accepted the file as it was passed to him. "Thank you, Sir."

"Now. I can tell you. There is one man in particular who you don't need to get on the wrong side of. At the time he was in his early twenties, but his influence in the village was apparent in a big way. Like the villagers throughout were afraid of him."

"Do you have a name?"

"Oh, yes. Billy Evans. Believe me. Don't get on the wrong side of that man. I know he will be in his sixties now, but from what I hear, he is still the big man."

"Well, I can tell you Mr Brittain, that it is my job to do quite the opposite of what you are telling me in order to get to the truth."

"Then watch your back. He described himself at the time as *'The meanest motherfucker in the village'* and told us even if he did know anything that he wouldn't tell us."

"Nice."

Colin nodded. "Billy had his *'gang'* which actually included Robert Gabriel that I mentioned just now."

"Well thanks for this, Mr Brittain. I have some bedtime reading. I had better get to Pontycymer and see my house."

"You are welcome, young man," Colin replied as he stood up with no problems, knowing that at his age many older folk would need some aid of some kind. "And don't be afraid to call me if you need anything else. But as I said. Watch your back."

"You must let me take you for dinner one evening as a thank you."

"That sounds wonderful," Colin acknowledged.

Tony nodded.

*****

The house in the Avenue had already been restyled and new furniture put in. The newspaper that owned it had rented it out several times over the past forty years since Christopher Fallon was ousted out by the lynch mob in 1982. Many of the locals had said that the place was haunted, that when Fallon was killed had put a curse on the whole street as standards in the area deteriorated and the economy of the whole Valley plunged. In reality, the die-hard residents knew it was because of the closure of the mines, and that the sightings of the ghost of Christopher Fallon were just what the people wanted to believe.

Michael Fallon arrived in Pontycymer and settled himself into the fully furnished place just two days after the boys bodies were found in the cemetery. Instantly, curtains opposite the house were twitching, two of the residents stood in their small front gardens taking note about who was moving in. They saw that it was just one man. In their eyes he had to be single. Just him. The delivery van that had taken furniture in the day before had also taken his mountain bike inside. Perhaps he was here to explore the countryside, the mountains, the trails which were frequented by mountain bikers from all parts of the UK. Babs Williams knew that she would be first to know. He would have parcels delivered and she was always the one to take them in for her direct neighbours if they were out. She would get the lowdown in no time at all.

It had been left to Michael Fallon to make up his own story about who he was, where he had come from, what he was doing there. He had his real Mum and Dad as well as his professional ones who he had agreed to work with back at the newspaper. He decided not to give away any information about his own direct family. Mum and Dad to him from now on would be Vicky and Ryan back at the paper. He was single having just

113

come out of a relationship. Bought the house as it was cheaper in the Valley as opposed to the town of Bridgend. Working at McArthur Glen as arranged by his Editor-in-Chief. Friends mostly lived in Cardiff where he went to University. He was a musician which he knew would have been picked up by the two nosey neighbours opposite as he had brought his electric guitar and amp with him. He had this wrapped up from the start, he told himself as he looked out from behind the net curtain at the two old women who he knew were talking about him because of the nodding heads in his direction. As a reporter he also knew that they wanted to get information about him, but it was going to be the other way around. He was the one who wanted to know them. Time for a walk around before he had to *'unpack'* he told himself.

The two elderly ladies were still outside their front doors talking about their new neighbour. Anthony crossed the road. He had chosen to adopt his bosses surname so as not to show any link to the tenant from forty years ago who, depending on how long they had lived here, they would know of. He walked across the road to introduce himself to the two busy bodies. "Hello. Tony. Tony Newton. I believe we are going to be neighbours," he exclaimed as he held out his hand for them both to shake.

Babs Williams and Fran Fudge were instantly impressed with the gentleman. "Barbara," the eldest lady, a widower by all means who looked like she loved the best of life with her glowing face and healthy look. "Known as Babs."

"Nice to meet you," the newcomer replied politely as he returned the gesture to the Bab's neighbour.

"Francis Fudge," she said as she also shook his hand.

"So what's it like around here?" Tony asked as he looked up and down the street. "I've only looked briefly before buying this place. It was the scenery that did it for me. Mountain walks and I have my bike as well. Might even get myself a dog, who knows."

"It's okay. Nothing much happens really, does it Babs?"

"No. I guess you have seen the Co-op?"

"Yes, on the way here," Tony said with a smirk as he knew that the Co-op was the only supermarket in the area and that apart from a few convenience stores, that was it. "That's okay. I work at McArthur Glen and can use Sainsbury's." He smiled at the two ladies whilst knowing that he had given them a good impression from the start. "I'm going to have a look around. Do you two ladies want to come with me?"

They both chuckled. "We will leave you to it young man," Babs said whilst still chuckling.

Tony headed down to the main road. He had read all the transcripts about both his Grandfather's mission and disappearance in 1982 and also the deaths of the teenagers that were happening now. All he needed now was information. He had to show his worth as an investigative journalist. Firstly he found the waste ground with the five trees. He guessed from the reports that this was where his Grandfather was killed. He stood looking at the scene, trying to imagine just what it would have been like those forty years ago. He shook his head as a tear came to his eye. Bryn Stores was his next port of call. Where else to get the gossip than from the local convenience store?

He walked into the shop via the sliding door which seemed to open even before he got there, and it surprised him a little. "Hello," he said as he looked to the left and saw the staff member behind the till, noticing that she was in her thirties and busy talking to one of the customers. "I'll be out for a ciggy in a minute," she commented to her friend. "I'll just see to this customer."

"Bread and milk?" Tony asked nicely as he looked around the store which appeared to have everything stacked close with little room to manoeuvre.

"Milk is behind you and the bread is just past the fridges on the right," the assistant replied. She heard the groceries being moved around and guessed that he was trying to search for the loaf with the longest shelf life which was usually at the back of each pile. Then she heard him thinking loudly down one of the aisles and quickly looked at the CCTV to check where he was. *'Biscuits'*, she thought to herself. *'Hurry up, I want a fag'*.

"Sorry, Got to have something to dunk in my tea. I've just moved in, and I haven't got anything yet," he said as he placed the three items on the counter.

"Welcome to Blaengarw," she replied as she pressed the buttons on the till. "Why here?"

"It's cheap and I'm working locally. Have you been here long?"

"Too long," she replied. "Ever since I was born. That will be five pounds forty-nine please."

Tony opened his wallet. He had cash. He didn't want anyone to know his real name and that included by using his cards. "My mate at work tells me you have had a few murders recently."

"Yeh. Somone is killing all the brats around here. I would like to say it was me. Most of them shoplift."

"Do the Police have any suspects?" Tony enquired, trying to push her for more information without appearing too forward.

"They are bloody useless. Billy Evans is more informative than them."

"Billy Evans?" Tony asked inquisitively with a confused face. He had heard the name before whilst reading the case files from forty years ago, and Colin Brittain had also mentioned him in conversation. He wondered if it were the same Billy Evans whilst knowing that there were probably a lot of people with the surname of 'Evans' in the Valley.

"Oh. Talk of the Devil. Here's your man now."

"Do I hear my name being taken into vain?" the big man asked as he walked through the door dressed in his normal check shirt that the villagers often wondered if it was the only shirt that he owned.

The assistant obviously knew him well. "We were just saying about the murders. This man," she pointed at Tony. "He is new to the area. Sorry I didn't catch your name."

"Tony. Tony Newton." He held out his hand towards Billy who accepted the gesture.

The big man looked at the stranger. He didn't like strangers in the village especially after Christopher Fallon all those years ago. "Where are you from, Tony?"

"Plymouth originally. My family moved to London some years ago. I've come down here for the peace and quiet."

"You won't get that here at the moment," Billy exclaimed whist still staring at him, trying to read him through his facial expressions but not at all succeeding. "So where in the Garw are you living?"

116

"I've bought a place up in The Avenue. Didn't believe my luck. £75K for a three-bedroom place."

Billy started to panic inside. He knew which house was going that cheap due to the history behind it. He needed to confirm it. "Oh what number? I'll have to pop up for a cup of tea."

"Number sixty-six."

"Oh Lord," the shop assistant commented as though she were frightened of something. "That one has got quite a history behind it."

"QUIET!" Billy ordered whilst staring at the woman with widened eyes and a look of anger. Then in a less angry and quieter voice he said, "I'm sure Tony here doesn't want to know the history of the house."

"Oh it's okay. I know. The estate agent told me, and I always like to know the history of the area. It doesn't worry me." Tony decided to change the subject a little, expanding on his last comment. "It must have been a very industrial area all those years ago when the mines were here. I've seen the photos."

"If only you knew. You should have lived here back then!" Billy Evans decided to also change the subject. "Well if you need any information about the area, I'm your man. Have you registered with a GP surgery yet?"

Tony shook his head. "No not yet." He knew where the surgery was but thought that he would gain Billy's confidence by letting him tell him where to go. "Where is the nearest one?"

"It's about half a mile down the road on the right. You can't miss it. There is a rugby club right next door and two chemists."

"Okay. Thanks. So are you close by just in case I need to knock on your door and ask anything else? Dentist? Post Office?" He laughed at his suggestion but deep inside was getting more information about the man. He could tell already that there was something not quite right with him. He seemed to be in control, especially with his outburst at the shop assistant, who, he noticed, took heed. Tony was also good at weighing people up.

"I'm closer than you think," Billy exclaimed. "Just two doors down." He pointed in the direction of Victoria Street.

117

"Thanks." Tony went to leave. "Nice meeting you both. And don't forget. Cup of tea!" He exited the shop, the slide doors once again swishing sideways.

Billy watched him disappear around the side of the building, nodded his head before turning his attention back to the assistant and giving her an evil stare. "Didn't your parents tell you to keep our business in the villages?" She ignored him. "He could be anyone. He could be an undercover Police Officer or even a reporter. We don't know. And we don't want any outside interference in what we can handle ourselves. Understood?"

The assistant nodded her head but said nothing.

Chapter 10

Catrin Kean's partner Poli waited patiently for her to arrive back from the dog walk. He knew that she had an important lecture that very afternoon and she wasn't normally that long, although sometimes when she went on a *'hike'* with Rhian they tended to put the world to rights, and both forgot the time of day. They would also document every walk on social media which made him laugh because both of them had more than enough photos of their dogs to last a lifetime. He did have Rhian's best friends telephone number. Perhaps Catrin had gone back there first. But she had to come home and get showered and changed because normally she was covered in mud and sometimes wet right through after being out with the dogs. He was now getting worried. It was only an hour until her lecture, and she had to travel to Bristol. She wouldn't make it. He bit his lip and looked out of the window and then down at his mobile. He picked it up and tried to dial Catrin. It went straight to voicemail. He tried again and the same happened, so this time he scrolled down to Rhian's number and tried that one. The same happened. Once more. Rhian. It went to voicemail again. He became slightly worried so made a last attempt at Catrin. Voicemail. This time he looked down the contacts for Rhian's best friend, Mike. The phone rang and was finally answered.

"I'm at work, bud," the voice said quietly as though he wasn't supposed to answer the mobile there.

"Mike. It is important. I haven't seen Catrin or Rhian back from their walk."

Mike looked at his watch. "That's unusual," he exclaimed as his face filled with slight confusion. "Have you tried calling them?"

"Yes. Both phones go direct to voicemail."

"Okay. That is strange. Listen. I'll take my break now and go out the back to try and get an answer from one of them. Ring you back in a sec."

Just a minute later, Poli's mobile burst into life, the screen showing it was Mike. "Any luck?"

"No. I'm beginning to think that they might have had an accident. Fallen down one of the steep drops or something."

"I'm going to take a walk up there," Poli exclaimed whilst feeling frantically worried about the pair, and even more so that neither could be contacted.

Thirty minutes later Poli was at the entrance to Blaengarw forest at the top of Pwllcarn Terrace. He looked around at the beautiful hills and greenery on the left and the farmer's fields on the right surrounded by the high hills. In the distance he could hear the sheep and the cows together with the sound of the running water in the streams. But nothing else. Quickly he walked up the incline reaching a junction of paths which turned left. He knew that they went back down finally to the stream and then further down to the old football field. He also knew that Catrin usually avoided that way as it could be quite treacherous when wet or just after it had rained, so he continued upwards. He always felt that this route was never ending. Just when you thought that you had reached the top of an incline, around the corner was another.

"Catrin! Rhian! Are you here?" There was no reply so at the top of the first incline he headed to the left continuing on the single path knowing that the two girls would never opt to go off route. He increased his speed, somewhat wishing that he had changed his shoes before venturing out. Then he had an idea. Perhaps he should call for the dogs. If the girls had had an accident, the dogs would stand a better chance of survival as they were nimbler, especially the younger one, Sula. "Sula! Raffi! Layla!" Nothing. So he continued upwards until the path began to level and head right. "Catrin! Rhian! Are you here? Sula! Raffi! Layla!" He stopped and listened. He could hear something. Someone else was around. It could be another dog walker who could have seen the girls and the dogs. He listened again and started walking quickly along the darkened path. The mist had continued to settle, and it was colder than back down in the village. He couldn't see much ahead of him, but as he got closer to the mine entrance he could hear something. The dogs. There was a distinct wining and yelping. As he got closer the mist dispersed. Raffi was limping towards him, crying as though he was hurt.

"Raffi! Here boy. Here!" As the poor dog got closer, Poli could see cuts which were leaking blood. The dog came in for reassurance although didn't manage the usual wag of the tail. "What's wrong boy? What has happened?" Poli took off his sweater as he realised that one of the wounds on the dogs leg needed dressing quite urgently. He wrapped it around and pulled the arms of the sweater tight. Raffi let him do it, obviously feeling the relief from the pain of the cut. Poli looked ahead. "Where are Layla and Sula baby?" He looked again and then laid Raffi down insisting that he rest the injury. "You stay here, boy. STAY!" He raised his finger as he noticed the sorry eyes of the dog look at him as though they were saying, *'Don't leave me'*. Poli leaned over and gave the dog a kiss and then looked further down the path. Then he started walking. He could hear the yelping of the other dogs the closer that he got. Raffi didn't listen but slowly followed his *'Dad'*.

"Catrin! Rhian! Where are you? Catrin!" There was nothing, just the sound of one of the other dogs who was yelping in pain, but he couldn't tell which one. He saw both of them laying on the ground and ran as fast as he could, skidding to a halt whilst noticing the wounds. He knew that he had to get all three of the dogs to the vets as soon as he could. But where was Catrin? He looked around. "Catrin. Where are you?" Then he noticed something. Just ten metres away. There was a trail of blood that just didn't appear to belong to any of the dogs because the amount of blood was just too much. It spread from one side of the path to the other, the seat on the left and over to the stream beside the mine entrance. He saw Betty and Otto who were patiently just sat by the bench, and as soon as they saw him they headed over. "Hello," Poli said to them both as he rubbed their heads before noticing that It looked like something had been dragged. Just what was going on, he asked himself.

He quickly walked along the blood trail. Then he looked into the water. "Fuck! FUCK!" Rhian's body was face down in the shallow water, the water reddened. Poli reached into the cold water and grabbed the girl's arm whilst hoping that she could still be alive but as he did he let out a huge gasp of breath and backed up, slipping on the ground with both feet as he reversed in fright whilst on his backside. "Arrrggghhhh!" he screamed. "Arrrggghhhh!" She was dead, her body maimed and mutilated beyond recognition. He became hysterically frantic, not wanting to touch Rhian's body anymore. But where was Catrin? He looked over and saw that Otto and Betty were still casually looking around as though they weren't affected by anything.

"CATRIN! CATRIN! WHERE ARE YOU?" Ambulance. No. Police. Both. His mind was as frantic as his behaviour and Poli found himself unable to think straight. He needed to find Catrin. Where was she? He took his mobile out of his pocket. 9-9-9.

"Emergency. Which emergency service do you require?"

"Police!" Poli snapped. "No. Ambulance. Both!"

"Putting you through to South Wales Police."

"South Wales Police.

"Call from 07856223154." The operator said urgently.

"South Wales Police emergency. What is the problem?"

"There is a dead body. On the mountain. My partner is missing. Dogs are hurt. We need an ambulance!"

"Where are you located, Sir?"

"The forest at Blaengarw. Please. Come quickly. I can't find her."

"A unit has been assigned sir. Now stay with me on the line."

Poli nodded. "Yes. Yes."

"Now you say there is a body?"

"Yes. In the water," he snapped back frantically and somewhat hysterically which was showing in his voice.

"Male or female?"

"Female. It's Rhian."

"You know the victim?"

Poli nodded as though the operator could see him. "My partner is missing."

"Is the person in the water definitely dead?"

122

The man started crying. "Dead. Yes. She has been hit. Her body slashed to pieces. Help. Please. My dogs. My partner!" Suddenly he turned around, alerted, felt as though someone was watching him. He did a complete 360 degree turn but could see no one. The branches behind on the uphill section were crackling as though someone was standing on them. But he couldn't see anyone. He could feel it though. But the feeling stopped and so did the noise. Poli shook his head and told himself that he was imagining things. He went back to look at Rhian and shook his head, his body was shaking with fear. "CATRIN!" he shouted once more hoping that all she was doing was hiding away from whoever had killed her friend. There was no reply. He looked at his watch. Where were the Police? Where was the ambulance? Once more he choked up tears whilst feeling useless because he couldn't do anything. Where the hell was Catrin?

"Hello, Sir. Are you still there?" the Operator enquired. "Sir?"

"Yes. Yes. Help. Please."

"Someone is on the way, Sir."

The Police had arrived down at the entrance to the Blaengarw forest but could not get any further in their vehicles because the gate was closed and secured by a heavy-duty padlock. Sergeant Andy Rollinson was first out of the vehicle and looked in the direction of Pwllcarn Terrace as the sirens and flashing lights from the ambulance arrived behind them.

PC Lestyn Jones had checked the padlock and rushed back to the Sergeant. "It's locked Serge. There's no way we are getting through there."

"What about from the other side?"

"I know that is inaccessible. Me and the Mrs have walked it with the kids. You can get so far but then it is a narrow mud path and thick metal barriers to stop the motorbikes and buggies getting through."

WPC Caron approached the pair. "What do you want to do Serge? Shall I try and get the Welsh Forestry Commission up here ASAP?"

"Good idea," Sergeant Rollinson exclaimed as he saw the paramedic approaching. "Hello there."

"Conor Morrisey," he said as he introduced himself. "I guess we can't get access?"

Rollinson shook his head. "Not a chance."

"We had a report of a dead body, is that right?"

"According to the witness who is up there," Rollinson said. "Looks like we are going to walk it."

"Do we know the whereabouts of where the casualty is?" Conor asked as he looked around at the mass of green and brown trees that overshadowed the area.

"The report was it was near the old mine entrance."

"Is it clear and accessible for the air ambulance to get close?" Conor looked at the Sergeant as he tried to remember what it looked like. "PC Jones. Could an air ambulance land near the mine entrance?"

Lestyn Jones shook his head. "Not a chance. It is a clearing though and so it could hover without having the hazard of any trees close. Apart from that it is an uneven incline, quite steep in some parts."

The paramedic nodded his head. "I'm going to radio through and get air support." He disappeared back towards the waiting ambulance.

Rollinson noticed two more Police cars arriving at the top of Pwllcarn Terrace. Inspector Geraint Thomas and PC Gareth Evans exited the first vehicle and Rollinson intuitively knew that Inspector Thomas would take over as SIO. As the senior Officer approached he noticed that the PC's in the second back up vehicle were WPC Rowlands and PC Lewis. "Guv."

"What have we got, Andy?" Inspector Thomas asked as he also looked around the area.

"Casualty reported as deceased up at the old mine entrance. At the moment it is inaccessible to vehicles. Paramedics are trying to get the air ambulance to attend."

"How far is it?"

Rollinson looked over to PC Jones for information once more who had overheard the question and jumped in with, "Fifteen to twenty minutes' walk, Sir. It is all up hill."

"Can we get India-99 in as well?"

"Well there is a field down at the bottom of the road where the helicopter could land for some Officers to join but we cannot land at the scene of crime PC Jones informs us."

The Inspector shook his head. "Let's get walking then."

Rollinson turned to all the Officers who were patiently waiting and announced the Inspector's decision. "Listen up team. We have to walk it. Let's get going. Quickly!"
*****

Poli was still in shock and was sat cuddling the three dogs and nursing the visible injuries whilst randomly shouting for his partner. "Catrin!" Suddenly in the distance he could see a figure heading towards them. At first he couldn't see who it was because of the mist which had now settled over that part of the forest. But as the figure came closer, he noticed that it was someone in Uniform. Police. The Officer came rushing towards him and Poli recognised the community Sergeant.

"Help!" he exclaimed as the Officer knelt down to see how the three dogs were.

"I heard the shout over the radio. What's happened?" Sergeant Llewellyn asked frantically.

"Rhian. She is dead," Poli exclaimed as he nodded his head in the direction of the stream over by the mine entrance.

"Rhian. What Otto and Betty's owner? Rhian Bevan?" He got up as Poli nodded and walked back towards the stream. Noticing the body he put his hand over his mouth. "Oh my God." He grabbed his radio. "548 Sergeant Llewellyn to Sierra Oscar."

"Go ahead, 548."

"Can you let the team on the ground know that I am at the scene up at Blaengarw Forest. One confirmed deceased. Woman in her '40's. Victim has been attacked and body unrecognisable."

Sergeant Rollinson overheard the message and jumped into the conversation. "Mike. It's Andy Rollinson. We are on our way up now."

"We are also going to need assistance to transport three injured dogs as soon as possible. It looks like they have been attacked as well."

Andy instantly began to wonder what action to take with the dogs. He knew that one of the local vets operated a mobile service. "Okay. I'll get that arranged."

Catrin's partner Poli jumped in before he could speak further. "Catrin is not answering. She was with Rhian. They were

125

out with the dogs." He started choking up again as he worried and panicked.

"Andy. We have one woman deceased and looks like one missing."

"We have the air ambulance coming in. I'll get the Inspector to request India-99 and scan with the infra-red heat seeking equipment."

"How far away are you?"

"I guess about ten minutes," Sergeant Rollinson replied, although he sounded as though he were out of breath whilst not expecting to be walking up a hill on this day. "Did you have a short cut or something? How did you get there so quickly?"

Michael Llewellyn smirked psychotically. "I know the mountain. I know all the short cuts!"

"I wish that you could have shown us," Rollinson replied whilst appearing to still be out of breath. "Is there no clues as to the whereabouts of the missing woman?"

"Nothing."

"Okay. We won't be long."

*****

Anthony Fallon was down at the Co-op in Pontycymer picking up some shopping. As he came out of the store he heard the sound of two helicopters flying over from the direction of Nantymoel, He looked up, shielding his eyes from the bright light with his free hand in order that he could try and see them. From what he could make out, one was a bright red which usually meant it was a medical flight such as the Air Ambulance. On the other he could just make out the writing which looked like 'Police' to him. He turned to the person beside him who was also doing the same.

"I wonder what that is all about," he asked inquisitively.

"Something is going on. That's all we seem to have these days. Trouble." The stranger moved on, ending the conversation with a shake of his head.

Tony knew that he needed to get closer to the action. He quickly walked back to the Avenue and as soon as he got inside he changed his shoes to his hiking boots and put on his North Face jacket just in case it was cold up on top amongst the mist and trees. He rushed down to the path, crossing the road near the Chemist and then moving down the eighty-one steps towards the lower lake. He went over the small footbridge and looked to his right. He could hear the propellers of both helicopters hovering over the mountain on the Blaengarw side. He headed the other way, rushing to the path on his right that took him up the mountain. It took him ten minutes to get to the flag and seat at the top. He felt thankful that he was quite fit and only saw the need to stop once to catch his breath halfway up. He kept looking to his right. Yes, he thought to himself. Something was going on. He was a reporter. He had to find out what.

*****

The paramedic had abseiled down to the scene of the crime and rushed over to the body in the water which had been already surrounded by the Uniformed Officers who had managed to reach the area. He walked over carrying his medical pack but was stopped by Sergeant Rollinson who immediately put his hand up which touched the paramedics chest as if to stop him going any further.

"I don't think we will need you at the moment," Rollinson exclaimed as he looked back and forth at the corpse. He noticed the paramedic stare down at the blood-stained body.

"My God. I'll report back and tell the C.O. that we will be needed at some point but not until later. Way later."

Rollinson nodded as he watched him head back and put the harness on, talked into his radio and was then hoisted back up. The Sergeant turned his head. "Right. Let's clear the area. We will need CID and SOCO up here."

"I'm doing that now," his fellow Sergeant Martin Pugh exclaimed with his radio already at his mouth.

Catrin's partner was stooped down looking after his three dogs but was also listening in to what was going on around him. He grabbed Sergeant Rollinson's attention. "What about my Catrin?" he asked concerningly. "She is missing. I have tried her mobile. It is still going to voicemail."

"I am going to get a unit to search the immediate area. But at the moment we have nothing to say that she is harmed in any way." He stared at the man, knowing that because of his accent he wasn't from the area. "Leave it with me." Poli went back to giving the three dogs the love and attention that they needed. Rollinson meanwhile had a hunch, and when his copper's nose had a hunch it was usually right. The woman had also been attacked. "Right listen up. PC's Lestyn Jones, Brydon Jones, Gareth Evans, Mark Nefydd, William Powell, and Michael Eastman." The six of them all become alert and headed over to Sergeant Rollinson.

"Serge," all six exclaimed as they stood in front of him.

Rollinson looked over at Catrin's partner. "We have a missing woman. We need to search and scan the surrounding area for her. Her name is Catrin Kean. Three head to the left and three to the right. Leave no stone unturned." He watched the six Officers mumble between themselves and then get into their teams.

Sergeant Michael Llewellyn headed over to the centre of the action. "What's happening Andy?"

"I've just arranged a search party for the missing woman. Martin there has called for CID and SOCO. We are going to have to get India-99 to land in that open space down there at the bottom of Pwllcarn Terrace and meet some of the team to get up here until the Welsh Forestry Commission opens that bloody gate. We also need to get the three injured dogs down and to a vets ASAP." As he said that WPC Caron came over to him.

"Serge. The gate has been opened by the local Ranger. We can now gain access."

"Good. Mike do you and WPC Caron here want to head down and direct the teams up here? Maybe seal off the gate from any potential hikers or dog walkers?"

Sergeant Michael Llewellyn knew that was a good idea. For him to get away from the scene even though he had been the first Officer on scene due to him not actually being extremely far from the scene of crime in the first place. "Come on then, young lady."

"Serge," WPC Caron responded whilst showing that she was all ready for the walk back down.

*****

Tony Fallon had reached the top of the hill on the plains where it was completely open. He looked across to the far end. There was no action over there. Being a stranger to the area he wondered how he would get to where the ariel action was to his right. There were paths going downwards that looked like trial bikes and buggies of some kind had been up there, but they didn't seem to head over in the direction that he wanted to go. He walked on and noticed a gap in the trees further ahead. What he didn't know at this particular moment in time was that the path was the one that the first three victims' bodies had been found strung up. But then he saw the remains of the *'Police – do not cross'* tape and the thought crossed his mind. Briefly he stopped and looked around. He had read the reports that had been made by his colleague at the paper. He continued walking upwards and finally came to the junction at the top. It had to be to the right he told himself, but he would have to be careful and knew that at any moment, if there was a problem and there was Police presence then there would be a cordon of some kind.

He spoke too soon as he approached the green barrier. "You will have to go back Sir," WPC Baines exclaimed. "The path is closed today."

"What is going on?" Tony enquired, knowing that the usual protocol was for them not to say a word. "It must be quite bad because of the helicopters."

"Just turn around, Sir. You will need to go back the way that you came." She looked at him seriously whilst not knowing just who he was. She would have never guessed he was a reporter because of his youthful looks.

"That's no problem," he replied. "Stay safe."

"Thanks. You too."

Tony headed back in the direction that he had come and once he was out of sight of the WPC he took his mobile out of his pocket. His call was answered almost immediately. "Dad."

"Tony. Have you got something for me?" Ryan Parry enquired as he dropped everything, clicked his fingers to quieten those around him so he could hear the undercover reporter.

"You may want to get someone up to Blaengarw forest. Top of Pwllcarn Terrace. There's something going on. Two helicopters. One Police. One air ambulance that has not long returned over towards Nantymoel."

"Pull what?" Ryan asked whilst not understanding the name of the street that Tony had told him.

"Pwllcarn Terrace. Papa, Whiskey, Lima, Lima, Charlie, Alpha, Romeo, November."

The senior reporter scribbled down the name. He knew that he had a contract reporter in Bridgend who could be there in twenty minutes and would hopefully beat the competition because they wouldn't have someone like Tony Fallon on the ground. "Any ideas what is happening?"

"No. I can't get close. It's cordoned off. But I'm going to try in any case."

"Try not to blow your cover. Remember you are there to cover the bigger picture." Ryan stood holding the receiver hoping that his advice was getting through to the younger man.

*****

Half an hour had passed. Sergeant Llewellyn and WPC Caron had sealed off the main entrance to Blaengarw forest at the top of Pwllcarn Terrace and were stood talking amongst themselves but suddenly alerted as a car approached the dead end and, instead of doing the usual thing of using it as a turnaround, parked up. Two men got out of the car and as walked across to the cordon, one reaching inside his jacket whilst the other prepared his camera.

"It's started," Llewellyn exclaimed concerningly as he prepared himself for the start of an onslaught. "The vultures are here."

"Officer," the reporter exclaimed as he looked around and noticed the Police helicopter flying over and still hovering above the crime scene.

"Get in your car and go," Llewellyn ordered. "There is nothing to see here."

"Tom Hussey, The Sun." He held the digital recorder out in front of him. "Can you tell me what is happening here? There are Police cordons all over the area, so we have been told. Police helicopter up there," he pointed up to the sky on the left. "We have seen the air ambulance as well. Has another body been found. Victim of the serial killer?"

"We have nothing to say," Llewellyn stated as he was suddenly startled by the photographer who appeared to be taking random snaps of the helicopter, the area, and the Officers at the cordon. Llewellyn didn't want his photograph taken but knew that he couldn't stop the photographer as it wasn't against the law to take them outside. "I'm sure that there will be a press conference at some point to keep you informed."

"Has another teenager been found up on the mountain, Sergeant?"

"Best move on," WPC Caron added. It was too late. Coming up the hill the two Officers could see a convoy of cars and vans racing up the dead end. "Shit," Caron said as she nodded her head in the direction of the arriving traffic. "Serge."

Llewellyn shook his head. "Yes. Shit." He watched the barrage of reporters and TV crew all jump out of their vehicles, some with pen and notepad, some with digital recorders just like the Sun's reporter and the TV Crews with cameras following some of the well-known presenters. He could see the vans. Sky. GB News. BBC. ITV. The questions from the reporters suddenly came thick and fast from seven others and the four television stations.

'Sergeant. Why are there helicopters hovering over the mountain?'
'Has there been another murder, Sergeant?'
'How many victims this time?'
'Are the victims male or female?'
'What are the Police doing about the murders?'

Llewellyn said nothing but picked up his radio. "548 Sergeant Llewellyn to Sierra Oscar."

"Go ahead, 548."

"I'm at the lower cordon at the top of Pwllcarn Terrace. Can you let the team know that the press have arrived expecting a press statement."

"I'll let the SIO know now."

"Thanks. Out." He overheard one of the television reporters taking two and two and making five and knew that it would only be a matter of time before they knew the truth.

'We are at Blaengarw Forest where it has been reported that there has been another murder. Police are present in mass and there are two helicopters in the area, possibly because the mountain is hard to access. It is unknown if the victim is male or female. Blaengarw has been hit with a spate of murders in the last three months, all teenagers. We are expecting a press conference at any time now.'

Two of the reporters tried to come around the side of the large metal gate to access the path. Sergeant Llewellyn made his way over to them immediately and pushed them back but as he did, two others tried to get over the other side. Then one underneath the barrier.

"STAY BACK BEHIND THE CORDON!" Llewellyn ordered officially. "You will be arrested for breach of the peace I can tell you that!"

"Serge!" WPC Caron shouted across to her senior Officer as she realised that she too was having trouble controlling the gutter press. The only good thing was the TV cameras were staying behind the fence.

"I SAID BACK!" He got on his radio. "We are going to need back up ASAP down at the main forest entrance!" He shouted into the hand piece hoping that Inspector Thomas would hear him. One of the reporters, Keith Waterhouse, tried to scarper up the path whilst the others took the two Officers attention away from him. Sergeant Llewellyn gave instant chase and rugby tackled the man to the ground. He wrestled with the reporter and pulled both arms around his back. Seconds later the reporter was in handcuffs. "NAME?" The Sergeant demanded to know although there didn't appear to be any answer forthcoming. "I ASKED YOU YOUR NAME." Llewellyn tightened the handcuffs that little bit more.

"Ahhhh. You are hurting me!"

"That's Police brutality," one of the other reporters shouted as the four TV cameras zoomed into him.

"NAME!"

"Waterhouse! Keith Waterhouse!"

"Keith Waterhouse. I am arresting you for breach of the peace. You do not have to say anything. But it may harm your defence if you do not mention when questioned something which you later rely on in court. Anything you do say may be given in evidence." He looked across at WPC Caron who was still having trouble and then turned his attention back to the arrested man. "Now you stay there!"

Caron couldn't believe the Sergeant's aggression with the reporter but then told herself that it probably had to be done. "BACK" She ordered once more.

Llewellyn got up and joined her knowing that his prisoner wouldn't be going anywhere soon even though he was still letting out cries of pain because the handcuffs were too tight. "DOES ANYONE ELSE WANT TO BE ARRESTED? NO? THEN GET BACK BEHIND THE CORDON! NOW!"

The Sky News reporter raised her microphone and signalled for her cameraman to alert.

'We are here at the cordon still where it appears that the Police are losing control of the waiting crowd who are mainly press officials. One man, a reporter named as Keith Waterhouse from the Daily Mail has been arrested and the threats have been made that there will be further arrests if those present, including reporters, if anyone tries to break through the cordon. At the moment, Mr Waterhouse is on the ground.'

The camera zoomed into the Daily Mail reporter and overheard him saying, "These handcuffs are too tight! They are bloody hurting me!"

WPC Caron whispered into her Sergeant's ear. "Serge. Shall I loosen the cuffs a fraction? They do look too tight!"

"No. Let him suffer. He was warned."

Caron's forehead filled with confusion as she disagreed with Llewellyn's decision, but she didn't want to go against her order to leave the cuffs as they were. Her attention was taken away as she noticed another vehicle approaching them. "Serge. Animal ambulance?" she asked confusingly. "Is that for the three injured dogs?"

"Yes," Llewellyn stated in an urgent manner. "Let them through." The van pushed its way through the line of reporters and the Sergeant banged on the roof.

"Sergeant. We have a request for pet ambulance?"

"Yes. Follow the path up. Ignore the first turning on the left. Just keep going up. The path bends around. Look for the flashing lights. I think you have three casualties. Severely injured. Ridgebacks."

"Thank you," the vet replied as he put his foot on the accelerator and raced up the gravel track.

*****

Back at the crime scene the search was on the way for the missing woman. PC's Lestyn Jones, Brydon Jones, and Gareth Evans had headed back in the direction of the main entrance to the forest, scanning the roughage each side of the path for any clues that the missing woman had been there.

"We could really do with the dog unit," PC Lestyn Jones said to his fellow colleagues as he used his baton to touch and move the greenery. "They would have more of a chance of finding anything. I mean, either way. She may have escaped and ran off. She may just be hiding."

Gareth Evans looked at him. "I would say that she is dead somewhere." He looked further down on the right. "This is hopeless. Hold on." He clicked the radio on his lapel. "Sergeant Rollinson."

"Go on, Gareth."

"This is like looking for a needle in a haystack, Serge. Could we not get the dogs up here?"

"I was just thinking that," Rollinson exclaimed thoughtfully. "I'll just check with the Inspector. He is SIO."

*****

Down at the cordon, Sergeant Llewellyn and WPC Caron noticed more cars approaching. He noticed the driver, DS Peter Ellis, and was thankful that CID was there at last. DCI Gwyn opened the window and held out his warrant card just in case the Sergeant didn't recognise them.

As Llewellyn opened the gate he waved the crowd to step aside and shouted, "Step aside! I said Step aside!"

WPC Caron herded them aside joining her Sergeant in shouting "Step aside!"

"What's the story, Sergeant?"

"One dead body, Guv. One missing. It's not a pretty sight."

"Where is the crime scene?"

Llewellyn pointed in the only direction that it could be, giving the same instruction that he had no long given to the vet. "Follow the track. Ignore the turning on the left and just carry on. You will see the blue flashing lights."

Suddenly a van appeared behind the CID vehicle. "Forensics are behind us. Let them in as well."

Sergeant Llewellyn fully opened the gate as the members of the press once again shouted questions but now at the CID Officers in the car. "Vultures. The lot of them," he said as the car and van drove through.

Chapter 11

The two intelligent springer spaniels, Bella, and Charlie, both brown, were led out from the back of the handler's van and instantly became alert to the surroundings but in their normal playful way. Bella just wanted her ball which she used to get as a reward for doing her job. Charlie was simply happy with the attention and the cuddles.

"DCI Gwyn. Nice to see you again," Mark Lemin said as he controlled the two dogs, one on each hand.

"Mark. I'm glad it's you!"

"What's the story? I just got the call saying there was a missing person."

The DCI nodded. "We have already had one dead body. That man over there is missing his partner who was out walking the dogs with the deceased." He nodded towards Poli Cárdenas who was busy assisting the vet getting the dogs into the back of the pet ambulance.

"Okay. I'll get the dogs on it right away. Do we have anything to which they can relate? Clothing or anything?"

"Hold on. I'll ask him." DCI Gwyn walked over to Catrin's partner who was still sat down on the stone bench, frantically looking all around him as though he was going to see her walking towards him at any moment. "Mr Cárdenas. We have the search dogs here to help us find Catrin. The handler wants to know if you have anything of Catrin's on you?"

Poli thought for a moment and then shook his head. "No. But what about something from me? We hugged before she left this morning. Her smell might be on my jacket."

DCI Gwyn looked over to Mark Lemin and waved his hand. The dog handler came over to them. "Mark. Mr Cárdenas doesn't have anything, but he and his partner had contact this morning. He wants to know if the jacket will suffice?"

Mark nodded. "Possibly. We will try it. Otherwise we will be looking for general smells. Possible blood." He bit his lip knowing that the offer of the jacket lowered the chances, but it was still possible. "We will try it." Poli removed his jacket and passed it over to the dog handler and then watched him head away from him and DCI Gwyn in order that the scent didn't get confused with him. Mark scruffled up the garment and held it in front of the two dogs. They started barking. He let them off their leads and they sniffed around the direct area. They ran from side to side in all directions. The dog handler knew that it was probably going to be difficult for them what with all the smells and scents around at that moment in time. Then Charlie must have caught something as he headed towards the path that led to the entrance of the Blaengarw forest, the path where Catrin had been chased. Mark called to Bella. "Bella! There!" He pointed in the same direction that Charlie was headed, and Bella took the command and ran over to her canine colleague. The pair of them sniffed from side to side of the path a little distance away from the action. They continued sniffing the ground. Bella suddenly sat and looked in the direction of the dark forest. Charlie joined her and also sat.

DCI Gwyn looked down. "Looks like they have found something."

Poli Cárdenas overheard the conversation and jumped up frantically whilst hoping that it was good news. "They have found something?"

Gwyn watched as Mark Lemin quickly walked in the direction of the pair. Then he followed whilst calling over to his DI. "Morgan. Take care of Mr Cárdenas here." Gwyn knew that nine out of ten times the dogs were right. If there was a further scene of crime he didn't want any interference. It had to be kept as sterile as possible for forensics.

DI Harris headed over and put his arm in front of Catrin's partner just in time as he was about to follow the DCI. "Best leave it to them, Mr Cárdenas."

"Yes. But …"

"Please," Morgan Harris exclaimed. "They will investigate. It may be nothing."

"I just want to know where she is," Poli said as he backed up onto the bench once more. "I can't stand it. My Catrin. She may be in a ditch somewhere like Rhian." He started to sob again and placed his head in his hands.

"Or she may not," DI Harris said with hope in his voice.

"But the dogs have found something."

"Yes. But we do not know what it is yet."

Poli continued to watch the sniffer dogs just as the pet ambulance left and headed back down towards the main gate. He had to make the decision what was more important, being there for Catrin or going with the dogs.

DCI Gwyn followed dog handler Mark Lemin down to the dogs. They continued to look into the darkness of the huge trees. "Shall we?"

Mark placed the two dogs back on their leashes so he could pull them away in time if they did find anything. Slowly the dogs lead the two forward, quite deep into the darkness. There was quite a huge drop to start, and the two men managed to get through the brambles although DCI Gwyn slipped a little on the mud. He looked at his once clean shoes and shook his head.

Just as Catrin had found out before she reached her demise, the woodland evened out to a slope. The DCI looked around for any evidence that there had been someone come down that way; broken twigs and branches and blood where any potential victim may have been hurt. He also realised that once they may come across anything, the area would become a scene of crime. He knew Matt Robinson's view of contamination of a crime scene and also knew that he would never hear the last of it. Suddenly both Bella and Charlie started barking. "DCI Gwyn. Here."

The DCI walked over towards the handler and his dogs. His eyes lit up with a mixture of horror and fright. What was left of a body, blood splattered everywhere. An unrecognisable corpse, mutilated, stomach ripped open, face missing. Gwyn knew that it was a complete replica of the murders that had happened close by, although this body had not been hung in the trees. His copper's nose instantly began to think. Was the body too heavy for the killer? Is that why she wasn't lifted up? Did the killer not have ropes to do it and therefore were the kills not planned? Were both kills opportunistic or planned? The woman had to have been chased. "Okay Mark. Let's get back to the path. I need to get this cordoned off. This is now a crime scene."

Mark passed Bella her ball and ruffled Charlie's head as the two jumped up to him as if to say, *'we are good dogs, we found it.'* Then he followed the DCI back towards the path, the two of them trying their hardest to take the exact route that they had done on the way in. "I think you have problems, Bill. I don't need to be an expert to tell you that whoever did this is dangerous. A madman."

"Or woman," the DCI responded as he shook his head. "At the moment we are at a loss. Hardly any DNA. They leave coal dust at every scene. But we are not sure if that is to put us off the scent of the real criminal." They both reached the path and DCI Gwyn picked up his radio. "Morgan. Radio silence for you." He knew that he could still be with the partner and that he didn't want him knowing that they had found anyone. That would make him frantic and risk the chances of contamination of the crime scene.

"Yes, Guv," DI Harris replied near silently.

"Sergeant Rollinson. We are going to need your boys and girls down here to set up another cordon."

"Bad news, Sir?" Andy Rollinson replied concerningly.

"We have found another body. Can you let forensics know?"

"Guv."

Poli Cárdenas was not stupid. It didn't take exceptionally long for him to put two and two together to make four as he watched the exodus of half of the team of both Uniformed Officers and CID head down towards the direction of the entranceway. He looked up at DI Harris. "What is happening? They ..." He stood up and started to push forward as DI Harris tried his best to hold him back.

"Please. Please . Stay back. It is a crime scene, and I can't let you close."

"It's my Catrin!"

"We don't know that," Morgan replied as he watched Poli start to cry frantically and then place his head in his hands.

"NO! IT'S MY CATRIN!"

DI Harris needed to get down to support the DCI and so nodded over to two of the PC's who came right over. "Can you take care of Mr Cárdenas. He must stay clear."

"Yes Guv," PC Powell exclaimed before turning his attention to the hysterical man as DI Harris headed down.

Inspector Thomas was overseeing the find of the first body and before Harris could disappear, he stood up in order to get an update. "I heard on the radio that they have found a body."

"Yes, Guv. Just going down there now."

"I'll stay here and take command of this one but keep me informed."

"Guv," Harris responded as he had a serious look on his face which showed a sign of worry about the current situation. He headed down quickly.

*****

Tony Fallon had found a way of getting closer. He walked along a path at the bottom of the trees and followed them along although they were fenced off and so unless he attempted to jump over and probably hurt himself in the process then he knew he couldn't go through. He took his small binoculars out of his trouser pocket and scanned over towards where the action was taking place but the power in them didn't show much so he knew that he had to get closer. Momentarily he wished that he had brought a more powerful pair with him instead of a pair that resembled those that his Gran used to use when she went to the theatre. He remembered going with her one day and seeing Keith Harris and Orville in a pantomime In Blackpool. He also remembered her slipping a pair into her handbag. He shook his head. Suddenly there was something happening ahead. He raised the binoculars once more although everything in the lens seemed small. It gave him the will to get that little bit closer. He moved on, watching his footing in the mud which seemed to be deeper and wetter the further that he went towards the other side of the valley. "What is going on?" he Mumbled to himself. But he knew that his position was wide open where he was and that he had to find some sort of cover, perhaps from the forest beside him on the left. Otherwise he would be spotted and who knows he may even become a suspect. He didn't want to blow his cover. He decided to hop over the fence and into the trees. It seemed to be damaged, and the barbed wire was broken which reduced the chances of him getting hurt in some way or even damaging his clothing.

Tony edged through the darkness whilst watching his every step because of all the dead wood on the ground. He reached the very edge and leaned against the fence, resting his elbows on the top and looking through the binoculars once more. It was a lot clearer. Police everywhere. He smirked as he thought that there were more Police here than there were in the whole of Bridgend. It must be serious. He took out his mobile and used the zoom on the iPhone. Then he clicked rapidly from one side to the other. He could see the mine entrance. There seemed to be something being lifted from what he could make out was a ditch of some kind. Tony raised the phone once more and snapped more photos. The rest of the action was happening behind the trees on the far right which blocked any chance of him seeing anything there. That was enough for the moment he told himself. Otherwise it would only be a matter of time before someone saw him. He had headed back over the plain and towards the flag. Then he made his way down the steep rocky path. At the bottom he could see the Pontycymer lake. As he approached the path he felt himself feeling relieved not only because of the strenuous and sometimes treacherous journey, but also the fact that no one had seen him. But that was going to change. He didn't see the bench to his left.

"Much going on up there?"

The voice made him jump a little. "Billy. Didn't see you there. I'm beginning to think that you are following me," he laughed whilst trying to make light of his comment to why Billy responded with the same.

"Well? Much happening up there?"

"Couldn't get close. Police everywhere." He looked at the older man. "You are not going up then?"

Billy Evans chuckled. "Forty years ago, maybe. But now? I'm lucky if I can make it up those eighty-one steps without stopping half a dozen times to catch my breath." He nodded towards the climb opposite them which took whoever was walking up them to the Doctor's surgery and chemist.

"Well I came out of the Co-op and saw the helicopters. Just had to get close."

"Yeh. Gave you your exercise for the day, I suppose," Billy responded without giving any eye contact to the newcomer. "Listen. You are new to the village."

"What difference does that make?" Tony's face filled with an inquisitive frown, and he squinted his eyes.

"You will learn, as I told the shop assistant earlier, that what happens in the villages stays here."

"Yeh?" Tony replied whilst feeling that he was being both bullied and warned at the same time. "Even if it means breaking the law?"

Billy clasped his hands and turned his head to look up at the young man. "Exactly. You know nothing. That is the best way."

"I'm happy with that," Tony replied whilst knowing that he was telling Billy Evans exactly what he wanted to hear. "From what I can make out, you have quite an influence in this place."

"You could say that. I was born and bred here. I am one of the originals."

Tony smiled although he looked straight ahead at the lake and did not make any eye contact whatsoever. "I've only been here a while. Already I have seen that influence. The shop assistant. You soon shut her up. Now you are trying to make sure that I follow the same protocol."

"Huh," Billy quickly laughed again although Tony could immediately tell that it was fake. "It's like I said ..."

"What happens in the village stays in the village," Tony snapped in. "So if she can't tell me, perhaps you can. She mentioned that the house I am living in has quite a history. Are you going to tell me what it is? It must be something that the estate agent didn't tell me." He knew that the latter comment was a lie because he didn't actually buy the house. It belonged to the newspaper.

Billy pushed his heavy frame upwards using the arms of the bench for support, and then brushed himself down after feeling the dampness from the bench where the rainwater had previously soaked it. "Keep yourself to yourself and you will get on just fine." He walked away towards the bridge that led to the bottom of the steps.

Tony watched him leave, staring at him to see if the big man turned around to look at him with his piercing eyes. It was quite the opposite. Billy just walked away with no expression. Something wasn't right. He then began to wonder if he had any suspicions about him. Moving into number 66. Stranger from out of town. There was a major story being covered by the press about the murders. But then he told himself that he had a job to do. He needed a drink. It was too far to get to the major chains like Starbucks or Costa. The café. He had seen a café right at the end of the shops in Oxford Street on the way in. That would be his next point of call. Slowly he started walking in the opposite direction although stopped to look back to the steps. Billy had stopped just like he said that he had to. Tony continued down over the bridge at the lower end of the lake, again stopping briefly but this time to look at the ducks who had swam his way with an expectation that he had food for them. He smiled and walked on. Down past the Co-op, across the road and into the lower end of Oxford Street. The café was still open luckily, so he walked in and right up to the counter. There was a female with her back to him washing some dishes at the sink. She noticed him.

"Hiya," the girl exclaimed as she grabbed a hand towel to wipe her wet hands. "What can I get you?"

"Oh. Latte and someone told me that you do bacon rolls to die for."

"We do."

"I'll have one of those as well then please," he said as he watched her key in the pounds and pence on the till and then passed her a five-pound note.

"If you would like to sit down I'll bring it over."

Tony guessed that the food was freshly cooked as he watched her turn to the kitchen section. He looked around and saw that he was the only one there. He could talk freely without any interference from people like Billy Evans. "I've just moved here," he said. "Already I see there is something going on up on the mountain."

She turned around whilst also flipping the bacon as though she was an old hand and could do it without even looking. "At the moment there is always something happening.

143

You have heard about the kids that have been murdered, have you?"

Tony nodded, not sure if she had seen him do so. "Yes. I am beginning to wonder if moving here was the right thing to do. Do you know if they have any suspects yet?"

"I don't believe so. But the deaths of the kids have been weird. They say that each time they have found coal dust at the scene. Makes me wonder if one of the old miners has come back to haunt us!"

Tony laughed to join in the joviality. "That would be funny in tragic circumstances. But it must be terrible for the parents. Losing their kids, I mean."

"I live next door to one of the families whose son was murdered. They are obviously devastated."

He nodded once more as he watched her place the bacon inside the roll and then edge herself around the counter and over towards him. She placed the plate on the table. "Coffee?" he asked.

"Oh God. Head like a sieve me," she replied as she went back to the counter and fired up the coffee machine. "So are you in Pontycymer then?"

"Yes," he replied as he eyed up the sandwich with a view to taking the first bite. "Just up in the Avenue."

"Lovely. It's quiet up there. Bit of a swine to park though."

"Yeh. Don't I know it." He bit into the roll. "Someone told me it has quite a history."

"Well I've only lived here nearly ten years. No one seems to talk about it. But from what I can make out about forty years ago there was a child killer in the village. The Police weren't sure if he was the one whose body was found one night burned to smithereens at the end of the Avenue. In fact, he lived in the same street."

Tony knew what she was talking about. His Grandfather. Hardly a child killer. "A child killer you say?"

"Yes. It appears that everybody thought it was him, but the Police couldn't prove it. Then one morning one of the villagers found the burning body. In fact, as rumours go, the so-called child killer lived in the Avenue." She came over with the cup of coffee. "There we go. How's the bacon roll? Have you died yet?"

Tony stopped eating briefly but then got the *'to die for'* reference. "What about the latest murders? Obviously, it can't be the same guy if he is dead."

She shook her head as she leaned one hand on the table to take the weight off her feet whilst she continued the conversation. "All we know is that the kids who were murdered all those years ago and the kids who have been murdered recently were all trouble makers."

The undercover reporter then began to wonder if the woman knew of the village rules that Billy Evans had threatened him with. "Well. That was lovely. Now for the coffee. I'm Tony by the way. I'm sure I will be down here quite a lot as I drink far too much coffee. And now it looks like I will be eating far too many bacon rolls!"

"Sue," she replied as she shook his hand. "Spread the word about the bacon rolls. We could do with a few more happy customers."

Tony swigged down the coffee. His Father always used to tell him that he had guts of steel because he could drink anything no matter how hot it was. "Any chance of a refill?" he asked as he jumped up and took the empty cup back to the counter.

"Of course. Have this one on me," she replied as she once more fired up the coffee machine. "Welcome to the Garw."

He took out his phone as he watched Sue head back towards her kitchen. Then he emailed his boss the photos that he had taken up on the mountain with the message, 'Managed to get close. Photos from the incident on the mountain.'

Ryan Parry replied back, 'Thank you young man!'."

*****

Matthew Robinson and Olivia Higgins were both on their knees leaning over the second corpse that had been found. They had left their colleague Stephen Garwood back at the first scene near the mine entrance. The SFO was somewhat happy in a way that the only contamination of the crime scene would have been from DCI Gwyn, the dog handler, and the dogs. The chances of anyone else coming this deep into the clump of forestry would be very remote. The only other DNA found, if any, would be that of the perpetrator. The first thing that they wanted to do was check if there was any ID on the body. Using his probe, Matt lifted the edge of the corpses track suit trouser pocket. Nothing, although there was a rattling of something like keys in the same pocket.

"Well we can tell that it is a woman," Matt said from behind his mask. "The breasts had been separated by whatever sharp tool had been used to mutilate the body. Rigi Mortis has not yet set in so it would coincide with the timescales of the woman who is missing."

Olivia nodded in agreement. "Looking at the wound edges, there are no animal tooth marks either on any cartilage or bone. Again, in this environment it would indicate that the body hasn't been here long."

"We need to get the body back to the lab for a full post mortem. It is in such a bad state we may have to rely on fingerprints or teeth to get a positive identification." He watched as Olivia continued to take swabs and blood samples from the wounds. Meanwhile Matt took out the digital camera from his bag and started taking photos of the wounds, the position of the body and the surrounds. "Unlike the other corpses it looks like this one was killed here. Not moved."

"Yeh. I was looking at the splatter patterns on the ground and on the surrounding trees," Olivia replied. "Quite a change in MO from the others. This kill appears more frenzied."

"Well. Head and perineum mutilated. The clothes were torn at places more-so on the area corresponding to perineum. The dead body is beyond recognition so the sooner we remove it from this place the better." Matt slightly lifted the body to ascertain if there was any further wounding on the back of the torso and Olivia lowered her head to try and see.

"The wounds on the head look exactly like the wounds on the other victims found in the area."

Matt nodded. "The head and face this time though. She was hit with some force. That is why the blood mainly splattered in that direction. The perpetrator is right-handed." He stood up and carefully walked over whilst trying his hardest not to catch any aspect of his Tyvek suit on twigs or branches on the ground. "God. What is that?" he asked whilst trying to guess the distance from the body to the tree where he was stood. "Six metres?"

"Yes. About that."

"I've found her face. Or what is left of it. Six metres. That was one hell of a hit. Whoever did this is one strong person."

"I think we can say it is the same killer, Matt. Look." Olivia held up some fragments of black dust from under the torso as the SFO walked back to her.

"Coal dust?"

"Possibly."

He leaned down once more and knelt on one knee. "Well. Multiple split lacerated wounds on her occipital area, parietal area, temporal area, and forehead. Several depressed fractures on her skull bone underlying the lacerated wounds. The body hasn't been here long as there is no decomposition. Looks like some brain matter missing from the exposed cranial cavity, but I guess we will find that over on the tree." He pointed towards the position he had just found the facial residue on. "I would say that the cause of death was opined to be due to the head injuries consequent upon some hard blunt force impact. She was dead when the mutilation took place, just like the others. The manner of death appeared homicidal as most of the injuries are on the vertex area. Looks like the dismembered ends have some sharp cuts and some irregularities suggesting the use of a knife as alleged."

"Or the pick."

"Yes," Matt replied. "Or the pick." He hesitated whilst looking at the corpse which he never found in the least bit disturbing. He knew that many people wound flinch and even urge when looking at such devastation. "Let's get this body back. Let the DCI know."

Chapter 12

Superintendent Saunders had requested every CID Officer of every rank into the incident room at Bridgend Police Headquarters. Without any argument because they may have been on rest day or even on leave, Saunders found the room was full of concerned Detectives. He knew that each one knew what was coming. Someone from up above was still going to be demanding action and that the case was closed soon. Five teenage murders in the past three months. Now, although the murders may not be linked, the team had the addition of two adult murders to cope with. Every one of the Officers who were patiently waiting in the briefing room knew that still they had little to go on and were no further ahead than they had been when the first three boys were killed. DCI William Gwyn cleared his throat as if to try and bring the room to some order and stop all the chit-chat. DI Harris flanked him behind and Gwyn could tell that his mind was working overtime trying to piece what they had together. Gwyn could always rely on Harris to do just that. Harris had an inquisitive and analytical mind. Gwyn also knew that the Garw case would be eating Harris up inside because he couldn't come up with answers.

Gwyn looked at the whiteboard behind him and placed the names of the two latest murders on the right-hand side. Because he didn't know that there was a link at the moment even though he could guess that there was, he didn't draw any lines towards the question mark in the middle. The question mark indicated the unknown killer. He picked up two of the whiteboard markers before turning back to look at his team and listened in to their individual conversations before deciding to bring things under control for Superintendent Saunders. "Right

148

ladies and gentlemen. Bit of quiet please. The Superintendent wants to take control of this meeting." The room went silent as mumbles of *'Sir'* and *'Guv'* echoed around the room.

"Thank you, DCI Gwyn," the Superintendent responded authoritatively. "Ladies and gentlemen. We need to up our game. The situation up in the Garw Valley is getting out of hand. It has been three months since the first three murders yet still we are no further forward. The powers to be above me in rank are still asking questions and I can only tell them what we have which, it appears, is extraordinarily little. So, we are going to brainstorm. Go from the beginning. See if there is anything that we are missing by pooling ideas, using hunches." Alun Saunders sat down. His promotion had taking its toll on him. No longer was he as operational as he used to be, and his new rank had ensured he was now attending more dinners with the upper ranks and having less exercise than he used to. Needless to say, what with the long hours, he was finding it hard to keep his weight down.

"Well, Guv," DI Harris jumped in, "We know that up until today the target seemed to be teenagers. The first three were found in the Blaengarw forest. Their bodies totally decapitated and mutilated. We identified them, as you know, as Derryn Jones, Kyle Griffiths, and Robert Hartland. Aged fourteen apart from Robert who had just turned fifteen."

DS Peter Ellis perked up. "We also know that they were the three boys suspected of setting the forest and surrounding woodlands on fire several times and guessed that they were going to do the same again on the morning that they were found."

"Yes, Guv," DC Dewi Ceredig, whose size seemed dwarfed by his fellow CID Officers as he was only 5'4" tall, mentioned as he looked around hoping that the rest of them would take notice. "The two WPC's first on the scene told us that there were accelerants as well as fireworks left close to a North Face rucksack where the bodies were found."

The other Officers nodded. "They were well known troublesome delinquents. Perhaps one of the villagers decided enough was enough." DC Aled Tello knew that he had been at the crime scene and had the responsibility of looking after the lady dog walker who had found the three boys.

149

"We don't need assumptions, DC Tello!" the DCI snapped in politely.

"It does all point to someone who knew the area though Guv," Tello replied whilst trying to make a point about his previous comment.

"What about the door-to-door?" the DCI enquired importantly whilst continuing to stare down his team.

DI Harris nodded before stating, "We have worked hand-in-hand with Uniform, not only interviewing the residents in the properties directly around the area, but also requesting their footage from their video doorbells and any CCTV. The point being the boys went up the mountain that morning and so their attacker must have gone up sometime the same morning."

"Unless it was a random attack and the killer was already up in the forest," DC Ceredig mentioned. "In which case they could have come from any direction. Or maybe even on a bicycle."

"I don't think it was random. It was too precise. Someone somewhere knew what they were up to and made it their business to put an end to it." DS Ellis scribbled into his notebook whilst joining in the conversation without looking at anyone.

"The weapon used," DCI Gwyn said whilst trying to move along in the conversation. "We had the results back at the time. I hear that Stephen and Olivia thought that the murders of the three boys, the fourth and fifth victims were linked by the murder weapon."

Peter Ellis nodded his head. "Sharp item was used to disable the five victims by hitting them on the head. The suggestion has been made that the size of the blow indicates the possibilities of it being an old miner's pick."

"What is a miners pick?" the younger Acting DC Jon Nafydd questioned, his lack of knowledge showing from his youthful looks at the age of only twenty, just out of the Police training at Hendon.

There were chuckles around the room and friendly banter before DS Ellis replied, "It's like a small pickaxe. The miners would use it to break the coal away down the mines." He turned his attention back to include everyone else before continuing, "They also mentioned the use of another sharp object which was used for the injuries on the neck and stomach wounds. Possibly a sharp knife with a clean blade."

"The fourth victim," DCI Gwyn continued whilst shuffling his papers and looking for the name of the victim. "Betson Morris-Evans. She was found face down in the overflow pipe near the top lake at Parc Calon Lan. Again, skull smashed in and mutilation exactly like the three boys."

DI Harris nodded. "She was also a known troublesome delinquent. Vandalism, drunk and disorderly, theft from local shops, affray."

"All at the very young age of fourteen," DC Tello added.

"And Delme Greening who was found in a coffin at the cemetery was the fifth victim, also mutilated." DI Harris shook his head, his face filled with a train of thought. "But why not kill the other boy? Why place him under the fifth victim in the same coffin?"

"Perhaps the killer was getting a thrill from it," Ceredig suggested although he didn't know why he had suggested it. "Is it in some way sexual? Not in a sexual assault kind of way, but a sexual excitement for the killer?"

ADC Rees decided to chip in. "Surely there is a common denominator here. The fact that they were all troublesome teenagers?" He crossed his arms and leaned back on the table to rest his legs.

"Possibly," DCI Gwyn replied. "Well up until today in any case. The five up until their demise were all known to Police. As was the one victim who is still alive and in Police protection in the hospital." There was a momentary hesitation. "But that was a slight change in MO. The boy who was found in the cemetery and is still alive. The only injuries he had was severe bruising to the side of his head which forensics have linked to a shovel found nearby. His friend had the same injuries as the first four murder victims, but the sixth boy nearly suffocated by being placed in the coffin with the fifth victim on top of him and the bones from the body that was originally in the coffin under him."

"Why was it a change in MO, Guv?" DC Tello asked being it that this was the first that he and many of the Officers in the room had known about the attempted suffocation.

"This must not go out of this room. We do not want the press getting hold of this information. At each crime scene, coal deposits in the form of small fine black powder was found."

"What has that got to do with the murders, Guv?" DC Tello enquired further.

"When we questioned the friends and family of all the victims, one of the boys stated that he had left them on the evening that they were last seen and that they were heading towards the Gelliron cemetery in Pontycymer."

DS Ellis looked seriously at his boss. "I guess we found coal dust there as well?"

The DCI nodded back to him. "No joking here, but we couldn't use the cadaver dogs to initially search for dead bodies in the cemetery." He smirked with bringing a little bit of humour into the situation. "But at the time we did use India-99, get a location of body heat then get some of the boy's clothes to use the sniffer dogs once we had pinpointed an area where they could be. They indicated that the boys were there and pointed out a possible location where they could be buried."

"So do we know the significance of the black coal dust at every scene, Guv?" DS Ellis enquired with an inquiring frown appearing on his forehead as he crossed his arms.

DCI Gwyn shook his head. "I'm open to suggestions," he replied. "We know that this is an old mining area. Perhaps the culprit has something to do with the mines. Old miner, or relative of an old miner. We can only speculate at this moment in time. What we do know is there seems to be an air of silence right over the villages. No one is talking."

"Uniform have tried several times, Guv. Requested any CCTV and video doorbell footage."

"We need to be more demanding, people," Superintendent Saunders intervened. "Follow it up, people. Threaten them with perverting the course of justice. If need be we will make an example out of someone."

The DCI shook his head. "Now the latest two murders. Again. It seems to be a complete change in MO. This time two adult females. The only thing that is linking this with the teenage murders is coal dust found at each scene."

"What about DNA, Guv?" DC Elfyn asked from the back of the room, leaning around the Officer stood directly in front of him in order that he could be seen.

DCI Gwyn shook his head. "That's it. There has been nothing at any scene. We are yet to find out if there is any at the latest murder scene. Forensics are working flat out to analyse the samples taken."

"Do you think that the culprit may be forensically aware if that is the case, Guv?" Elfyn continued with a confused look on his face as he continued with his suggestions. He watched the DCI nod lightly and saw that there was an element of thought on the senior Officer's face.

Superintendent Saunders looked at each and every now silent Officer and wondered just how many were thinking positively. "Let's brainstorm. Suggestions. No matter how small or inconsistent."

"Well," DI Harris mentioned. "DC Elfyn has already said that the culprit could be forensically aware."

"If that is the case, Guv," DC Morris who was stood beside DC Elfyn and looked at him as he continued, "Perhaps the culprit could be something to do with one of the emergency services?"

"Forensics have suggested that the killer has to be particularly strong. Lifting bodies that have a dead weight, especially into the trees, takes some doing. Especially for one man. Or woman as the case may be." DI Harris again shook his head whilst looking for inspiration.

"Perhaps there are two." Superintendent Saunders threw the spanner into the works.

"Guv. We need to be the first to interview the boy who survived." DCI Gwyn looked at the team.

"Well at the moment he is in a coma," DI Harris responded. "He is being induced by the Doctors and so we do not know when he is going to come out of the coma."

"But you are right, Morgan. The boy may know something. Get onto Uniform straight away," the DCI exclaimed with a serious look on his face. "Meanwhile, the residents are arranging another meeting. I am afraid that they may take matters into their own hands. They may have someone in mind who they think is responsible."

153

"Did you need me to find out when the meeting is and attend it Guv?"

"You read my mind Morgan. If you can spare the time. I know you have been spending long hours on this case." DCI Gwyn knew just how long and knew that Harris was at the moment getting little sleep.

"I'm sure I can manage a couple of extra hours, Guv," DI Harris responded whilst trying to show promise.

"Just don't go expecting any overtime. Budget is stretched as it is." Harris laughed, knowing just what a spendthrift his boss was and knowing that budgets in the Police in this day and age meant everything to those above. "But thanks for volunteering," DCI Gwyn replied as he watched his DI nod his head. "Take three other Officers with you once you have the info."

Superintendent Saunders cleared his throat. "Right. Come on people. Let's up our game and show everyone just what this team is made of!"

The office emptied as one by one each Detective left and went back to what they were doing.

*****

Police Sergeant Michael Llewellyn was at home. The television was on. Every station was reporting on the spate of murders in the area especially the latest crimes with the deaths of the two females. He didn't know what to do. He didn't know if he had been seen. The DCI had already questioned him on how he was first on the scene and how he had heard about the murder at the entrance to the old mine. He had given the excuse that he raced there when he heard the call on the radio. But he didn't know if he had been believed. He was paranoid. He needed help. His Father would help, he told himself. He walked up the stairs and once more pulled down the loft stairs with the hooked pole. Carefully he ascended the ladder-style steps and turned on the light.

"Dad. Are you here?" he asked quietly and inquisitively. There was no reply which began his thinking that the last time he had heard voices, he was only tired and overthinking. "Dad?" Still

154

no reply. He lowered his head so as not to bang it on the rafters and headed over to the box. He had returned the artifacts to the box but kept the journal on top. Each of his kills Michael had added to the empty pages after the entries that his Father had written inside. Then he remembered that his Dad had indicated on one of the pages that he didn't work alone. There was another. He flicked through the pages to find what he had previously read. He found it. No name mentioned. But there was a telephone number.

The man who can help. 01656 286654.

That's all that was written. Michael looked at the entry. His Father had help committing the atrocities and had passed the baton for him to continue which he had done. He had now made mistakes. He needed help. Pulling himself upright he headed back over to the ladder carrying the journal. He didn't know whether the phone number still existed. Did he have the nerve to call the number? Would it be the same person who had helped his Father, maybe even given him the names of the victims in order that they were dealt with forty years ago? He didn't know.

Michael clambered down and went back down the stairs to the living room, immediately slouching down in his Dad's old Chesterfield chair. Once more he opened the journal and hesitated. He reached over to the small table which he kept beside the chair usually to place his coffee cup on or his magazine. His mobile phone was there. Slowly he dialled in the number, and he waited patiently for it to ring. Finally it was answered.

"Hello?"

Michael didn't recognise the voice. He didn't know how to approach the situation or ask for the help that the journal had told him to ask for. It may not be the person who he had to ask for the help, he old himself once more.

"Hello? Whose there?" the voice asked.

"I need help," Michael said with some trepidation and worry in his voice. "My Dad tells me that you are the one that can help me."

The line went specifically quiet before the voice continued, "Michael. Is that you?"

The man on the other end of the line knew his name. How did he know his name? At first Michael started to panic but then told himself that this must be the man that can help him as it said in the journal. He decided not to say who he was. It could be a trap. "I've made some mistakes. One of my targets is still alive. A boy."

"Yes. I know."

Michael began to wonder if that's all the voice was going to say. He still didn't recognise the voice on the end of the phone. He didn't know who or where it was. The dialling code was a Bridgend dialling code, but it could be anywhere. Perhaps it was another Policeman. He didn't know. "The boy may have seen my face. He needs to die. Can you help me?" The line went dead. Michael began to panic. His stomach felt as though there were butterflies in it, just as it did when he went on a date for the first time as a teenager, but this felt like indigestion. Like his heart was going to explode. Suddenly his phone rang. Hesitatingly he picked it up but did not speak.

"Go to the hospital. Make yourself known. The suspicion will be removed. Do it now." The line went dead once more.

Momentarily Michael hesitated once more but then jumped up and headed to the front door, picking up his car keys from the hallway table as he headed out. He crossed the road and got into his car. Then he sped down the road towards Bridgend town, just as the voice had told him to do.

Chapter 13

Reporter Tony Newton reread the transcripts from the Police investigation in 1982. It mentioned several individuals and contained several witness statements, most of whom had said nothing or claimed not to know anything. He began to cross reference the names with the people he knew were still alive and still in the village today. Top of the list was Billy Evans. Tony was very suspicious of him not only because of the influences that he seemed to have in the village, but the warning that Ex-DCI Colin Brittain had given him prior to him coming to Pontycymer. Then there was Lee Jones. That seemed to be the only two. But Tony then remembered what Colin had told him. "What was the name of that criminal in Blackmill?" he asked himself. He checked all the statements. That was it. Robert Gabriel. Moved out of the area soon after the incident involving his Grandfather. Two other names who were linked to Billy Evans. Ron Howells and Trefor Idle, who also didn't live in the area but had done so at one point in the eighties. Lastly there was a Julian Evans. Same surname, Tony thought. But a common name.

He read on. The local Police Officer was Dafydd Llewellyn. Tony began to wonder if Dafydd Llewellen was related to the current community Officer Michael Llewellyn, although just like Williams, Evans, and Jones, Llewellyn was quite a well-known surname in the Welsh communities. Perhaps he could just ask the Officer in passing conversation. There were two more names of persons that statements had been taken from. Peter Hoskins, who it mentioned was eighty-two at the time of the 1982 murders. He gave a statement to say he heard commotion coming from the direction of the fire. Problem was, he was eighty-two back then so the chances of him living another forty years were remote. Very remote, Tony told himself with a smile and then a laugh. Damn near impossible. The other statement came from a dog walker. Stewart Gilmour. Tony read the transcript. He was walking his dog. He came across the burning remains of a body. Tony looked forward. The same body that the Police couldn't identify. The body that could be his Grandfather Christopher. There was no more. It looked like a page from the statement was missing. Quickly the reporter flicked through the pages to try and see if the page had been misplaced or misfiled. There was nothing. But what it did have on the top page that he had was the address of Mr Gilmour. He looked once more at the opening statement. Stewart Gilmour was forty-three at the time. What were the chances of him still being alive forty years later? He had to find out.

Minutes later, Tony found himself knocking on the door of Stewart Gilmour's old house in Victoria Street. On the way it humoured him that all the streets seemed to be named differently even though it seemed to be just one long road in and out of Blaengarw. He was hoping that he would knock on the right door. He did.

"Can I help you?" the woman in her fifties asked as she stood cautiously in her hallway.

"Oh hello. I was looking to speak to Stewart Gilmour. Does he still live here?"

The woman looked him up and down, obviously trying to suss him out and wondering why someone would be asking for her Father at this time of his life. "Why do you want to see him?"

Tony became relieved. Her last question proved he was still alive. Now how was he going to convince his daughter to let him speak to her Father? "I'm investigating an incident that happened in 1982. Mr Gilmour was a witness I believe."

"Oh God, not this again," she exclaimed angrily. "You had better come in." She opened the door wider.

Tony began to think that by his word 'investigating' that she may have thought that he was a Police Officer, but he hadn't actually said that he was. He never even gave the impression that he was so knew that he couldn't get in trouble. "Thank you," he said as he wiped his feet.

"Come this way. Why it is being looked at again I'll never know. Bloody Billy Evans has already been down hassling poor Dad." She pointed into the living room where the old man sat in an orthopaedic chair staring into a lit coal fire, photo's covering the mantelpiece of days gone by in the village, the mines, the miners all covered in dust, and streets filled with economically fulfilling villagers.

"Billy Evans? Was that recently?"

"Just yesterday. I told him that Dad has Alzheimer's, but he insisted on speaking to him about the same thing that you are about to question him on."

"I am sorry for the intrusion. It's just if Mr Gilmour remembers anything about the day however small, it would aid my investigation."

"Well why bring it up after all these years?" The daughter was becoming slightly irate, standing in the doorway to the kitchen, one hand resting against the doorframe and her head shaking in amazement.

"I can't give much away," Tony replied calmly. "But I am linking the murders back then with the murders that are happening this year. I can't say anymore at the moment."

She hesitated and bit her lip as if to withhold her slight anger. "Well. Take a seat. I'll be surprised if you get much out of him. Billy didn't. He seemed insistent to Dad that he didn't know anything in the first place."

"Really?" Tony replied suspiciously as he sat down.

"Can I offer you a drink? Coffee? Tea?"

"Oh. Tea please. Two sugars."

"Sorry. I didn't catch your name," she asked as she placed the kettle under the tap.

"Anthony Newton." He was hoping that she didn't ask anymore and realise that he wasn't an Officer of the law and try to stop him talking to her Father. "Can I take your name?"

"I'm Vicky Stone. His daughter. Different surname but that's down to a failed marriage. I take care of Dad now."

Tony heard the kettle making a noise and decided to say no more to her but to speak to the old man. He turned to face him and tried to get some form of eye contact with him. Then in a soft voice he said, "Hi Stewart. My name is Tony." He looked for any type of response or movement but there didn't seem to be any. "Stewart. I like your photos. The mines. Did you work down them?" Slowly the man's head turned to look at him. Tony knew that talking about something in their past could trigger memories in someone with dementia. He remembered speaking to his uncle who had the same condition and who didn't recognise anyone but could speak to you in detail about his days as a lighthouse keeper and how the lamps worked. It used to amaze Tony when he was younger and who used to say, "Tell us about the lighthouses, Uncle Jim," just to get a conversation from him.

"Who are you?" the old man struggled to ask.

"Tony. Where you a miner then?"

There was a slight silent pause but then Stewart burst into life. "Twenty years! Up and down that bloody mine shaft. Those were the best years."

Vicky brought the cup of tea through, one for Tony and one for her Dad. She looked at him face to face. "Dad. Cup of tea. On the table."

"Who are you?"

She looked at him and shook her head. "I'll leave you to it," she said as she walked back towards the kitchen.

"Stewart. Someone told me you had a dog."

"Dave! Dave! Where is he?" The old man started looking around his chair for the dog that had died in 1987. "He's out the garden."

"Do you remember the trees on fire, Stewart? You were out with Dave."

"The trees. Smoke." He started to slightly panic as though it were that moment that the incident was happening. Vicky decided to intervene.

"It's okay, Dad. It's not happening now."

"The trees. Bones. Everything burnt." He started to blow with his lips as though he could put out the flames, just like a child blowing out the candles on a birthday cake.

"I bet it was you that called the fire engine," Tony added. "Did you see it arrive? Where there flashing lights?"

"Police. Dafydd. Police," he responded worryingly.

"Dafydd. Was that the community Policeman? Dafydd Llewellyn?"

"Billy. He's talking to Billy."

Vicky intervened once more as she saw her Father getting frantically worried about the past experience. "I think it's best that we end it there," she said as she took hold of Stewart's hand.

"Yes. I understand." He turned once more to the old man. "Thank you Stewart." Tony picked up his cup of tea and realised that perhaps Vicky might know something about that day. If she were in her fifties now she would have been a young child at the time. Her Dad may have told the family. Children eave's drop. "I bet your Dad must have come home panicking on that day."

She nodded. "I was twelve. Like most kids I just wanted to get down and see the fire engines and the Police cars."

Tony sipped his tea. "How do you cope. With your Father I mean. It takes an incredibly special person to care for someone with Alzheimer's. Speaking from experience of seeing my aunt do the same."

"Well you will know then that sometimes it is hard going. But he is my Dad. When he was younger up until the time he became ill, he cared about other people. Just like that day that you questioned him about."

Tony nodded. "Yeh. No mobile phones or computers back then."

"No. He came back panicking. Luckily, we had a phone in the house. Most of the neighbours didn't have one and the nearest red box was up the road."

Tony swigged back the last of the tea. "Well thank you for your time. I will leave you in peace." He got up to leave but then frowned as he remembered something that her Father had said. "Your Dad said about Billy and Dafydd seeing the fire. Did he mention anything to you about that?"

"Only that he thought that the pair of them were there on the other side of the trees. Dad rang the fire brigade just in case."

"Yes. The statement at the time stated that it was your Dad that called them." He frowned once more. "Thank you Vicky. Might see you again." He left but paused outside the front door as she closed it behind him. He was worried. He had only been there a few days and he was finding out more and more about Billy Evans than the Police had done since 1982. But one thing crossed his mind. If Stewart Gilmour had seen Billy Evans and Dafydd Llewellyn at the scene, why didn't they call the emergency services?

*****

Michael Llewellyn arrived at the hospital once more, this time in his plain civvies. He was 'visiting' Jamie Arnett but this time giving the impression that he was there not only as the community Policeman but as a friend as well. He had bought the boy some magazines about the PlayStation whilst knowing from witness statements taken that Jamie played the PS5. He managed to get through the security intercom and walked down the corridor to reception just as he had done on his previous visit. He saw the receptionist behind the desk.

"Here to see Jamie Arnett," he said whilst holding up his Police warrant card.

"Yes," the nurse said pointing to the left but before he could continue, Michael chipped in.

"On the left. The one with the Police Officer outside."

"You've been here before!" the nurse smiled as he watched Michael head done towards the private room.

The plain clothed Officer noticed the PC outside the room who automatically became alert to the stranger. "Can I help you, Sir?"

Michael held up his warrant card once more but for two reasons. The man who was helping him told him to make himself known. The PC on duty would take heed of his presence and have to record him as a visitor together with the date and time of his visit. "Michael Llewellyn. Just going to visit the family if that is okay. I'm both the Sergeant in the village and a friend."

"No problems, Serge."

Michael tapped on the door and pushed it slightly ajar. "Hello," he said in the direction of the worried parents who were still sat by their son's bed.

"Sergeant," Jamie's Father replied as he turned his head. "Thanks for coming. Come in."

"Just thought I would pop in to see how the boy is doing," he replied as he stepped closer to the bed. But it was on his mind what *'the man who was helping him'* was up to. Why did he need to be here?

"The Doctor says that he is stable. Not sure if you have heard but he is in an induced coma." The Father looked around for a spare chair for Michael to sit in, found one behind him and dragged it across the floor. The feet of the chair made a bit of a noise on the surface. "Here. Take a seat."

"What a terrible thing the boy went through." He lifted up his hand that had the magazines in. "Oh. I brought these for when he wakes up." He passed them to Jan, Jamie's Mother, who put them on the bedside cabinet.

"Thank you, Sergeant," she said as she noticed that they were about her boy's favourite games console. "He will be over the moon with them."

Michael Llewellyn was still worried about being recognised by the boy when he came out of the coma. He tried to remember if and when he had removed his mask. Had the boy seen him? He didn't know. But it was too dangerous for the boy to come to and tell the DCI and his team that it was him who did this. He looked around the room. Just how would he get in here, he asked himself. Officer on the door. If he were to use his authority as Sergeant and muddle with the fluids that were being pumped into the boy's body or turn off the machines then he would be recognised as the last person to go in there. "Is there any news on when they will wake him?"

"The Consultant has been around a few times. He said that whilst in the coffin the oxygen didn't get to the brain. But he does think that there wasn't a dangerous amount of damage. He is hoping that next week they can start to bring him around." Gareth Arnett looked at his boy whilst talking, hoping that in some way Jamie could hear that both his family and those in the village were worried about him. He had also been told that familiar voices aided comatose victims in their recovery.

Michael smiled falsely. Next week, he thought to himself. That didn't give him much time. But possibly he wouldn't remember much right away. Or they would take whatever he said as some type of confusion, especially as he was there when the boy was saved, and he was here with the boy's parents now. He might have simply confused the Police Uniform on the evening with the darkness of the mask. Either way Michael thought, the boy had to die. He had failed once, and he wasn't going to fail again.

*****

The next morning the Police Sergeant heard a loud banging on his front door. It woke him and he looked at his smart watch to check the time. Six-twenty, he noticed as he stretched his arms up. The banging continued. Someone was obviously trying to wake him. He got out of bed and walked down the stairs, his feet banging on each one as he thought, *'This had better be good'* as he descended. The banging continued as he approached and opened the door. He saw a familiar face, one of the parents who regularly attended the football matches on a Saturday afternoon.

Frantically, Robert Gough stood there looking worried and becoming erratic in his behaviour. Before Michael could even say *'hello'*, he exclaimed, "Sergeant. It's Brandon! He hasn't been home all night!"

"Hold on," Michael said as he looked around outside to see who else could hear them. "Come inside."

Rob did just that. "Brandon. He hasn't been home."

"When did you last see him?"

"Last night. He went up to play football with his friends. But we didn't realise that he hadn't been home until this morning." The man was panicking. The thoughts going through his mind of the murders that were happening in the villages around. "His bed hasn't been slept in since Jenny made it yesterday."

"Have you called his friends? He might have just stayed at his friends or something." Michael knew that he hadn't been involved in any action on the previous evening as he was at the hospital visiting Jamie Arnett. But then he started to think about *'the man who was going to help him'*. He could see just how worried the parent was as he stood in front of him.

"Yes! Yes!" he replied loudly as if the Sergeant thought that he wasn't thinking for himself. "I did that just now. All his footballing mates."

"Okay. Why come here? Why didn't you dial 9-9-9?"

"I don't know. Just that you live just opposite us I suppose."

Michael couldn't understand the sense in his madness but saw his reasoning. "I'm going to call the station for you. We will then recall his friends, this time from an official point of view, namely me, and then if there is no success there, we will arrange a search."

"Thank you, Sergeant. Oh thank you," the panicky parent exclaimed as he watched the undressed man go into the kitchen and disconnect his mobile phone from its overnight charger.

*****

Half an hour later, Police Constable James Larkin and WPC Lisa Clarke were knocking on the door at the address of the Goughs in Victoria Street. They had been assigned to investigate and collate information on the teenager who had been reported as missing from the evening before. The door was opened almost immediately by what appeared to be a distraught and worried parent who was overshadowed from behind by a now fully dressed and Uniformed Sergeant Michael Llewellyn.

"PC Larkin. This is WPC Clarke. Hi Serge," James exclaimed as he pointed to his colleague. "I believe your son has not been home all night?" He looked at the woman and noticed that she appeared to be in her early thirties. She opened the door wide for them to enter.

"Yes," she exclaimed as she invited them in. "Please, go in to the living room." She pointed to the left and the two Officers took up her invitation.

"Can I take his name?" Lisa asked as she took out her pocket notebook and pen to take down any information that they were given.

The Mother nodded, her face filled with worry after the previous reports of the missing teenagers and their demise. "Brandon. Brandon Edwards."

"And you are his Mother?" PC Larkin enquired as he watched Lisa continue to take down the case notes.

"Yes, although my surname is different as I remarried. It is Jenny Gough."

"So when did you last see Brandon, Mrs Gough?"

165

Sergeant Llewellyn chipped in. "His Stepfather has said that his bed hasn't been slept in, so they guess that he hasn't been home all night."

WPC Clarke started to write down everything, including what the Sergeant was saying. "So you last saw him last evening I guess?"

Jenny nodded and then heard the noise of a key being put into the lock on the front door. "Oh," she said hastily. "Here's my husband now."

Robert Gough came right into the room. "Ah. The Police are here."

"Any luck?" Sergeant Llewellyn enquired knowing that he had been just up the road to two of Brandon's friends.

"No. They were playing football until about eight and then they all went their separate ways."

PC Larkin knew that things were getting confused in their questioning mainly due to the stepfather's own intervention and Sergeant Llewellyn being present. "So what actual time did you see Brandon, Mrs Gough?"

"He came home for his tea after school at about four yesterday, did his homework and then went out with his friends about five-thirty. He took his football. They normally go up to the football pitch for a kickabout."

Lisa scribbled in her book. "Can we have a description of Brandon? Most of all, do you have an up-to-date photograph?"

The Mother turned around and grabbed a framed photo of her son from the top of the fireplace, removing the back and handing the photo to WPC Clarke before returning the empty photo frame to its rightful place. "He is about five feet ten. I know that because I always joke that he is getting taller than me. He is quite slim. Mousy brown hair."

"And do you know what he was wearing last night?" the female Officer enquired.

"His dark blue Adidas tracksuit. The type with the white stripes on the arms. No doubt under that he had his red Liverpool top and red shorts on. He always does."

PC Larkin went to leave. "These friends that he may have been with. Do you have their details?"

"All I have are their names. Although his best friend James Murphy lives two doors up. Number thirty-six."

"I've been to see him," Rob Gough exclaimed. "He hasn't seen our Brandon since last evening either."

"Okay Mr and Mrs Gough. If you could write down the names of the friends and then we will try and find your son." James Larkin watched as the worried Mother disappeared into the kitchen and he heard her scribbling on a piece of paper.

"So what happens now?" she asked worriedly as she returned and passed the male Officer the list.

"Well, we will check with his friends if they saw him or if he has stayed with one of them over night. It is often the case."

"But he hasn't called," Jenny exclaimed frantically. "He always calls if he does that. His mobile is going straight through to voicemail. It is so unlike him!" She shook her head and placed her hand over her mouth. "What if the child killer has him?" She started to cry with worry and leaned against the back of the sofa.

"Let us look for him, Mrs Gough. I understand your worry. We will be in contact."

Michael Llewellyn nodded at the pair. "I will stay with them. If there is any news you can relay it via the radio to me. He nodded at the two PC's as if to acknowledge their intervention. "I will get the ball rolling and keep in touch with you both. I'll call my two PCSO's."

"Thanks, Serge," Larkin replied as he led the way back out of the front door and down the steps, nodding to WPC Clarke to follow him up to number 36. It was early in the morning and the sun was just appearing over the hills and lighting up the area.

"I guess we are checking with his friends?" Lisa Clarke enquired as her colleague didn't actually mention his plan.

"Oh, sorry. Yes. I'm in a world of my own here," he replied as he reached the bottom of the steps at the Murphy's house. "Ladies first," he said lightly whilst pointing his colleague up the steps. At first Lisa thought he was being a gentleman but as she reached the top of the steps realised that he had an alternative motive and just wanted her to take the brunt of the anger if the Murphy's were still in bed when they knocked on the door, especially as they had not long been woken by Brandon's Father.

Lisa pressed the button at the bottom of the video doorbell and then took a step backwards. There appeared to be no movement inside and so she pressed the button once more.

As she did the door opened slightly and a man looked around the door whilst rubbing his eyes at the same time. "What?"

"Hello Sir. WPC Clarke and PC Larkin. Does a James Murphy live here? If so, is it possible that we could have a word with him?"

"Is it that urgent that it couldn't have waited until later?" the man asked as he widened the door and finally showed his unhealthy-looking body to the two Officers with his beer belly shape showing through his tight white vest. "Hold on," he bellowed as he didn't get a reply to his question and turned to look up the stairs. "I've just had Brandon's Father here. We need to sleep, you know!"

The two Police Officers looked at each other and without saying a word, smiled at their common in-car joke about 'Yeh but, no but' from the TV series Little Britain. "I'm sorry Mr Murphy. But this is important."

"James! James! Get your arse down here. There are two Police Officers that want to speak to you!" He looked back at the pair. "He won't be long. I'm sorry about my outburst. I'm the sort of person who needs his sleep!"

"It may be easier if we discuss this inside, Mr Murphy. It is quite a delicate matter," PC Larkin exclaimed as he watched James Father widen the door and without speaking indirectly inviting them in.

"You can go in there," he said pointing to his left. "James! Move your arse. NOW!" There was movement, a thump on the floor which sounded like two feet stamping down and moments later the teenage boy appeared in the doorway of the living room.

"Don't worry, you haven't done anything wrong," WPC Clarke immediately mentioned hoping to put the boy's mind to rest as she saw a sudden look of worry on his face.

The tired boy rubbed his eyes. "Mmmm. Is this about Brandon? His Dad has just asked me if I have seen him."

"You are friends with him, is that right?"

James nodded his head. "Yes. We play football together. We even go to school together."

"I believe that you saw him last night?" PC Larkin asked whilst giving the boy a look that made the boy see that the matter was quite important.

He nodded. "Yeh. We were up the football field. About seven of us."

"Did you all leave together?" WPC Clarke asked as she started noting what the boy was saying in her book.

"Brandon left before us. He said he had some homework to do by Monday and his Mum would kill him if he didn't get it done."

"I don't suppose you know what time that was?"

The boy shook his head whilst staring alternately at the two Officers. "No idea." He began to wonder what was going on, telling himself that the only reason why two Policemen would arrive was if there was a problem. "Is everything okay with Brandon?"

"Well," PC Larkin added as he closed his book. "Brandon hasn't been seen since last evening. You may have been one of the last to see him."

"Oh no. Do you want me to ring the rest of the gang to see if he stayed there?"

"It may be easier if you can give us some names and addresses for the boys who were with you last night. Telephone numbers as well if you have them. We already have some from Brandon's Mother, but if you know who was actually there last night that's even better," Larkin exclaimed. "Brandon's Mother says that his phone is going straight to voicemail."

"I can give you their mobile numbers off my phone," the boy exclaimed, a look of worry for his friend appearing on his face as he became uneasy about the situation. Larkin nodded and watched as the boy headed over to the stairs and ran up, although not for long. He appeared in the doorway. "I'll write them down for you," he said as he walked over to the dining room table, grabbing some scrap paper and a pen from the side as he did so.

James Father, who up until now had remained silent and just eave's dropped in on the conversation, perked up. "It's very unlike Brandon," he said worriedly. "That boy lives and dies football. It's all he does."

"Well hopefully all he has done is stayed with one of his friends and forgotten to ring home. Maybe his phone has run out of battery."

The Father nodded as James came back holding the piece of paper in his hand and holding it out for PC Larkin to take. "There we go."

"Thank you," the Officer replied as he pulled a card out from his pocket. "This is my number," he said. "If you do hear from him in the meantime, can you either get him to call us or you can call."

James nodded. The thought of the recent murders was going through his mind, and he was scared that something had happened to his best mate. He knew that it was unlike Brandon not to go home.

Chapter 14

Adam Dutton was the proud owner of a very playful and boisterous Boxer dog who always seemed to be up to no good. He would always take the dog up to the football field first thing in the morning before he went to work, mainly to let his pet run around like a mad dog, but also to check on the football ground because he was involved with the local team. The morning was so far quite bleak, drizzly rain starting to fall and the usual mist coming in over the mountain top. Adam looked at his watch, realising that he had a bit more time than usual so decided to start on the football field at Blaengarw and then perhaps head towards the old football field further up the path. He knew that the crazy mutt was an outdoor dog and used to enjoy going to work with him as well.

They reached the side entrance to the football field. "Bugger!" he said as he wrestled with the rusty bolt on the gate. Several times he had told himself that he was going to either mend it or loosen it with WD40. He looked to the right where there was a public footpath that was thin and quite treacherous when wet and muddy. Suddenly his eyes caught sight of someone, and as he focussed through the misty rain and the mesh fencing, he gasped loudly. Someone had been tied to the fence. At first Adam thought it was the teenagers in the area playing pranks by tying one of their friends up. He squinted his eyes once more as the rain was making his vision blurred. But then it hit him. "Fucking hell!" He looked at his dog whilst finally managing to slide the bolt on the gate across. Then he took his mobile phone out of his pocket as he rushed over towards the hanging body. Adam froze. He looked at his dog. "Buster! Here!" Then he worriedly dialled 9-9-9 but as he did started to sob. He

171

recognised the red Liverpool top. Even though the body hanging was unrecognisable, he knew about the teenage murders, and he knew who wore that Liverpool shirt. He gasped out loudly once more. "Oh my God. No. Please no!"

"Emergency. Which service do you require?"

"Police."

The Police raced up the road towards the field some minutes later whilst having to only come from Pontycymer where the two Officers were conducting enquiries into the disappearance of Brandon Edwards. The lights were flashing and sirens wailing as they screeched to a halt on the gravel just in front of the gates. PC James Larkin and WPC Lisa Clarke jumped out of the marked Police vehicle as Lisa noticed the ambulance arriving behind them.

"Mr Dutton?" James enquired seriously. "You have reported a body?"

Adam was quite shocked, his voice trembling as he pointed over towards the bloodied body hanging on the fence at the far end of the pitch. "Yes," he stuttered. "There."

Larkin and Clarke looked down. "Better get CID down here Lisa. I think we have found our missing boy." WPC Clarke stared at the body, somewhat taken aback by what she saw and for a moment it was like she had switched off from what was happening around her. She had heard what her colleague had said but it didn't register for her to do anything. "Lisa?"

She came to. "Oh. Oh. Sorry." She turned around and clicked her radio. "452 to Sierra Oscar. We are up at Blaengarw playing field. Request urgent CID presence and need Uniform back up as soon as possible. We have a dead body."

"Thank you 452. Will inform."

Sergeant Llewellyn heard the call over the airwaves. Luckily, he had left Brandon's house and was no longer in the company of the boy's parents. "WPC Clarke?"

"Yes, Serge. Better come up to the football field. I think we have found the boy."

"I'm on my way," Llewellyn exclaimed. He changed direction and walked across the pedestrian crossing whilst beginning to wonder whether this was what his helping hand was talking about. Giving him an alibi.

Up at the field Adam continued to look down towards the mutilated body. "I guess you want me to hang on?" he asked the Police Constable beside him.

"Yes. We will need a statement from you. Is there anybody that could have the dog?" PC Larkin realised that the playful canine would soon become bored with hanging around.

"I'll call my wife."

"Try and meet her away from the crime scene." He watched him nod silently. WPC Clarke arrived back and stood beside him. "We need to get the area cordoned off which will be quite difficult I guess because of all the trails around."

Lisa Clarke nodded. "I have asked for back up as well as CID, I'll make a start though." She turned away and headed over towards the squad car, opened up the boot and pulled out the crime scene tape. As she did she looked around and noticed that there were already people arriving close to the field having seen the blue flashing lights and hearing the commotion from the path down below the field. She knew that she had to act fast and hoped that the backup would be there soon. She looked over at her colleague and noticed that he was already attempting to slide the rusted bolt across in order that he could secure the field to prevent anyone coming in. The entrance at the side had already been blocked with a man-made barrier earlier in the year by the football club officials, although there was a slight gap in the fence at the far end of the field.

PC Larkin knew that there wasn't any chance of the boy being alive, but he also knew that he had to check because stranger things had happened. He edged his way around the outside of the field whilst carefully looking at the ground to see if there was anything that could be evidence that he should avoid as he slowly walked down. He looked on the ground, in the surrounding bushes and on the fencing itself. It appeared to be clear. Larkin knew that the inclement
weather didn't help and when the forensic team did arrive they would see that the rain would wash away any potential evidence such as fingerprints or imprints from footwear especially in the open ground like the football field.

The two CID Officers, DI Morgan Harris, and DS Peter Ellis, were speeding along the narrow lanes towards the three villages that appeared to be the target of the major crimes, in particular Blaengarw where the latest body had been reported as found. There was silence in the cars as both of them were trying to think of who could be the guilty party for the horrendous crimes and why they were happening. At that moment in time the *'coppers nose'* wasn't working although the investigation was still ongoing and now three months since the first murders. The DI knew that they had to try and wrap it up sooner rather than later. Suddenly the senior Officers mobile burst into life.

"DI Morgan," he answered quickly.

"Guv, it's Aled."

"Give me some good news, young man," Morgan replied to DC Tello. "We certainly need it."

"You know that the team have been circulating for CCTV and video doorbell evidence in the area. We were given one last night in Pwllcarn Terrace dated on the morning of the deaths of the two women. I think you need to see it."

"Okay. We are currently en route to Blaengarw football pitch. Another possible victim." Harris looked into the side mirror on the car to see that the forensics van was right behind them. "We will need more Officers on scene. Can you come up to Blaengarw playing fields as soon as?"

"Yes, Guv."

"We also need to continue with the requests for CCTV. The more evidence the better."

"Yes, Guv. Like I said, we only have the one piece of video doorbell evidence." He had seen the pictures but only on the link to the owners mobile. He was hoping that it wasn't what it looked like but knew that only the DI or DCI could confirm that. "We have arranged for a few Uniform to join us in the area later today to continue door-to-door requests for information just as the Superintendent ordered. We are using the heavy-handed approach."

"Okay. If you can meet us at the field. Forensics are behind us, and we have a couple of marked cars with their blues and twos on behind us as well."

"Is it the missing boy reported this morning?"

"Most possibly. We have a body. We have a coincidence. That is all we have at the moment."

DC Tello paused. "We will be there soon, Guv." He ended the call.

DI Harris turned to his DS who was busy navigating the parked cars that were causing the roads to be restricted to one lane. He faced oncoming traffic many times and had to pull into whatever space was available. "Did you hear all that?"

Peter nodded his head. "At least whatever is on the footage will be a start. The ten percent rule."

"Ten percent of anything is worth its weight in gold."

Finally the four vehicles, aided by the sirens from the two in the rear of the convoy raced up the incline towards the field and skidded to a halt just before the cordon tape. The Senior Forensics Officer was first out even though his vehicle was the second in line. He wanted to make sure that apart from what should be a limited number of people going close to the body, that he was one of the first.

DI Harris saw him heading over to the PC near the gate. "You beat me to it again, Matthew!"

"This bloody rain," Matthew moaned as he looked to the dark grey sky. "It plays havoc with my crime scene."

"YOUR Crime scene," Harris joked in return whilst Matt Robinson ignored the comment, or at least pretended to ignore it.

The SFO looked over to the van that he had arrived in and saw his two juniors pulling equipment out of the side door. He knew that he never had to tell them what had to happen. If they needed to know something or needed something clarifying, they would always ask, he knew that. "Olivia," he shouted. "We need a tent."

"I've got two," she shouted back as she slid the door closed and without checking to see that it had actually fully closed she headed over to be with her boss who was waiting for the bolt on the gate to be opened for him in order that they could access the field.

"I guess we have to wait, Matt?" DI Harris said in a joking manner whilst knowing how the SFO and his team operated.

"You know the drill, Guv," he replied. "Perhaps you could rustle up a couple of coffees for us," he said cheekily with a smirk on his face. They went into the field and over towards the body.

DI Harris stood shoulder to shoulder with DS Ellis, DC Tello, and DC Lewis, the latter two who had earlier been canvassing the area for the CCTV and video footage. It had been nearly two hours since the forensics team had secured the scene around the body, erected tents not only to protect the body from the elements but also to stop any press coverage from taking photographs. Finally, Matt Robinson evolved from the tent, brushing himself down and removing the top set of sterile gloves. He always wore two pairs at a time *'just in case'* he always said. *'Just in case one splits and cross-contaminates the evidence'*. His team always saw sense in his madness and had considered doing the same several times.

"Morgan! You can come in now."

"Thanks, Matt," the DI replied as he started walking over closely followed by his three CID Officers. The SFO pulled back the entrance on the tent for them to enter. The DI tool a look at the corpse. "My God. Another."

"Well," Matt Robinson exclaimed. "You could say that at first glance. You know I have attended all of the murder scenes so far."

"Yes," Harris replied inquisitively, wondering what the *'you could say that'* quip was hinting at.

"Well either our killer if it is the same person is getting lazy or it is not the same one."

"Lazy? Tell me you have something," Harris exclaimed excitingly. "Please."

"Obviously I have to fully analyse the findings, but Olivia here pointed something out whilst we were examining the corpse."

"Yes, Guv," Olivia said as she knew that Matt would be wanting her to explain. "There are no injuries on the cranial area like there were on the previous victims."

"So it could be a different killer?" Harris watched Olivia shrug her shoulders before looking back at Matt. "And you said lazy? In what way?"

Matt held up two plaster shoe imprints. "These. Fresh as the morning dew. All around the body and in positions that indicated a struggle."

DI Harris's eyes lit up like a child on Christmas morning looking at all their presents. "So you are saying that the victim may have fought back?"

"I'll have to examine the body fully, but as Olivia pointed out, unlike the previous corpses, this one wasn't killed by a blow to the head. This one was killed," Matt pointed to the throat area. "By some type of sharp blade across here whilst being held from behind. The blood clotting and scatter patterns say that the majority of the blood lost was from the slicing of the carotid artery. The trademark mutilation of the torso was done after the effect."

"But wasn't that the case on the others?" Harris enquired confusingly as he frowned, put his hands on his hips and looked at Matt eye-to-eye.

"We know on the others that the weapon used was probably a pick. No such weapon has been used here. Yes, the others had their throats cut but as a last resort. This one had his throat cut to end the victim's life."

DI Harris nodded whilst looking at the rest of his team. "I can guess the victim is male. Age?"

"I would say between twelve and fifteen. Going by the reports I think it is more than likely the missing boy. He is wearing a Liverpool top with a name tag inside. Brandon Edwards."

*****

Tony Newton was returning home after his morning trip to the newsagents to get 'The Sun' newspaper which always amused him. The fact that he read and worked for the same although he could imagine the stick he would get if he walked into the office carrying one of the rival papers.

He edged his way along the street. He had heard the sirens and told himself that there seemed to be more happening in this small community at the moment than there was in the whole of London. He changed direction and headed down towards where he thought he had heard the action and saw the blue flashing lights up on the hill beside what he knew was a sports pitch of some kind. He didn't get far as he noticed a crowd of people at the bottom of the incline where the two cycle paths split. He saw the Police pushing the onlookers back further than they originally were, although at times struggling with some of the crowd who didn't want to do as they were being requested to do.

Tony looked around and noticed that many dog walkers were stopping and inquisitively wondering what all the commotion was about. They were asking the two Officers who were guarding the cordon. The resident's from the houses on the left going up towards the sports pitches had been confined to their homes. No one was going in and no one was getting out at the moment.

"I wonder what is going on here," Tony said to a complete stranger beside him, leaning down to stroke the man's dog before getting back up again.

"Must be bad," the man replied as he looked at the two Officers. "All those Police cars that have gone up." Suddenly there was a siren from behind the crowd who all seemed to look back to catch the glimpse of an ambulance. They all moved aside, and the cordon barrier was lifted. "Might be another murder."

"It wouldn't surprise me," Tony said as he noticed a familiar face approaching from the cycle path coming from Blaengarw. "Billy. Fancy seeing you here," he said sarcastically.

"You seem to be following the trouble, Mr Newton," the big man replied to him as his eyes looked suspiciously into those of the reporter, squinting as they did so.

"Well. I'm beginning to ask myself why I bought a television. There's more action here, only this is live."

"I'm beginning to wonder why you have more than a passing interest in what is going on in this village," Billy snapped whilst still maintaining his suspicious tone. "Coming down from the mountain when the two women were killed, and now here for this."

"For what, Billy?" Tony questioned, thinking that the way Billy had questioned him gave the impression that he knew something about what was going on up at the field. But how would he know? Who had he managed to speak to? "I'm just a really suspicious person in reality."

"Really," Billy said in a non-friendly sort of way. "Remember what I told you."

"You have lived here all of your life, haven't you?"

"Oh yes," the stranger who Tony had been speaking to moments ago before Billy had arrived, quipped. "He is like part of the furniture."

"What's that? About sixty years, Billy?" Tony knew that he was riling the older man up, but it was intentional as though he wanted to let him know that he just wasn't going to get the upper hand or bully him as he had done with many of the other villagers.   He watched as Billy turned his head and gave him an evil angry stare which spoke a million words, mainly *'Don't fuck with me!'* "It's just someone told me about some murders that happened between 1982 and 1984. Eleven teenagers wasn't it? Then it appears the guy who lived in my house up at the Avenue disappeared in 1982. That must have been quite a year." There was no reply, so Tony continued, "Then one of the old villagers told me that at the same time that man disappeared, there was the smouldering remains of a skeleton found just down from the farm at the end of the Avenue. Of course it may be coincidental." He looked at Billy's face as it started to turn red, although Tony didn't know whether it was from guilt or anger, or a mixture of the two. He decided to push him further. "I'm surprised what with you being so inspirational with the residents here and living here all those years that you don't know something about it."

Billy snapped and moved towards Tony as though he wanted to fight him. "Listen here you fucking wanker!" Instantly two of the villagers who were in the group stepped between them both which angered Billy even more. "Get out of my way! Out of my way!" He screamed at them both before turning his attention back to the new face. "You listen to me. You know nothing! You know nothing!" He shook away from the hold whilst continuing to stare angrily at the man who had just riled him up. Then he walked off back in the direction of his house whilst swearing under his breath.

Inside, Tony told himself that he had succeeded in doing exactly what his impulse decision had told him to do. But he also knew that he had got on the wrong side of the wrong man. Would the villagers do anything for him or where they just frightened of him? Did he have a hold over the older ones of some kind? He kept looking behind him to check on the bigger man. Billy was doing the same and Tony could tell that underneath his breath, Billy Evans was swearing. His attention was taken away by the many cars and vans that were racing over towards the cordon which blocked Tony's view of his now nemesis. The press were here. Some of them might recognise him, he thought to himself. Time to exit right. He did, just in time and headed up the cycle path towards the Blaengarw end. He knew that there was a path from the cycle track up to the football field. Could he get closer, or would that be cordoned off as well? There was only one way to find out.

*****

Billy Evans climbed the steps up to his front door and fumbled with his keys, failing to get the key into the Yale lock and then getting annoyed with himself for not being able to aim it in the right hole. Finally he stepped inside and slammed the door behind him.

"Fucker! God!" he exclaimed as he felt angry not only at himself for doing what he always told himself that he shouldn't do, but angry at the newcomer to the village. There were so many thoughts going through his mind. Who was this man? In such a short space of time he had caused so much trouble and questioned Billy so much about things that didn't concern him. Or did they? He picked up the handset to his home phone and speed dialled his brother.

"Long time no speak," Julian Evans exclaimed whilst knowing that after the death of Christopher Fallon those forty years ago, he and his brother had agreed to keep their distance. Julian had moved over near Nantymoel, which although not that far was far enough to be distant just in case something happened. Now it had.

"I think we have a problem," Billy exclaimed angrily. "Someone is asking questions. We need to meet. Get the rest of the boys together as well. We may need to fix a problem."

"When and where?"

"Somewhere that we won't be seen and won't be heard," Billy replied with a sense of urgent anger.

"I was taking the dogs over to Southerndown this afternoon. What about there? At the café? We can sit at the picnic tables."

"Sounds good. Three O'clock. No excuses."

*****

It was sunny but chilly down on the South Wales coast. The beach was quite crowded with a mixture of swimmers brave enough to battle the cold waters, and the dog walkers whose pets didn't care how cold the water was. Billy Evans arrived first, paid his £5 parking fee to the man at the entrance and then parked up on the right in the main car park. He noticed that he was the first and so walked across to get a cup of coffee from the hut. He stood holding the cup in both hands whilst looking back up the hill to wait for the others to arrive. He didn't know what type of car any of them drove, not even his own brother. The only one of the six of them that he had seen since that fateful day in 1982 was his best friend Lee Jones. Ron Howells had moved to Merthyr Tydfil, Robert Gabriel to Blackmill, and Trefor Idle over to West Cross in Swansea.

Robert Gabriel was the first to pull up in a space right next to Billy's Toyota. As he got out of the car, Billy waved his hand and tried to get his attention, which finally Robert saw, even though he didn't directly recognise Billy as he had put on weight since they knew each other forty years previously. He headed over to the refreshment hut first, looking around as he stood waiting for his drink to be served and being extra vigilant just in case someone was watching them. As he walked over towards Billy, four other cars arrived in convoy, although not intentionally so.

Billy wasn't sure if the occupants of the cars were the members of the lynch party that he had summoned. The lower car park was now full and so all four cars got directed to the upper overflow car park. It was a few minutes before they all started walking down the steps towards the refreshment area. Billy realised that they had all felt the importance of being there. Julian's phone call had worked. He watched as his brother was the only one who went to get refreshments whilst the other three headed right towards them where he and Robert were now sat. "Lee. Robert. Ron. Trefor. Good to see you all."

"This had better be important, Bill," Trefor snapped.

"Is this what I think it is about? What you said the other day?" Lee enquired as he watched Billy nod his head.

"Julian mentioned that someone is sniffing around." Robert looked over to Billy's brother who was just about to sit down.

"Thanks for coming gentlemen. I know we all said that we would never contact each other again." He looked at them all as most of the party were looking around as though they were being watched.

"So what's the problem, bud?" Julian enquired as he approached the table with his drink in one hand and the dog lead wrapped around the other. He looked at his chocolate brown Labrador who was busy demanding cuddles from everyone. "Sit down, boy." The dog did as he was ordered, and Julian looked back at his brother. "You said someone is asking questions."

"We have," Billy continued slowly whilst twiddling his fingers and looking down at what he was doing, "A newcomer in the village. I've got my suspicions. I think he is either a reporter or a private investigator."

"Why do you say that?" Julian enquired confusingly. "You don't just think that you are being paranoid? I mean that has happened in the past."

"There's just something not right. He has moved into the same house as Christopher Fallon," Billy exclaimed worriedly. "He seems to be interested in everything that is wrong about the Valley at the moment. The murders. Plus, he has a knowledge of what happened in 1982."

"Ah, yes," Ron Howells, who was aged the same as Billy but who had managed to keep himself in trim unlike his old friend. "1982. The year that you told us that Fallon was the serial killer which we all believed until the murders continued after we had killed him."

"Just remember that I was told he was a key suspect by PC Llewellyn."

"Being a key suspect doesn't make you guilty," Trefor added angrily. "We should have realised that at the time. Didn't you say that old Peter told you after the lynching that Fallon wasn't the killer? You disagreed didn't you?"

Billy could sense the animosity amongst the six of them, like someone was trying to apportion blame but most of it in his direction. In effect, his actions had made them all murderers and all of them had lived with that since it happened. He got the impression that none of them actually wanted to be his friend anymore but just his acquaintance. "May I just remind you that we are all to blame! We all agreed that it was the right thing to do. We all had a part to play. It was the four of you that went into the house to lynch him."

"And don't we know it," Robert exclaimed angrily. "We have been looking over our shoulders ever since." He continued to scan the area for anyone who may be watching them. He too felt like he was being paranoid.

"I have been watching this individual," Billy interjected whilst trying to show his seniority to them all as the organiser, although after forty years his leadership had thinned out and the others felt that he may have influence still in his village but not over them. "He has been making enquiries in the shop. Talking to the staff. That is where I first met him. There's something not quite right, believe me. He has been up the mountain on the day of the murders of the two women. Something that a reporter would do to get a story. In fact all of the newspapers reported on it and most had photographs."

"Like you said Billy. All of the newspapers reported on it," Lee stated whilst looking ahead and not wanting to express his opinion by sharing a look of worry. "So just say he is a reporter. For which of these newspapers does he work? They all printed the story!"

Billy banged his fist on the table but then realised that he was getting angry and that he could be drawing attention to their meeting, so he lowered his voice. "There is something going on at the football field today. Another murder. He was there at the cordon taking an interest."

"As were most of the villagers were no doubt," Lee snapped in once more.

"He was ridiculing me. Telling me about everything that happened at the burning. Asking me why I didn't know about it if I was living in the village. Believe me. He knows something!"

"It could be completely innocent," Trefor said positively. "He might just want to be a busy body neighbour who wants to know what is going on. Especially as he is new in the village."

"Or it could be something more," Julian said In support of his brother. "I can see where Billy is coming from. What if there is more in it? We always said that we would keep the secret hidden. Command the old school villagers to keep their mouths shut. But we all know that secrets can sometimes backfire on those who hold them. Secrets can kill."

"I have told him several times that he needs to keep his mouth shut. About the way we do things in the Valley." Billy said whilst readjusting his position on the bench to make himself more comfortable. The damp wood on the seats of the picnic style benches was making him ache around his buttocks. "He isn't listening. He needs to be taught a lesson!"

"Not another lynching then," Ron asked sarcastically whilst trying to put the point across that they had wrongfully done that once and were paying the price for it.

"No. I'm open for suggestions," Billy replied. "In the end it is up to you. You either believe me that there is something going on involving this individual or you leave it and hope for the best."

Tony Newton had followed Billy Evans from Blaengarw, watching his every move since their altercation at the cordon. He parked at the car park at the top of the hill, quite far and out the way from where the six older men had parked and congregated. Then he had walked down along the coastal path, trying to mingle in with the other walkers. Once he was in view of the beach, he sat down where he didn't think that he could be seen. This time he had a more powerful set of binoculars with him. He took them out of the pouch and looked around the area with them looking for Billy Evans. The only problem was the crowds that were around him were sometimes blocking his direct line of vision. The dogs that were off their leads also interrupted him several times looking for him to either cuddle or play with them. He didn't mind. It gave him cover.

He looked over to the other side of the beach where there were walled gardens which he then thought would have given him a better position if only he had gone to the car park over that way. But where he was at the moment left him wide open to be spotted. He had to fit in. He put the binoculars on the grass and took out his digital camera from the bag. He changed the lens in case he had to get photographs from a long distance. To test, he started taking shots of the coastline, the boats out in the water, the dogs running on the beach. To those around him he was just another amateur photographer out for the day to learn how to use his new toy. He thought he saw Billy. Quickly he lowered the camera and picked the binoculars up to his eyes although pretended once more to look out to the ocean. But then he turned them around and looked at the gathering of men. The only one he knew was Billy Evans. It looked like things were getting heated. Words were being screamed rather than spoken. Fists were being banged on the bench tops. Fingers were pointing. Something was going on, but little did Tony know that the something going on was about him. Once more he changed to the camera, zoomed in to the party of six and clicked away on the multi shot setting.

Down at the refreshment area, the six were still arguing. The heat came to a standstill as all of the men suddenly silenced and looked away from the man that they blamed for practically ruining their lives. The only one who seemed to care for Billy Evans at that time was his friend Lee, and even he seemed to be stressed with the situation.

Ron Howells was stood up and ready to go back to his car. "We should never have met," Ron snapped angrily. "Meetings like this are only bringing attention to us as a group. You don't know if the Police are investigating you, Billy? This man could be a Police Officer. Undercover."

"He's right, Bill," Trefor added somewhat more calmly than Ron. "I think initially this is your problem."

"Not anymore," Ron perked up urgently. He noticed a glare of light, a reflection from the sunlight on binoculars pointed in their direction. "I think we have problems," he interjected into the group of criminals who suddenly all went silent.

185

"Wh...at?" Robert enquired as the only one to ask the man what he meant by his statement.

Ron looked over in the direction of the glare. "Someone is watching us." He made it no secret that he was staring back and was showing his awareness of being watched, pointing in the direction of the unknown man.

"Where?" Billy asked as he also jumped up off the seat, a move that was echoed by the rest of the men.

"Up there," Ron exclaimed as he continued pointing up towards the grass bank that Tony was stood on. "I've just seen the sun glare. Someone is watching us through binoculars." He raised one hand over his eyes to block out the sunlight. "He now has a camera aimed at us."

The reporter noticed them all looking at him and knew his time was up. He had been seen. He needed to get back to his car. He replaced his binoculars into their pouch and then looked down at the six of them who seemed to be angrily stirring. He told himself that they couldn't do much if they did catch him as there were too many people around. But still he quickly grabbed his zoom lensed camera, aimed it in the direction of the six and snapped pictures of them all together before making a move back up the coastal path towards his car as quick as he could.

All six men were stood up, watching the man take-off up the hill. They dropped everything, not even bothering to pick up and dispose of their litter in the bin much to the dissatisfaction from the kiosk staff who watched them all head back in the direction of the car parks.

Tony ran as fast as he could knowing that it was only a matter of time before they caught up with him either on foot or in their vehicles. He had to reach his car before they did. In minutes he heard the sound of racing engines coming from behind, but luck was slightly on his side as the road down to the beach was only a single-track road and two cars were on their way down to the beach. The cars coming up had to stop and give way to them both. It gave him valuable time. There were also cars in front of them leaving the area which slowed the assailants down. He jumped over the slate wall and into the car park, quickly opened the car using the radio-controlled key fob and jumped in the driver's seat. He pressed the start and then looking left and right to check the way was clear, he raced out of the car park entrance and up towards the main entry road, turning right at the Three Golden Cups pub and heading towards Bridgend. His foot hit the accelerator. He knew he had to get away and the odds of six to one were against him. He raced through the lanes. Minutes later there was a car behind him. He looked in his rear-view mirror and noticed that he was being tailgated. He could see several cars behind the lead car. There was a *BUMP!* and he felt the car behind shunt his car hard which caused him to lose momentary control and he skidded slightly whilst trying to get back control. They were travelling at 60mph through the country lane and Tony was hoping that nothing was coming towards him from the other direction because there was nowhere to pass, and he wouldn't be able to stop in time. The car behind hit him once more, then again. Then again. Tony continued to look in his rear-view mirror to try and see if he could get a look at the driver. He couldn't, the sun visor was down covering the top part of the driver's head. The car behind hit him again, only this time harder. Then again with the same force. This time Tony's car spun around, and the shunting car didn't stop. It continued forward and hit the side of Tony's car at speed, its engines revving high as it pushed the reporters car sideways. Seconds later Tony's car flipped over three times, the crashing sound echoing right through the lanes and the accompanying fields around them. It stopped with a final crash of the roof on the ground and the car behind skidding to a halt whilst blocking the lane.

Julian Evans stepped out of his car. He was the lead. The first car to chase the reporter. The car that had shunted him. He signalled to the five cars behind him to turn around and quickly go in the other direction in order to get away from the accident before walking over to the damaged car to check on Tony. The windows were all smashed in, and the car was on its roof. There was no other traffic around at that moment. He knew he had to be quick. He too had to get out of the area, hopefully without being seen. But he needed the camera that they had been photographed with. He also needed to see if there was any ID on the unknown man.

Julian stood at the side of the damaged car and looked at the driver, who was still secured with the seatbelt and therefore in an upside down, although awkwardly so, position.

The car's airbag had activated, and his bloodied face was resting on it. The unknown man was unconscious, not making any sounds.

The camera case was now on the roof of the inside of the car. Julian reached in and grabbed it. Tony was out of it and didn't realise what was going on. "Let this be a warning!" Julian snapped. He then ran back to his car, camera in hand, smiling as though his mission was complete. What he didn't realise was that the photos taken had already been emailed back to his boss at the Sun Newspaper using the Wi-Fi facility in the camera. Tony Newton had some evidence.

*****

All six cars had escaped in the other direction. Nothing had passed them on the road from the direction of Southerndown which they all felt was a benefit, although Julian's Volvo was damaged at the front. He told himself that Volvo's were built like tanks and hopefully on the way home no one would take much notice. He could get stopped by the Police, he thought to himself. They might think that the car was unroadworthy. He would have to face that problem if it happened. He could say he was taking it to the garage to get it fixed.

Within time, all of them reached the junction of the M4 and all went their separate ways. One car towards Cardiff. One towards Swansea. Robert and Julian left the party at the junction further down the road and headed out on the Nantymoel turning. Lee Jones led the way for him and Billy to get back to Blaengarw. All of them told each other that hopefully they wouldn't need to see each other again. Ever.

Chapter 15

It was late evening. For the second night running Jamie Arnett's parents had left their son and gone home on the understanding that if there was any change in their son's condition the hospital would call immediately. Gareth Arnett had insisted to his wife that they go home and get some much-needed rest, have a nice shower, a change of clothes, and talk to those who had been asking about Jamie. He knew that if the Police needed to talk to them as well, they knew where they would be.

He was dressed in blue. Mask on his face. Head gown. Surgical gloves on his hands. Unrecognisable. There with a purpose. It was now or never. He had watched the parents leave for the second time. The only hurdle he now had to get past was the Police Officer guarding the door. It was sink or swim for the disguised Michael Llewellyn. But it had to be done. He stood near the entrance to the children's ward, watching, waiting for his chance to enter without actually pressing the security intercom himself. He didn't want to speak. It was five minutes before one of the nurses headed towards the door and clicked the security code into the keypad. Sergeant Llewellyn rushed over behind her, stethoscope around his neck to make it look like he was a Doctor coming into the ward. He didn't say anything as the female nurse held the door open from inside whilst thinking that he was there to come to see patients on the ward. He nodded his head at her and then followed her into the ward and headed down to reception. The nurse behind the desk didn't see him but was too busy on the telephone, looking in the other direction and at files on her desk in front of her.

Sergeant 'Doctor' Llewellyn had got past the second hurdle. Just the Police Officer now. He walked calmly towards the private room. He knew that he could probably get away without speaking once again. Some Doctor's were arrogant like that, looking down on someone like a simple Police Constable. He walked up to him and just like the nurse when he had entered the ward, he nodded his head as he reached down to the door handle and just walked into the room. Then he stopped. Stared. The boy. The one he missed. Now in his grasp. He had him in the palm of his hands. One problem, he didn't know what any of the machinery around the boy actually did. He looked at the fluids, the bags hanging and being filtered through tubes and into the boys arm on either side. He also had a tube of some kind in his throat. Llewellyn knew what that was. It was helping him breathe.

The Police Officer outside of the room turned and looked through the window to check just what the 'Doctor' was doing. Out of the corner of his eye, Michael noticed him and so immediately took the stethoscope from his neck, placed the two plugs into his ears and then pretended to listen to the boy's chest. He had seen how to do that on the television. He looked out of the corner of his eye once more. It looked as though the Officer had accepted the fact that he was medically examining the lad and gone back to being alert outside the door.

Michael looked at the tubes and tried to ascertain where each originated from. He knew that there were alarms that echoed around after a short time of each being disconnected in any way. If anything, if he didn't kill the boy, perhaps he would inflict more damage to the brain. Just enough to make sure that he didn't talk to the Police when he finally came around. That he didn't say that he had seen the Sergeant's face if indeed he had. Llewellyn couldn't take that chance. He looked up. He was sweating under the mask and gown whilst trying to think whether or no he was going to get it right. To disconnect the right tube. The life support tube that went into his mouth. There appeared to be a valve that looked like a smaller version of a water pipe that you would find connected to the washing machine. Something that would just block the water from going into the machine. It was the same. The valve would block the oxygen in the tube. That was it. Decision made. He turned the valve, briefly looked at his handy work and then turned to leave. He opened the door, closed it behind him and then casually and silently exited in the other direction to his left to make it look like he was visiting other patients.

It was several minutes before the life support machine alarm kicked in. The Police Officer outside the room was the first to stir but then saw two nurses heading towards the room from the direction of the reception desk with some urgency and rushing into the room.

"What the hell?" the Charge nurse exclaimed, immediately recognising that it was the life support alarm and checking the connections.

"There! There! The valve has been shut!"

The charge nurse reopened it and the pump started working once more. "Who the hell did that? Has someone been in the room?" He started checking the patient as the other nurse went out to the Police Officer.

"Has anyone been in the room?" she asked with important urgency.

The Officer looked at her. "Yes. The Doctor."

"Doctor? He's not due a Doctor's visit until the morning. Shit! Which way did the Doctor go?" she demanded to know whilst realising that no one had passed the reception desk in the past five minutes, or so she thought.

"That way. I thought he was on his rounds."

"How was he dressed?" the nurse asked frantically.

"Well. Like a Doctor. Blue trousers and top. Mask. He had a stethoscope around his neck."

She went back into Jamie's room and, showing urgency that someone had breached the security she shouted at the Charge Nurse, "We have a breach. Bogus Doctor. We need security up here. Are you okay there?" The Charge Nurse nodded his head and watched his junior talking to the Police Officer. "You had better call this in," she exclaimed as she headed back to the desk where the telephone was. "Security! We need you to the Children's ward. We have a bogus Doctor who has targeted one of the patients."

*****

191

Tony Newton started to come around from his semi-conscious state and suddenly realised that his body was hurting all over. He looked at his hands and then his clothes which were all bloodstained. He lifted one of his hands up to his head which, although hurting, had already received attention from the medical staff in the ED. He knew who had run him off the road. Did he want to say anything if the Police were to ask him? His camera had sent the photos to his *'Dad'* at the paper. Soon enough Ryan Parry would be calling for an update on what was happening. Perhaps if the hospital staff were to ask if they had to contact anyone, he could tell them to contact the entry marked *'Dad'* in his phone. One way or another he would have to let his handler know what had happened. But would he be taken off the case if he did because of the risk to his life? Maybe not.

"Hello, Mr Newton?" the junior Doctor stood over him. "I am Doctor Sendell. Do you know how you got here?"

Tony appeared semi-conscious and wanted his cover to remain that way in order that he wouldn't have to answer any probing questions. He shook his head. "No," he answered as though he were in a dazed state.

"You were in a car accident. Your car was overturned. There was no one else around. Now I'm going to send you for some tests and X-rays. The Police also want to speak to you."

He nodded his head but gave the impression that he didn't know what was going on. In a way, he didn't, but he also knew that to a certain degree he was play acting. "Where am I?" he Mumbled back at the Doctor as though he hadn't heard a word that had been said to him.

"Princess of Wales Hospital in Bridgend," the Doctor replied. "You are in the Emergency Department. You were in a car crash." The Doctor looked at the casualty, and then started signing some papers in a file. Then turning to one of the nurses, he said, "X-rays and then get him to the MIU overnight."

"Yes, Doctor," the nurse replied before pulling the curtain back around the bed to give Tony some privacy.

*****

The security Officers at the hospital were going through the CCTV footage to try and locate the bogus Doctor and his movements in and around the ward. They also wanted to know if they could get an ID on him in time for when the Police arrived.

"There!" Nick Prosser said as he looked at the screen. "He just walked in," he pointed to the screen as his colleague David Tucker stood behind him. "Right past the reception." He flicked a few buttons and the CCTV aimed at the corridor where the Police Officer was stood outside. "And the Police just let him walk right in!"

Suddenly there was a knock at the CCTV office door. David turned around and opened it, noticing one of the porters stood there being flanked by two men in suits. "These are Police Officers, Dave," he said. "I'll leave them with you."

"DCI Gwyn and DC Mitchell," the DCI stated as he held up his warrant card.

"Thank God you are here. We are just looking at the CCTV. Your patient who is under guard on the children's ward had an attempt on his life about twenty minutes ago as you know." Nick Prosser twisted the joy stick and then paused the image for the two Officers to see.

"The culprit walked right past the Uniformed Officer outside the door?" DC Mitchell questioned whilst appearing quite angry that it had happened and shaking his head in disbelief.

"It looks that way," the security guard replied whilst feeling amazed that there was actually a lack of security as opposed the high level and vigilant action required, especially in the Children's ward.

"Is the boy okay?" Gwyn asked worriedly whilst knowing that he could be an important witness when he woke up from the coma, so they needed him to be alive.

"As far as we know. Now this is the man we are looking for. Looks like he exited out of one of the fire doors towards the rear of the hospital."

"Can we get any close up on his face?" DC Mitchell asked whilst staring at the CCTV screen.

"I'm trying to get a good picture somewhere along the route that he took. Whoever it is seems to be very CCTV navvy. Keeps his head down where necessary." Nick continued to play around and get images from all angles. "No. Nothing."

"Okay," the DCI said importantly. "Can we get copies of the CCTV in order that our tech boys back at the station can take a closer look?"

"I'll do that now for you. Put it on a data stick for you."

"That will be great. Meanwhile, DC Mitchell and I will be up on the Children's ward talking to staff and our very observant Police Officer." He sounded sarcastic as he mentioned the last words about the Uniformed Officer. They headed out of the security office and back to the hospital entry level.

"Whoever it was had some barefaced cheek, Guv," Mitchell stated with some anger. "How could he just have the tenacity to bypass a Uniformed Police Officer, dressed as a Doctor and try and kill a child whilst that Officer was literally metres away?"

DCI Gwyn shook his head. "It makes me wonder just who is responsible for all what is going on. Firstly the murders and now the attack on a potential witness. Young Jamie Arnett must definitely have something on the culprit." They passed the elevators.

"Guv. The lifts are here."

"We will walk it," Gwyn replied nervously. "I have a thing about lifts. It stems from being stuck in one when I was a teenager. Four bloody hours."

DC Mitchell nodded although he was hoping that there weren't too many stairs up to the MIU. Minutes later they were heading in towards the Children's ward which was now on a high security alert. Mitchell pressed the intercom, and both Officers produced their warrant cards. The door was no longer being opened electronically but by the Senior Charge Nurse who was checking everyone that was coming in and going out. "DC Mitchell and DCI Gwyn." Mitchell noticed that the warrant cards were thoroughly checked.

"Down there to the left. Your Officer is still outside the room."

"Thanks," DC Mitchell replied authoritatively as he headed down to the room.

"Yes, thank you," DCI Gwyn added to the conversation and directions before following his junior Officer. His anger was brewing. He wanted to give the Uniformed Officer a piece of his mind. He was wondering how someone could be so lax and stupid. But then he realised that he wasn't there. He didn't know the situation. Someone dressed like a Doctor could have fooled anyone. It was a hospital. There were Doctors and nurses walking around at all times of day and night. It may have been a mistake on the Uniformed Officers part, but it could have been a fatal mistake. Once more he held up his warrant card and he found the PC was now extra vigilant as he looked at the card in detail. "DCI Gwyn."

"Sir," the PC replied whilst looking like at that moment in time he was standing to attention in front of the senior Officer.

"I'll talk with you later. Now I want everyone, and I mean everyone, security checked before they come into this room. Is that understood?"

The PC nodded whilst feeling like he had received his first dressing down of many. "Yes, Sir." He watched DCI Gwyn and DC Mitchell go into the room.

Inside there was a genuine Doctor checking the boy over and a nurse who was assisting him. The Doctor looked around. "Can I help you two gentlemen?"

"DCI Gwyn and DC Mitchell. South Wales Police," he said whilst once more holding up his warrant card. "How is the boy?"

"I can tell you that he was incredibly lucky. The alarm went off in time and the actions of the two nurses ensured that there was no immediate damage done. We will have to carry out essential tests. The boy had relevant damage to the brain in any case due to the lack of oxygen when he was found. Let's hope that this hasn't caused further complications."

DCI Gwyn felt slightly relieved, not only for the patient but also for the case. If the boy did have information then he might be their only lead. Yet someone wanted him dead. Someone was worried. Worried enough to make an attempt on a child's life. "Right Doctor. I am going to change the guard on the door to an armed guard. Can you tell me when the boy is likely to come around out of the coma?"

"Well it wasn't supposed to be until next week. But I feel because of this incident we may have to stop the comatose state a bit sooner. So it could be in the next forty-eight hours."

Gwyn looked at DC Mitchell and slightly nodded his head as if to say. *'We are getting closer'.* "Uniform are currently searching for the bogus Doctor who was responsible for this but more than likely he has long gone. I think with an armed guard we can rule out any further attempts on the boy's life and give the staff a bit more security as well. Especially now that there will be more vigilance."

They watched the Doctor finish his examination of Jamie. "Well. The incident on face value doesn't appear to have caused much damage. I will be ordering some tests in the morning just to be on the safe side. C T scan etc."

"Okay. Meanwhile we will get that armed Officer up here as soon as possible."

Doctor Syms nodded.

*****

The ED was bursting at the seams or so a more alert Tony Newton thought. He hadn't been in one for years and had no idea about the amount of patients that they had to deal with at one time. He smirked as he thought that he could only tell by what he had read in the papers, thinking that he himself worked for *'the papers'* as he had put it to himself. He looked around for a member of staff.

"Nurse!" he exclaimed as he saw one of the busy-body women rushing to and fro. "I need to make a phone call."

"No mobiles allowed in this department, Sir. You will have to wait until we get you up to the ward. It shouldn't be long."

"Ward? Which ward?" Tony asked confusingly whilst knowing that all he wanted to do was get home.

"You have a head injury, Mr Newton. We are keeping you in overnight at the MIU."

It was two hours before the porters transferred him to the next floor up and into the MIU. Tony was glad because the hustle-bustle of the emergency department had started to make his head hurt, although he wasn't sure if it was that or the fact that he had a head injury due to the accident and told himself that it was probably due to the latter.

He looked at the porter who was behind him pushing his bed. "Do you have my mobile there, bud?"

The porter held up Tony's bag of possessions that he had come into the hospital with. Wallet, binoculars, mobile. Tony realised that there was no camera. "Is there any chance that I could have my mobile phone. My Mum and Dad will be worried sick about me." He watched as the porter opened the bag and took out the phone.

"There we go," the man said as he continued to push the bed along the route to the ward.

Tony scrolled down the contacts and then speed dialled 'Dad'. The phone rang for nearly thirty seconds before it was answered.

"Tony. What's up?" Ryan Parry wasn't expecting a call from him and knew for his reporter to contact him would mean that he had something important.

"Hi Dad. I've had an accident. My car was hit and rolled over."

Ryan alerted himself and gave the call immediate urgent attention. "Are you okay? Was it deliberate?"

"Yes. Listen Dad I have sent you some photos by email. Hope you like them. I took them down at the beach."

"Who is on them? Suspects?"

"Yes."

"Was it them that ran you off the road?" Ryan asked in his normal suspicious manner that every good reporter had.

"Yes. I'm alright. Don't worry. I'm in the Princess of Wales Hospital in Bridgend. I'm being taken to MIU for overnight observation."

"Okay. I'm thinking on coming down. There is a lot happening that needs a reporter on the ground in any case. So I can also be closer."

"Right Dad. I'll see you later then," Tony answered whilst being somewhat thankful that he wasn't being recalled off the case but then he would have back up. He ended the call and then looked upside-down at the porter behind him once again, reached up with his mobile phone. "Thanks," he said. "You can put that back in the bag for me please."

The muscle-bound man took it, his hands so big that he could have probably crushed it in the palm of one hand. Tony smirked at his last thought. Yes, he thought. Crush it as he would crush a drinks can. That easy.

*****

Billy Evans knew that Tony Newton wasn't going anywhere soon. His car had received quite a blow from his brother's Volvo. So much so that Tony's vehicle was probably a write off. What it did do was give Billy time. Chances are that Tony was in hospital and would be there for at least twenty-four hours observation. Or at least for the night in any case. Unless he was seriously injured and then it would be a lot longer. It gave Billy time. He left his home and walked along the street to the grass patch where his memories started coming back from forty years ago. In his mind he could imagine the burning trees, the screaming from the victim, the neighbourhood joyously watching the burning just like a scene from 'The Wicker Man'. They had burned their sacrifice. Billy walked past and then headed up the path towards the Avenue. He found himself stopping twice to catch his breath, and then again stopping at the top briefly before turning right into the long road.

"Billy, how's it going, butt?" One of the villagers who lived down near him asked. "Are you alright? You look like you are going to keel over!"

"It's that bloody hill. That and the fact that I am not getting any younger!"

"Well I didn't want to say anything," the man joked. "Catch you later."

Billy watched him disappear down the same slope that he had just walked up. He looked around. He had a plan. He needed to find out a bit more about Tony Newton. Could he get into the house that he was living in? It was too open to do it from the front and he knew about the two nosey neighbours Babs and Fran who never missed a trick. Perhaps he could try the back door. He laughed as he realised that to get around the back would mean that he had to clamber up another incline. There was no time like the present, he thought to himself. This needed to be done. Perhaps Lee should be there with him. Lee could bring some tools. Lee was more experienced at breaking into properties than him. Yes. He would call Lee. He took out his mobile.

"What's up big man?"

"I need you up here at the Avenue."

"What for?" Lee enquired whilst hoping that Billy wasn't going to do anything stupid that could bring attention to them all.

Billy lowered his voice showing a sign of paranoia and worry. He put his hand near the mouthpiece as if to shield any speech from anyone who might be listening. "I need to find out more about Tony Newton. We need to get into his house."

"Bloody hell, Bill. Are you for real? I thought we were trying not to bring attention to us all."

"Like I told you at the meet. There's something not quite right. I need to check to see if there is anything that may incriminate him." Billy heard the momentary silence. "Bring some tools. We are going in the back way."

Lee Jones sighed. He wasn't going to agree but knew that once Billy Evans had something in his head, nothing would change his mind. He was like that as a teenager when they were growing up and he was still like it now. "Okay, Bill. But be it on your head! I'll be there soon."

It took him ten minutes. Billy waved to him as he approached whilst guessing that he was going to come from the other direction to what Billy had taken. Walking in front by quite a distance, he headed up the side of the end house towards the lane at the back of the terrace. Lee had soon caught up with him being the fitter of the two men.

"Do you know which one it is, Bill?"

"Yes. Twelfth one along. I'm counting them as we walk. What did you bring with you?"

"Crowbar. Drill." He looked inside the bag that he had with him. "Hammer. Chisel. We should be able to get in somehow."

"With as little noise as possible. We don't want the neighbours calling the Police."

"We don't want to be seen!"

The back door on the dilapidated kitchen extension prised open with little effort from the crow bar, the UPVC door frame just falling apart. The two men looked around to see if anyone had heard the noise. There didn't appear to be any interest from neighbours and the next row of houses was some distance away with a lane in between. The two men quickly pushed themselves in, Lee closing what was left of the door behind him to make it look as though it were closed. There was another door going from the extension to the actual kitchen, but it was only an internal wooden door. Billy shouldered it but he didn't really need to as it wasn't locked in any way, and it made Lee laugh as Billy nearly fell flat on his face as he stumbled in. Both men turned their small torches on and pulled their hoods up over their heads.

"What are we actually looking for?" Lee asked although the volume of his voice was slightly lower than normal.

"Anything," Billy replied as he headed into the living room. "We will make it look as though he has been burgled to hide the fact that we are looking at any documents we might find."

"It doesn't look like he has a lot," Lee exclaimed whilst looking around.

"Yes. Strange that, isn't it?" Billy looked back into the kitchen. "You check the drawers in the kitchen," he said as he nodded back into the room. "I'll start here." He went into the living room. There was a pouffe beside the sofa and Billy recognised it as one where the lid came off and there was storage space inside. On top of the lid there was a part-drunk cup of coffee. He didn't care. What was left of the cold coffee spilt out over the carpet and the side of the sofa. He heard the drawers opening and closing from the direction of the kitchen. "Anything, Lee?"

"Nothing. Usual kitchen utensils. Plenty of batteries."

"Pull the drawers out and empty everything onto the floor." Billy looked at the papers in the pouffe, but it was just a film magazine and a few letters about the Council Tax together with his contract of employment with the shop at McArthur Glen. He checked the name. Anthony Newton. The same name that he had given him down at Bryn Stores. He tipped the rest of the contents out over the carpet. To the side there were two guitars, one electric and one acoustic together with a guitar amp. Billy stood up and kicked them both. The acoustic damaged easy because it was wooden. The neck snapped. The electric guitar was more difficult and so Billy picked it up by the neck and smashed it on the ground several times.

Lee appeared in the doorway and looked at his friend's handiwork. "Nothing. Let's try upstairs." He went out of the living room door and shone his torch to the right up the stairs. The two of them walked up whilst trying their hardest not to make too much noise with their feet. Lee knew the layout more of less because his house was exactly the same. Bathroom directly in front. Small room to the right. Up around the banister, the first room on the left was the spare bedroom. Down at the other end of the hall was the main bedroom. "You check in the spare room there," Lee said to the man behind him. "I'll check this one. There seems to be a desk in there."

Billy Evans went into the ridiculously small room. There were boxes in there which were still unpacked. One by one he emptied them out onto the floor, checking any lose piece of paper that he could see for any evidence of who this newcomer was. Nothing. So another box was emptied. Again, nothing. Books, envelopes. Lots of pens. There was a record player and a number of vinyl LP's which Billy took great joy in smashing. "Have you found anything?" He shouted into Lee.

"Nothing. Bloody Covid test kits. Hold on." Lee picked up some tablets in a vacuum pack. He looked at the name. "Shit Billy. You had better come in here."

Seconds later the big man entered the room and looked confused as his mate past him the box of tablets. "What am I looking at?" he asked inquisitively.

"Look at the name."

Billy read the label and his face dropped. "Fuck. Anthony Fallon. Fallon. I knew there was something more to him that met the eye."

"Are you thinking the same as me? Fallon? As in Christopher Fallon? The man we executed?"

"It's more than a coincidence don't you think?" Billy froze and looked at Lee, then looked back at the box of tablets just to make sure that he had read it right. "My God. What is he doing here?"

"Was Christopher Fallon his Dad?"

"If he is related it would be more like his Grandfather. What with the age difference." Billy shook his head. "But why now? After forty years?"

"Revenge?" Lee asked worriedly. "Perhaps he is here to exact revenge."

"Or perhaps he is a copper. Undercover."

"Fucking hell, Bill. I hate this. What do we do? If he is a copper, we have just driven him off the road. We can't do any more to him."

"He is pushing and pushing when you speak to him. He is just waiting for me to slip up in some way." Billy stared ahead, his mind working overtime as his eyes pierced the wall behind the desk, the cogs in his brain grasping for intervention. "He may be here of his own accord. He may not be a copper at all."

Lee's eyes widened and he began to appear frightened and worried. "Let's get out of here, Bill." He was first to move out towards the door and run down the stairs, not worrying about the loud footsteps on each stair this time. Billy was slower than him. As the both of them stepped back into the living room, they stopped. Lee stared at Billy. What they didn't see was the small CCTV camera on the window sill in the living room picking up their every move, every conversation. It was also following them with its motion sensor, listening and recording their voices as they spoke. "I'm really worried, Bill," Lee exclaimed, the worry showing in his facial expressions.

"What about?"

"If he is playing a game with you, he may know more than he is letting on. He may know that we arranged for that Christopher Fallon to be executed. Fuck. He could be after us all!"

"It was you that sliced him open. Slit his throat!"

"I know. I know. Did he survive the attack at Southerndown today?"

"I don't know," Billy said worriedly, his face frowning and he started becoming more distraught that he was upstairs. "I will have to check. Make a visit."

"Come on. Let's get out of here." Lee closed the back door the best that he could and then they headed up the steps, through the overgrown garden and out of the back gate. Both men casually walked towards the Blaengarw end of the lane whilst not wanting to draw any attention to themselves.

*****

Tony Newton had at last been given a bed in the MIU albeit in a mixed ward with five other patients. The porter placed his belongings into the bedside cabinet beside him. In what little awareness he had, he looked at the television and noticed that he had to get a card of some kind and prepay in order to activate it, although he was allowed thirty minutes free each day. He couldn't be bothered at that moment in time. But suddenly his mobile phone beeped, and he realised that it was neither the ring tone nor the message tone. This was different. He had heard It before. He moved his body over slightly in order that he could reach the bag of his belongings and after opening the small door pulled it out. He grabbed his mobile phone. He unlocked it with his thumb print on his left hand and looked for which notification was highlighted. Tapo. It was either the SMART lights he had set up or the camera. He opened up the app. It was the camera. His eyes widened. There was someone in his house. He opened the historic images that the camera had recorded on movement. The camera had picked up several images. He closed the first and opened up another. Then another. The face was slightly covered by the hood. But the hood fell down as the burglar was smashing his electric guitar on the carpeted floor. There were voices. He listened in to the conversations that the two burglars were having. Then Tony nodded his head and smiled as though he had won the lottery. He saw Billy Evans. He saw Lee Jones. He heard them both. "Gotcha!"

Chapter 16

Dylan Chiswell was frightened and had been so since the attack on his two friends. He couldn't get over the fact that Delme, it appeared, had been the victim of the serial killer and lost his life, whilst Jamie was in a pretty bad way and in hospital. Dylan was also feeling pretty selfish that he had escaped with his life just for not being there. For making the right choice. If only his two friends had done the same that night. But he chose to carry on the best that he could. He had his Mum and Dad to protect him.

He held his PS5 controller in his hand, attempting to play the Star Wars game that he had been given some time ago but only played once or twice. Attempting was the word. He was failing dismally. He couldn't concentrate what with the other things on his mind. Both of his parents had gone to bed. He had the usual orders to make sure his games console and the houselights were switched off and both the front and back doors were locked. He had the living room light off to give the effect of the game that little bit more colour, the graphics echoing around the darkness. He had tried and tried to get through the current level so told himself that he would have one more attempt. Which usually turned into two. Or three. Or four. His X-Wing fighter was destroyed once more but as he clicked through to try again, he noticed something in the reflection of the screen. It panicked him but he didn't want to make any sudden movement. Inside his body was frozen. But slowly he turned his head towards the window. Something, or someone, was outside. He stared; his face filled with the horror. The blackened figure outside made no attempt to move. It stood still, feet firmly on the ground, hidden eyes staring at the boy. Dylan could feel them piercing him, wanting him.

Something went through his mind. His Mum had told him to make sure the doors were locked. Did that mean that they were unlocked? He looked over to the doorway that lead to the stairs and then back at the dark figure. It was still there. It hadn't made any move towards the door. Had the door already been tried? Perhaps they found that they couldn't gain entry and so decided to try and scare him instead? But Dylan was too frightened to move away or call his Father. His body was still, apart from his head turning he didn't divert from his position. He slowly looked back over in the direction of the stairs once more, then back towards the window. He started to choke up with fear, and tears came to his eyes. He looked back to the stairs. At first he didn't want to make any sudden movement just in case the black figure tried something more than he was doing.

There was movement upstairs. Dylan could hear the thud of footsteps. Within seconds he heard the noise of someone urinating into the toilet. It was his Dad. The noise stopped. The flush was pulled. Now was his chance. He needed help. He was frightened. "DAD! DAD! HELP!" Dylan made a run for it. Jumped up and headed for the stairs.

"What's up?" his Father asked as he saw the look of horror on the boy's face. Dylan ran up into him and put his arms around his Dad. Then hysterically he started to cry. "There's someone outside! THERE'S SOMEONE OUTSIDE!" He shouted. He could hear his Mother stirring and when she heard her son screaming she jumped up quickly.

"What's all the screaming?" she asked as she appeared in the doorway of the bedroom.

"Call the Police, Sue!"

"Wh.."

"CALL THE BLOODY POLICE!" Michael ordered. "There's someone outside."

"Fucking hell," she screamed as she ran back inside the bedroom to look for her mobile.

Dylan wouldn't let go of his Father. "Dad. Dad," he cried.

"Let go son. I've got to go downstairs."

"NO. NO! He will kill you!"

Michael tried to prise his son's arms from around his waist. "It's okay. I'm going down to look."

"He's looking through the window!"

"Yes." Michael replied whilst trying to calm his boy down a little and stop him being hysterical. "Now let me go. Your Mother is calling the Police. They will be here soon." Dylan started to ease his grip and finally his Father could cautiously go downstairs, back to the wall, looking just in case whoever it was had got inside the house. Michael was a big man, and he knew that he could handle himself, but an unknown assailant could be bigger and stronger, have weapons. He didn't know. There was only one way to find out and he had to protect his family. He forced his way into the living room and looked around, looked out of the large window. Nothing. There was no one there. He wanted to go outside and check but told himself that he would just secure the doors and windows downstairs and wait for the Police to arrive. Slowly he headed over to the openers on the front window. Secure, he told himself. Now the back window and the door in the kitchen. He walked over, sweat forming on his forehead and to a certain degree he was himself frightened. He didn't know what lengths whoever it was doing this would go to. He tried the window locks and then the back door lock. All secure. They didn't look like they had been tampered with in any way. Now for the front door. Cautiously he headed through the living towards the bottom of the stairs on the right and the hallway with the front door on the left. Slowly, step by step, he edged forward. There was no time like the present he told himself. He rushed forward. The door was secure. Locked. Now he needed to get back up the stairs and protect his family.

"Dad! Dad! Did you see him? Did you see him?" Dylan demanded to know.

Michael shook his head. "No. He's gone. Did you see who it was?" He asked as he grabbed each of his son's arms and looked directly into his face as he leaned down.

Dylan shook his head. "The face was covered in black, Dad."

"The Police are on their way," Sue said as she came out to the two of them. "Hopefully they will get here soon."

Michael nodded as he hugged his rather worried son. "We will be okay." He spoke too soon. He listened to the noise coming from downstairs. Something was happening. There was a breaking of glass. "Quick! Get in the bathroom and lock the door!"

"What about you?" Sue asked whilst feeling worried that her husband wasn't doing the same.

"GO!" he ordered as he looked over the banister and down the stairs whilst trying to work out who was making the noise. He couldn't see anyone. He listened in as there was more noise, but he couldn't make out what it was. Suddenly he found out exactly what was happening. He could smell something. Then smoke started filtering through into the hallway from the living room. "Oh shit!"

Sue was just about to shut the bathroom door. "What's up?"

"We need to get out. The house is on fire!"

"WHAT?"

"Whoever it is has started a fire downstairs!"

"Dad! Dad!" Dylan was even more worried, frantic, and scared and he stepped around his Mum to get to his Father. He also looked down and saw the smoke. He started sobbing which together with his frantic behaviour started making him impossible to talk to.

"Dylan! DYLAN!" His Dad shouted at him as he grabbed both of the boys upper arms and shook him.

"He's going to kill us! He is burning the house down!"

"DYLAN! I need you to be brave for your Mum! We both need to take care of her." Michael knew that the boy loved his Mum and would do anything for her. "We need to get Mum out of here! Okay?" Dylan nodded. "Right. Let's go!" Michael looked down at the smoke. He could feel the heat as he led them down the stairs, but he couldn't see any flames at that moment in time. He became worried that this was just a ploy to get them outside of the house. "Where the hell are the Police?" he asked as he made the decision on safety grounds to open the front door. He looked left and right. The neighbours were gathering, some dressed in their nightgowns and pyjamas. He dragged the boy and his wife outside and down the steps with some urgency. In the distance he could hear sirens outside as Dylan's Dad thought that one of the neighbours might have heard the commotion and seen the smoke or flames and called the fire brigade. They didn't have as far to come as the Police because the fire station was in Pontycymer opposite the Co-op. "Sue. You and Dylan go up to Karly's house. You will be safe up there." He waved up the road as he noticed the exact person he was talking about stood in her front garden making a hand gesture for them to do just that.

Sue turned around to see who he was waving at. "Good idea," she replied as she grabbed her son's hand. "Come on."

The Firefighters stepped out of the engine and instantly started to take control of the situation. They too could not see any flames but took it that the fire must have been started at the rear of the house. Michael started banging on neighbours doors to get them to evacuate just in case.

"Does this house belong to you?" the senior fireman approached Michael.

"Yes. Someone was trying to break in I think. My son saw a face at the front window. Then moments later there was smoke."

Sergeant Llewellyn suddenly made an appearance beside the pair, fully dressed in his Uniform. "What's the problem, Mr Chiswell?" He asked importantly, looking around the increasing number of people, mostly residents of the area.

"Ah, Sergeant. We dialled 999. Dylan was being stared at through the window by some peeping tom."

"Okay. Where Is Dylan?" The Sergeant started looking around but did not spot the boy.

"He is with his Mother. They are going up to Karly's. Just up there." Michael nodded up the street and the Sergeant turned his head to see that they were stood in the small front garden of one of the neighbours on the other side of the street to where their own house was.

"Okay. As long as they are safe. I'm going to try and control this crowd." He looked at the congregation of neighbours and onlookers. "BACK! PLEASE!" He shouted whilst trying to let the Firefighters do their job. "YOU NEED TO GET OUT OF THE WAY OF DANGER!"

Michael Chiswell watched as the hoses were carried up to his front door. He overheard the conversations of the Chief.

"Can we get access to the rear garden?"

"Yes chief. Unit two is negotiating the back lane now!" one of the crew replied.

The flames finally appeared, quite heavily so, booming into the sky at the rear of the row of houses and looking like they were going to spread quite easily onto the neighbouring houses. At each cordon, the residents looked on, hoping that their properties would be spared any damage, and their possessions wouldn't be destroyed. The water from the engine at the front of the house was activated, the hoses filling. There was a lot of activity with Firefighters coming to and fro from the house. The flames now bellowed out of the roof. Michael walked up towards his wife, a tear coming to his eye as he realised that everything they had was not going to stand a chance of being saved from the fire.

*****

Ryan Parry was sat at Tony's bedside. The casualty had managed to get to sleep, albeit broken because every couple of hours one of the nursing staff would wake him to complete various tasks such as taking his pulse, blood pressure, alter the flow of fluids that where going into his arm and regulate his temperature. He opened his eyes and tried to focus on what was around him.

"Hello young man," Ryan exclaimed as he moved into the line of sight so Tony could see him.

He knew the voice in any case. It had shouted across the office that many times that everyone knew Ryan Parry's voice. "Hi."

"You've had quite an escape."

Tony nodded slightly, although he had started to feel the pain from his injuries as the pain relief that the nurses had given him had started to wear off whilst he was sleeping. "Ow," he cried as he raised his hand to the back of his head and neck. "I think I'm getting close."

"Too close!" Ryan exclaimed knowing that he had to make a decision on what was going to happen next. "Vicky wants me to pull you out."

"No! No! You can't! Where's my phone?"

"You are not ringing her to argue, Tony!"

"No. Ryan. There is something on my phone. In the cabinet there."

His boss opened the small doors and looked for the mobile. Then once found he passed it to the casualty. "This had better be good."

Tony found himself becoming more alert as his body woke up. "Someone burgled me last night. The security camera picked it up." He momentarily went silent as he opened the phone using his thumb print and then activated the Tapo app. "But I think I may have the beginning of the story I want." He pressed the play on the historic video and turned the phone around so Ryan could see the picture and hear the audio.

His boss stared. The cold feeling went through his body as he looked and heard everything. He grabbed the phone.

"What are you doing?" Tony enquired.

"I'm sending these to my phone. We need it backed up. This is getting dangerous. If whoever this is finds out that you have this, they will go to more lengths to make sure that you are silent."

Tony nodded. "There are six of them. The same six that run me off the road, perhaps trying to kill me, and took my camera. The photos. From the camera. They should have automatically been emailed. They should be the same images as these two who burgled me. The two in the video are Billy Evans and Lee Jones."

"So you are saying that the six, not just these two, could be linked to the death of your Grandfather?"

"Billy Evans," Tony watched as Ryan replayed the video, "The bigger man in the images, both photos and that video, met them all at Southerndown beach. They saw me and chased me in their cars. The last thing I remember is being shunted several times by one of these six. They all know something that they don't want anyone else to know about!"

"What do you want to do, Tony? We could go to the Police now with this evidence."

"No. No. We want the rest of the story. I think this goes bigger. Just why did they pick on my Grandfather?" He grabbed the back of his head and neck once more. "I wish they would give me some morphine again."

"Do you want me to call the nurse?" Ryan enquired whilst realising that his junior was in agony and may need some additional pain relief.

Tony shook his head. "No. I need to have my wits around me. Who knows what they will try next. If they wanted to kill me by shunting me off the road, but find out that they didn't, they may be back for more."

"I have to tell Vicky what I think."

"Please," Tony asked frantically. "I should be out of here in the morning. Give me more time. I'm sure there is a link between the murders and the death of my Grandfather."

Ryan nodded his head although he showed signs of being cautiously apprehensive. "By the way. I'm still your Dad. I mean to the hospital staff. That's the only way that they would let me in."

Tony tried to readjust the pillows behind his back. "Good. My Dad can take me home in the morning then. Maybe stay whilst I am recovering."

Ryan nodded.

*****

The action at the Chiswell's had started to calm down. The fire had been brought under control, although it looked like the Chiswell's house and the neighbouring houses each side had been severely fire damaged and uninhabitable to live in. Michael Chiswell stood as close as he was allowed by the Fire Chief and shook his head. Inside he was feeling choked up. Suddenly Sue came down from the neighbour's house to support her husband and also take a look for herself at the damage.

"Where's Dylan?" Michael enquired whilst wondering just who or what was outside the window when he had shouted to his Father. "We need to tell the Police what he saw. This all happened immediately after that."

"He's up at the Bateson's. He's quite safe. Karly and Gareth are taking good care of him."

Michael nodded. "What is happening in this place, Sue? What the hell is going on?" He looked back at what was left of their home and started to sob. "What or who were they after? Dylan? Me? You?"

The two parents were interrupted. "Mr and Mrs Chiswell?"

"Yes. That's us," Michael exclaimed whilst looking at the two men dressed in suits standing in front of them.

DI Harris held up his warrant card for them both to see and this was echoed by DC Tello. "DI Harris. This is DC Tello."

"CID?" Michael enquired worryingly. "Isn't Sergeant Llewellyn handling this?"

"The guys from central called us to say that you had someone looking in the window before the fire." DI Harris looked at Dylan's Father. "Is Dylan around?"

"We were just saying he is up at the Bateson's place," Sue Chiswell replied as though the events had taken their toll on her, her eyes baggy and tired. "Shall I go and get him?"

"It may be best if we have a word with him behind closed doors," Harris continued. "Do you think that your neighbours would let us in?"

"I'm sure they will," Sue said in her tired voice. "Follow me. I'll take you up there."

Morgan Harris nodded at DC Tello to indicate for the DC to follow as well. "Come on, young man," the DI said softly. "I think that our young Mr Chiswell might have seen the same figure as the other teenagers who were murdered. If so, he is in danger."

"Should we tell the DCI, Guv?" Tello enquired as he walked side by side with Harris.

"He is busy still at the hospital. God. It is all happening today." They reached the Bateson's house and Sue Chiswell banged on her front door.

"Hi Karly. These Police Officer's want to speak to Dylan. Thanks for looking after him." Sue noticed that Karly was looking at her as if she didn't know what her friend was talking about.

"He left a couple of minutes ago, Sue. Said that he needed to be near you and his Dad." Dylan's Mum started to panic inside. They hadn't seen him. Hadn't passed him or anything on the way up the street. "Have you not seen him?"

Sue shook her head. "Where has he gone now?"

"What's this?" Michael jumped into the conversation.

"Dylan has gone looking for us."

DI Harris became instantly suspicious. "Mr Chiswell. We may have just missed him. Best get back down to where you last were and see if he is looking for you." He watched Michael

212

Chiswell head back down to the cordon and then looked at Sue's friend Karly. "Was there anyone with him, or anyone around that you didn't know?"

"I watched him go out the door and turn left. That was about it."

Sue Chiswell shook her head. "I told him to stay with you! The little shit. Why the hell can't he do as he was told for once?"

DI Harris looked at Tello. "Follow Mr Chiswell down. See if anyone has seen the boy." He looked on and then turned back to the Mother. "So what exactly did Dylan tell you about the incident, Mrs Chiswell?"

"He shouted up to his Father and said that there was someone looking at him through the living room window."

"What happened next?"

Sue stared forward whilst trying to remember the incident but at the same time showing worry over Dylan. "We called the Police. Meanwhile my husband told us all to get upstairs. But then there was smoke. So we had to get out."

"Did anyone else see the figure outside the window, Mrs Chiswell?"

Sue shook her head. "No. Just Dylan." She looked in horror, her anxious mind working overtime as she realised that Dylan was originally one of the three boys. The other two were attacked. One was dead. One in hospital. Was someone now after the one that got away? Namely her son Dylan? "Oh my God. They are after him. Dylan."

"We don't know that for sure," Harris exclaimed whilst trying to put the Mother's mind at ease. "Dylan could just be looking for you both."

Karly Bateson intervened. "Gareth is going down with Mike to see if he can see the boy," she told Sue.

"Thanks Karly," Sue replied as she noticed her friend's husband brushing past his wife and putting on his jacket at the same time. "Thanks Gareth."

Two minutes later Gareth saw his friend. "Any sign, Mike?"

"No. Strange. He might have missed us and just be amongst the crowd." He continued calling for his son which was quite hard due to the amount of noise from both the gathering crowd and the fire engines. "Dylan! Dylan!" There was no reply.

Gareth joined him. "Dylan! Dylan Chiswell!"

"This isn't funny, Dylan!" his Father bellowed loudly. "And you better have not gone to one of your friends to play PS5!" Still no reply but he doubted under the circumstances that he would have gone especially as he had seen a ghostly black figure outside and the fire had started.

"I don't think that he would have, Mike. He was quite scared and just wanted to be with you both. Dylan! Dylan!"

"Is everything alright?"

Both men turned around to see the local community bobby behind them. "No, Sergeant. Dylan seems to have disappeared. He left the Bateson's house," he pointed to Gareth Bateson, "and was headed down to see Me and Sue at the cordon."

"He seems to have disappeared. It is a bit worrying."

"Yes. Especially as the thing was looking through the window at him before the fire."

"Okay. I'll tell the Bridgend Central Police Inspector. See if we can help look for him," Llewellyn said as he turned around to now look for the senior Officer. "Give me two minutes."

"Where the hell is he?" His Father questioned worryingly, a sign of stress on his face as it filled with a wrinkled forehead.

"I'm sure he's not far. Dylan! Dylan!"

Sergeant Llewellyn walked back with Inspector Geraint Thomas, a typical Welshman who looked like he had been in Wales all of his life and never travelled further than the old Severn Bridge apart from going to Hendon for his training. "Hello, Sir. I believe that you can't find your son."

Mike continued to look around with a hope that he would see Dylan and then without looking at the Inspector, he continued, "He was up Gareth's house, here." He pointed at his friend. "Now he has just gone. Nowhere to be seen."

"Yes," the worried friend said whilst joining Mike to look around and not looking at the Inspector. "Suddenly he said that he was going down with his Mum and Dad."

"Okay. I'll get some Officers on it right away. What was he wearing?"

"Well believe it or not, his pyjamas! Super Mario printed all over them."

"He should be easy to spot then," Inspector Thomas said as he looked for spare Officers. "Leave it with me. Sergeant Llewellyn, you stay with Mr Chiswell."

"Yes, Guv."

"I'm sure he would call back if he saw us," Mike Chiswell said to the Sergeant. "He's a good, sensible lad. Well, at times."

"I guess this is your house that is burning then, Mr Chiswell?" The Inspector added before he walked off completely.

"Yes," Michael replied sorrowfully whilst surveying the damage that was already beginning to materialise. "I should say that this was my house. As I told Sergeant Llewellyn here, Dylan saw a black dressed figure outside of the living room window. The next thing we know, our house is on fire!"

Two hours had passed. Mike and Sue Chiswell, Gareth and Karly Bateson, Sergeant Llewellyn and the assigned Uniformed Officers had checked everywhere, even the accompanying streets as close to the fire that they could go. The Fire Chief was happy that the fire was under control. All they had left was the burning black ash that seemed to reignite now and again when it found something to burn but was soon doused with water. The fire had spread into the accompanying houses each side. The Firefighters had tried their best to control it the best that they could. Everyone had continued to call the boy's name. Unsuccessfully. The early morning darkness had fallen. Dylan had disappeared.

*****

The dark figure stood over the boy. It had been quite a risk placing a cloth with chloroform over the boy's face when there were so many people around and then placing him in the boot of the Police car, but Sergeant Llewellyn managed it, telling Dylan that his parents were going over to the Police station to make a statement and that he would take the boy to meet them in the car. He raced up the old Bridgend Road. No one took any notice because there were so many emergency vehicles around that

215

one more wasn't going to make any difference and in any case it was now 01:35 in the morning. About a mile along, Sergeant Llewellyn turned right into the Forestry Commission car park, but he didn't intend on stopping there. He had the keys to the gate from a previous incident involving a lost group of hikers and had just forgotten to return them to the Ranger. He closed the gate behind his vehicle and then slowly drove up the gravel path whilst trying his hardest not to have any flick backs onto the car. The path curved around to the right and then downhill towards a bridge over the stream. Luckily for him there was no one around at this time of night. He headed right just before the bridge. There was another gate, but he didn't need to go that far. On the left there was an opening, a series of 'stepping stones' which crossed over to grass on the other side of the stream. Many teenagers used to go there and set up man-made barbecues surrounding the fires with rocks from the water. Dog walkers would take their dogs down for them to swim and have a drink of the fresh water which, unlike the water in the lakes at Pontycymer and Blaengarw, was exceptionally clean and clear.

Sergeant Llewellyn opened the boot. The only light he seemed to have was that of the moonlight and so he grabbed his torch. Dylan Chiswell was just semi-conscious and coming to, getting over the effects of the chloroform as the Police Officer lifted him out of the boot. He was carried down to the edge of the water and placed on the ground whilst Michael Llewellyn went back to the boot of the car to get his weapons and dress in his protective suit. The more time that the Sergeant was taking the more that Dylan was coming around.

The boy started to focus. Where was he? He felt the coldness of the water to his left. It was dark and yet he could just manage to see the moon up in the sky above him. He didn't understand why he was there or what was happening. The last thing he could remember was being taken by Sergeant Llewellyn to the Police car. Then he suddenly jumped as he realised just what was happening. Everything was hazy and no matter how many times he tried to stand his legs just wouldn't support him. He looked around. He knew where he was. He had been here before with his friends. How could he escape?

Michael Llewellyn slammed the car boot shut and then headed back down the small slope towards his next victim. He smiled psychotically as he realised that Dylan was alert. Good, he thought to himself, as he likes the victims alive to start with. He grabbed the pick, the blade glistening in both the moonlight and with the glare from the torch. The tall killer stood in front of his next victim. It was the first time that he had ever given his kill the time to think about what little life they had left. He stood looking into the eyes of the frightened boy, staring, but with no conscience whatsoever, he didn't care.

Dylan was frightened, so much so that he started to urinate in his trousers. "Please. Please. Sergeant." He started to cry whilst guessing what was about to happen. The same had been done to his friend Delme.

"Please? Say it again!"

Dylan looked at him. If he said please again would he be spared? "Please. Please." He held up his right hand as though he were going to protect himself from anything that was going to happen. He saw the pick and lightly shook his head, his eyes widening and staring in fear, his whole-body trembling. He knew that he had seconds to try and escape. But the effects of the chloroform still slightly rendered him useless.

Llewellyn raised the pick above his head, his face filled with a psychotic smile. The boy kicked out, attacking the Police Officer's shin. It hurt his attacker. Dylan could feel the life coming back into his body, in particular his legs. His kick to the shins had slightly toppled Sergeant Llewellyn off balance and he had slipped on the muddy surface. The boy turned and with all the energy he had started to scramble across the stepping stones.

"Arrghhhh!" the injured Officer screamed as he stood up straight and grabbed the handle of his pick. He looked at his potential victim who was nearly over the other side, knowing that he had to disable him in some way. He couldn't let him escape. He looked over. The boy was nearly fully steady and getting to his feet. He grabbed the handle and threw the pick at the boys back. The sharp end pierced Dylans shoulder.

"Arrghhhh!" the boy screamed out in pain. He fell down face first. He knew that he still had to try and escape. He also knew it was too late. He tried to reach around to his lower shoulder and see if he could grab the handle and try to remove whatever it was that had hit him.

217

Michael Llewellyn carefully manoeuvred the wet stepping stones. He placed his left foot on the boys lower back as heavy and hard as he could and then leaned down to do what the boy couldn't. Pull out the sharpened pick. He did. "Do you know something?" He raised the pick and slammed it down into the boy's left side, smiling psychotically as he heard the boy's screams that no one else could hear. "There are four kinds of Murder." He pulled the pick out from the wound and slammed it into the boy's right side. Then he shouted. "Felonious!" The pick went into the boy's left leg. "Excusable!" Into the boy's right leg. "Justifiable!" Into the base of his spine. Llewellyn removed it as listened to the pain coming from the boy's screams. He took pleasure in standing over the body and making the most of what little life was left. Then he raised the pick high above his head and slammed it down into the back of the boys skull. "And praiseworthy!" He heard the skull crunch. "Yours will consist of all four ..."

The blood started to spurt everywhere, most of it trickling down into the water and making the stream reddened in colour, the moonlight shining onto the water and making Michael Llewellyn think that it actually made the water that little bit more beautiful. But that made him more aggressive. He raised the pick once more and started to hit the body with full force, once, twice, three times, in random places. Every hit with the pick forced the blood to splatter in every direction. Michael Llewellyn was making a frenzied attack on the body of the boy. He knew Dylan was dead, but he didn't care. Finally he stopped. He looked at his handywork. "That will teach you to kick me."

He didn't need to mutilate the body anymore. He stared at it for what seemed like minutes, smiling, turning his head, eyes widening as he admired his success. Then he bent down and rolled what was left of Dylan Chiswell into the lower section to the left of the stepping stones where the water was deeper. Someone would find him, he told himself.

Chapter 17

DC Tello banged on DI Harris' office door. Something was on his mind. Something that had been bugging him for days. In the last team briefing that they had it had been suggested that the killer may be forensically aware. He had remembered the doorbell CCTV image that he had seized from one of the residents in Pwllcarn Terrace covering the morning of when the two women were murdered.

"Guv. Just wondering how we are getting on," he asked as he watched the DI look up from his desk and stop writing.

"Slowly but surely, Aled."

Tello could tell that the senior Officer was tired through the look on his face. "Something has been bugging me, Guv."

"Fire away. My ears are always open."

"Did you get the chance to review that Ring doorbell footage?"

Harris shook his head. "It is on my list, young man." Tello didn't move but bit his lip and looked perplexed. "Why? Something on your mind?" He looked up. "Come in. Close the door." The young Detective did just that and walked over towards the desk. "Take a seat."

"That doorbell footage shows someone resembling Sergeant Llewellyn heading past it."

"Yes. He heard the call for assistance and raced up to the scene."

"So he says, Guv. If you look about five minutes before what I think is Sergeant Llewellyn passes the camera, two women pass the same. You hear dogs barking in the background."

Harris gave him a look of worry. Something was on one of his Officer's minds. Something he couldn't ignore in case the Officer was right. "Let's take a look." He reached over for the file and pulled out the data stick that was in an evidence bag attached to the inside. Then he slipped it into the free USB slot at the side of his laptop. Each segment file was timed. Tello looked over his shoulder and pointed to the first video that he wanted the DI to look at.

"There. It's short and sweet but the motion detector picked it up because the front doors lead straight out onto the pavement."

DI Harris looked at it. "I don't think that you can say for sure that it is Sergeant Llewellyn. It's just someone in black carrying some type of bag on their back."

"Have a look at the one before, Guv," Tello asked politely.

DI Harris smirked as he felt that he had to do as he was told, like a naughty schoolboy, but then laughed the thought off. He pressed play on the clip. "Well you can tell that it is two females. One is calling their dog. What was that? Raffle?" He strained to listen to the audio.

"Raffi. It's the name of one of the Ridgebacks that was injured."

"Right. So what are you saying DC Tello?"

"I can't say anything Guv. I'm just putting forward a scenario. These two video clips are five minutes apart. It would have taken the two victims about fifteen to twenty minutes to get to where they were murdered." He pointed back at the screen. Now Poli Cárdenas, one of the victim's partners, said that she left home at 08:00 hrs and was normally back by 10:30 in order that she could have got to her lecture by 13:00 hrs. The two victims past the Ring doorbell at 08:25. Just say that this is Sergeant Llewellyn. He went up five minutes after them. So all going well, the victims got to the crime scene at about 08:45. Now Poli Cárdenas said he became concerned at midday because Catrin Kean hadn't returned home in time to get to her lecture. He called into the emergency services at 12:47 hrs. Again. Hypothetical situation. Sergeant Llewellyn was the first Officer on the scene. He said he heard the call and used a short cut to get there. But, hypothetically he went up the mountain at

08:30. Yet the time he called it in to say he was up there was at 12:57. I don't know of any short cuts that could take me to the mine entrance from the bottom in ten minutes." He raised his eyebrows as he finished his analysis.

"So what are you saying, DC Tello?" DI Harris was becoming more and more worried. He liked theories, and in his own point of view, this was one hell of a theory. He also knew that the suggestion had come across that the killer was forensically aware. That suggestion would fit in with Tello's theory. "What you are in fact saying is that Sergeant Llewellyn was already on the mountain and not down in the community at the time when the two female victims were murdered."

"I don't know Guv. I've met Sergeant Llewellyn close up. I've seen the doorbell footage. I would like to say that it is not him, but to me, I cannot rule it out. Fact is, he says he was down in the community when he heard the call. So he would have got from one of the villages to the top in ten minutes. Quite impossible really."

The DI nodded. "Okay. Take it down to the tech boys and see if we can get a clearer still."

"That's not all, Guv."

"You mean there's more?"

Tello nodded. "When Delme Greening and Jamie Arnett were found, Uniform conducted door-to-door enquiries. They interviewed a ..." His head filled with so much information at that time, Aled had to look at his notes. "Tracey Edwards who owns the fish and chip shop at Gwaun Bant. She stated that one of the victims had told her that she was surprised that Sergeant Llewellyn hadn't seen the two boys because she had seen the Sergeant up near there on that very night whilst she was out walking her dogs."

"Then she is murdered?" The DI enquired as he began to wonder whether this was reality or as ludicrous as it sounded. A killer cop? He told himself that if this were America he would have jumped at the chance to believe it. But this was in the Garw Valley where nothing much happened usually. Where the headline on the Garw Hub was usually *'Someone has stolen my bucket handle'*. "Okay. This is how we are going to handle this. Listen to me. It is only a theory until we have evidence. Now you seem to have done some of your homework but not all of it. I need you to prove to me that what you are saying has some relevance. Evidence!"

"Yes, Guv."

"Have you mentioned this to anyone else?" Tello shook his head. "No? Good. Keep it to yourself for the moment. In this job, an Officer making an accusation against another Officer is seen as a taboo subject. If anyone finds out, word will spread thicker than an Australian bush fire. You will be blacklisted amongst your colleagues, especially if the accusations are unjustified. So this goes no further than you and me, understood?"

"Yes, Guv. And thank you."

"Don't thank me yet. Prove to me what you are saying. I will then back you all the way. Then you can thank me. Here. Data stick. Tech boys. Copy it first just in case they lose it."

"Lose it, Guv?" Tello asked worryingly.

"I was joking," DI Harris replied as he shook his head in disbelief that DC Tello had fallen for the quirk. He watched him leave and then leaned back in his chair to think about what the young DC had just explained to him. To a certain degree it made sense, he told himself. But Sergeant Llewellyn had been a Police Officer for many years, had received many commendations for his bravery and even run clubs for teenage offenders at his last station, teaching them how to keep cars in top condition, getting local businesses in to show them how to do general mechanics on engines. Harris just couldn't explain it. But nobody was whiter than white, he thought to himself.

*****

Ryan Parry had picked up Tony Newton from the hospital as he was being discharged. He had been given the all clear as long as there was someone else at home with him and so his boss had drawn the short straw, Tony thinking that his *'Dad'* was about to become his *'Mum'* for a few days at least. After climbing the eight steps up to the front door, Ryan having to carry the injured man's bags although it did cross his mind that Tony could have been *'milking it'*, they went inside. Ryan walked in first and instantly saw the mess when he entered the living room on the right.

"Is your place in London this untidy?" he asked whilst trying to put some light on the fact they knew that Tony had been burgled.

"No. But then again I haven't got Billy Evans living down the road from me."

"Are we going to call the Police about this? They are coming around in any case to interview you about the accident." Ryan looked at the invalid who was struggling to sit down as he manoeuvred his way onto the sofa using the one crutch that the hospital had given him.

"Well, If I gave them the footage, it would certainly rile our Mr Evans up that bit more. It may even let the villagers around here see that he is not the sweet little man that he claims to be."

"I thought they already knew that," Ryan exclaimed as he headed out to the kitchen area. "Where's your coffee?" He asked as he looked around the room.

"On top of the microwave in the corner," Tony replied.

"Of course. Where else would it be?" Ryan shouted back in a jokingly sarcastic tone. He filled the kettle with water and then switched it on. Whilst waiting for it to boil he positioned himself in the doorway between the kitchen and living room. "Of course. We could play another game with him. To see what his next move may be."

"What game is that then?"

"Let's just say that a copy of the video footage of him involved in this burglary of your house, without sound, falls on his doormat." Ryan smirked and then went back to complete the coffee duty.

Tony tried to make himself comfortable on the sofa. "Perhaps he would come and offer to pay me the three grand to replace my electric guitar."

"Funnier things have happened," Ryan shouted through before appearing once again only this time with the two coffee mugs, one of which he placed on top of the pouffe at the side of Tony.

"It makes a change for you to make me a coffee. It's usually the other way around."

"Yeh? Well don't get used to it too much!"

"So, Dad. What effect do you think that giving Billy Evans a no-sound copy of the burglary will do?" Tony could only see more trouble ahead once he received it. He had already been shunted off the road, what would he do next if he were riled once more?

"Well. We give him a no-sound copy first and see how he reacts. Then a bit later we give him a copy with the sound. With the confession from them both that they killed your Grandfather."

"Why don't we just give it to the Police now?" Tony enquired whilst knowing the answer but just wanting Ryan to confirm his suspicions.

"We need to know who the serial killer is. It may be Billy Evans or any one of the other five that he met yesterday. If they are capable of running you off the road and leaving you for dead, they are capable of anything."

Tony nodded in agreement. "Did you say the Police are coming around about the accident?"

"Yes. Tonight, I believe. But you will need to call them about the burglary. You will need a crime reference number to claim back from the insurance company for the guitar."

"I can tell you now that the sight of a Police car outside will get back to the almighty one in no time at all."

"That is the objective," Ryan replied. "You are lucky to have me here. Two heads are better than one."

Tony took a swig of his coffee, feeling surprised that his 'Dad' actually knew how he took it considering he couldn't remember when the last time was that Ryan had ever made him one back at the office. "Right. Let's get the Police here then." He dialled 1-0-1. It took over a minute of ringing before the phone was answered.

"South Wales Police."

"Hello. I've just come home from spending a night in hospital and it looks like I've been burgled."

Three hours passed. The operator did say that it may take time due to the fact that it appeared that the burglars had gone and there was no real threat, and that units were busy elsewhere in the town. But Tony had explained that he had been the victim of a hit and run on the previous day and thought that the two incidents could be related. So they didn't just pile him off with a crime reference number and no visit.

The doorbell rang. Ryan curtain-twitched to see who it was and when he realised that it was the Police he went into the hallway and unlocked the front door. "Mr Newton?"

"No. No. I'm his boss. Mr Newton is in the living room on the right if you would like to go through." He closed the door behind the two PC's.

"Hello, Sir. PC Jones. This is WPC Caron. Looks like you have been in the wars."

"You could say that," Tony replied whilst acting as though he was in deep stressful pain, which, to a certain degree was right because the meds had already began to wear off.

"So what has happened? Were these injuries the result of the reported burglary?" PC Lestyn Jones enquired whilst looking at the bruised and battered face.

"No. I was forced off the road by some idiot, yesterday. In fact I think there is another unit coming around to take a statement in a short while."

PC Jones turned his head and looked at his colleague, giving her a smile that spoke a million words, but mostly, 'Why didn't they handle both incidents?'. "So were you hospitalised, Sir?"

Tony nodded his head. "Only for twenty-four hours."

"But then we came back to this mess," Ryan intervened as his hand indicated all the damage that had been done.

"I guess you haven't touched anything?"

"Only the kettle," Ryan added. "We haven't been upstairs yet. But looking through the kitchen window it looks like they smashed the back door in through the conservatory." He headed over to show the window view through to the back door. WPC Caron took heed and looked through. She put her gloves on and then walked out to the conservatory. Without touching anything she looked at the lock on the back door, and all the damage to the frame where the crowbar had been used to wedge the door open.

The female Officer came back in. "They came in through the back. Looks like they used a crowbar or something similar," she said to her colleague.

225

"Do we know the time that this happened? I know you were in hospital."

Tony shook his head. "No. I'm afraid not. I was recovering for most of the time."

"What about you, Sir," PC Jones asked Ryan. "Would you know?"

"Well no. I received a call from Tony telling me he was in hospital. I was working in Cardiff at the time and drove down immediately."

"So what is it you both do?" PC Jones continued with the questions.

"I'm a salesman at McArthur Glen. Ryan is my area manager." Tony stared at his boss with wicked eyes. What he wanted to say was that he was Ryan's toyboy and they were lovers, but he thought that would be taking the role play a little bit too far.

"Okay," PC Jones continued. "I see you have a camera. Do you know if that picked anything up?"

Tony shook his head. "It may have, but I've only just moved here, and I hadn't put the SD card in. So it wouldn't have saved anything. It usually alerts me, but with me being out for the count in a hospital bed, I didn't hear anything."

"Okay. We will just take a look upstairs for you. Check what damage is done. I will then give you a crime reference number."

"No one coming around to fingerprint the place?" Tony enquired whilst knowing the answer because of the number of complaints the paper get on a daily basis about the Police having to prioritise their workloads due to budget constraints.

"Well chances are whoever did this were wearing gloves. The only time we get success on burglaries these days is when we pick a criminal up for other reasons and they want other crimes to be taken into account to make it look as though they are cooperating with the Police to the Judge." PC Jones shook his head as though he disagreed with the procedures but had to abide by them.

"You go and do whatever you need to," Ryan said to them both.

The two Officers 'investigating' the burglary had left the crime scene to go back to the station and make their reports. Ten minutes later there was another knock on the door. Ryan repeated his task of looking through the curtains and then going out to meet the second batch. He also noticed the curtains twitching on the opposite side of the road as he walked towards the front door.

"You have nosey neighbours then," he mentioned jokingly.

"Babs and Fran," Tony replied as he nodded and laughed.

Ryan opened the front door. "Hello, gentlemen. Before you ask, I'm not Mr Newton. He is the invalid in the living room on the right!"

"Someone is in good spirits," PC Evans said as he wiped his feet. "I'm PC Evans. This is PC Powell. I think we spoke to you in the hospital, but Mr Newton was sedated at the time."

"Yes, that's right. I remember now," Ryan replied gracefully. "Did you manage to get anything from the car?"

"Well yes, actually," PC Evans exclaimed in his deep Welsh accent. "Quite a significant discovery. Mr Newton had both a front dash cam and rear-view camera," he replied as he walked through to the living room, instantly spotting the casualty.

"Oh. Mr Newton. At last you are awake!" PC Evans said jokingly as he looked at the state of the casualty all battered and bruised.

Tony nodded. "Yes, hello."

"I was just saying to your friend here that you had a dash cam and a rear-view camera."

"Yes, that's right," Tony answered whilst hoping that it had picked something up.

"Well the good news is that we have analysed the camera footage of both. We have a good image and registration plate of the driver and the car that forced you off the road."

"Bloody hell," Ryan jumped in. "Do you know who he is?"

"Another unit has gone down to interview and if necessary arrest the driver as we speak, I believe," PC Powell said as he smiled at the positivity. "But I can tell you that the suspect is known to us."

227

"So all we have to do at this point is take the statement, and then we will be off," PC Evans added as he took out some paperwork from his folder.

Tony and Ryan looked at each other. Tony knew that it was one of the six men who had run him off the road and more or less written off his car. They had that. They had the photos that Tony took of the six, and they had the burglary footage. The gun was loaded, and the bullet was ready to be fired.

*****

The Chiswell's were frantic beyond belief. What more could happen. Their son had just disappeared in a crowded street. The Police had made urgent enquiries, interviewed everyone who was there at the time, showed them a photo. They had knocked on the doors of all the neighbours who weren't directly affected by the fire. No one had seen him or heard from him.

DI Harris had specifically chosen DC Tello to partner up with him for the day. The more that he had thought about Tello's theory, the more he thought that it had possibilities to being right. He had been told that the family were currently staying with the Bateman family because of the house fire. In a way he thought it would save them a bit of time because all the main witnesses would be in the same place. Harris knocked on the door and Karly Bateson answered. "Hello," he said as he held up his warrant card.

Karly looked at the card but could tell that he was a Police Officer because of his attire, his precisely ironed shirt and his tie neatly secured with a standard knot around his neck. "You had better come in," she said in her tired voice that sounded like she hadn't slept since her friend's son Dylan had left to find his parents and never arrived. "Through there."

"My name is Detective Inspector Harris. This is Detective Constable Tello," he said as he put his card back into his suit jacket pocket. "It's good that you are all here because I believe that the four of you were the last to see Dylan."

"That's right," Karly butted in before anyone else. "One minute he was saying that he was going down to the barrier to find his Mum and Dad, the next minute nothing."

"We searched and searched," Michael Chiswell said whilst also sounding as though he was exhausted and hadn't slept since the incident. "Have the uniformed Officers had any luck with any cameras in the area?"

"Well as you probably know, there is no Council CCTV at all for miles. We are relying entirely on neighbours handing over their CCTV and doorbell footage." Harris shook his head in disbelief that there was no public CCTV. "The Officers have asked all of the residents to look at the footage and if they see something suspicious to let us know."

"Where the hell could he be?" His Mother asked as she started to cry once more. Michael Chiswell knew that she hadn't stopped crying since Dylan disappeared because she was thinking about the dark figure that Dylan had said was looking at him through the window and then the house fire. They were under threat. "We told the other Officers about the stranger looking through the window at Dylan and then our house being firebombed straight after."

"So what is happening? What are you doing to find our son?" Dylan's Father asked forcefully. "I mean you had the helicopter out for Delme and Jamie."

"The problem we have, Mr Chiswell, is that we do not know where to start looking. We had information about Delme Greening and Jamie Arnett that they were last seen in the vicinity of the cemetery."

DC Tello thought he would jump in with the explanation. "That's right, Sir. The helicopter uses infrared heat seeking equipment but in a limited area." He looked over towards the DI and they swapped eye contact. "Sir, was Sergeant Llewellyn helping you on the night of the fire?"

Both Michael and Gareth Bateson nodded their heads. "Yes," Gareth replied. "I saw him. Did you, Mike?"

"Yes. He was down at the edge of the fire with us. Well he was here, there, and everywhere. He even helped look for Dylan," Mike exclaimed with a frown on his forehead. "Why?"

Tello had to think of an answer almost immediately without touching on his theory. "Oh, we can talk to him as well to see what was happening with the search when you first found the boy gone. Being the Community Policeman, he knows the ground."

DI Harris looked over at his DC as if to say, *'good reply off the cuff'*. "Is there anywhere that you can think of, and I'm asking you to rack your brains here, where he might have gone?"

Both parents shook their heads. "Well one of his best friends is dead and the other in hospital," the Father answered politely whilst looking at the floor and shaking his head.

"Was he happy at home? No problems?"

Again, both parents shook their heads. "He was terribly upset about Delme, and frightened. Scared that whoever it was would come after him."

"I'm sorry to ask this, Mr Chiswell. No family problems?"

Michael realised that the question had to be asked and so it didn't upset him, but looking over at his wife he could see that it had upset her, so he chose to quickly jump in with an answer and end that line of questioning. "Quite the opposite. We always talked and said that if there were problems we would sort them among us as a family. I always brought him up to not be afraid of us and tell us if something was wrong."

Harris hesitated and looked at the two parents whilst trying to weigh them up which he did in every situation to try and use his experience to tell if they were lying. It didn't appear that way in this case. He could sense that they were loving parents. Not perfect. No parent was. "Okay, Mr Chiswell. I know Uniform are continuing their door-to-door enquiries. I'm going to get a team together to search the wider area."

"Thank you," Michael replied. "But tell us one thing. Do you think that the serial killer has taken him?" He had a look of worry on his face that everyone could see.

DI Harris had to think of a diplomatic answer quickly. "I don't think that we should assume or speculate at this moment in time. Please." He went to leave. "We will keep you informed. Have Uniform arranged a Family Liaison Officer for you?"

Both Sue and Michael nodded. "He is actually on his way."

"Make the most of him. He is there to help you and answer any questions you may have."

*****

230

PC Lewis and PC Eastman parked up outside Julian Evans house in Dinam Street, Nantymoel. Lewis knew that the suspect wouldn't be able to argue because the image they had from the rear-view camera of Tony Newton's car was crystal clear. One of the advantages of having an expensive unit with HD quality.

"Arrest him immediately, Alun?"

"Yeh, why not. Give him the chance to lie about where he was and then take him in," PC Lewis jokingly replied. He banged on the door and almost immediately a female answered. "Hello. Could I speak to Julian Evans, please?"

The woman looked at him, giving the impression that she should be stood there with her hair in rollers and a cigarette hanging out of the side of her mouth. "Jules! Police for you!"

The male face appeared around the side of the door. "Yes, gentleman. How can I help?"

PC Eastman stepped forward and pulled his handcuffs from his utility belt. "Julian Evans. I am arresting you on suspicion of attempted murder. You do not have to say anything. But it may harm your defence if you do not mention when questioned something which you later rely on in court. Anything you do say may be given in evidence."

"Attempted murder?" Julian snapped knowing what the Officer was talking about but only expecting the charge to be dangerous driving.

"Turn around," PC Eastman demanded.

"Are you fucking joking? Attempted murder?"

"I said TURN AROUND!" PC Eastman ordered. Still, Julian took no notice but continued arguing against what he was being arrested for. "ALUN!"

PC Lewis stepped forward. "Let's get him on the ground!"

"Fucking attempted murder? You have got to be fucking kidding me!" Julian shouted as he continued to struggle and kick out with his legs.

"Leave him alone," the suspect's wife shouted at them both.

"Right, listen to me. You are two seconds away from being tased. Now on the ground. Face down! Hands behind your back!" PC Lewis ordered as he kicked the man's legs to the side and watched him go down with some force.

231

"Fucking get off him!" The woman screamed as she stepped forward.

"You will be joining him in a minute! Now get back!" PC Eastman ordered whilst looking at her seriously. He then managed to lean forward and grab the suspect's arms, pulling them tightly together and slapped on the cuffs.

"Owwww. They are too fucking tight!"

"Shut up. If you had done as you were told it would have been a lot easier," Alun Lewis told him. "Now we are going to stand you up." He nodded to his colleague who got around the other side of the prisoner. "After three, Mike," he said as he nodded his head. "One. Two. Three!" Julian Evans was upright and being led towards the back seat of the Police car. PC Lewis opened the door. "Right in we go!" He pushed the man's head down, covering the top of the head with his hand in order that the prisoner didn't bang it on the door surround. Once he was in, PC Lewis slammed the door shut.

"Wankers!" the woman shouted at the pair of them.

"Grow up! How old are you?" PC Eastman responded before getting back in the passenger side of the vehicle. He looked at his colleague who had finally got inside. "That was easier than I thought."

Alun Lewis laughed as the prisoner in the back kicked off once more. "What's this attempted murder shit?" he demanded to know.

"Save it for the interview!" PC Lewis shouted back.

Chapter 18

Ryan Parry took his laptop and placed the SD Card that contained the footage from the burglary into the side, then copied the videos to his hard drive. He looked into his bag. Should he really start to take the piss? He thought to himself. He had several promotional USB sticks with the name of his newspaper stamped on them. Now that really would hit the nail on the head, he smirked. Just for Billy Evans.

He ran back down the stairs. Tony was still feeling sorry for himself, sat on the sofa, and watching television. "Got it. Time to notch the plan up a gear."

"Don't expect me to walk down there yet," Tony said as he nursed his own sore ribs and then removed his neck brace. "Bloody thing. So uncomfortable." He placed it down beside him.

"You said that the old man's house is near the shop?" Ryan enquired whilst placing the USB stick into an A5 size envelope. On the front he just wrote, *'Billy'* with a black marker pen.

"Two doors down from Bryn stores," Tony replied whilst trying to turn his head to look at his boss but struggling to do so.

"You should keep that neck brace on. At least for today."

"I'm beginning to think that." Tony picked it up and looked at it for a few moments. Then he wrapped it back around his neck. "So as you look down toward the Coop from Bryn Stores it's the second house on the left. Victoria Street. Be careful though. Otherwise you will be next." Tony pointed to his neck brace.

Half an hour later, Ryan walked back through the front door and smiled at his colleague.

"All done," he said with a smile. "This should stir things up."

"Well he has tried to kill me once."

"We can get more of a confession out of him. I'll be in the kitchen out of sight by the back door. Digital voice recorder in hand. Story of a lifetime!"

*****

The big man came back from his shopping trip, getting off the bus at the bus stop opposite his house and crossing the road, up the steps and then he fumbled with his front door keys and found that he had to drop his bags in order to get the key into the lock. Before he picked up the bags he noticed that he couldn't open the door easily. He thought that the postman must have been as he noticed the package inside blocking the door on the bottom. He picked it up, looking at the *'Billy'* written on the front and thinking that it must be something from one of the neighbours. He stepped back outside and picked up his bags and then went back in, closing the door and locking it from the inside. On the way to the kitchen he dumped the package on the dining table.

He had put his frozen foods away. Back out to see what was in his package, a frown appearing on his face as he opened it and all that dropped out was the USB stick. But then he froze as he saw the logo on the stick. *'The Sun'*. He looked around for his laptop, walked over and sat down on his living room chair as he saw the laptop, lid closed on the coffee table. It came to life as he opened the lid. He placed the USB stick into the side, and it auto played on the video app. As the video came up Billy's eyes opened wide, fresh with worry, the blood ran cold through his body, and he started to panic, slamming the lid of the laptop closed so hard that it was a wonder that it didn't break. He bit his lip and looked to the side and then up towards the wall in front of him, his mind working overtime on how he was going to get over this. Hold on, he thought. It was only an image. There was no sound. The worst that could happen would be for Tony Newton to pass it to the Police and Lee and him getting arrested for breaking and entering. They didn't actually take anything. Just

234

smashed the place up. He tried to remember just what they had said whilst they were there. It didn't matter. There was no sound. Perhaps the CCTV didn't record sound. It was time to visit Mr Newton or Mr Fallon or whatever he was really called and see what he was going to do. He would call Lee first. Two heads were better than one.

Lee's mobile rang and it was several seconds before it was answered. "Billy. What now?"

"We have a problem, Lee. I've just had a USB stick put through my door. It is a copy of the CCTV from Newton's house."

"And?" Lee began to listen and pay attention immediately rather than think *'Bloody Billy is calling again'*.

"It is an image of you and me stood in the living room."

"Fuck. Fuck! Did he hear what we were talking about? Because I'm not sure if you remember, but I do!"

"There is no audio on the recording. Not sure if there is. I thought that we need to make a visit to see him. See what he is going to do. But the other worry is that I think I have found out for whom he works."

"How did you work that out?" Lee enquired worryingly whilst deep inside panicking like he hadn't done for years.

"The stick. It has a logo on it. The Sun newspaper."

"Only the biggest fucking tabloid with the widest distribution in the UK!"

Billy was still panicking, trying to work out which one of them was more frightened of the situation. "I know! I know! Listen. I think we need to go up and see him. Try and find out what his plans are. Put the frighteners on him a bit more."

"We? You want me to go with you?"

"You are on the CCTV image as well," Billy snapped. "It's your livelihood as much as mine. Now get down here ASAP!" He ended the call whilst knowing that Lee would be as worried as him and would do as he was ordered to do.

Ten minutes later the pair were walking up towards the end of the Avenue. Both were completely silent and not knowing what to say. Inside, both of them were trying to think of the consequences. Had Tony Newton ne Fallon already gone to the Police? If he were a reporter as Billy thought, he would be after a story and to solve it himself in order that he could print it as

'Investigative Reporter' and then ask for Police comment. Finally they were outside.

"How are we going to handle this, Bill?" Lee enquired.

"He already feels threatened by me, even more so since we ran him off the road. So we will warn him to keep his big mouth shut!"

"And you think he will accept that?" Lee asked as he widened his eyes and frowned. "He has the upper hand."

"Come on," Billy exclaimed as he couldn't believe his ears at the cowardice of someone who forty years ago had ripped a man apart with a ballistic knife. He shook his head and then lead them up the eight steps. He hesitated before banging on the door, his finger pointing at the doorbell, but then pressed it.

The injured man struggled to the door on the one crutch. As he opened it, he smiled with an expression that more or less said, *'One nil to me'*. "Billy. I was expecting you to wear a stripped jumper and have a beret and a facemask over your eyes," he said sarcastically and with a wicked smile. "You had better come in."

Billy wiped his feet and Lee followed suit whilst closing the door behind him. "Thank you for the USB stick. Quite a show on there."

"I can't believe that you were that careless," Tony exclaimed. "Oh, and thanks for arranging for one of your goons to ram me off the road."

"My pleasure," Billy replied as he watched the injured man take his seat at the end of the sofa next to the window.

"If I didn't know otherwise, Mr Evans, I would say that you had something on your mind," Tony said whilst still being sarcastic.

"So what are you? A reporter? The USB stick showed your newspaper."

"Oh yes. That. Okay I'll come clean. I'm down here investigating the murders."

"Yeh?" Billy snapped whilst knowing that there was probably something more than that because of the coincidence of the surname of *'Fallon'*.

"Oh, that and the disappearance of my Grandfather forty years ago. Perhaps you could help me with that. I mean you were a resident and known to be the man who fixed problems back then."

Billy became angry because once again Tony was riling him up, but Lee suddenly intervened just as Billy was about to answer back. "Now listen here ..."

"NO! YOU LISTEN!" Tony exclaimed. "I am closer than you think. That video on the USB stick isn't the only copy file. The one with the sound, yes, there was sound on the original copy, is back at the newspaper." He looked at the worried eyes of the two men who were now looking at each other as if to say, *'shit'*. "That and the images that were taken of the six of you at Southerndown. You see, The man who rammed me may have stolen the camera, but it is so state of the art that it automatically emails images direct to my office. So I have all of you. Now I know that you were the leader at the execution of my Grandfather, Billy." He turned his attention back to Lee Jones. "And you. I know that you put the finishing touches on the murder."

"We are saying nothing more," Billy snapped. "But let's just say that your Grandfather was in the wrong place at the right time."

"What? Pontycymer at a time when you needed a scapegoat to take the blame for the murders of those boys? But it didn't work, did it? The murders continued!"

"Yes, they did."

"And you know who was responsible for them, don't you? And I bet you know who is responsible for the latest spate of mutilations!"

Billy's face went bright red with guilt. "I'm not saying anymore."

"From now on you leave me alone. Understand? Otherwise my boss opens the files. Both the video and the photos. Knowing him he will contact the Police and you both go down for a long time with the other four who you met yesterday." Tony stared at the big man in particular. "Well, one of them is already in Police custody, no doubt."

"What?" Billy asked confusingly.

"The Police came around about the accident. What you all didn't realise was that I had both a dash cam and a rear window cam installed on the car. Your thug who stole my camera forgot to remove them. Vital evidence. A clear image of the culprit and his car it appears."

Billy looked at Lee and both of them began to think that this was the start of their worlds coming crashing down around their feet. "Let's go," he snapped at Lee. "We are saying no more."

Ryan Parry stepped around from the hidden doorway leading from kitchen to conservatory. "You don't need to," he said as he held up his digital recorder. "We have everything that we need. It will make a cracking story."

"Who the hell are you?" Lee enquired whilst feeling very worried with butterflies gathering in his stomach. "Bill. Who is he?"

"Say no more!" Billy exclaimed. "Let's go!"

"Before you do, I want the camera back! Plus, Mr Evans. The guitars. The Gibson is valued at £3200. The acoustic £570. Cash only as I don't trust you no further than I could throw you!" Tony looked at his boss as the two men left and banged the front door on the way out. "I think the both of us won't be getting a Christmas card this year from them."

"We will have to watch our backs. They will now be trying to get rid of the evidence. The evidence being you and me. Just like they did with your Grandfather. Maybe he knew more than the Police found out."

Tony nodded as he bit his lip. "We are still not quite there yet. Something is missing."

"Which is why we don't go to the Police quite yet. This is our story."

Billy stormed back towards his home and found himself walking faster than he had ever walked before. His anger had risen, his face was red, and he knew his blood pressure that the Doctor had told him to keep an eye on, was at an all-time high without even measuring it. He grabbed his mobile phone as he was walking.

"Hold on, Bill," Lee snapped as he saw him dialling on the phone. "What you doing? Who are you calling?"

"Julian. If a rear-view camera did pick up the person that rammed that cunt then it would have picked up the face of my brother. If the Police have arrested anyone it will be him!" He had the phone to his ear. It went straight to voicemail. It was either out of battery or switched off. "Nothing," he exclaimed as he tapped the top of the phone on his bottom lip. He scrolled through his list of contacts. "I'll try his Mrs."

"Bill. I've been trying to get hold of you," Laura exclaimed.

"What's happened?" he asked as he heard the hysterical behaviour of the woman.

"The Police have arrested Julian. Attempted murder. What the hell is that about?" she screamed down the phone. "Has this got something to do with you? It normally has."

"Attempted murder? Oh fucking hell. They have evidence, Laura. Rear view camera footage."

"What has he done?" Julian's wife enquired whilst only knowing part of the story which she had got in broken conversation directly from her husband and by listening into his phone conversations.

Billy didn't know whether to tell her but then thought that she would find out soon enough in any case. "He rammed someone off the road on the way back from Southerndown the other day."

"Is that why our fucking car was damaged?"

"Yes. Listen. Did they say which station they were taking him to?"

"No," Laura replied sternly. "They just came and took him away."

Billy hesitated, in some ways stuck for words and not knowing what his next move could be. Hopefully, Julian would keep his mouth shut. Hopefully, he had a solicitor. "I'll get back to you," he exclaimed as he ended the call abruptly.

"What did she say?" Lee asked as they reached the bottom of the steps that led up to Billy's front door. He didn't reply how Lee had hoped.

"Go home."

"What?"

Billy raised his voice, shouting, "I SAID FUCKING GO HOME!" He noticed Lee looking at him. "I'm sorry. This is getting to me. I have to sort a few things. I'll call you later."

Lee walked off in the direction of his home, somewhat angry that his friend was keeping him in the dark. "You are just unbelievable sometimes, Bill," he shouted back as he walked at speed away from his friend and partner-in-crime.

*****

It was early morning. The mobile phone was on the bedside cabinet with its charger cable attached to ensure that it had power for the day. The morning was just dawning, the light shining through the gap in the centre of the bedroom curtains. Police Sergeant Llewellyn knew that he wasn't on duty until 09:00 hrs when he had a briefing with his two PCSO's and was also welcoming the Go Safe mobile enforcement camera in the area for the day to catch any speeding vehicles in Blaengarw and Pontycymer. Also on his agenda was the continued search for Dylan Chiswell. He was leading the search in a different direction to where he had left the body, aiming around the area where the boy lived. He was going to suggest that today the search party look up around the area in the mountain where the majority of the other murders had taken place. He knew that it was only a matter of time before Dylan would be found by someone, but the later the better.

His mobile suddenly burst into life. In a tired voice as though he wasn't quite ready for human interaction at that moment in time, he answered. "Hello."

"Sergeant Llewellyn."

He recognised the voice having dealt with the man many times. But he was hearing voices all the time and many of them always sounded like that of his Father, Dafydd. At first he thought it was his Father, but then shook his head and realised it was Billy. "What can I do for you at this time of the morning?"

"My brother Julian has been arrested."

"What the hell for?" Michael enquired whilst also wondering why Billy Evans had contacted him as there was little that he could do because he was only the community copper for the Garw.

"It's a long story. It would be better if I came over and spoke to you about it."

"I had better get some clothes on then," the Officer said to him as if to say, *'Why can't this wait?'*.

"Five minutes," Billy said as he ended the call.

Michael Llewellyn quickly changed out of his pyjama shorts and t-shirt and put on his Adidas tracksuit to try and look a bit more respectable. He was just in time as he noticed a shadow approaching his front door. He opened it whilst not giving his visitor the chance to ring the doorbell.

Billy barged himself in without even being asked. "Coffee, two sugars," he said to the Police Officer who closed the front door and followed him through to the kitchen area.

"Anything else? Would you like biscuits? Or maybe some Cornflakes with milk."

"My brother Julian has been arrested."

"What for?"

Billy looked suspiciously around. After his visit to Tony Newton's home on the previous day he was becoming paranoid that he was being recorded by either video or audio. "Attempted murder."

"Who the hell did he attempt to murder for God's sake?"

"You know that new guy up in the Avenue? Tony Newton?"

"Well I've heard that someone moved into the house. I haven't actually met the guy."

"Well it appears that Tony Newton the salesman who supposedly worked at McArthur Glen is really Tony Fallon the reporter who works for The Sun newspaper." Billy sounded seriously worried.

Michael Llewellyn started to make the coffee that Billy had requested. He too needed one. If he was a reporter, why was he here? "What has he got to do with Julian's arrest?"

"This reporter was riling me up. He seemed to have something on me from when your Dad was alive. He was putting two and two together about the community. Asking too many questions. So I arranged for the gang to meet up and see what we could do about it."

"And Julian decided to murder him? What was he on?" Llewellyn exclaimed whilst not being able to believe that Billy could let it happen.

"No. We all met out of the way at Southerndown. He followed us there without our knowing. He was taking photographs. We gave chase." Billy shook his head. "He is piecing things together gradually. Julian ran him off the road. Shunted his car which flipped over in the lane whilst heading back to Bridgend."

The Police Officer shook his head, but he knew that he was just the community bobby for the Garw. There was nothing that he could do. It would look suspicious if he started poking his nose into attempted murder investigations being handled by CID. "I will try and find out as much as I can."

"There's something else. It's bad. Blown up big time."

"What is worse than attempted murder? Apart from murder itself." The kettle boiled and Michael poured the hot water into the mugs, realising afterwards that he had forgotten to put the coffee and milk in the actual mugs before filling them with water.

"Whilst this Tony Newton was in hospital, Lee and I broke into his house to try and find out more about him, because I knew that there was something not right. It was during that break in that we found his medication with his real name on the label. Tony Fallon."

"And this is relevant how?" Michael asked as he passed the mug over to Billy with coffee now fully made inside.

"Lee and I recognised the surname. Fallon. You have probably heard the stories about the man that was executed by a group from the villages back in 1982."

"Everyone in the village heard about that! I was ten at the time and even I heard about it," Michael snapped.

"Everyone thought that our kids were being murdered by this Christopher Fallon. It turns out that we were all wrong. We had murdered the wrong man. He was actually a reporter as well. We found out that he was here to report on the closure of the mines in our support against the Thatcher Government."

"Shit. I should arrest you for this, Bill. You are confessing this to a Police Officer."

"It's a mess. But when I tell you more, you won't want to arrest me. You see. It was your Dad that told us that Fallon was a suspect in the murders. After we killed Fallon we hoped that the teenagers murders would stop." Billy was trying to work out how to tell Michael Llewellyn the next bit of the story.

"I know the rest. I found my Dad's journal in the loft. The killer was my Dad. Which is why the murders stopped in 1984.

Dad died in 1984." A tear came to Michael's eye. Then he became nastily angry. "Do you know why he murdered all those teens?"

"Not exactly," Billy replied. "He never said anything until his last moments. We told him he should have stopped when we assassinated Fallon. We could have actually blamed it on Fallon then."

"He contracted coal workers' pneumoconiosis. The dust scarred his lungs. But it also made him lose his mind. The oxygen wasn't getting to his brain because his breathing was irregular."

"My God," Billy said as he took a swig of his coffee.

"The journal tells it all. Even down to the fact that he was angry over Mum's death. She was mugged by a group of teenagers down by the Pontycymer mine. For all of two pounds. He was also angry at the British Government for not giving the miners who were diagnosed with the various diseases associated to working down the mines, specialist medical treatment. He killed all those youngsters."

"I feel partly guilty."

"Why?"

"I was giving him the names of teenagers in the area who were problematic. I thought that he could sort them out as a Police Officer. But he was sorting them out in a different way. To avenge your Mother's death."

"So the blood is on your hands."

Billy nodded. "You could say that." He hesitated. "But it is also on yours now."

Michael Llewellyn felt instantly guilty. "What?" he questioned whilst feeling slightly amazed at Billy's comment.

"Are you not angry about your parent's deaths? You can tell me. I am the man who can help you."

The Police Officer froze and stared at the big man. He was silent, didn't move for what seemed like several minutes. "It's you. You are in Dad's journal."

"I gave you an alibi. Told you to go and visit Jamie Arnett and be seen. Meanwhile another boy was murdered."

"Brandon."

Billy nodded. "It's okay. Your secret is safe with me. I am the only one who knows. Well, at the moment."

"What do you mean by that?"

"That Tony Newton. Or Fallon. Whatever he is called. He has someone there with him. They are getting close. We thought that they were speculating about Lee and me being involved with the murder of Tony Newton's Grandfather, Christopher."

"Which you were," Llewellyn snapped back.

"Yes. But when we burgled the house, we didn't realise that there was CCTV inside. The CCTV picked up audio as well as visual. It caught me and Lee discussing the murder."

"And I guess they are after a story that will sell newspapers as opposed to giving the collar to the Police."

"Tony Newton is after my blood. Lee's blood. I can tell you that." Billy shook his head as he put his empty mug down on the table. "You need to help us. The six of us that were responsible for his Grandfather's death."

"You are the one that fixes problems," Michael said whilst feeling that he didn't want anything to do with what Billy was suggesting. "Why don't you do it?"

"I'm the one he suspects. He is following me. Everywhere I go. The only reason I know that he hasn't followed me here is because he can't walk far without having to sit down at the moment."

The Sergeant shook his head. "I'm not sure about this, Bill."

"You did away with those two women who were interfering. Now is the time to do away with two investigative reporters who could find out about you. Prevention is better than cure."

Michael stared ahead. Then he nodded. "Leave it with me."

Billy got up. "And Julian?"

"He will probably have to accept whatever is coming his way. I can't perform miracles. Only the impossible."

Michael saw Billy out of the door. He had to give this some thought. The two reporters knew about Billy and Lee. Plus the other four. But he didn't know about him. He had read the journal. He knew the exact depravity of his Father's murder spree although at the time he was only a boy who was unaware because he was too young to understand. Perhaps the blame had to be apportioned elsewhere.

*****

The sun was rising. Nicola Stone, an avid hiker, had arranged to meet three of her friends and walk around the forests around the next two Valley's over from Pontycymer and Blaengarw towards Maesteg. She had checked the weather forecast and it was due to be a beautiful and warm day. Nicola dressed herself in her shorts which, although not long, because of her short legs they looked like they were knee length ones. Her rucksack looked twice the size of her, but this didn't deter her. She was strong, both in her legs and arms. You didn't argue with the little hulk.

The four ladies walked down the path after climbing up from Pontycymer, heading past the flag and then right down the other side to a long downward path. As usual the four were talking women's talk and having a laugh whilst they were at it. It took them nearly thirty minutes to reach the bottom of the hill. They didn't know that they were at the scene of the murder of Dylan Chiswell.

Nicola had a bottle that cleanly filtered water from a stream and made it drinkable. It didn't even require the old system of tablets. "Hold on. Just going to top up my water," she shouted as she headed right and away from them. She knelt down at the water's edge and prepared her bottle, at first not taking any notice of her surroundings. Then she looked down. The body was blue, cold, face down. Nicola screamed. Her friends came running down to see what was wrong.

"Oh my God!" Rhiannon said as she stared at the body. "Call the Police!" No one seemed to be listening as they all stared at the body in shock. "CALL THE POLICE!"

Nicola finally broke from her shock and took her mobile from her jacket pocket. She checked for a signal as they were deep in the Valley. "I haven't got a signal," she exclaimed. "Anyone else?" All three searched for their phones and then one by one checked the signal bar.

"I'll run up there," Tracey said whilst nodding up towards the path which went over towards Pont-y-Rhyl. As fast as she could, she walked up the incline, every few metres checking the signal bar at the top of the phone. She had to walk quite a

245

distance, so much so that she could see the village and the main road down to her left. Finally, a strong signal. 9-9-9.

"Which service do you require?"

"Police. Urgently! We have found a body. A boy."

Chapter 19

Police Sergeant Michael Llewellyn knew that things were getting out of hand. He sat in his Chesterfield chair whilst looking at his watch to check the time knowing that he had a busy day ahead. He stared at the nothingness, thinking about one person. Billy Evans. That man could destroy him. He could put paid to his Father's good standing legacy as the long-term community Policeman, even though deep down inside he was a mass murderer. Michael had also followed in his Father's footsteps. But Billy Evans was on edge. He could end everything. Tell all, even though he himself was a murderer. He had the blood of Christopher Fallon and the youngster Brandon Edwards on his hands, and that was only two that Michael knew about. Who knows. there could be more.

He knew that Billy Evans was after Tony Newton. He knew that Tony Newton had someone with him, although at the moment it was unknown just who the man that Billy had mentioned was. If Tony Newton was a reporter as the big man had claimed, then maybe his visitor was also in the same trade. Or he could just be a relative taking care of him after Tony was forced off the road.

He needed a plan. He looked at his watch. 08:20. Was it too early to make a visit to Tony Newton? Would he be up and about or sleeping? He would have to make out that he didn't know anything about him, his real name or his meeting with Billy and Lee. He could try and get some information just by visiting as a concerned community Policeman. He knew that he had to be at the station no later than 08:55 but it was only down the road from the Avenue. He ran upstairs and quickly got dressed in his uniform, grabbed his keys and before going up to the Avenue he thought he would make a quick visit over to Billy to let him know just what he was going to do about the situation. He crossed the road, walked up the steps and banged on the big man's door.

"That was quick," Billy exclaimed as he opened the door, his face filled with an angry look that more or less told the Sergeant that they were no longer friends.

Llewellyn pushed himself in. "It's okay. I'm not staying. Just thought I would tell you my plan."

"Yes?" Billy replied as he turned and led the way into the living room, plonking himself down into a chair that looked like the shape had moulded itself to the shape of the big man and that he had been sat in it for years.

"I will find out about your brother. Like I said there is not a lot that I can do. They have the evidence. But I will find out and let you know." Llewellyn looked at the bigger man with a sense of discontent at what Billy had said to him earlier that morning. "Now I am just going up to visit the two reporters and introduce myself as the community Police Officer. To give them the support for their recent mishaps. Maybe something will go missing. Something with finger prints, if you get my meaning."

Billy smiled psychotically. "Oh yes. I get your meaning. I like you're thinking."

"Right. I can see myself out. Don't get up." The Sergeant looked at Billy again with eyes that more or less let him know that they were no longer friends. As he walked out to the hallway, he saw Billy's wallet lying beside his keys on the table to the right. Pulling down his sleeve over his hand, he picked it up. "I'll be in touch."

"Bye." Billy shouted at him.

Five minutes later, Sergeant Llewellyn was stood outside number 66 The Avenue. He walked up the steps and took a look to see if he could see any sign of life but then decided to knock on the door in any case.

"Oh hello," Ryan exclaimed as he noticed the Uniform Officer stood there.

"Mr Newton?" he enquired whilst not knowing if this was the visitor or the resident.

"No. No. He is inside. Injured. I'm his Father. Please. Come in. Are you here about the accident or the burglary?"

"Well, neither. Or both as the case may be. I am Sergeant Llewellyn. The community Police Officer. I heard about both and thought I would come up and show my support."

"Please go through." Ryan looked at his junior reporter who was sat in the chair watching the television. "Tony. This is Sergeant … sorry I forgot your name already."

The Officer leaned forward and held out his hand for Tony to shake. "Llewellyn. As I told your Dad here, I'm the community Officer. I heard about the accident and your burglary."

"Did your colleagues contact you?"

"Yes and no. I'm afraid in this community nothing stays secret for exceptionally long. Word soon spreads! But yes, I also read it on the station report. I just thought I would come up and show my support. Just say if I can do anything, let me know."

"Well, thank you Sergeant. I guess you are based down at the station down by the chemist."

The Police Officer nodded his head. "Although I'll give you my card as that station is no longer operational. It's just a base for me and the two PCSO's." He reached into his jacket and pulled out the card, dropping it onto the coffee table. "So my colleagues have been around to see you, I take it?"

"Yes. I believe that they have arrested someone for the so-called accident."

"He rammed you off the road the report said."

Tony nodded as Ryan intervened. "Prat didn't realise that Tony here had a rear-view camera," he said as he shook his head.

"What about the burglary? Do you have any idea who could have done it?"

Both Tony and Ryan shook their heads even though they were lying. "They didn't actually take anything. Well apart from my pills. They just smashed the place up. You can see the state of my guitars." Tony nodded over towards the broken pieces. "It's okay. They are insured."

"Okay. Well I had better get off. There is a speed camera being set up on the main road this morning. I have to meet them."

249

"Thanks for letting me know," Ryan exclaimed with a laugh. "I'll remember to keep to the speed limit."

"I would," Sergeant Llewellyn replied whilst joining in with his humorous reply. "And remember Tony, if you think of anything else, please do not hesitate to call." He got up and looked at Ryan. "It's okay. I can see myself out. Good to meet you both." He walked out down the steps and headed down, crossing the road, and turning right into the lane that would take him down right opposite the station. On the way he shook his head. If what Billy was saying was true then the two of them that he had just been to see were lying. Why lie? Why couldn't they just confirm that Billy and Lee were the burglars?

He went to work. He would keep in his 'friend's' good books, trying to find out the latest on Julian Evans. He sat down at the station desk and then searched through the Police directory for the direct number to custody. He had a few minutes to kill before everyone started to arrive, so he picked up the phone and dialled.

"Custody."

"Hello. This is Police Sergeant Llewellyn. I'm based in Pontycymer. I believe you have a Julian Evans in your care."

"We sure do. Feisty little devil he is. How can I help?"

"I've had his brother approach me asking for an update. Is there something that I can tell him?"

"Let me have a look." The custody officer clicked on a few buttons on the keyboard in front of him. "Right. His Solicitor has requested bail which has been granted for the attempted murder charge because he will be released pending further investigation. However, we kept him in as CID want to interview him with reference to the murders up around your place. So they have rearrested him. They have," he looked at his wrist watch. "Five hours left. Otherwise they must charge him or ask for an extension to the judge."

"They must suspect him. It could be that we have the murderer then?"

"Don't build your hopes up yet, Sergeant. Personally, I think that CID may be clutching at straws."

"Really?"

"Oh yes," the custody Officer replied sarcastically.

250

"Haha. Okay. Thanks for that. I'll pass the information on to the suspect's brother that he is currently being interviewed and will hopefully be bailed later. That will get him off my back for a while."

"The joys of rural Policing."

"You said it. Thanks again." He ended the call and then looked at his watched. The two PCSO's were just arriving. Suddenly his radio beeped.

"Sierra Oscar to 452."

"452."

"Sergeant. We have had reports of a body found in your area. We are not quite sure of the location, although we are using GPS to locate the caller. Can you attend?"

"Where did they say they were?"

"On a track which goes down to the forest where there is a bridge and a stream. It is near somewhere called Pont-y-Rhyl."

"I think I know it. Tell the unit to meet me at Pont-y-Rhyl village. I will go there now."

"Will do. Thank you 452." He clicked the radio as his two PCSO's pushed the door open. "Morning. Don't get too comfortable. We have reports of a body found over from the old Bridgend Road."

Janine started to look distraughtly worried. "I hope it's not that boy," she mentioned. "The poor parents were going out of their minds when I spoke to them."

"Well, it's not looking good," Llewellyn stated. "Let's get over there. Two minutes. In the panda."

Ten minutes later, the local team were sat at the small parking space in the centre of the Pont-y-Rhyl village, Sergeant Llewellyn in the driver's seat. He could see the blue lights heading down the Valley, lighting up the normal tranquil surroundings and which caused everyone along the way to wonder what was going on. Their sat navs brought them exactly to the village and the two units attending drove onto the gravel of the car park, skidding to a halt.

"Sergeant Llewellyn?"

"Yes, that's right," Michael exclaimed as he jumped out of the panda.

"PC Evans. This is WPC Baines. I believe that you have an idea where to take us? I can see someone waving to us up on top of the hill."

"Yes. Follow me. Luckily, I have the key to the gate." They all got back into their cars. The two central cars followed the panda containing Sergeant Llewellyn's team, turning the sharp left into the forestry car park as if they were doing a U-turn. The Sergeant jumped out whilst his engine was still running, undid the padlock and swung the green metal gate back around before getting back in his car and continuing the journey. They soon reached the top and were flagged down by Tracey Edwards who had run up to get the phone signal and call it in.

"Hello, Tracey," Llewellyn said as he lowered his window and recognised her from the local chip shop. "You reported a body? You had better jump in, girl," he said as he indicated for her to join Peter Lloyd in the back of the car.

Tracey did just that and was thankful that there were two people with him. Since Catrin and Rhian's deaths she was very weary of the Sergeant after what Catrin had mentioned although several times she had told herself that it may be nothing at all. "It's bloody terrible," she said. "You can't see who it is."

"Do you know if it is a boy or girl?" The Sergeant enquired as he sped off in the only one direction that they could go whilst looking at Janine Brockway beside him.

"I think it could be that missing boy," Janine exclaimed worriedly. "Look at it sensibly. That is the only missing person we have on our books."

"Well whoever it is has been attacked by a madman. Pieces of them all over the place in the stream," Tracey exclaimed.

Peter could tell that she was getting frantically distraught, shaking with the shock of seeing the corpse. He indicated for her to come closer for him to console her, which she did. "It's okay. It's okay," he said as she started crying out and the car sped down the long drive towards the bridge.

Sergeant Llewellyn noticed the three other ladies stood over by the gate at the bottom of the hill, waving to the Police cars, even though he himself knew exactly where the body would be. All three vehicles skidded to a halt on the gravelly path as he recognised all three of them who appeared to be in the same state as the one in his car. He got out and then opened the door for Tracey Edwards who had been sat directly behind him, not acknowledging her in any way but letting PCSO Lloyd continue looking after her. He then looked at the two Officers whom he had spoken to at Pont-y-Rhyl get out. "WPC Baines. Can you look after the four ladies? Start getting statements from them?"

"Yes, Serge," she replied as she walked over to the PSCO and the two of them led a terribly upset Tracey Edwards over to meet her other friends. They all appeared to be in a state of shock, were all huddled together, hands covering their faces as though they didn't want anyone seeing that they were crying and sobbing.

Nicola Stone shouted over to Sergeant Llewellyn and pointed her arm down to the stepping stones. "Down there!"

The Officers in the second Police car came running over. "WPC Rowlands, Serge."

"PC Nefydd."

"Welcome to hell," the Sergeant replied commandingly. "I think we need to get cordons set up. The tree felling lorries operate constantly in this area, and we get cyclist and hikers down here on a regular basis. So we will need something on all three entrances." Individually he pointed to the three road paths. "There, there, and there. Can I leave that to you?"

"Yes, Serge," Rowlands and Nefydd both answered at once.

"Janine!"

"Yes, Serge," the woman answered as she came running over.

"Can you assist these two Officers in setting up the cordon and then man one of them so each three are secure, please."

"Yes, Serge," she said as she turned around and joined the two, somewhat happy that she wasn't going to be involved in anything that would make her even more squeamish that she already was.

"PC Evans. You are with me." Llewellyn noticed the young PC nod at him as he walked over. "Down to see what we have, and then we will have to call it in."

"Serge."

They both slowly walked down the path towards the stream, Llewellyn taking the lead whilst watching his step just in case there was any evidence that the four woman hadn't seen when they innocently went down to the water. As they were in view of the stepping stones, the young PC Evans gasped and the Sergeant could tell that he hadn't handled anything quite as bad as this before, whereas he was used to it in many ways.

"Oh my God," PC Evans exclaimed as they moved closer again.

"Well I think we can say that there is no sign of life," the Sergeant said as he scanned the area to check that he hadn't left anything behind that he may have missed when he had committed the atrocity. "We need CID, SOCO and forensics as soon as possible. Use the radio. Doubt whether we will get a phone signal." He watched PC Evans move away from the edge of the water and walk up towards the top of the path. Llewellyn kept looking around. From inside his pocket he took out Billy Evan's wallet that he had stolen earlier, then threw it into the water beside the body. He knew that forensics would find it at least. His plan was coming into fruition. It was time to pass the blame, to make it look like he wasn't responsible for the murders but was investigating them.

PC Evans soon returned. "Serge, They are on their way. Sierra Oscar has informed them."

"Thank you young man. We are not going to disturb the crime scene any more than we have done already. Let's join the guys at the cordons and wait for backup."

"Yes, Serge."

It was over half an hour before the CID department turned up in force led by DCI Gwyn. DI Morgan Harris, DS Peter Ellis were in the lead car, whilst four other DC's filled up the car following them. They drove around the path that led downwards to the crime scene and initially were stopped at the cordon's but on Sergeant Llewellyn's instructions PC Nefydd lifted the tape as high as he could to let the two cars through. DS Ellis parked behind the panda that had been driven down by Uniform and DC Mitchell pulled up behind them.

"Sergeant Llewellyn. We meet again," DCI Gwyn exclaimed authoritatively as he walked over to him. "What do we have?"

"I think it is the missing boy. Not a pretty sight. Worse than the others, I can tell you that."

"Okay. We had better clear the area for forensics," Gwyn shouted to them all. "Stay on the cordons!" He looked at Morgan Harris. "We need a fingertip search. Anything that appears out of place."

Over the horizon there were more flashing lights and Morgan Harris looked up to the top of the drive where they themselves had driven in. "Forensics are here, Guv." He watched as a minute later the van pulled in where PC Evans had directed them.

The three forensics officers got out of the vehicle and opened the back and the side doors, instantly removing their equipment. "Where to?" Matt Robinson asked although he then saw DCI Gwyn standing next to Sergeant Llewellyn, the latter waving to him. "It's okay," he said as he headed towards the pair, closely followed by Stephen and Olivia.

"Matt," DCI Gwyn said as the SFO approached. "Another one for you."

"I'm definitely earning my money these days," Matt commented. "Down there I guess?" he asked as he watched the DCI nod his head. "Thanks. As usual, keep people away from the scene. I will need to know who has been down here in order that I can alleviate them from any tests that are completed."

"Of course," DCI Gwyn answered, knowing of the forensics Officer's procedures, and knowing how meticulous he was. Until he gave the all clear, it was always 'his crime scene'.

"By the way. If anything, if it is the same person as the one who killed the boy up at the football field, then chances are we are looking for someone who wears a size ten shoe."

"We will scan the area for fresh footprints," Gwyn answered whilst waving over to DS Ellis who was busy with some of the Uniformed Officers searching the ditches and hedgerows for potential evidence.

"Stephen. Can we get this covered up somehow. Protect it from any more of the elements that want to get at it, although

255

looking at the body, it has been in the water for some time," Matt ordered his junior.

"Yes, I'll try and make something up," he replied.

"Right. Olivia. You and I will take a look. Bring the kit."

DCI Gwyn walked over to Morgan Harris. "Well the good thing is the press can't get here. Well, I wouldn't put it past them to hover over in a helicopter as soon as they hear about it."

"You know them too well," DI Harris responded whilst agreeing with his boss. "It won't be long. But at least the gate is secured by Uniform, and the cordons are in place."

"Right. It's all a waiting game. As soon as we get confirmation that it is a child, one of us will have to visit the Chiswell's to tell them we have found a body."

FO Stephen Garwood had managed to erect a covering over the crime scene the best that he could considering that part of it was on land and part in water. He had drawn the short straw, thinking that it must be his day for getting all the shit jobs. He walked back to the van, closely watched by both senior Detectives, as though he were going to tell them something, but he walked right past them. He started to dress himself with waders as he had to get into the water itself, and then he headed back, again without saying anything to the DCI.

Gwyn and Harris listened hard and heard the slight splash of water, they guessed that Stephen had jumped in the three-foot deep cold water. They could only hear slight voices among the three. Two hours passed and Olivia emerged. The DCI saw his opportunity because he had a better working relationship with her than he did Stephen. "Any news, Olivia?"

She tilted her head, a slight look of horror on her face. "I'm just going back to the van now to get a body bag. We are going to try, and I mean try, to get the body out of the water in the least number of pieces that we can."

"That bad?"

She nodded back at him. "I'll see if Matt will let you see the corpse before we move it. I guess it was only seen face down in the water."

Gwyn nodded. "Yes. By the Sergeant over there. And of course the four witnesses who found it."

"Well I would say that compared to the others that this is a more frenzied attack, a bit like the attacker being wound up about something as the weapon was used. Either that or they were on something illegal." She looked at him, not knowing if she was going to get a reply. "Anyway. Got to get back. But standby."

Both Gwyn and Harris nodded their heads as they watched her go down to the makeshift covering. But it was only a minute before Olivia waved to them both. "Oh. Here we go," the DCI mentioned. He immediately led the way down towards the tent. Olivia passed them both suits and masks to wear. Once they had put them on, Gwyn led the way as Olivia pulled the 'door' aside. The body was cut into several pieces, with the arms only hanging on by what looked like ligaments, the legs by skin and some muscle. The head was smashed open, bodily organs showing throughout.

"Oh my dear God," DCI Gwyn said as he looked on. "Male or female, Matt?"

Matt Robinson shook his head. "I can only say Male because Stephen found a set of genitals further down the stream on a beach of rocks." He looked up at the DCI. "I have never seen anything so bad. Whoever did this has to be caught soon or later."

Suddenly Stephen Garwood, who was still looking for both body parts and evidence in the water and surrounding area, shouted out. "Matt! I have something!"

"Excuse me, gentlemen," he said as he disappeared out of the other side of the covering. Whilst he was outside, DCI Gwyn and DI Harris both reversed themselves out of the tent to get back on the path. Both looked at each other but said nothing. "Olivia. Evidence bag!" he called out to the younger FO.

"Hold on," she exclaimed as she reached into her kit bag and took one out, Then she passed it through the gap, listening as she heard something quite heavy dropping into the bag. She pulled the makeshift door back and was greeted by him as he had just got up off of his knees.

Matt went through the gap on the other side to see Gwyn and Harris. "Gentlemen," he said as he held up the evidence bag. "You might be interested in this. It's a wallet. Young Stephen found it jammed amongst the rocks on the bottom of the stream, exactly where some of the body was found."

DCI Gwyn started to get excited as he looked at Harris. "Is there anything in it?" he asked as he continued looking to and fro from Harris to the evidence bag and back.

"Everything. Bank cards. Driving license. Even a photograph. Unfortunately, any of the DNA would have probably been washed away depending on how long it has been in the water," Matt said whilst knowing that it could be a crucial piece of evidence in the case. "I can't let you have it until tests are done. But you are looking for someone called William Evans. Can't read the house number very well, but it is an address in Victoria Street, Pontycymer." He thumbed through the edge of the wallet in order that the DCI could see the driving license and more importantly the photo.

Both Detectives hesitated and looked at each other. "This can't be coincidence, Guv," Harris said whilst somewhat shocked that they may have a lead at last. "That's Billy Evans. The leader of the pack!"

"If this is our man, then the killer has been right in front of our eyes. Billy Evans. He organises the neighbourhood. He was the one arranging the searches for the boys who were found in the cemetery." Gwyn felt slightly sick inside, as shocked as Harris that they had something at last, although also thinking of the state of the latest victim. His thoughts went to the case of Ian Huntley some years ago who had murdered two young girls and yet acted innocent by joining in the searches.

"Closer to home than we thought," Harris exclaimed.

"Thanks for that, Matt." He was just about to continue when Matt Robinson cut him off.

"I know. As soon as possible."

"Well we may need the wallet for interview."

Matt nodded. "I'll make that a priority."

"Thanks," he replied as he started leading the way for DI Harris to follow him back up to where the cars were parked. "Okay, Morgan. Take Sergeant Llewellyn with you seeing as he knows everyone in the village. Arrest Billy Evans on suspicion of murder."

The DI smiled and since the start of the murders felt like they had made a step forward. He walked over towards Sergeant Llewellyn who was checking on all the cordons, although at the moment there appeared to be no one around. "Sergeant!" he called out importantly.

"Yes, Guv," Michael said as he turned around. What the DI didn't know was he was hanging around waiting for the moment that the evidence that he had planted was found. "Cordons are all secure."

"Never mind that. Tell me. How many William Evans are there in Victoria Street?"

He thought for a moment and counted his fingers on his left hand. "Three. Yes. Three. Why?"

"We have a lead. Wallet found at the crime scene. DCI wants you and I to arrest William Evans."

"Do we know which one? Do we have an address?"

"I've seen the photo. It is the community leader. Do you know the house?"

"Well, yes. He lives literally opposite me! Are you sure it is his wallet?"

"One hundred percent," the DI retorted. "We need to get him in for questioning. Check his alibi's for the date of each murder."

"I can't believe it. I mean I know the guy is a pain in the arse. But. The murderer?"

"Well, we will find out. You can drive. We will go in your panda. I will call for a van to transport him back to the nick."

Sergeant Llewellyn nodded his head with wide eyes and then without saying anymore headed over towards his Police car. His face filled with a psychotic smirk as he opened the door and sat in the driver's seat whilst waiting for the DI who at the moment in time was talking on the radio. The plan was so far working, he told himself.

*****

DI Harris, Sergeant Llewellyn, PC Powell, and PC Eastman had arrived at Billy Evans house in Victoria Street. Already there were neighbours outside of their front doors talking and when they saw the two Police cars arrive, their tongues were wagging even more as their topics of conversation changed instantly.

Harris banged on the door. At first there was no reply and so he repeated the bang only this time with more force that made it slightly louder. "Mr Evans! It's the Police!" He could hear movement inside.

"Alright, alright. Give me chance butt!" Billy exclaimed as he finally opened the door.

"Billy Evans?" the DI questioned although he recognised him from the photograph on the driving license and from the residents meeting and so knew he was right.

"Yes. That's me."

"William Evans I am arresting you on suspicion of murder. You do not have to say anything. But it may harm your defence if you do not mention when questioned something which you later rely on in court. Anything you do say may be given in evidence. Do you understand?" He then looked at PC Powell and ordered, "Cuff him!"

"Murder?" Billy exclaimed as he looked at Sergeant Llewellyn as if to say, *'This has got something to do with you!'*. "What murder?"

"Leave it for the interview, Sir," PC Powell exclaimed as he pulled Billy's arms behind his back and latched the handcuffs together before dragging him to the car.

"It's not me that you should be arresting," Billy shouted angrily as the PC pushed his head down to get him into the back of the van. "It's him!"

Chapter 20

Billy Evans had been in a cell for three hours before the duty solicitor finally showed up. He asked for the duty Solicitor mainly because he never had one of his own, he had never had the use for one in the past apart from when he purchased his home. He sat on the rather uncomfortable bed in the cell patiently waiting. But deep down inside he was steaming. Was this something to do with Llewellyn? Or the two reporters at The Avenue? In the meeting earlier that morning with Sergeant Llewellyn, many secrets had been exchanged, some on a rather desperate level. Yet Tony Newton and his colleague had so much on them as well. He had yet to find out.

The cell door opened. "Mr Evans?"

"Yes. That's me!" the big man exclaimed whilst not knowing who the man was that had just been let into the cell. He didn't know whether it was a Police Officer or the duty solicitor that was stood in front of him, but then guessed that it was the latter due to the case and the paperwork that he was carrying.

"David Boyle. I'm the duty Solicitor. Sorry I'm late. I've just picked up the disclosure from the investigating Officer." He sat down beside Billy on the bed.

"I don't even know why I have been arrested. On suspicion of murder? Who am I supposed to have murdered?"

"Right. It appears four hikers came across the body of what the Police think is a young male. Also found nearby was your wallet."

"It can't be. My wallet is on the hallway table at home." He suddenly started to think and put two and two together. Sergeant Llewellyn came across to tell him about his brother

Julian this morning after their heated conversation. The wallet was on the table from last night and that is where he last saw it. He hadn't been out since and hadn't had the need for it or the need to check that it was there. Suddenly it was found at a murder scene.

"So how do you think it got to the murder scene?"

"I went to the shop last night and used my card there. Then, as usual, I threw the keys and the wallet on the hallway table. Who is it I am supposed to have murdered in any case?"

"Well, they don't actually know at the moment," David replied as he continued to take notes. "The body was so badly mutilated that they cannot identify the victim."

"I am being set up here," Billy shouted angrily. "This morning I went over to see the community Police Officer who lives opposite me to see if he could get any information about my brother who was arrested yesterday. Ten minutes later he came over to me. That must have been when the wallet went missing. It's him. The Police Officer!"

"Okay. So why would he do that?"

"I don't know. I really don't." Billy shook his head innocently, even though inside he was thinking, *'I'm going to get you for this'*.

"Well listen. All they have is the wallet that could have been lost there at any time. They have no identification as to who the victim is. No DNA evidence at the moment. If what you are saying is true, they will not be able to link you to the scene of crime."

"They won't. Unless that bastard Llewellyn stole something else."

"We will face that if and when it is mentioned. I know that they have searched your home. There is nothing in the disclosure to say that they have found anything that would implicate you." The Solicitor continued with his notes. "I am recommending that you give a *'No-Comment'* interview throughout at this moment in time. Understood?"

Billy nodded. "Yes."

"Don't get angry at anything they say. Just no comment. Sit back and relax." He widened his eyes as if to clarify what he said. "Okay. I will go and tell them that we are ready for the interview."

The lights were quite bright in the interview room of Bridgend Police Headquarters. DI Harris has specifically requested DC Tello for the interview mainly because of his views on Sergeant Llewellyn being involved somehow and wanted Tello to question Billy Evans on this. Tello placed the two tapes into the machine, pressed record, and then turned to face the accused. He waited for the beep to stop signifying that the tape was now ready.

"Interview with William Evans. Also present are, please state your name for the tape," Harris said to the solicitor.

"David Boyle from Simey and Jones."

"Officers present are me, Detective Inspector Morgan Harris."

"Detective Constable Aled Tello."

"Interview commenced at 15:53 hrs. Billy, first of all I must caution you that you are being interviewed on suspicion of murder. You do not have to say anything. But it may harm your defence if you do not mention when questioned something which you later rely on in court. Anything you do say may be given in evidence. Do you understand?" DC Tello looked at the accused and there was no response.

DI Harris intervened. "Billy. It is okay if I call you Billy. I know that is what most of the village call you in the area where you live." He looked at the suspect but didn't get any response. "There have been quite a few murders in the Garw recently. We found a body today. Do you know anything about that?"

"No comment."

"We are currently searching your house, Billy. Will we find anything incriminating?" Tello enquired in what appeared to be quick-fire questions.

"No comment."

DI Harris looked as though he were the one playing the bad cop in a good-cop-bad-cop scenario. "Introducing item DC1, a wallet belonging to the defendant. Is this your wallet, Billy? I think it is. It contains your details, bank cards, driving license."

"No comment."

"It was found at the crime scene. Did you murder the boy?" Harris asked aggressively.

"No comment."

"Gentlemen," the solicitor perked up. "As far as I am concerned and according to the disclosure, you were unable to determine the sex of the deceased due to the state of the body. There were a set of genitals close by, but these weren't determined to have belonged to what was left of the corpse. Therefore I cannot see how you can ask my client if he murdered, may I quote, 'The boy'. Unless you have the forensic results back and wish to share them?" He looked at the two Officers who were staring at each other. "No. I didn't think so."

"What about the other murders Billy. Where is the weapon that you used?"

"No comment."

DC Tello hesitated which was a trick he had learned in his training and from his old DCI when he was an ADC. "Okay. You can tell us. Why teenagers Billy? Do you have a thing for children?"

Billy remembered what his solicitor had said. Don't get angry. They will try and make you get angry. He looked at them and smirked. "No comment."

"You smiled as I asked that question, Billy," Tello continued. "Did I hit the right note there?"

"No comment."

DI Harris uncrossed his arms and started taping his pen on the table hoping that it would annoy the suspect. "Did you have anyone else with you, Billy? I mean. Lifting a body is quite a hard task on your own."

"No comment."

"Are you hiding the other person's name Billy?" Tello added whilst looking directly into Billy's eyes to try and see if there was any body language fluctuation.

"No comment."

"Is it someone in authority, Billy?"

Billy paused and looked at DC Tello before very slowly answering "No comment."

DC Tello knew that he had hit the right note. "Why the pause, Billy? Is it someone that we know of already? Is he helping you murder children?"

"No comment," Billy snapped back almost immediately, realising the mistake he had made previously by answering slowly.

DI Harris took over the questions. "Brandon Edwards. His body was found on the football field a few days ago. Did you murder Brandon, Billy?"

"Gentlemen, gentlemen, gentlemen," the solicitor intervened sarcastically. "You know that you must keep the questioning within Section 24 of the Police and Criminal Evidence Act 1984. If you wish to interview my client about other murders then full disclosure of the other murders must be given prior to interview."

DI Harris and DC Tello knew that until the house search was complete and they had the full results back from Matt and his team at forensics, then it would be hard to proceed any further. Harris gave it one last try. "What size feet are you, Billy?"

"No comment."

"Gentlemen. I think you have ascertained by now that you have no real evidence. A wallet belonging to my client found at the scene which could have been lost anywhere in the stream and washed down to where it was found. You have come forward with nothing more. I have advised my client to give a 'no comment' interview throughout until such time that you have evidence. Is that understood?" He watched both Harris and Tello nod at each other.

"Interview terminated at 16:07." DC Tello reached over and stopped the tape.

"Right. We are going to put you back in your cell for a while," the DI exclaimed.

"My client is here, still innocent until proven guilty, and I demand that due to the lack of evidence that you release him with immediate effect." David Boyle stared at the two. "Put it this way, if you put him back in that cell I will request a meeting with Superintendent Saunders and make a complaint about your style of questioning and the fact that at the moment my client is innocent and should not be locked up with a hope that you can try and get more evidence. You have none."

"Okay, Mr Boyle. If you and your client would like to stay here," Harris said as he jumped up, pushing the chair back with the back of his legs, "I will arrange for Mr Evans to be released pending further investigation."

"Thank you." David looked at Billy and smiled, then watched the two Detectives leave the room.

"Hold on," Billy exclaimed quite desperately. "I will speak to you off the record."

Billy's solicitor quickly intervened. "Mr Evans, I wouldn't recommend that you say anymore, either on or off the record."

Billy continued without any reply. "Well?" He watched Harris and Tello look at each other and then DI Harris placed the case papers back on the desk.

"Go on," Harris said whilst wondering if this was just going to be a pack of lies to get them off track.

"It's not me you want to be chasing. I'm breaking the code here. But if it means saving my arse then so be it. Rumour is out that the man you want for everything is one of yours. Sergeant Michael Llewellyn."

"And you know this how?" Harris enquired, watching as Billy's solicitor stood shaking his head.

"Just word of mouth. Mouths are talking. I heard in the shop the other day that he keeps a journal. It is in his loft together with the weapons that he uses for the kills. Get that journal and the weapons and it will clear me. He stole my wallet this morning. He planted the evidence. I bet he was at the crime scene, wasn't he?" Harris and Tello looked at each other which more or less confirmed his question. "Yes. He was. He is your man. One of your own and he has been one step ahead of you all this time!"

"Thanks for that," Harris said as though he had heard enough and in any case, *'off the record'* meant that it didn't hold up in court and they couldn't ask the judge for a search warrant. They left the room.

Outside, DC Tello made sure the door was closed and then looked at his boss. "Guv. You know he just confirmed my suspicions."

Harris nodded. "The copper's nose. You have it at last. But in the wider picture I don't think that our Billy Evans is clean. There's something wrong. He is scared. Which is why he wanted to clear himself, *'Off the record'.*"

"So what's the next step?"

"We tail Billy Evans. If someone has set him up and he suspects who, he is going to react."

*****

266

Ryan Parry stood at the living room window and looked out over the mountain where the sunlight was lighting up the green trees and beaming down on the rock surface of the quarry.

"Tony, mate. There's something going on. There is a helicopter hovering over the top of the mountain, slightly on the other side."

Tony reached into his bag beside him at the end of the sofa and pulled out his binoculars. "Here," he said. "See if you can get a closer look." His boss grabbed them and then headed towards the front door.

"I'll go out the front," he said. Slowly, Tony followed him whilst holding onto his one crutch.

"Anything?"

"Well," Ryan said, pausing for a bit. "There is definitely some action. That helicopter is not Police or air ambulance or even mountain rescue." He looked through the lenses once more. "That is Sky News. There is something going on. In the next Valley."

"Let's get over there," Tony said as he reached up to the coat hook for his North Face jacket.

"What about your leg?"

"The story is more important. I'll suffer afterwards." Tony responded. "Grab your car keys."

Minutes later the two of them were heading down the Avenue towards the main road.

"How do we get over there?" Ryan enquired whilst wanting to know if he had to turn left or right.

"Well, if it is something and the Police are present, I guess the area will be cordoned off, So the answer to your question will be, with great difficulty. Right just after the supermarket and then follow the road." As they approached the turning off the Bridgend Road they both noticed that the entrance was chock-a-block with cars and television camera vans. The police were maintaining a cordon whilst the reporters were already there, the television cameras at the ready. Ryan and Tony had to park up on the road which along with other cars already parked there just left enough space for other cars and small vans to pass in single file. "I hope we aren't too late. Have you got your camera, Ryan?"

"Of course. I sleep with my camera!" They headed around the corner and joined the rest of the gutter press, realising they were just in time as a Police vehicle was coming down the stretch of gravel drive and then stopped at the gate.

DCI Gwyn was flanked by two Uniformed Officers as he approached the heavy gate which he stood back from and used it as the barrier between him and them. "Ladies and gentlemen." He knew that he would have to shout as the questions came thick and fast. The cameras were already clicking and the Television reporters giving their viewers presented news headlines.

'Has there been another murder?'
'Is it the body of the missing boy, Dylan Chiswell?'
'Do you have a suspect?'
'Why are the Police dragging their feet on this investigation?'
'Was the killer taken away in the Police car a few hours ago?'
'What is his name?'

"LADIES AND GENTLEMEN," Gwyn shouted loudly which surprised everyone there. He paused as he noticed the helicopter hovering above the trees of the forest to his left, looking briefly upwards and then back at the crowd of reporters. "A bit of hush please. I have a statement to make, after which there will be no questions answered due to the stage at which the investigation is at."

'Early this morning, Police were called to an area on the other side of Valley. An unidentifiable body was found in the water. The forensic team are removing the body and taking it back for further analysis. We will give a further, more detailed statement from Bridgend Police Headquarters once we have more. Thank you.'

As he started walking back to his Car, the two PC's assisted the Officer's at the cordon with keeping the crowd under control and even stopping some of the reporters trying to get around and under the gate to get to the DCI.

DC Mitchell watched his boss jump in the passenger seat and then asked, "Back to the station, Guv?"

"Yes, please. We need to see how far DI Harris has got with the suspect."

Mitchell honked his horn at the cordon for the PC's to open the barrier. It took some time, and the gutter press were all blocking the path of the car as it edged forward, camera's flashing and taking shots of the DCI, faces right up against the glass, questions still coming thick and fast. Mitchell continued to honk on the horn. He knew that he didn't want to knock anyone down but with some reporters more or less sitting on his bonnet, he would have no choice although it wouldn't be his fault. Finally they got through and headed to the right at the old Bridgend Road.

*****

DC Tello had grabbed the assistance of DC's Elfyn and Morris for the surveillance on Billy Evans, telling them to get dressed in civvies and meet him in the reception. He himself went to the locker room and quickly joined them in his scruffs. They were just in time as outside; Billy Evans was stood talking to his solicitor in what appeared to be a heated discussion on why Billy had disobeyed his advice with the *'off-the-record'* conversation.

"That's your man. Billy Evans. Lives in Victoria Street in Pontycymer. He is on suspicion of murder, but both the DI and I suspect him of something more."

"Why is he out if he is on suspicion of murder, Aled?" Eirlys Elfyn enquired knowing that usually suspected murderers are kept on remand.

"Let's just say he has a good solicitor, and we haven't got the evidence as yet. Looks like we interviewed too early. Hopefully, his time will come."

"So what do we need?" Iwan Morris asked whilst staring out at the suspect.

"DI Harris wants everything. Where he goes, who he meets. Usual stuff. What time he changes his underwear," he laughed jokingly as his two fellow DC's joined in with him.

"How many skid marks he has?" DC Morris added.

"Phew! You've always got to go one step too far!" DC Elfyn said with a smile and a chuckle as he looked at Morris.

"Keep me in the loop," Tello asked. "I have some business to attend to with the DI." They both nodded back at him.

"Right. He's off. Let's go," Elfyn exclaimed.

Back inside, DI Harris was thinking about Billy Evan's *'off the record'* statement and was wondering why he would say such a thing. Why pick on Sergeant Llewellyn who was a man with a meticulous record and several commendations under his belt? But Harris wanted something that he would be able to go back to the suspect and tell him that he was bullshitting. Even if it were true, he couldn't get a search warrant with just hearsay. Perhaps Sergeant Llewellyn would allow him in to search voluntarily? He was here in the station, Harris thought to himself. If he had nothing to hide and it was just down to some animosity between Billy Evans and himself then he had nothing to worry about. He went into the staff canteen where he knew the community copper was having a cup of tea. Harris grabbed one himself and then sat down opposite him.

"All done, Guv?"

"We have had to let him go. Lack of evidence at this stage."

Sergeant Llewellyn panicked inside knowing that Billy Evans would know that it was him that set him up. "No DNA?"

"Still being analysed. All we have is the wallet which, his solicitor said, could have washed down from anywhere."

"Pending investigation then?"

Harris nodded. "Yes. I need to ask you something just to be able to go back to Billy Evans and tell him to his face that he was lying."

"What's that?"

"He made an off the record statement accusing you. He says that you have a journal at home, together with the weapons that were used in the murders. Supposedly in your loft."

"Come on. He is trying to buy time!" Llewellyn responded whilst feeling angry inside and telling himself that he wished he had made Billy Evans one of his victims a long time ago. He also felt thankful that he had seen something like this coming. He chose to hide the box containing all the incriminating items in a place where no one would think of looking and any of his own clothes that had managed to get soiled under the black outfit he had burned. "I suppose you want to have a look at my place?"

"It would help us. Just so we could stick our two fingers up at Billy Evans and call him a liar. Wipe that smirk from his face. Although he has got the sort of face that you would like to smack."

Llewellyn laughed. "I agree with you there." He reached inside his trouser pocket. "Here. My keys. You go and search anywhere you like. I warn you now, I haven't changed a lot since Dad died in 1984. It's his furniture, an ancient as it can be, and the loft. Chock-a-block with both of my parents stuff so good luck with that."

"Don't want to lose the memories," Harris commented whilst trying to show his good side.

"Something like that. Let me know when you are going, and I'll follow you back in the panda and go in and do some paperwork at Pontycymer station."

"I'll just get Aled Tello and then we will go. Yes?"

"Sounds like a plan," the Sergeant replied although he was really thinking, 'Billy Evans. You are dead.'.

"Right. Stay there. I'll come and collect you."

"Great," Llewellyn answered as it didn't for one moment cross his mind that DI Harris actually suspected him of being involved. "I'll grab another cup of tea!"

DI Harris went back into CID office where DC Tello was busy typing away at his laptop putting in his notes for the day and ensuring records on the PNC were up to date. The junior Officer didn't see him.

"We are on, Aled. Get your coat."

"He agreed?" DC Tello enquired excitingly as he locked his screen and then took his coat from the back of his chair and put it on.

"Quite easily. Not a guilty concern whatsoever."

"That doesn't mean that he's not guilty. That just means the evidence is somewhere else."

Harris looked at him. "You have your teeth firmly inserted in this theory don't you?"

"It's just something nagging at me. I told you, Guv."

DI Harris nodded and then threw the car keys at him. "You can be my chauffeur."

*****

Billy Evans got on the number 72 bus at the Bridgend bus station. Individually and at different times DC's Elfyn and Morris also got on the same bus both sitting in different sections, Elfyn in the back seat and Morris two seats back from the suspect.

"Lee. I'm on my way to yours. We have another problem." Billy stated after taking out his mobile that originally had been seized but returned after the complaint from his solicitor.

"Okay, Bill. Where are you now?"

"Just left Bridgend on the bus. I'll explain later."

"No worries." Lee ended the call.

DC Morris started writing a text.

Morris: *'Did you hear that? He is going to someone called Lee's'.*

Elfyn: *'Yes. I'll see if I can find out who it is.'*

DC Elfyn was hoping that DC Tello could shed some light on the name Lee. He text the fellow Officer who at the time was driving in the same direction as the bus.

Elfyn: *'We are on the bus heading towards Pontycymer. Evans has just called someone called Lee and said he is going there first. Any ideas?'*

DC Tello heard the text sound on his phone and realised that it could be important. "Guv. Can you check that message for me? It may be one of the two that are tailing Billy Evans."

DI Harris looked at the notification on the screen. Realising that he couldn't reply on Tello's phone due to it being locked and Tello currently driving, he took out his own phone and decided to answer.

Harris: *'Lee Jones. Evan's best friend and partner-in-crime.'*

272

Elfyn: '*Thanks Guv.*'

It was over half an hour before the bus arrived at Nanthir Road and Billy jumped off the bus acknowledging the driver as he did so. DC Morris got off just behind him leaving DC Elfyn on the bus to get off at the next stop around the corner outside of the shop. Morris headed up Pretoria Street towards James Road whilst keeping a close eye on Billy Evans who walked up past the William Trigg centre and then tapped on a door not far in from the junction.

Harris: *He's gone into the third house from the main road.*

Elfyn: *I'm on my way back down. Look out for me.*

Lee Jones had opened the door and let Billy inside. He was still fuming from the arrest but now he was sure that someone was following him, although at this precise moment in time he was probably just feeling paranoid what with all that had happened.

"So what's up, Bill?" Lee enquired as he could see that the big man was nervous.

Billy went over to Lee's living room window and looked out. He was unsure about the two strangers on the bus whom he had never seen before. "I'm sure there was someone following me."

"Where?" Lee asked as he watched Billy step away from the window but then walked over himself less diplomatically opening the blind to look out. "Can't see anyone mate," he said as he dropped the blind back down. "So what's up?"

"I've just got back from the Police Station."

"Julian?"

"No. I was arrested on suspicion of murder," Billy exclaimed angrily.

"What? For the Christopher Fallon thing forty years ago? Has his Grandson given the Police the tape?"

"No, no, no," Billy replied shaking his head at his friend. "This morning Sergeant Llewellyn came across to my house to tell me what he had found out about Julian. Whilst he was there,

273

we had some heated words. I didn't know it, but my wallet disappeared."

"He took it?"

Billy nodded. "I dumped it on the table as usual last night. This morning it was found at the crime scene. I think that they found the young boy that is missing. I told the Police off the record about Llewellyn. The journal and the murder weapons in his loft. The wallet."

"How the hell did the wallet get there?"

"Our community Policeman was the first Officer on the scene, that's how it got there." Billy was biting his lip angrily and looking as though he was gunning for someone, in this case Sergeant Llewellyn. "He is out to get me. He is up to something. I have a feeling that he is going to squeal along with that damn Fallon guy. I will go down. Which means you will go down. Which means everyone will go down!"

"Hold on, mate! We agreed if one were caught then the silence would continue, no matter what. What are you saying now?"

"I meant that you are also on the video recording when we burgled the Fallon house. We both admitted to it. They will look at your guilt as much as mine."

"Fucking hell. I can't go to prison, Bill. I'm fucking sixty-two years old."

"You are not the only one," Billy replied seriously, his face filled with just as much worry as his friend. "We need to tell the others. We need to get rid of anyone that may drop us in it. Our Sergeant Llewellyn first. He has got to go!"

"How? Surely if we kill him then the suspicion will automatically come on you because you have told the Police it was him."

"Not if we are careful and give each other alibi's. That is why we need the six of us."

Lee nodded. He could see the sense in the madness. "I'll give them a call. Get them here."

"It is the only way."

Chapter 21

Tony Fallon and Ryan Parry had returned to report on the latest killing, even though they couldn't get close to the scene, they could get a headline in the paper and link it to the other murders in the Garw. Tony looked at all the papers all over the table and floor. Luckily, he had kept everything in the boot of his car and therefore the burglary hadn't meant that Billy Evans and Lee Jones had seen anything. He placed corresponding potential evidence on top of the right potential links.

"I think that we should follow Billy Evans again."

"So the two of us can get run off the road?" Ryan enquired as he looked at his junior.

"It's all part of the game. He was involved somehow, we know that. We know that he and that Lee killed my Grandfather. He burgled me. Just what else is the man capable of?"

"Hold on," Ryan exclaimed as he picked up one of Tony's organised 'piles'. "What was that community Sergeant's name?"

"Sergeant Michael Llewellyn. Why?"

"I'm looking at the hard copies that you printed off from the mesh for the times of your Grandfather's murder. The community Police Officer back then. I'm sure that he had the same surname. Llewellyn."

"There are loads of people with that surname in the Valleys," Tony exclaimed. "Have we got anything else to link him?"

Ryan shuffled some more papers, then opened up some pages on his laptop. Typed in the search on Google. "Here it is. Police Constable Dafydd Llewellyn in the Glamorgan Gazette obituaries for 1984. Husband of Gwyneth and Father of Michael aged twelve." He turned the laptop around for Tony to see. "Look. The community Police Officer in 1982 is the Father of today's community Sergeant!"

"Shit! So as well as Billy Evans and Lee Jones being our suspects, there could be another one?"

"Michael Llewellyn would have only been about ten years old back then. So I guess not. I think we need to stir things up a bit though. Give our Sergeant Llewellyn a copy of the video tape containing the burglary complete with audio. See what he does."

"Are you thinking what I am thinking? If the father were involved in the murders, including the murder of my Grandfather in 1982, could the son now be avenging his death with the help of Billy and the gang who were also involved at the time?"

"It's a theory. And it has substance," Ryan added with a surprised look on his face. "Where was that business card that Sergeant Llewellyn gave you? I'll give it a call; say we have something important for him from the camera footage on that day. Meanwhile, you burn off a copy for him to take away."

Tony saw the plan. He also saw the story of a lifetime that Vicky Newton had requested. He looked in his bag for a USB stick, pulling another corporate one advertising his newspaper from the side. Quickly he plugged it into the USB slot on the side and started the copy.

"Hello. Sergeant Llewellyn? It's Ryan Parry up at number 66 the Avenue."

The Officer recognised the voice. "Hello, Sir. How can I help?"

"I was wondering if there is any chance that you could come up? We have something for you that was on the CCTV camera on the night of the burglary. You might want to take a look and give it to your manager."

The Sergeant knew exactly what he was talking about. Billy Evans had already told him about the CCTV that would bury him if it became public. He smiled. Something else to bury the big man with. Firstly the wallet and now the CCTV. "I'm not far actually. I'll call in on my way back from the station."

"That would be great. You should get a promotion with this," Ryan exclaimed, trying to impress the man and gee him up that he would be the responsible Officer for putting Billy Evans away.

"That good eh? I'll see you in five minutes or so."

*****

DI Harris and DC Tello had searched high and low, not only in the loft of Llewellyn's house but also the other rooms. There was nothing. Not even a piece of paper that would implicate him in anything. Harris knew that would probably be the case, but the junior Officer was somewhat disappointed.

"Either Billy Evans is lying through his teeth to buy time, or as is usually the case, the stuff that has been mentioned is elsewhere. A lock up. Ot the boot of a car."

"Or it could be that I was just wrong," Aled Tello said shaking his head and looking at the DI.

"I don't think you are wrong, lad," the DI replied reassuringly and meaning what he was actually saying. "The guy is too smug not to be bent in some way. Even if it is murder." He gave the place one last look around. "We had better phone our fellow Officer and tell him that he can have his house back."

DC Tello nodded.

*****

One by one, the four other men who participated in the execution of Christopher Fallon arrived at Lee Jone's Home. The two Detectives who had been assigned to follow Billy Evans became alert as four cars arrived and parked in the street filling all the available spaces. They had positioned themselves on the opposite side of the road looking through an archway that led to a grassed area from the main road. This time DC Morris decided to call the DI.

"Iwan. Tell me you have caught him and extracted a confession!" the DI joked before laughing.

"If only, Guv. No. Lee Jones has had four more visitors. I'm thinking they are the same four that added up to the six that that guy up in the Avenue mentioned when he was run off the road," Morris replied.

"If you get the chance, use your mobile to take photos."

277

"Yes, Guv. Something is going down. It's like a gangland meeting."

"Just keep your eyes on them. Stay with Evans at all times if you have to choose."

"We don't have transport, Guv. We followed him on the bus."

"Okay. Aled and I have just finished our search of Sergeant Llewellyn's home. We are not far. We will park on the hill. Let me look at the map. Pretoria Street."

"That's affirmative. Good location."

"Five minutes." The DI ended the call.

DC Morris turned to his colleague. "DI Harris and DC Tello are coming to back us up."

DC Elfyn nodded. "I guess we stay back and do not pursue the others. I heard him say just Evans."

"He is the main target I suppose. As soon as forensics become available they will probably re-arrest him. But out he is a flight risk."

"I don't think that will happen. He is a Valley's man through and through. He has probably never been past Cardiff." Elfyn looked right over at the house where they were all congregated. "God, I wish there was somewhere around here to get a cup of tea."

"Just think of your bladder," Morris replied back.

"I am," his partner retorted as he patted his stomach. "At the moment it's empty. Nothing since breakfast."

*****

The six men all gathered in Lee Jones house, some made themselves at home and instantly sat down either on the sofa or on the dining chairs. Ron Howells and Trefor Idle chose to remain standing whilst hoping that they didn't have to be there long.

"What's this all about, Billy?" Robert Gabriel enquired with a serious look on his face. "Twice in one week? The order to never have contact again has gone out of the window."

"We have problems," Billy replied whilst looking at each in turn. "Julian here has been arrested and charged with the

278

attempted murder of Tony Newton after we chased him a few days ago. He is on bail."

"What evidence do they have?" Ron asked, hoping that the evidence didn't actually include any of the other five, in particular him.

Julian intercepted. "Rear cam footage showing both me and the number plate on my car very clearly. The Detective has said I will be going down for this. So I'm making the most of being on bail."

"One down," Trefor commented much to the dismay of those around. "Well. In my opinion at this rate we will all be going down soon. You don't know if someone is watching us."

Billy went to the window and looked out once more whilst still showing signs of his paranoia. "The other problem. I was arrested today on suspicion of murder."

"What the hell are you doing out of a cell then?" Robert enquired seriously, wondering just how he got away with not being on remand.

"Thanks for the concern, Rob," Billy snapped. "There was no evidence. Just hearsay."

"Who from?" Trefor enquired.

"Our friendly neighbourhood Police Officer here in the Garw."

"What Llewellyn?" Trefor continued nastily. "Why the hell has he done that?"

"He also stole my wallet and planted it at the crime scene," Billy snapped, shaking his head at the same time, and feeling himself getting angry. He stared ahead, but his attention was taken away as his mobile telephone rang. "Hold on. Withheld number. I wonder who this is." He pressed the answer button. "Hello."

"Hello Billy," the voice said psychotically.

"You. You're plan didn't work you fucking wanker!"

"No. But this one may," Llewellyn stated with the intention of keeping his phone call short. "Check your messages." The line went dead.

Billy fumbled with the buttons on his phone and then saw there was an attachment to the message. He opened it and played the video. It was the same video that Tony Newton had given him. Only this time it had the sound on. His phone beeped once more.

Withheld: *'Quite a performance. Breaking and entering. Then admission to murder.'*

He couldn't reply. Withheld number, Billy threw his phone onto the ground in anger and screamed, "Arrrgghhh! That fucking man has to go! He is going to destroy me. Destroy you! He knows too much!"

Ron Howells picked up the phone and replayed the video that was still on the open screen. "What's this?" he enquired as he started becoming more and more worried. "What have you two done?" He looked at Billy and Lee in turn.

"We broke into that Tony Newton's home to try and get more information. We found out he is possibly the Grandson of the man we murdered in 1982, Christopher Fallon. Newton is not his real name. He shares his real name with Christopher Fallon."

"What the hell is he doing around here then?" Trefor asked sharply whilst just like Ron showing concern and worry on his face.

"He is a reporter. There is a guy with him who we think is also a reporter."

"Fucking hell," Trefor shook his head and unfolded his arms. "I'm outta here!" He went to head towards the door.

Billy stopped him by standing in front of the internal door that led to the hallway. "We have to end this. Now. There are three people that can destroy us and probably have us all put in prison for life. Even more."

"What are you suggesting, Bill?" his brother Julian asked.

"What I am saying Bruv is, if there are no witnesses, then chances are that you will get a lighter sentence. Or the DPS will not proceed with the case and so you may not get anything at all." He watched his brother nod. "The rest of you are all accessories to the murder forty years ago and the attempted murder of Tony Fallon last week." Billy again stared at each one of the gang individually. "We are all in this together. We all started it. We must all finish it."

"What the hell is Sergeant Llewellyn up to?" Julian enquired. "Why doesn't he just take the video to his boss?"

"Because I have something on him, although CID do not believe me. I have told them there is a journal and weapons in his loft," Billy exclaimed whilst changing his worried tone to one of part-satisfaction.

"Journal? Weapons? What do you have on him?" Trefor asked inquisitively, a forehead filled with wrinkles from a mixture of his age and the worry.

"We killed the wrong man forty years ago as we know. The murders continued for two years. Until the death of PC Dafydd Llewellyn!"

"God!" Robert snapped in amazement.

"Are you saying what I think you are saying?" Ron asked as he looked at Billy nodding his head silently.

"Dafydd Llewellyn was the one committing the murders of all those kids?" Trefor continued. "Well we missed that one, didn't we."

"There is more," Billy said with a psychotic smile. "I found out that our Sergeant Michael Llewellyn is the one committing the atrocities now. He is following in his Father's footsteps."

"Why haven't the Police arrested him?" Ron snapped as he banged his fist on the table. "And he has the fucking cheek to set you up and send you that video."

"I have no evidence. Unless they find the weapons and journal if and when they search his house. He is setting me up for the murders that he has committed."

Julian grabbed his coat that he had previously taken off and hung on the back of a dining room chair. "Let's get it right this time. Let's kill the right man. Who is coming?"

"Where?" Ron enquired.

"Yes, where?" Trefor also wanted to know.

"To put an end to our problems and the end to the murders in the Garw. Llewellyn has to go!"

They all agreed and started to move towards the front door.

*****

281

Across the road, DC's Elfyn and Morris were just about to run across to the DI's car when they stopped, noticing all six men leaving the house and arranging to go in just two of the cars instead of individually.

DC Elfyn speed dialled the DI. "Guv. There's movement. Six men leaving Lee Jones' house. In two cars."

"Okay," Harris exclaimed. "Take down the registration numbers and the type of cars being used. Then get over to us."

"Guv."

"They have gone, Eirlys. Driven down in the direction of Pontycymer."

"Right. Let's go." The two of them started to run across the road to Pretoria Street where the DI was parked. They noticed that Aled Tello had already started the engine ready for when they got there. Each Detective jumped in the back seats.

"Strap yourselves in," Harris exclaimed even though DC Tello had already started moving and turned left onto the main road.

"Something is going down, Guv," DC Morris stated worryingly. "It's all blowing up."

"We may need back up at some point. But I don't want to rely on the local Police," Harris said whilst giving DC Tello a bit of a sly look. "Right now, let's see where they have all gone."

*****

They used Ron Howells and Lee Jones cars. Billy was sat in the front seat of the latter, and it didn't take them long to reach the front of Michael Llewellyn's house in Victoria Street. Billy jumped out.

"Park around the back, Lee. Out of sight. I'm sure that the Police are around."

"Okay," Lee replied quickly as Billy closed the door. He immediately sped off and turned right opposite the Bryn Stores in towards the industrial units. He thought that the best place would be directly at the rear of the Sergeant's house in case he escaped from the back garden.

Billy walked across the road and started banging angrily on Llewellyn's door. "Open up you fucking wanker. You set me up! You are fucking dead!"

*****

Tony Fallon and Ryan Parry had decided to stake out Billy Evans once more. Just in case they needed a vehicle, Ryan drove down and parked in the car park outside of the plastics factory at the rear of Victoria Street. They both got out, Tony deciding that it was too late to hide the fact that they were following the big man. He knew. He knew who they were.

"I can hear someone screaming," Ryan exclaimed as they cautiously walked along the main road towards the shop.

"Yes," Tony replied whilst nodding his head towards the action. "There. It's our man! Come on." He went out in full view of Billy who in between shouts to the Police Officer, saw them both.

"You! You two! You are fucking next! What have you done? Given that video to the cops? Arrghhhh!" he screamed out and banged the door angrily with his fist as he looked up above him before turning back and kicking Michael Llewellyn's front door. He pointed at the pair.

"I think we have upset him," Ryan said jokingly.

"What makes you think that?"

*****

The unmarked Police vehicle arrived at the start of Victoria Street. DI Harris instantly noticed the suspect Billy Evans stood in front of Sergeant Llewellyn's house whilst looking to his left and shouting abuse at someone.

"Park up," Harris said to Tello. "Car park over there on the right."

DC Tello turned without even slowing up to do so and skidded to a halt on the gravel just near where Ryan and Tony had parked. The DI rushed out of the car and headed up the street back towards Billy Evans. Then he saw the two reporters stood taunting the big man.

"Stay where you are!" the DI shouted. "Hands where I can see them!" He rushed over to both men closely followed by Elfyn and Morris who had followed him. "Who are you? ID. Now."

Both Ryan Perry and Tony Fallon pulled out their 'Press' cards and handed them to the DI. "I'm Anthony Fallon. I'm an investigative reporter, as you can see. I work for the Sun."

"Ryan Parry. Assistant Editor of the Sun."

"What the hell are you doing here, gentlemen?"

"The same as you by the looks of it," Tony responded as he nodded and pointed down the street at Billy. "Mr Billy Evans. Has Sergeant Llewellyn passed you the video yet?"

"What video?" Harris questioned as he nodded towards the two DC's behind them to release their grip on the pair.

"I'll take that as a no, then," Ryan exclaimed seriously. "Let's just say that it gives you the evidence that you have been grasping for on Billy Evans!"

*****

The big man's mobile rang. Billy knew that at any moment he would be apprehended by the Officers and so answered the call.

"Hello, Billy," the voice said. "You can stop knocking on my door. I'm not there."

"Llewellyn. Where the fuck are you? I'm going to cut you up into little pieces for what you did!"

"You had better tell your goons to get up the mountain. Tell them I will wave to them whilst sitting on the bench by the flag. You see, I have what the Police were looking for. The journal that you so nicely told DI Harris about. The weapons that I used. You didn't think that I would be stupid enough to keep them in the house, did you?"

"Fuck off!" Billy ended the call and looked down the road to see where the Police were. He had time. He quickly dialled Lee Jones. It was answered almost immediately.

"Bill?"

"I have trouble. The Police are approaching. The fucker is up the mountain, by the flag. Save your arses, Lee. Get rid of him!" He ended the call as Harris, Tello, Elfyn and Morris all approached him.

284

"Mr Evans. We meet again. Need to speak to Sergeant Llewellyn do we?" Harris enquired whilst more of less guessing why, after what Billy had told him *'off-the-record' back* at the station.

"No one does this to Billy Evans and gets away with it! I want a word with him!"

DC Tello looked at his boss. "Of course Guv it could be seen as interfering with witnesses, especially after what the two reporters have just told us."

"Llewellyn is the killer!"

"We need proof, Billy!

"He is up there on top of the mountain. He has all the evidence that you need! The journal! The pickaxe! The knife!" Billy was getting frustrated.

"If I were you, Mr Evans, I would go home. It's not far," Harris said as he nodded towards the other side of the road.

"Hold on, Guv," DC Tello said enquiringly as he looked at Billy with a frown on his face. "Where are the other five of your friends, Billy?"

"No fucking comment!" Billy bellowed in the same style that he had given at his Police interview.

Aled Tello looked to the right side to try and see if he could look at any part of the mountain and then looked at Harris. "Guv. I've got a funny feeling!"

"Call for back up! We will need an ARV as well. If there are weapons, SO19 will need to intervene."

"Yes, Guv. I'll arrange it. I'll also let the DCI and the rest of the team know. We may need them here."

Harris looked at DC Tello. "Ask DS Ellis to attend as well. We need everything that we can throw at this one. It's time we got a result."

"Guv."

*****

The five men, all in their sixties were finding it hard to ascend the rocky path in the direction of the top of the mountain. The early evening was coming in fast, the mist descending onto the tops of the tall trees and starting to hide any signs of the wind turbines which, on a clear day, stood as tall and proud as the green pines.

"Doesn't fucking Billy know how old we are?" Ron snapped as he stopped and held on to the fence post for what seemed like the tenth time. He looked up and saw that they weren't even half way up. But they could no longer see the Sergeant.

"I can't see Llewellyn anymore," Robert exclaimed as he stopped. He was the leader of the pack and was rushing up more than the rest because he felt that he had a lot more to lose than the others. His freedom for one. But he also had several convictions which carried suspended sentences.

Julian looked down towards the lake. "Looks like the Police are organising themselves to make the journey up here as well."

"They will probably use the helicopter," Trefor said as he stood beside Billy's brother and joined him in looking down towards the Pontycymer lake.

"Let's get moving then," Julian said as he turned and started walking again.

*****

Billy Evans had made it look like he had taken DI Harris's advice and started to cross the road where he climbed the steps, opened his front door, and disappeared inside. He knew that he had to get up there with the rest of them. He needed to take his revenge out. It was eating him up inside. No one betrays Billy Evans. He had an idea. He looked outside of his front window whilst hiding behind the net curtains. The crime scene where the latest body was found. Would it now be clear? Had they secured the gate at the junction of Bridgend Road? He could drive up around the gravel paths and get as close as he could. He headed out his back door so he wouldn't be seen and turned left out the back in the lane, then left again and down towards the convenience store. He noticed a lot of the neighbours stood outside all looking down the street towards the commotion that he had caused. Quickly he crossed the road, hoping not to be seen. He walked around the back of the houses and looked for the two cars that they had all arrived in.

As he approached he looked inside each of the driver's side windows. "Thank you very much, Lee!" he said to himself as he realised that his mate had left the keys in the ignition. He jumped in, started the car, and then exited into Victoria Street in the direction of the Co-op. He took the immediate turning after the store and then put his foot down heading into Bridgend Road. He knew that he was taking a risk but also acting on a hunch. Minutes later he turned right onto the start of the gravel path. The Police Cordon staff had gone. The *'Police – Do Not Enter'* tape was still stretched across the entrance, but the gate was open. He sped up and snapped the tape. The gravel was flicking as he wheel spun at every turn. He knew the way. He knew every path. He'd lived there all of his life and seen the development. The changes. It wouldn't take him that long.

*****

The five men were nearly at the top. Julian and Trefor continued to look down at the action near the lake. It looked like there had been reinforcements as mass of blue and black looked like it was making a lake of its own.

"Has anyone seen sight of Llewellyn recently?" Rob asked.

"Nothing," Ron exclaimed. "Personally, I think that we should have all stayed at home and let Billy Evans do his own dirty work. I mean, where the fuck is he now?"

"Yeh," Trefor added. "Looks like we are going to get in the shit for misdemeanours for which he is majorly responsible."

Julian shook his head. "Just remember he is trying to save your skins as well. Accessory to murder still carries a life sentence."

"Hold on," Lee jumped in, holding up his finger as if to silence the four others.

"What is it?" Julian whispered to his ear whilst standing beside him.

"I thought I heard branches breaking." He looked to his left and saw a smaller path heading through the overgrown woodland. "Ron. You and I check this way. The rest of you get up and check around the top."

"Okay," Julian said in agreement. "Keep in contact. Mobiles on silent because we want to surprise this bastard." He watched the two disappear cautiously into the overgrown path and then directed the other two who were left, up the last incline to the flag.

*****

DI Harris was assembling the search party at the bottom of the hill, not wanting to authorise any Officer to go up until SO19 were present because of the possibility of weapons. He also held on to DC Tello's theory about the involvement of Police Sergeant Llewellyn. Where was the Sergeant now? Surely he would have heard all the shouts over the radio network. Just what was he dealing with? Decades of conspiracy? And just how deep did the conspiracy go? He and many Officers before him had heard the term, *'What happens in the village stays in the village'* so many times. He was hoping that by getting Billy Evans out of the picture a lot more people would come forward, although by doing so they may implicate themselves.

The press had once again started to gather even though the Uniformed Officers had already set up the cordons at some distance. He had let Ryan Parry and Tony Fallon come inside the cordon although they had to sit on the bench at the bottom of the eighty-one steps just to observe. But he needed to know more about the video that they had passed to Sergeant Llewellyn, so whilst waiting for SO19 he walked over towards them.

"DI Harris," Ryan said as he saw him approaching. "Any news yet?"

"Keep this between us. But no. I have asked for an armed response vehicle and won't let anyone up the hillside until they arrive."

"Good idea," Tony said. "I have faced their wrath and know how it feels."

"Yes, so I have seen," the Inspector said sympathetically. "Listen. I need to know more about the contents of that CCTV video." DC Tello suddenly appeared beside them.

"You mean the one that Sergeant Llewellyn hasn't given you?" Tony said worryingly as he shook his head. "Of course he may have just not had the time yet."

"So what was on it?" DC Tello enquired whilst hoping that it was something that perhaps confirmed his theory.

"It was the burglary at my house," Tony said as he looked to the lake and smiled. "On the way out, Billy Evans and Lee Jones admitted to the murder of my Grandfather forty years ago."

DI Harris and DC Tello looked at each other in disbelief.

Chapter 22

The valley was now covered in a veil of ghostly-white mist. All around it was eerily silent as Lee and Ron carefully edged their way forward through the trees. The ghostly denseness wrapped the mountain up so no one could see. The mist was there, an age-old enemy to both nature and the human race. Further into the trees the mist was spook grey. It was lifeless and motherless. Elements of the mist drooped down to the Pontycymer lake and grasped at the calm water enclosing the shrubs around it. On this early evening, the mist was there to kill rather than to comfort. The two men looked left and right, listening to every piece of silence and every fleck of noise. Branches creaking in the slight wind and the echoes brushing through the gaps of the pine needles. The trees that both men were walking through were veiled in the densest of mists, their trunks sombre brown. Both men looked forward and then to each side of the small path, eyes travelling to the edge of the woodland as they become silhouettes against a blanket of white. It was only daylight where they stood but outside of the forest the night time air was dropping. The moon was just hours away and ready to encircle them with twilight. Suddenly there was an unusual crack as though someone or something had stood on a piece of deadwood.

"Did you hear that?" Ron whispered to his friend who was leading the two.

Lee nodded his head but did not say anything. The mist was making him feel that little bit nervous and scared. Neither man could see hand in front of face. "It has just suddenly got cold," he whispered back to Ron.

"There it is again," Ron said worryingly. "There is someone here." He didn't stand a chance. The pickaxe was thrust sideways into his head as it propelled in just above the right ear. There was a loud 'crunch' as it pierced the bone and the body instantly fell sideways, laying in the half-light, utterly still, eyes open as if admiring the heavens. The assailant disappeared back into the dense trees.

Lee Jones screamed as he turned around to find out what had caused the noise, a cursory glance being enough to know that Ron was dead. His lips blue, skin grey, eyes dull with exploded pupils, he is as lifeless as the pre-autumn leaves that gust around him, though they at least get one last dance amongst the mist. But then Lee panicked and started to cry out, became hysterically frantic, wanted to run but didn't know in which direction. Forward, he told himself. RUN! He didn't last long. From the front the bloody pickaxe was thrust blade first into his face, which seemed to explode on impact and his body joined the deadwood on the ground. The mist had claimed its first two victims of the day. The dark figure had to finish his kills. He hacked away at the torso's, the blood of the victims spraying all over nature. The dark figure then escaped through the trees.

Julian, Rob and Trefor finally reached the flag and the bench which Rob felt obliged to sit on and rest. Whilst Rob looked out over the Valley and took in its beauty, the other two looked around to see if they could try and find Michael Llewellyn. Rob briefly noticed something to his right.

"Hey," he said almost silently to his two friends as he nodded his head over to the grove of trees. "There!"

Julian and Trefor both looked sideways, not bothering to hide the fact that they had seen the man that they were looking for. "He is taking the piss!" Julian exclaimed angrily. "We had better tell the other two that we have spotted him. Quick Trefor. Call Lee."

Trefor played with his mobile and then listened in to the dialling tone. "No answer," he said. "It's going straight to voicemail."

"Try Ron. Lee might have his phone on silent."

"Same. It rings but then goes to voicemail."

Julian knew that he had to make a decision. They had to do away with the one man that could destroy them. "Right let's go. We know where he is hiding." But then he stopped. His mobile was ringing. "Billy. Where are you?"

"I'm on my way up to join you."

"We have found him. He is taunting us."

"Where?" Billy enquired, his face getting red with anger, and starting to trap his soul in bitterness. He knew that until Llewellyn was dead, he could not move on. The moving on would be his rebirth.

"The forest looking in the Bridgend direction from the burnt-out car on the top."

"Okay. I'll find you."

As the phone call ended, the three started running as fast as their old legs would take them, Julian telling himself that when the body and brain both are on overload and running is the only chance to survive, you run. Their survival depended on getting to Michael Llewellyn as fast as they could. As they got closer, Julian realised that the man wasn't afraid. He was taunting them. At first Julian didn't feel fear of the one man who didn't appear to fear his pursuers, but then he realised that fear is shackles, fear is a knife in the gut slowly twisted, fear is a constant hammer on the head. Yet fear also evaporates like the mist that was engulfing the trees and forest that they were about to run into in order to chase the man that felt no fear.

They reached a fence at the edge of the large grove of trees, each leading on either side of the muddy, rocky path that had burned shrubbery on the right and a dense forest further on both sides. Cautiously the three edged forward, looking left and right just in case the man jumped out at them. Rob noticed a path that went into the burned section of the small pine trees and silently with his fingers he indicated that he was going that way to look. Julian did the same hand signals to tell him that they would continue forward. They walked on slowly, both taking their ballistic knives out from their sheaths ready to attack if the need was there.

Robert Gabriel heard the crack of footsteps on branches to his left. That was the last thing that he heard. The pickaxe swung in instantaneously and struck him in the side of the head, the blood spurting, although not in a constant flow, but in time with the beating of Rob's heart. At first it came thick and strong, flowing down his dead body which was falling to the ground and through his fingers as the last thing that he did was clasp the ripped flesh and crushed skull. The lifeforce left him. The dark figure stood over him admiring his kill and smiling under his blackened costume of death. He completed his ritual of ripping the torso apart and then moved away, looking back at the body which was being engulfed by the deadly mist that had made the kill look almost invisible.

Julian and Trefor edged on. They had lost sight of Michael Llewellyn but knew that he couldn't get that far ahead and in any case, he was looking for them as much as they were looking for him. Julian began to wonder if they were the hunters or were they being hunted? He decided to try Lee's mobile once more to see if they had seen the Police Officer.

"Trefor. Keep watch," he whispered as he put the phone to his ear. "Trying to get hold of Lee." He watched Trefor nod as his mobile connected and started to ring at the other end. Nothing. After a series of rings it went to voicemail once again. He tried Ron once more and the same happened. Then he looked around to see if Rob had finished his search and then speed dialled him. The same. It rang and went straight to voicemail. Julian became worried, started to panic slightly. The only one he could account for was Trefor who was now more than a little way in front of him. Julian took his attention away from Trefor in order to look back for Rob. It gave the dark figure enough time to grab the fourth victim. He unexpectedly pulled the man sideways into the trees to the left with the edge of the blade on the pickaxe. Trefor lost his balance and fell to the ground.

"Juli..." His call was cut short, and the weapon was brought down with force into the top of his head, again the sound making a crunch as the skull was smashed.

Billy's brother heard the momentary cry. Once again he panicked. He could not get hold of Lee or Ron. Rob wasn't answering and now Trefor was nowhere to be seen after it sounded like he had cried out. He edged down to where he last saw Trefor and looked around, the dense mist making it hard to see anything around him, even on the ground. He heard something on his left-hand side and through the mist he squinted to see what it was. A hand. A leg. Julian stepped forward into the trees. His body froze. He dropped the knife to the ground and raised both hands to his mouth. Trefor was dead. His body on the ground. His head opened up and crushed. The contents of his chest and stomach oozing out over the ground. Blood everywhere. The gore bringing a wave of sickness within that went far beyond anything that he had seen since the death of Christopher Fallon in 1982. He had to get away. He had to run. His brother would be there soon. He reversed back out onto the path whilst still looking at the decapitation. Then he started running as fast as his elderly body would let him. Back towards the gate that they had jumped over to get into the forest area. From there he would be able to see the burnt-out car that he had told his brother about.

The dark figure walked out from the trees just as he started running. Julian didn't see nor hear him. All he heard was the swishing sound from behind and a few seconds later he felt the pain. The axe had hit him and impaled his back, had crushed part of his spine, immobilising him as he fell face first. The pain from his back overcast the fact that he could no longer feel or move his legs. The blade from the pickaxe was thrown so violently and powerfully that the tip had gone right through the body and pinned him to the ground as he fell. Yet at that moment he was still alive, gurgling blood, unable to speak. Trying to scream out loud with a hope that someone would hear him.

The dark figure casually walked up to the body. He removed the mask and let the victim look at him. Michael Llewellyn shook his head slowly.

Julian spoke his last words, struggling to get them out of his mouth because of the pain and the lack of able movement. "Y...ou. Y...ou. Ar...e in...sa...ne."

Michael Llewellyn placed his left foot on the base of the dying man's spine. "Really. That is a nasty thing to say. My Father. Now he was insane. Me. Well my Mother and my Father were both taken away from me along with my present, my future, and the very essence of me. Of course I fought to win, thinking I was just as insane as my Father. That it runs in the family. Who knows? I was always the boy who got up after every fall, always ready to go again full power, ask anyone. I survived the pain of

294

losing my parents. Crying was never on my list of options, and neither was insanity. The only thing I had on my bucket list was winning. Today, I have won."

He took his foot from the dying man's back and with all his strength pulled the pick axe away from the wound which caused blood to pump out. The blade on the pickaxe was sharp enough to cut flesh as if it posed no resistance. At once a fountain of red came from the wound, the ebb and flow in time with a terrified heart, and in no time at all the life left Julian Evans. Llewellyn stood watching as if he could not hear the screams of pain. He never moved at all until his mark was bled out, his red blood mingled with the gravel, rocks, and earth around him.

Michael Llewellyn stood looking at the man, admiring the signs of death, the wounds. He leaned over and placed his hand in the blood that had spilled out over the ground. Removing his hand, he lifted it to his face and licked it. The taste of life, he thought to himself. But he had one last thing to do. He raised the pickaxe above his head and then with force thrust it into the dead body. Again, he thought to himself. He repeated the thrust. Again. Again. Again. Violently. Frenzied. Brutal. Ferocious.

Michael Llewellyn walked away.

*****

The armed response vehicle had at last arrived. Firearms Officer Sergeant Andrew Cooke was first out and was instantly met by an anxiously waiting DI Harris.

"Sergeant Cooke, Sir. You requested armed response?"

"Yes. We have five or six individuals on the mountain all reported to be armed," Harris replied as he pointed up the path.

"Do we know what they are armed with?"

"No idea, although we think that five of them are trying to kill a Police Officer who is also up there. His name is Sergeant Michael Llewellyn. We have been unable to contact him. I need my men to be safe whilst performing search and arrests."

"No problem, Sir. My men will lead, and two FO's will take up the rear of the search party."

"Thank you."

*****

The dense mist continued to wrap itself around the forest, the eerily cold feeling rubbing itself on the arms of the big man who was only dressed in his regular checked short-sleeve shirt. Goosepimples were forming on his arms and Billy didn't know whether it was because of the cold or the fact that deep down he was slightly frightened. He had his mobile phone to his ear. Julian. It rang and went straight to voicemail. Lee. It rang and went straight to voicemail. Ron. The same. Rob. The same. Trefor. The same. Julian once again. The phone died. He headed over towards the area where Julian had given him directions to go once he had arrived. His age was getting to him, and he realised that he could not have walked up the mountain because his legs were already feeling like jelly just walking along the rough terrain. It took him ten minutes to get to the gate where he could access the forest that Julian had described.

"Julian," he called out hoping that his brother would answer him as there was no other contact available with any of them. "Julian!" There was no reply, so just as he had done when he tried to call them on the phone, he decided to try the others. "Lee! Where are you? Lee!" No one. "Rob. Ron. Trefor. Someone answer me!" He walked along some more, not being able to see anything now apart from shadows. Shadows of the trees reaching upwards towards the heavens, shadows of the birds firstly resting in the trees and bushes and then flying away after being disturbed by what was happening around them. Suddenly Billy froze, stopping dead in his tracks. He tried to focus at the shadow on the ground, momentarily squinting his eyes. Then he realised what he was looking at. "Lord. No!" he exclaimed as he rushed over to what was left of the body. He recognised the clothing. "Julian! Julian! No! No!" The pickaxe. Remove the pickaxe, he thought to himself. Do CPR! Just like the dark figure had done earlier, he placed his boot on his brother's back and with what strength and adrenaline he had left, pulled the pick axe from Julian's skull where Llewellyn had left it. Then he turned his brother over. Billy looked at the body and realised it was too late. He started to cry hysterically as he knelt down and wrapped his arms around his brother's body and hugged him tightly, then started rocking to and fro.

*****

Fifteen minutes had passed and SO19 together with DI Harris, CID and a squad of uniformed Officers had reached the top. Firearms Officer Sergeant Cooke had words whispered into his ear by one of his team.

"Sir. FO Porter has indicated that we have a vehicle over to the left, the doors are still open. I am going to send a unit in to clear the area and make safe. Then we can let you closer." He made hand signals to some of his team and four of them moved towards the vehicle, their Sig Sauer MCX rifles primed and in position. Slowly they edged forward, one eye looking through the sight, each one of the four surrounding the car from a distance, two on the left and two on the right.

"Cover me," FO Sam Morrison, who was the most senior of the four ordered. He walked slowly over to the open car door, and then saw no one. "It's clear!"

SFO Cooke looked at the Officers around him. "We can go."

The mist had thickened even more making any line of sight difficult at a distance. "We need to head in that direction," Harris announced as he saw the trees in between the clearing of the white fall. "If there is going to be any gunfire or otherwise, it will be in the cover of the forest rather than out here in the open."

SO19 led once again, rifles at the ready. As they got closer FO Logan Kershaw held his arm up indicating for the party to stop dead in their tracks. Sergeant Cooke walked beside him, and Kershaw silently tapped his ear and then pointed two of his fingers forward. Crying. They could hear crying, but they could not see anything because of the whitened grey around them. Cooke pointed at two of the other Firearms Officers and indicated for them to follow him. Their rifles scanned left and right as they headed down the track as an elite unit, covering any potential attack from all sides, although still the mist made it difficult for them to see extremely far ahead of them.

Suddenly FO Kershaw saw the outline of someone kneeling. "Stay where you are!" He ordered loudly and authoritatively. "Hands behind your head! I said HANDS BEHIND YOUR HEAD!"

"My brother. It's my brother!" Billy exclaimed as he took no notice and continued rocking back and forward whilst embracing the mutilated dead body.

The other three Officers quickly stepped in to provide cover once again, rifles pointing in every direction. "Hands behind your head! I need you face down on the floor. Back up from the body! DO IT NOW!"

Billy Evans still wasn't listening, wasn't even looking at the commanding Police Officer but was continuing to hold the corpse. "BACK AWAY FROM THE BODY!" Kershaw ordered. "This is your last chance. We will shoot!"

SFO Cooke made the decision. He forced his way forward at speed and aimed his rifle directly at Billy. "I'd do as I was told if I were you Sir. Otherwise he will fire!" He shouted as he stood at the side of him although a safe distance away. The big man turned his head briefly to look at the man who had made the command. It hadn't registered. Billy knew he had nothing to lose now. He grasped the handle of the pickaxe. All of the firearms officers became alert and aimed their rifles directly at the armed assailant, the red dot from each piercing every section of his head and torso. "PUT THE WEAPON DOWN NOW!" was the command from Cooke. Billy had now taken hold of the weapon with both hands. "WEAPON DOWN! GET ON THE FLOOR!" He wasn't listening. He just stared at all of the rifles that were pointed his way, his eyes looking like he couldn't see or hear anything that was in his way.

Billy told himself that he had nothing to lose. At his age he wasn't going to spend any time in Prison. His psychotic eyes stared at SFO Cooke, who, in return was watching the assailants body language. Suddenly Billy Evans ran at him. "Arrghhh!" he screamed as he started to raise the pickaxe. It didn't even manage to get waist height. The shot was taken. Then another. Billy fell to the floor, blood oozing from both wounds, his body jerking.

SFO Cooke held his rifle on target and nodded over to FO Kershaw to check the body whilst under cover. The body now lay still, silent, motionless. Just like the mist around them. Kershaw placed his fingers on the man's neck whilst trying to search for a pulse, then turned to his Sergeant and shook his head. "Okay," Cooke ordered. "Man down. Life extinct. Let's search the area! DI Harris?"

"Yes. All clear?"

"All clear. Man down."

Harris stepped through the white and finally managed to see the two brothers laying on the ground. "Billy Evans," he said pointing at the man who had just been fatally wounded, "Julian Evans," he continued as he pointed at the other corpse. He looked over to some of the Uniformed Officers who were now on the scene. Then he called out loudly, "This is the Police! You are surrounded! Put your hands behind your heads and come out where we can see you!" There were no takers to the offer, so Harris repeated his request. "I said, put your hands behind your heads and come out where we can see you! There are armed Officers present who will shoot." He looked at all the Officers present. "Batons ready. Search. Sergeant Cooke. Can your guys provide support to each search team?"

"Yes, Guv."

Over the next ten minutes, the mutilated bodies of Robert Gabriel and Trefor Idle were found hidden in the trees exactly where Michael Llewellyn had left them. The sight of the bodies made some of the Officers who were searching feel like they were going to urge and be sick.

"Two still missing, Guv," DC Tello said as he returned to see the DI who was still at the scene with Billy Evans.

"Organise a search further afield," Harris ordered. "The mist on the mountain isn't helping at all," he said as he stood surveying the area, hands on his hips and his jacket brushed backwards. "Better get forensics up here as well. ASAP! They will most certainly have their work cut out." He looked upwards. There were two helicopters hovering at a safe distance above them. Sky News marked on one and another unknown. Did Harris think that it was over? He didn't know. He still had the question on his mind about the whereabouts of the community Police Sergeant Michael Llewellyn. He looked at DC Tello who had joined him in stepping back from the action that was going on at the crime scene. Both Officers shook their heads.

*****

Sergeant Michael Llewellyn made his way back to the Pontycymer station using routes that he knew like the back of his hand coming down from the mountain. The routes that others would have to stumble across by accident. No one would notice him. At the present moment in time he would fit it. Just another Police Officer on the misty mountain. He casually walked back into his office He had ditched the blackened gowns and facemask close to the body of his last kill. Part of the plan, he thought to himself. His knew that inner self had enjoyed wearing them, had enjoyed the thrill, the power, the sexual prowess. Further down the mountain he had removed the white Police Tyvek suit that he had worn underneath to protect him from the possibilities of DNA evidence being found at or around the murder scene. He placed it in a bag and took it back to the station with him, immediately taking it out the back of the station and into the old oil drum. He had no problems quickly burning the evidence before going back inside. He had to shower, he told himself, which he did, ensuring that he was scrubbed down and any sign of evidence that he might have not seen washed away, any sign of smoke from the fire in the drum that he had just lit and then thrown water on to put out.

Llewellyn quickly dressed into his clean uniform, then sat at his desk quite calmly, picked up his pen and started his paperwork as though nothing had happened. No one had seen him. Only the six that were dead.

Chapter 23

It was now deep in the early hours of the morning. The CID office at Bridgend Police Headquarters was in party mood although most of those present were stood looking tired after all the long hours worked that had ensured that most of them had bags under their eyes and made it look as though they had been out on the town. Superintendent Saunders and DCI Gwyn provided glasses of bubbly for all that had worked on and at last after all the hard work over the past months, cracked the case. Most of the Officers, both plain clothed and Uniform together with Matt and his team from forensics raised their glasses.

Alun Saunders twanged his glass to get some attention. "Ladies and gentlemen! It's over!" There was a large round of applause and cheers throughout. "After all these months of hard work, long hours, and bloody turmoil, it is coming to an end. The searches at the premises of Billy Evans has not only pulled up evidence from the murders now, but the cold case teenage murders from forty years ago."

DCI Gwyn jumped in. "Just to let you know, even though the suspect is dead, the evidence we have against him is dumbfounding. When searching Billy Evans house we found the boots worn which proved he was at the scene of the crime where young Brandon Edwards was found. The footprint casts taken by Matt Robinson and his team," he stopped speaking to raise his glass to the three, "matched the bottom of the boot, as did the type of earth analysed from the pitch and found plastered all over the wellington."

There were cheers all around. Apart from DI Harris and DC Tello who were both stood next to the two invited reporters Tony Fallon and Ryan Parry, who were equally unimpressed.

Superintendent Saunders kicked in, himself trying to take most of the glory for the investigation. "Then there was the CCTV from this man," he pointed at the reporter, "Mr Tony Fallon's house where Evans and Lee Jones after breaking and entering had unknowingly admitted on CCTV camera to killing his Grandfather Christopher Fallon all those years ago!" The room cheered once more. "I must add that whilst our sincere condolences go out to Mr Fallon, I am sure that he is as glad as us that the case can now be closed." He raised his glass, and the gesture was responded to by Tony. "Now Mr Fallon here, also provided photographs of Billy Evans and the other five men who were murdered today meeting at Southerndown last week. Proof that they all knew each other and as a result their homes are currently being searched for evidence." More cheers.

"The black outfit suspected as being worn by the killer was found thrown in the trees near the corpses of Julian and Billy Evans at the crime scene today. He looked at his watch and jokingly said, "Sorry. Yesterday!" Everyone cheered as their glasses were filled up. "The weapon. The pickaxe. Covered in Billy's fingerprints, recovered as he threatened Officers with it. The other weapon. The ballistic knife used to cut throats. Found in Billy's shed at the back of his garden, along with a bag of coal dust and a bag of 'trophies', panties, boxer shorts, mobile telephones, bus passes, wallets, and purses. Not only relating to the recent murders, but the murders in 1982, 1983, and 1984." DCI Gwyn raised his glass once more. "Forensics have their work cut out! A toast to them! A toast to you all and your professionalism." Everyone cheered and raised their glasses.

Neither Harris, Tello, Tony Newton or Ryan Parry wanted to spoil their moment of glory at that moment in time. All four knew that Sergeant Michael Llewellyn had thought of everything. The community copper had set Billy Evans up to die. "Don't worry," Harris mentioned quietly to the other three although with all the noise it wouldn't have mattered if he had shouted it out. "It's not over. His time will come. Maybe not now. But it will."

302

Epilogue

Relief had spread among the villages as though a burden had been lifted. The residents could talk once more among themselves about what was around them and what had happened in the past without the fear of being silenced and threatened. They all thought that the rumoured curse on the villages that had been given by the reporter Christopher Fallon back on that fateful evening in 1982 had now been lifted. Gone forever. How wrong they were. The curse had just been passed on to another generation.

The Mist on the Mountain will stay forever in the Garw Valley. If you take a look, it is still there ... watching, waiting for you, surrounding you ... invisible ... haunting ... murderous ... mutilating. A shroud of white and grey which wraps itself around you as you walk around the Valleys, taking your very soul in its hands and grasping every breath you take.

Keep looking behind you as you walk. It is there.

Also available from Stephen Knight
Available in Kindle, Paperback and Hardcover from Amazon

Why not check out the official website
www.stephensamuelknight.co.uk

<u>Acknowledgements</u>

To all the residents of the villages of Blaengarw, Pontycymer and Pant-y-Gog who volunteered to be a part of this book, and their dogs, including,

Kirsty Williams
Rhian Bevan
Otto and Betty, the Newfoundland's
Catrin Kean
Sula, Layla and Raffi, the Rhodesian Ridgebacks
Oreo the Staffy
John Rix
Stella Edwards
Tracey Edwards
Lynne Edwards
Poli Cárdenas
Karly Bateson
Gareth Bateson

Thanks to the following businesses.

Gwaun-Bant Fish and Chip Shop
Bryn Stores
South Wales Police

Finally, if there is anyone that I have missed. Thank you!

Stephen Knight, Author, 2024

Printed in Great Britain
by Amazon

38533635R00169